Garnett readied the twins for bed. He stared intently first at Gino, then at Dirk, to curtain off the private lessons of the day, making certain that the information was securely stored in their minds. They would have no memory of it the next day when they wakened. It would be catastrophic, of course, if their childish lips leaked any hint that he was training them to be Masters.

Garnett chuckled—how fitting it was that Kei's own grandchildren would carry on the work of the cult she and Simon had nearly destroyed! What luck to indoctrinate two apprentices at such a young age, when their eager minds could sponge up the limitless Satanic knowledge crucial to the dedicated Master. The twins would soon be adept at the black arts, the demonic blood would flow through their veins and they would undo the mischief that the Eagletons had loosed on the local cult . . .

THE ULTIMATE IN SPINE-TINGLING TERROR
FROM ZEBRA BOOKS!

THE
SPAWNING

BY FRITZEN RAVENSWOOD

ZEBRA BOOKS
KENSINGTON PUBLISHING CORP.

To "The Family"
and
the Fourth Corner,
wherever he may be

ZEBRA BOOKS

are published by

Kensington Publishing Corp.
475 Park Avenue South
New York, NY 10016

Second printing: January, 1989

Printed in the United States of America

PROLOGUE

A bone-gnawing October wind swept up from the Loire River, rattled the dry stumps of the grape stalks on the slopes of the vineyard, ruffled the surface of the moat circling the sleeping château, and set the tin banners vibrating above the conical roofs of the four corner towers until they whined and squealed on their rusty pivots. In the stable, a dog barked and scratched at the door until the hired hand, stumble-footed with sleep and enveloped in bed-smelling body warmth before the chill air sucked it away, came down and took the animal upstairs with him to his apartment.

Out in the oak grove beyond the meadow, branches creaked and danced over a moon-silvered mound of rubble and sterile ground where no vegetation grew.

"Sélène!"

A voice whispered down through the debris that partially filled the ruined grotto, moved along the webbing of roots woven through the soil, and reached toward an airless, rocky cavity where a figure, its knees drawn up in the agony of childbirth, had lain underground for three hundred years with its mummified feet, contorted like the talons of a great bird of prey, braced against a stone altar that had fallen on its side. On the ground between the corpse's legs curled a parchment-colored bundle of small bones and dried flesh. Stretched out to catch the last trace of dying air, the woman's neck tissues had turned to fragile shreds, and her skull balanced at an angle on the floor, trembling at the footfalls overhead.

"Sélène, I am the new Master," said the voice, "and I have come to give you life again!" As the words traveled down through the ground, the star-shaped snout of a mole brushed against the mummy's head and with a rustle the skull turned to the side, its empty sockets staring into the darkness and its papery lips drawn back from its sharp teeth in an eternal smile.

CHAPTER ONE

The dinosaur jaw of a bulldozer's scoop, reddish earth dripping from its teeth, bit down into the barren mound protruding from the forest floor like a giant's skull pushing up through the soil, gobbled up a mouthful of dirt and rocks, turned, and spat it into the back of a dump truck. With a roar of gears, the cab's mechanism swiveled around again on its carriage, and the scoop dipped down to grub up another load of the rubble that filled the ruins of the grotto.

Was there a body buried out there or not? And if there was, what in the hell was he going to do with it?

Simon Eagleton tapped his upper lip thoughtfully with a finger that was losing its summer tan and stared out the salon window at the workmen and machines that had been trying to dig out the grotto behind the château for two days now without making noticeable progress. Something or other kept breaking down and going wrong, as if the grotto itself were resisting being obliterated. But no matter how long it took, he was going to get rid of it. Dig it out, fill it in with fresh earth, level it, and build a folly—a gazebo—on top. The plans he'd drawn up for it were at his elbow, amongst the crystal decanters reflecting colored shadows across the sun-warmed rosewood counter of the bar by the window. He'd build a lacy white summerhouse out there in the oak grove, where guests could sit in summer twilights with tall drinks in their hands, listening to music and watching friends play croquet on the meadow that lay between the forest and the moat that circled the château. That would take the curse off the bloody grotto!

But if, as legend had it, the remains of the notorious Sélène were still trapped under the rocks and earth filling the cavity, how was he going to dispose of them?

Witches couldn't be interred in consecrated ground, and the only burial site in the tiny village of Fay-sur-Loire was the church cemetery. Still, if the followers of Sélène's Satanic cult hadn't stolen her body away sometime in the past three hundred years, there couldn't be much left of her now. A few bones and shreds of cloth, at most. So a small plot in the back pasture, unmarked to prevent depredations by the ghoulish or vengeful, might do as well as any spot for their final resting place.

No hope that Father Sarde would consent to say a word or two over the pitiful packet as it was lowered into its grave. Not when the villagers still blamed every miscarriage and stillbirth on Sélène's malevolent influence, filtering up through the soil back there. Father Sarde knew which side his paté de fôie gras was spread on.

"Why do I have to do everything *myself?*" Simon

complained to the empty room, feeling put upon. Because he never trusted anyone to do things as well as he could, that's why. He ran a hand over his thick, silvery hair and smoothed it down on the back of his head, puzzling over precisely what would be appropriate to say over the bones of a monster who had killed her own newborn babies to render their fat down into potent ceremonial candles, who flayed the skin off dissenters from her cult and then burned them, still alive and screaming, in wicker baskets on the meadow. It took some stiff mental discipline not to think of that whenever he looked out there, where the paths to the forest and the stable were squishy underfoot with wet leaves, and dust from the digging operation was glittering like gold powder in sunlight filtering down through the brown and russet trees beyond. He bitterly grudged saying anything as benevolent as "Rest in peace" over Sélène. Well, he'd think of something when the time came—*if* she was still mouldering underground where the bulldozer was groaning and rumbling, inching nearer and nearer the brink of the grotto.

Tall and square-shouldered, with eyes as dark as Greek olives and a distinguished outside shell that hid the soft-hearted person bumbling around inside, Simon stood slouching against the bar with his hands shoved into the pockets of his riding breeches, feeling persecuted and growly, while he watched two workmen and the driver of the dump truck standing on the edge of the pit and shouting contradictory suggestions to the man at the helm of the bulldozer. Thinking that Frenchmen had a way of turning every procedure into an impassioned contest of individual

9

viewpoints, Simon kept his eyes on the bulldozer, which seemed to be getting perilously close to the dropoff point, and reached for some peanuts on the bar. He had his hand almost to his mouth before realizing that he'd scooped up a bunch of cigarette butts instead. "God dammit!" he said and dumped them back into the ashtray and brushed off his hands.

A dragging sound overhead caught his attention. She was at it again! He snatched up the plans of the folly, crossed the Aubusson carpet in a few long strides, clicked rapidly over the foyer tiles, and took the stairs two at a time, arriving winded at the top. My word, one of these days he'd better start thinking seriously about cutting down on the two—no, be honest—three packs of cigarettes he smoked a day!

Catching his wife and Marthe, the cook and housekeeper, wrestling a huge antique armoire against the wall of the blue bedroom, he leaned gasping against the door frame and said, "Are you out of your tiny minds?" They froze for an instant and then turned to stare at him while dust motes danced down to the Tabriz rug. "You *promised* to get Hilaire in to do any heavy work," he continued accusingly, addressing his wife Kei, whose rangy clotheshorse figure was shrouded in one of his old workshirts, worn flapping over faded and paint-spotted jeans. Her sleeves were rolled up and she'd wrapped a red scarf printed with a large pink K—the sound of her name—around her shaggy beige-and-silver mane. Obviously, she'd been all set to make some major rearrangements, and the look in her long hazel eyes was not welcoming.

"Oh, shoot!" she said, pulling off the scarf to wipe her nose with it. "I'm not even two months along, Simon, and I'm not going to have the baby splat on the floor if I just push a few sticks of furniture around." She stuffed the scarf in a back pocket and began rolling down her sleeves, knowing what a fusspot he was where her health was concerned and that arguing was a useless exercise.

"Sticks?! That wardrobe's as big as a moose!"

"Now, don't carry on, I'm quitting. But I can't sit on a cushion and eat strawberries and cream all nine months, and it's too much bother to call Hilaire in from the grounds every time I want to do a little something."

"Jeanne-Marie said the first trimester was the touchiest, particularly for a forty-five-year-old woman. She's the best obstetrician in the district, and she can be presumed to know what the hell she's talking about," he said, walking over to smooth down a tail of hair that was sticking up on top of her head. "If yóu won't take care of yourself, I'll have to start laying down the law." He combed her tangled hair back with his fingers, trying to get some order into it.

"You never *stop* laying down the law," she said, smiling up at him. Women's lib be damned, it made her feel secure and cherished when he got bossy, so long as she could get her own way in the end. Which she could. Most of the time.

Marthe took up a corner of the blue gingham *tablier* she buttoned over her clothes to protect them while she did housework and began polishing up the long mirror on the front of the armoire, saying defensively, "I take the heavy end, you understand. She will not listen to me, so I take the heavy end at least." She smoothed down the *tablier*, pushed back a cloud of frizzy red hair from her forehead, and cocked her head like a robin peering down a wormhole while she straightened the cameo brooch on her pillowy bosom. Rearranging the furniture was not *her* idea! To her way of thinking, the tutor should not be put in a bedroom on this floor, where the family slept. One of the attic rooms, up where Monsieur Eagleton stored the paintings and art objects destined for his London gallery would be more correct for hired help. She looked up again to see her employer's hand straying from the top of his wife's head to the curve of her neck and then wandering down toward her shirt-front. Marthe coughed discreetly and, favoring her arthritic knee, edged her way around the newlyweds and left to see about lunch.

Just as he was undoing the second button of Kei's shirt, Simon was distracted by a shout from outdoors and glanced over her shoulder out the window. The two workmen and the dump truck driver were clustering around the bulldozer, trying to steady it as it teetered up and down on the edge of a gaping hole where part of the grotto had fallen in.

"Hold that thought," he said to Kei and started for the hallway. "Something's gone wrong again!"

Kei looked out to see what the trouble was and then followed on his heels, buttoning up her shirt as she tried to keep up with his long legs.

"They must be mad!" Simon exclaimed as they ran up the meadow path, seeing that the three men had jumped down into the crater and were trying to boost the bulldozer by pushing at its treads while the driver worked at getting some purchase on the ground so he could back the machine away. "That thing'll fall on them, the idiots! Kei, tell them to get out of there before they're killed!"

The men, whose blue work outfits were powdered pink by the reddish earth that rusted their hands and arms, stopped a moment when Kei called to them in French. One of them gave her an impertinent look, took out the cigatette butt that had been clamped between his lips, and tossed it down at his feet, keeping his other hand where it was. Orders from a woman were not to be taken seriously. They ignored her. Furious and sure that the workmen's strength was a ridiculous prop against the massiveness of the bulldozer toppling above them, Simon flopped down on his stomach and grabbed the collar of the man nearest him, pulling his grasp loose and getting a smart cursing for his interference as the man wrenched away from him.

"Get out, for Christ's sake!" Simon shouted, getting up and squatting at the edge as he rubbed his hand where the collar's cloth had burned it. The earth-clotted treads of the bulldozer dipped up and down, up and down. Then in a rattling avalanche of stones and debris, the whole machine slid into the grotto like an ocean liner being launched and fell with a crunch against the far side of the pit, pinning a workman on his back under its implacable weight with a sickening sound of snapping ribs. The man's mouth opened in a scream but was clogged by a gushet of blood that spilled out over his neck and denim jacket.

The man nearest Simon scrabbled at the side of the pit and was up beside him immediately, while the dump truck driver scrambled backwards to safety and then stood as if paralyzed, watching the bulldozer grind the crushed man down into the soft soil. Half thrown out of the cab, the driver of the bulldozer scrambled out through its window and clawed his way down its side with one hand as the other flapped loose at the end of his sleeve like an empty glove.

"You cretins, *help* him!" Simon vaulted down into the grotto as they stood and stared motionless at the man on the ground, whose hand was fluttering palm upward in a slow pooling of red that was soaking into the churned earth. Simon knelt by him, but no breath came from the blood-filled mouth, and there was no heartbeat under the sodden jacket. The hand trembled and slowly opened out flat, finally still.

The men shifted out of their static poses when they saw that the man was dead, one man removed his cap in respect, and another shook his head and wiped his nose on the back of his gritty hand. The driver of the bulldozer, as yet unconscious of pain, cradled his broken forearm against his chest like a pet animal and said, "Ah Sélène! Elle y est, vous savez, sous nos pieds." The other men looked furtively at each other with frightened eyes and then down at the ground hiding the relics of the witch's devil worship. "Sélène!" the driver repeated, whispering the word. All three men crossed themselves.

CHAPTER TWO

"Simon, I'm frightened!" Kei reached up for his hand, and he took it between both of his and sat down on the bed beside her. Trying to seem calm and reassuring, he swallowed to get his voice under control.

"Jeanne-Marie says the bleeding doesn't necessarily mean we're going to lose the baby," he said softly. "We'll have to wait and see."

"I wish I'd listened to you about not moving the furniture," she said, "but I really think it was the shock that did it. Seeing that man squashed like a fly under the bulldozer." She stopped, feeling a faint clenching in her lower abdomen, and wondered if it was only caused by screaming nerves or if cramps were starting that would terminate her pregnancy. Simon, who was watching her face closely, looked alarmed, and she forced a smile. "I'll be all right, you'll see."

"Of course you will," he said huskily. "And if . . . Jeanne-Marie said we could try again almost right away. If you're sure you want to."

Kei lay back against the pillows. She was too old

to be making babies! But Simon was too precious and rare a person to exist on earth for just a moment without leaving something of himself behind. She was ashamed of her cowardice. He'd never had a child, having married so late in life, and he adored children. She wanted to please him and, more than that, had a deep, primitive desire to carry a part of him inside her, to make a sort of replication of him. Still, if she aborted now, perhaps it would be a divine sign that she wasn't supposed to have the baby. Maybe something was wrong with it . . . some deformation. Her mind shied away from the possibilities.

Jeanne-Marie came in from the round tower off the bedroom, which had been converted into a bath, buttoning up her sleeves after washing her hands. "A little rest this afternoon, then only mild activity," she said briskly. "A daily nap. Then we shall see what we shall see. One must be patient."

With a wave of her hand, she shooed Simon down to the foot of the bed and then pulled up the sheet and folded it back neatly over the rich fur coverlet. "These animal skins! I would not have them in my house," she said sniffily. "Not sanitary! And as for all those collectors of dust. . . . " She glanced at the dark-faced Russian madonnas hanging in heavy baroque gold frames on the emerald velvet wall. "I ask myself what kind of a mind you have, Simon, to turn a respectable bourgeois bedroom into a place that looks like a brothel." She smiled old-maidishly at Simon, who opened his mouth to protest and then closed it again, sighing, knowing that she was trying to get a rise out of him to lighten the situation.

"Now," she said, raising a well-scrubbed finger with a square-cut nail at Kei, "please not to think negative thoughts. We can monitor the womb to see that all is progressing normally. It is no longer guesswork. The bad things happen sometimes because the egg has become old without being fertilized at the proper time. The infrequency of intercourse in the older couple, you understand. Then it is sometimes necessary to end the pregnancy. However, I am quite certain that Simon does not allow your eggs to grow old." She chuckled at his expression and gave a smacking pat to Kei's hand lying on the coverlet. "Let me know right away if you have large clots. I must return to the clinic now. Madame Villar's twins may surprise us with an early début. She is full to bursting."

Simon helped the doctor on with her coat and accompanied her through the hallway, down the winding staircase, and out to a caramel-colored runabout that was standing on the gravel parking area in front of the château, while Jeanne-Marie kept up a running monologue on Kei's care.

"I ask that you say nothing about this outside the family," she said finally, tucking a frosty strand of hair into the bun on top of her head. Her nose was turning pink in the crisp autumn air, and she dabbed at it with a tissue before pulling on her driving gloves. "The man in the grotto was killed and another broke his arm, no? So without doubt the people in the village would say that the witch Sélène has cursed them and your dear wife. I try to educate them from their superstitions, but. . . . " She shrugged and got into the car, rolled down the win-

17

dow, and added, "As you Americans say, do not increase the fuel to the fire, please, I shall be back again, but telepone me if the flow becomes abnormal. Immediately."

She stuck her hand through the window to give Simon's hand a shake and started the engine. With a squirt of gravel from under the tires, the car reversed sharply, charged over the little bridge spanning the moat, sped through the open wrought-iron gate, and made a squealing turn onto the highway leading back to Orléans.

Simon leaned against the large sculpture that stood by the glass front doors—a marshmallow-shaped block of spongy white stone on a hip-high marble base—and ran a hand over its rough surface, feeling as dismal as he ever had in his life. A queue of ducks trailed up from the opaque green water of the moat and crowded around him, gabbling and pecking at each other. He shook his head at them. His pockets were empty of breadcrumbs. Mitzi, the pony-sized mastiff of the house, appeared from nowhere and slid her silky head under his hand, sensing his mood. He patted her back, appreciating her sympathy. Then he went back up to check on Kei, who had fallen asleep, exhausted by emotion, with salty trails running down into her hair from the corners of her heavily-lashed eyes. He put his hand gently on her belly a moment before going back downstairs and out to the grotto, where a giant crane was wrestling the bulldozer out with a screeching of chains.

They'd had to dig the mangled body out from beneath the bulldozer with hand shovels, and the morning had been crammed with the busyness that

18

followed disaster: calling an ambulance, driving the bulldozer driver in to the clinic to have his arm set, taking care of the insurance papers, notifying the widow of the man who had died and quieting her hysteria until the doctor arrived to sedate her, arranging with her neighbor to give her children lunch, getting the body removed to a funeral parlor in Orléans, and getting in the crane. And then Kei had started hemorrhaging.

Damn the grotto and all the trouble it had brought swirling down on the household! Simon thought wearily.

That had been where Kei found Sélène's talisman years ago—the small black iron pomander ball pierced with tiny holes that emitted a nauseating echo of odors from the dried, clotted mass of magical unguents inside. Kei had taken it back with her to America, and the local Satanists had kidnapped her and tried to murder her in revenge after they'd stolen it back when she returned to the château this summer. She'd barely escaped with her life, but Mitzi's mate had not been so lucky: they'd left the dog's body twisting at the end of a rope hanging from a tree near the grotto. They'd tortured the prize bull to death and mutilated it afterwards, cutting out its tongue, heart, and penis. Simon's favorite horse had been killed as well, and they'd seen to it that their own Satanic Master died when his identity was exposed.

Thank God, the cult was now a thing of the past, destroyed in a holocaust at the old abbey near the edge of town! But now this! It was almost enough to make a person believe that the witch was still pouring out her poison from down in the grotto. But that was nonsense, of course. She probably wasn't even there any more.

Laboring noisily, the crane hoisted the bulldozer up out of the pit and slowly swung it, tipping back and forth in its harness of chains, to deposit it gently on its treads on the ground. A couple of workmen left off leaning against the fenders of the dump truck and came forward to slip huge iron hooks out of the links holding the chains, and one of them climbed into the cab of the bulldozer to test its gears, shouting Ça marche!'' triumphantly when it proved to be still in working order. Nodding above the treetops like a giraffe cropping leaves, the crane backed away. Now the operation could continue, Simon thought, and the gazebo's simple frame construction would be up before the snow flew.

Satisfied, he turned back toward the château, mentally preparing himself to deal with a chapter on the French film actress and the fraudulent Cocteau prints that he was dictating into the cassette recorder. Jeremy Kirbottle, his publisher at Landsend House in London, was beginning to get shrill about how far past deadline the memoirs were and was icily unsympathetic with Simon's problems in treading the treacherous line between including the lip-smacking details that made for best-selling copy and trying to preserve his own dignity.

Actually, Simon had always hotly resented the way the media pictured him as some sort of jet-set Casanova who was less interested in acquiring art works for his gallery than in seducing every glossy beauty who came down the pike, but in working his way through his personal history, he'd become less incensed at their viewpoint. There *had* been a surprising number of women in his past, if you lined them up, but he hadn't been counting. He'd seen them as individuals, friends and lovers, and he hoped he'd given as much as he'd taken, but damned if he didn't sound like a Don Juan trying to set a track record when he played the tapes back! Kei would have conniption fits when the book came out, even though it was in her own interest as chairman of the board at Landsend for the book to sell well. He was innately monogamous and she knew it, but she managed to be just as jealous in retrospect as she'd been when that old girlfriend who'd missed the wedding announcements had turned up expecting renewed fun and games. If, on the other hand, Kei *hadn't* been possessive, he supposed, he'd feel tepidly loved and undervalued. Marriage entailed a lot of contradictions like that, and he wondered if he'd ever resolve them gracefully, even without the storm that was sure to blow up when Kei read the book. Nervously, he'd kept the tapes that concerned his adult life under lock and key, but he looked forward to the publication date with major trepidations.

A spare-figured man in a black cassock was coming toward him up the path from the château, walking—nearly dancing along—on the balls of his feet as his skirt rippled in black scallops around the tops of his shiny boots. It wasn't Father Sarde, who rolled ahead without a bobble, like a black barrel on casters. As they approached one another, the priest ackowledged Simon's attention with a jagged-toothed smile and stuck out a hairless brown hand with long spatulate fingers, saying in a light, timbreless voice that sounded as if it were still singing mass, "May I introduce myself? Barteau, Jacques Barteau, Father Sarde's replacement." The words carried scarcely a trace of accent, but the intonations had a foreign ring.

"I didn't know Father Sarde had left," Simon said, taking the proffered hand in a proper French pressureless shake and being surprised by its warmth in one who appeared so ascetic and bloodless.

The priest's olive-skinned face was a triangle that broadened out to a high round forehead framed in gray tendrils of windblown hair, like that of a kewpie doll that had undergone severe spiritual rigors and very light lunches. His features looked quickly sketched in with a fine-tipped pen—a small chevron for the nose, tilted half-circles for the hoods over his gray eyes, another pair for the pale flat pouches below them, arches for the lightly-drawn brows above his glasses. Only his mouth appeared to be in full relief, sensuous, and with a full, smooth lower lip.

Hands clasped in the small of his back, Father Barteau strolled slowly back to the château with Simon, explaining that recurrent depressions and nervousness had occasioned Father Sarde's retirement. Obviously glad to have someone to talk to, he expressed his own misgivings about ministering to the backward, superstitious villagers in his new congregation. "I really wasn't prepared for this, and I have serious doubts about my effectiveness in dealing with such parishioners," he said and bounded lightly up the steps of the small bridge over the moat, then leaned on the railing and looked thoughtfully down at the shadows of little fish schooling beneath the surface of the water. "Foolishly, I discounted Father Sarde's analysis of the local problems, attributing his warnings to his agitated state of mind. I suppose it's not news to you that the people in Fay still believe in witchcraft and other medieval abominations."

"Hardly," Simon said sourly.

"The widow of the man who was killed this morning is demanding that I perform an exorcism out there." He nodded toward the grotto. "I never expected to have to use the *Rituale Romanum* in my career and, as far as I can see, performing the rite of exorcism would only encourage the strange climate of opinion here, lending credence to their notions." He turned around to face Simon and crossed his arms over his chest. "An unpleasant thing. The housekeeper found Father Sarde's copy of the *Rituale* under his bed, with the pages covered with what looked like dried blood and obscene drawings and symbols. She claimed it had something to do with his breakdown and burned it, so I couldn't check on her veracity. Certainly something must have disturbed her to make her go so far as to destroy part of a priest's personal library." He dropped his chin on his chest and sucked in his pink lower lip, looking thoughtful and dour. "It's absurd, but it makes me feel a little insecure in that place, as if my privacy might be invaded at any time, if someone did violate the book. One is a little apprehensive in any new location at first don't you find?"

"I know what you mean," said Simon, "but there's no need to worry yourself about the grotto.

23

Within a month, the whole area will be filled in, with fresh foundations, and a gazebo will be on top of it."

Father Barteau's eyebrows rose higher above his metal-framed spectacles. "A gazebo? A strange old man? That *is* the meaning, isn't it?"

Simon laughed. "I mean a summer house. Though it will be winterized with space heaters and storm windows where the screens will go in fine weather, in case the château gets an overflow of guests. Once the gazebo's up, no one will remember the grotto." He opened the doors off the gravel-surfaced bridge. "May I offer you a drink?"

"Very kind, but I have my afternoon round of calls to make. Yesterday I paid my respects to Mrs. Eagleton, so I'll be. . . . " He put a long finger on his upper lip as he searched for a word. "I'll be toddling along, thank you."

Before the priest could enter the foyer, a very small dark-haired boy in a turquoise corduroy jump suit burst through the doors on his way to see the machines working in the oak grove, stopped dead at seeing the priest, and teetered on his tiptoes while his eyes traveled up from Father Barteau's black boots all his long, narrow length to his ragged smile.

"Hello, nice lady!" the boy said sunnily and grabbed the priest around the knees.

"Nice *man*, Gino, nice *man!*" Simon said hastily, embarrassed, detaching the boy's starfish-shaped hands from the priest's skirts and putting his hands under the child's armpits to swing him up for a kiss.

"A natural error," the priest chuckled as Simon set the boy down again, reaching out to stroke a hand over the glossy brown Dutch cut the boy wore.

"Are you playing dress-up?" the child asked, puzzled.

Interrupting Simon's move to explain, Father Barteau said, "Yes, I do it all the time."

An almost identical child in a yellow suit popped out of the hallway and fell upon Simon for loving before he noticed the priest and did a similar double take. His twin took him by the hand and pulled him aside for a giggling conference in an indecipherable lingo. Then they raced down the steps and toward the oak grove.

"Don't go beyond the meadow!" Simon called. "It's dangerous out there!"

The boys stopped to confer again, heads close together, and, walking with exaggerated sedateness to show their step-grandfather that they were being obedient, went to the very farthest edge of the meadow to plump themselves down on the leaves and grass at the closest possible observation point and looked back at Simon for an approving nod.

"Chris must be here," Simon said. "She's dropping off the twins with us while she goes down to the Basque country to research for her M.A. at the Sorbonne. They're called Dirk and Gino. That was their own private language you heard. Nobody understands a word of it but them." He waited a moment to be sure they really meant to stay where they were parked before ushering Father Barteau into the hallway, which was decorated with a vast bouquet of autumn foliage fanning out from a tall Sèvres vase set on a refectory table below a baroque gilt-framed mirror. "I'd like to have you meet

Chris," Simon said, stepping into the salon to see if she was there, but the room was empty.

They found her in the dining room, helping the housekeeper sort the twins' wardrobes into piles of socks, T-shirts, pajamas, underthings, and pants while in fluent French she gave instructions on how to get into the house for more clothing if the boys' grubbiness outran the laundry. "J'espère qu'ils seront sages mais je m'en doute," she was saying, trying unsuccessfully to sound like a stern, fussy mother, when they entered.

In a good husbandly fashion, Simon resolutely skipped his eyes past the valentine-shaped behind whose khaki-clad contours were temptingly displayed each time Chris's slacks tightened when she bent over the table and fastened his attention instead on the thick blonde braid hanging down to the waist of her red plaid shirt. Chris was a tiny thing, and Simon hoped the twins wouldn't turn out to be short. They had her hair and the same big brown eyes with wet-looking spiky lashes that could turn a Caligula into a Mother Machree, the same clean-lined tilted nose that looked as if it had been carved out swiftly in a few swipes of a knife by a Benihana chef, but he hoped they'd get their height from Kei's side of the family rather than growing up to look doll-like.

"Chris," he said, and she turned, smiling as she saw him. Before she'd met Simon, she'd been appalled that her mother-in-law was marrying such an internationally notorious womanizer. Later, when she got to know him, she suspected that the predatoriness of the women in the moneyed set had created his reputation. They must have pursued him like a screaming band of harpies, talons out-stretched, because she'd never seen a woman since except Kei who could joggle him. Even at fifty-eight, he was gorgeous, she thought. Those melting eyes, that thick silver hair, those gobs of suave! Not as broad-shouldered as one might like, a bit too boyish in build, but that made his clothes hang well on him, and you can't have everything. What a pussycat he was, really!

And who was this in the priest's getup? Awfully cerebral-looking. Oldish face, young body. Maybe fifty? Boy, they didn't even look you in the eye, did they? Afraid all that pent-up stuff might burst out so they'd leap on you and ravish you, maybe.

"Chris, I'd like you to meet Father Barteau, who's taken over from Father Sarde. Christine Ronald, Father," Simon said, and the three of them proceeded into small talk, going into the hallway and leaving Marthe matching socks.

"The tutor should be by any time now," Chris said, picking her raincoat up off the newel post of the staircase. "His name is Garnett Tobol, and I think the twins will adore him. He used to be with the Kidwells in the village before he took off for Khatmandu or someplace. They say he's wonderful, makes marionettes and does ventriloquism, things kids love."

"Haven't you met him yourself?" Simon asked, disapproving that she'd hired someone sight unseen, as he helped her on with her coat.

"Oh, sure, but I wanted to check with the Kidwells, not just accept some written recommendation. They think the sun rises and sets on him. I

27

guess he finances his globe-trotting by doing this kind of thing for a few months a year." She buttoned up her coat and rummaged in its pockets for her gloves. "I kind of fell in love with him myself, he's so . . . I don't know, he's got that kind of seriousness, that older-man maturity that gets to me. Sort of brooding and Heathcliff-y, except that he's got reddish hair. If I didn't have to go off on this trip, I might have a go at him." She glanced mischievously at Father Barteau, who averted his eyes and studied the cherubs twining around the frame of the mirror. She pulled on her gloves and added, "Well, I'm off. Give Kei my love when she wakes up." She stood on tiptoe to kiss Simon on the cheek and whispered, "I hope she doesn't . . . you know. I'll pray for you both. And for the baby." After shaking Father Barteau's hand, she left for Spain.

Before the priest went back to his rounds, Marthe came out of the kitchen with a freshly-baked galette wrapped in aluminum foil and insisted he take it, saying he looked as if he needed some more meat on his bones. "He won't get it from the one who keeps his house," she said as she closed the door after him. "Her cuisine! Good enough for dogs only!"

Simon went into the study to resume dictation on his memoirs but remembered that the birds in the ceiling-high aviary in the end of the room behind the desk hadn't been fed, and he could happily postpone getting down to business for another fifteen minutes while cutting up a banana, refilling the seed trays, and freshening the water in the cups attached to the white wires of the cage. Banana still in hand, he suddenly thought of the twins and wondered if they were still sitting where he'd left them. He looked out the casement window over the moat and saw that they were now on the meadow with their toy rakes, gathering leaves into long piles to mark out rooms, as he'd showed them how to do when they'd made a leaf house a few days ago. The wind had disarranged the boundaries since then. Good! The bulldozer was chugging away again, and the dump truck was trundling off along the path by the stable, carrying a fresh load of dirt and rocks.

A tapping on the frame of the open door drew his attention from the window. Marthe was standing there, wiping her hands on her *tablier*. "Someone to see you," she said. "A friend of your nephew's, perhaps. A boy."

"Be right out." He cut up the banana and put the chunks on a feeding tray inside the bars but kept one and coaxed Mimi, the pink cockatoo over for it. She cocked her head to inspect it, ruffling up her apricot-colored crest, and then opened her beak for it, showing a thick gray tongue. Jesus, he was glad he didn't have a tongue like that in *his* mouth! Enough to make you sick!

There was no one in the salon, where the late afternoon sun was slanting across the carpet and picking up points of light on the rough paint of the heroic-sized Moody canvas filling one wall. The boy must be waiting in the foyer.

Standing by the front doors of the hallway, with a bright blue backpack and two large orange pumpkins on the tiling beside his engineer's boots, stood a man wearing jeans and a Fair Isle sweater with the sleeves pushed up.

29

Not a boy, thought Simon. Not by a long chalk. He had the solid, assured air of someone who had cut the apron strings long ago and gone out on his own to prove himself. Not the tutor either, quite evidently.

This fellow's dishwater blond hair was sun-bleached light on top, almost to platinum, and was longish but not unruly or raffish. He bore a close resemblance to one of Simon's prep school friends, the one who did everybody else's homework for them, and his straightforward stare before he broke into an open, square-toothed smile as Simon stretched out his hand promised that there wasn't a brood in his being.

"Simon Eagleton," said Simon, liking the man on the instant, "and you're . . . ?"

"Tobol. Garnett Tobol, the tutor." He seized Simon's hand in his paw with a firm grip that made Simon's signet ring cut into his finger. "I've come to take care of the twins."

CHAPTER THREE

Thank heaven Garnett had appeared just when she needed him, Kei thought, pulling her alpaca blanket shawl closer about her against the cooling twilight air as she sat on the bottom step of the bridge out back, one elbow on an upper step, and watched him eviscerate a pumpkin while the twins squatted, rapt, on either side of him. If there was one thing she hadn't been up to after the operation, it was baby-sitting two dynamos with enough energy to light up New York City for a year! But for Garnett, this afternoon they would have dragged her off to the village and made her take them on all the rides at the tinny, itinerant fair whose wheezing music was percolating through the bright trees by the Canal d'Orléans.

The jostling of the crowd would have brought her claustrophobia into full flower. Her miserable aim at the rifle range and the coconut shy would have caused her sweaty-handed embarrassment. Bumping around in those little cars that skidded around on electric poles would have given her a crashing headache while she worried about jarring her insides loose again. And she didn't even want to think about trying to hang onto two wrigglers like Gino and Dirk and nail them into their seats at the top of the ferris wheel while dizziness threatened to bring up her breakfast! Garnett had relieved her of that trial and didn't look the least tattered from the strain as he worked on the jack o'lanterns while telling them the history of Hallowe'en customs.

His cheerful sunniness was an antidote, too, to the melancholy that seeped through her days since having her womb scraped clean, ending her pregnancy after she'd hemorrhaged a second time. Blood had fountained down her legs when she'd been out at the grotto, watching the workmen pour concrete into forms laid over fresh fill in the cavity. Simon had rushed her straight to the clinic and Jeanne-Marie's waiting, starchy arms.

She'd known it would happen like that. The dream had been too vivid, the cold wetness of the leaves under her bare feet too real as she walked through the night toward the oak grove, telling herself that she was dreaming, trying to rouse herself from the tangle of sleep as her feet moved ahead in slow motion, heavy as if she were wading through syrup, unstoppable, unresponsive to her command.

A thick gray mist spiraled up from the grotto, swirling and eddying faster and faster, scattering leaves across the forest floor, forming itself into a pillar and gradually melting away along the outline of a form solidifying within it. Part of the mist curled across the ground into the dark undergrowth, while the rest flowed in smoky rivulets down from the woman's head, cowling her in luminous shadow.

The woman moved forward, and Kei flinched away from the smell of decay that drifted toward her. A long, greenish-white arm—so thin that every tendon and muscle stood out in painful relief—reached out from the gray pall, and a hand like a bundle of twigs touched Kei's belly, slid a razor-sharp fingernail down its length, and slit the skin. The icy hand moved about amongst her entrails and wrenched something loose. "Mine!" said the woman in a hoarse whisper like a wave washing against a pebbled shore, and held a bloody clot before Kei's eyes.

For interminable minutes she seemed to be swimming up out of the dream, as if she were struggling, drowning, up from the ocean's floor, until she woke, shaking, in Simon's arms. As he tried to calm her, she buried her face against his neck, snuffing up the smell of his skin—like clean fur and sunwarmed autumn leaves—to get rid of the charnelhouse reek that filled her nostrils.

So she hadn't been surprised when Jeanne-Marie had told her gently that no fetus had formed. There had never been a baby. Just one of Mother Nature's rotten, wry jokes.

Simon was taking it too hard for Kei to turn to him for comfort, keeping a firm stopper on his emotions and drinking a bit more than was good for him. None of Jeanne-Marie's assurances had really convinced him, Kei knew, that it wasn't his fault somehow, that something basically wrong with him hadn't damaged her in a secret, ineffaceable way—that next time everything would go all right. She had to let him fight it out by himself, loving him through it when he'd let her, without reaching out a

33

hand to him to steady herself. Why do *I* always have to be the strong one? she thought in a rush of rebellion. She smiled grimly. Because you can, she answered herself. That's the only explanation you're ever going to get: Because you *can*.

The flaking stucco of the château wall shimmered as she looked up past it with wet eyes to the sky. Blue like the dancing Mediterranean in a Dufy watercolor had changed to a pale heliotrope as the evening drew in. She glanced down again to the flash of the spoon's edge as it brought out a web of thready orange pulp and ivory seeds.

" 'Elp, 'elp, I'm losin' me brains!" complained a sepulchral Cockney voice from the interior of the pumpkin Garnett was emptying. Gino hopped backward in surprise and tumbled onto his soft, round bottom with a laugh.

"I saw you move your lips," Dirk said accusingly, pointing a small, coral-tipped finger shaped like an auger at his tutor's mouth.

Garnett smiled and shook his head. "Just chewing my gum," he said blithely and dug out a final spoonful. Kei was struck with how much he resembled the twins' father, and thinking of Stephen's death was another stone added to the burden of her sadness.

"Pumpkins can't talk. They're not alive," said Dirk with juvenile pomposity and turned the face of the other, fully carved jack o'lantern around to look at it sternly.

"Don't be too sure." Garnett whacked the spoon on a newspaper spread out on the bridge and took up a bone-handled knife to start tracing triangles where the eyes would go. "At any moment—when you're least expecting it—familiar objects can undergo a transmogrification.''

"Trans-mogri-fication," Gino repeated accurately, rolling the word over his tongue with relish.

"A change. A sort of magical change," said Garnett, who never talked down to the twins.

He knew how children savored elaborate words, Kei thought and hitched up the material of her taupe corduroy slacks at the knees, changing into a more comfortable position. She crossed the ankles of her boots.

Garnett had a knack for understanding children's minds. And why not? He was hardly more than a child himself. Look how pink his knees still were! The muscular legs bared by his tan cutoff shorts might be those of a man, but the glistening blond down on them made her think of fuzzy ducklings. That glossy hair the color of dárk honey, the high terra cotta flush under the skin of his Slavic cheekbones, and the contours of his physique—like Michelangelo's David—epitomized youth at its prime. He was like a juicy sunfreckled pear ready to fall from the tree into a waiting hand. And hands aplenty there'd be, once the village girls got wind of his presence at the château. Gays, too, from the local artists' colony, who were always sniffing around for a delectable lad, would nose him out eventually.

Was Garnett worldly-wise enough to fend them off and keep his balance? Oh, surely he'd been fair game since his early teens, if not before, and had learned how to handle himself. To enjoy the sport as well, Kei suspected. Sometimes she'd caught him looking at her with a sexual awareness that was disconcerting. In any case, Garnett's lovelife was none of her business. Just because he looked like her dead son Stephen didn't give her the right to mother him, which he probably didn't need anyway and would be offended by if she carried it too far. After all, *he* was the babysitter, *she* wasn't.

And where was Simon? Oh yes, in the study, dictating the final part of his memoirs onto tape and hating every minute of it. She'd have to curb her impulse to go in and distract him from doing what he didn't want to do, when Jeremy Kirbottle was calling from London almost daily to badger him for more copy. Simon must be sitting at his desk in the jungle of green plants in the front tower room, with the birds in the aviary twittering and talking to themselves, and his head must be bent slightly forward as he spoke into the microphone, exposing the defenseless-looking back of his long, tanned neck. The thought set off a jangle of tingles in all her vital spots. Tonight was the night! Waiting the prescribed time since the operation had been making them both edgy, in addition to their depressions, and they'd been quarreling more than usual because of it. But tonight, at last! Kei wriggled and slipped off into a reverie, remembering the dark rainy night when they'd gotten into a telephone booth and . . .

Which brought back the memory of another telephone booth and Robin phoning around for jump cables to start the car one February morning in Chicago while she stamped her feet by his, trying to keep warm. When he finally located a station that would send someone out, he'd been so elated that he kissed her. In precisely the same way that he'd *always* kissed her. Suddenly, she couldn't stand the monotony of Robin's kisses any more and jumped out of the booth, slammed the door and wedged it shut with a stick, while he pounded on the door and muffled words of bafflement came from behind the frosty glass.

Why did wives hang onto pathetic specimens like Robin? Because they'd put all their eggs into one flimsy, shabby basket and hated to admit to the world that they'd chosen a bad alliance? Or was it the daunting prospect of growing old alone that kept them stuck fast to men they no longer respected? It had taken her years to realize that she'd swallowed whole the notion that life for a single woman was arid and lonely. Not once in all those years had she questioned the intelligence of the minds that had foisted that concept on society. Then one Saturday morning—in a sunburst of illumination—she'd realized that public opinion wasn't shaped by wise heads, it was the pooling of ignorance by masses of mediocre people who often didn't know what the hell they were talking about!

Saturday was The Day on Robin's calendar. For all she knew, he marked it down in the plastic-covered pocket notebook from which he ran his life: *Saturday morning—Remember to screw Kei.*

He'd been rooting around inside her while she tried to dredge up a rape fantasy to spice up his dreary predictability, and her thoughts had kept returning to the fancy of putting up a wall chart to save him the trouble of laboriously thinking through the process each time:

37

I. *Fiddle with A for 10 seconds.*

   A. *Don't get rough or she'll be cross.*

   B. *They are not art gum erasers that you used to chew in first grade. Suave does it.*

II. *Doodle around with B for 15 seconds.*

   A. *Try not to look disgusted. Remember that women can't help it that they're not packaged as tidily as men.* Concentrate on this factor.

   B. *Be patient. The fun part is only two minutes away.*

She'd panted and groaned convincingly (she was, she thought at such times, a great loss to the stage) while trying to avoid the King of Spit's endless flow of saliva that dripped down his tongue into her throat, and when he gasped "Wowee!" as always, she restrained herself from giving him a knee in the groin and got up gratefully from the bed.

At that instant the revelation had burst upon her. She couldn't *get* any lonelier than she was with Robin! His emotions were as deep as a coat of paint, and was *this* kind of monkeying around anything she'd miss? The single women she knew had rich, fulfilling lives, and who *was* it who'd told her she couldn't make it happily on her own? Other married women, who were afraid to face the world! Kee-rist, what a sucker she'd been! What a lot of time she'd wasted on this poor simp!

When he'd honked her, it had been the final, absolutely and positively last straw! He'd reached out, squeezed her breast playfully, and said "Honk!" and—in a moment that still gave her delicious satisfaction—she'd let him have it smack in the kisser with the cold dregs of his beddy-byes warm milk.

She'd been packed and gone before he got back from his Faculty Salary Complaint Committee meeting. And never looked back.

Robin was as different from Simon as greasy French fries from Beluga caviare. To begin with, Simon was aware that there was more than one way to kiss a woman. More than one place, too, which would have boggled Robin's imagination. A man of infinite variety, Simon was elegant, stylish, a respected authority on art, passionate and devoted, rich, a little bit crazy, a lot behind on his deadline for the memoirs, and there he was, standing at the open back door, stretching and yawning and digging his fingers into his flaming white hair, massaging his scalp.

"I've thought it over," he said to Garnett, and twisted his head from side to side until his neck gave an audible snap, which seemed to relieve him, "and I think it's a fine idea."

Garnett looked up from the merry smile he was carving and said, "The folly? You're going to let me turn it into a playroom for the twins?"

"At least until summer, when our American and British friends start hankering for a trip to the continent and need a place to light. We might need the space then." Simon walked across the bridge and came down to sit beside Kei, jackknifing his long legs until his knees were shoulder height to accommodate the depth of the bottom step. Mitzi, the mastiff, came out from the foyer, nosed him down, and then abandoned him for the delights of the shrews and small animal life in the woods. Simon pulled up his black cashmere turtleneck to reach the pack of Players bulging in his shirt pocket, shook out two cigarettes, handed one to Kei, and lit both of them. "Space heaters would keep it warm in the winter. No use having it vacant for months." He let out a stream of smoke that swam horizontally across the still, crisp air like a water snake and paled away. "I might feel differently if they'd found Sélène in the grotto, but since they didn't . . . "

"You won't believe what I can do with that place!" Garnett said jubilantly. "If I can have a free hand with the decoration, I can get marvelous stuff from a window dresser I know in town. Wholesale."

"Do whatever you like," Simon said glumly, looking at the darkening forest, where concrete foundations were drying and ripening in a cleared area. The place looked innocuous, now that the barren dome of earth that had covered the grotto was leveled. "They're going to start building tomorrow, using double crews to beat the cold weather."

"We ought to give it a christening party when it's finished," said Kei, hoping to boost him out of his gloom. "Maybe a costume ball." She put her chin on his shoulder and scratched at the silvery stubble on his jaw, but he seemed not to notice and continued to stare out at the woods, where a clutch of ravens were creaking in the trees.

Finally he shook his head and crossed his arms on his knees. "That would be tantamount to dancing on the grave of the workman who . . . " Kei put a finger on his lips, mindful that the twins were listening. He took her hand and kissed it absentmindedly. "Can you imagine how that would make his widow feel? Besides, I don't feel in the mood for a crowd of houseguests right now. I don't even feel much like seeing Monsieur le Curé and Eagle at dinner tonight." He turned to look at her for understanding and said, lowering his voice so that the conversation was between him and his wife, "Sorry I can't seem to shake out of this, darling. You're the one who's suffered, and I've been sulking and bleating around like a lost lamb, but I just can't drag myself up out of the pit somehow." Kei put her arm around his shoulders and squeezed him gently. His head drooped. "If you were expecting a tower of strength when you married me, you ought to demand your money back."

Kei put her cheek against the thick silkiness of his hair and said, "What you need is to get away from here for awhile. I heard you talking on the phone with Bony Foxworth about scouting around Australia for some acquisitions for the London gallery. Why don't you go yourself? It'd do you good."

"It's too long a trip for you right now."

"I know, but you used to travel solo, and I'd rather do without you for a couple of weeks than watch you dig yourself into a serious depression."

He looked at her speculatively. They were doing paintings out there with colors that were barbaric and wonderful, fresher than anything coming out of Europe or America now. He'd picked up some things in the Outback a couple of years ago, in-

triguing primitives that were rather in the line of arti-
facts, but some young urban Aborigines who knew
how to handle oils and acrylics were producing
rough-edged, original concepts that some clever
dealer was going to make capital of sooner or later.
It would be a pity to let them slip into other hands.
And if he could bring back something truly out of
the ordinary, something that might have as revolu-
tionary an impact on the creative world as African
sculpture had had on Picasso and that crew. . . .

Feeling sheepish for the quick flicker of excitement
that the prospect gave him, he said, "I don't like to
be away from you for that long." He meant it
sincerely, but he also was afraid that if he didn't get
a chance to turn over the contents of his mind soon,
the way a spade turned over exhausted soil to expose
the fresh loam beneath, he was going to go off his
nut.

"Pish-tush, sillywhiskers," Kei said and tapped
her cigarette ash off into the air with a haughty
grande-dame gesture, "you're beginning to think
you're indispensable. A dangerous conceit."

Simon looked up at a rattle of newspaper as
Garnett gathered together the carving gear, having
finished his art work. Now the tutor lit a candle and
dripped hot wax down into one of the melons. Black,
oily smoke ribboned up from the wax, and a tingling
smell of scorched pumpkin made Gino hold his button nose between his fingers. When a pool of wax
had accumulated at the bottom of the lantern,
Garnett blew out the candle, skewered it inside, and
started on the other jack o'lantern.

"Maybe I'll just do that," Simon said, watching

him. "I'll give it a think."

Garnett put the lids on the pumpkins and handed one each to the twins. "All ready for Hallowe'en," he said. Dirk looked at his and bared his teeth at it in imitation of its sawtoothed smile. "Now run these things out to the kitchen and ask Marthe if she'll put them away for you." He parceled out the pulp-filled newspaper, the spoon, and the knife to the children and gave Gino a light smack on the bottom to get him going.

A tall black figure loomed in the dark doorway, blocking it. The twins pulled up short to stare at Father Barteau's long surplice with its row of buttons running down the front, the rabat at his neck with its two white tails hanging down like an untied bowtie, and the black beret covering his slatey hair.

"You're *still* dressing up," Dirk said enviously. "My mommy only lets me do it once and a while. You must have a nice mommy."

Forty-five-degree angles formed a smile at the corners of the priest's mouth. "My mother is the nicest mother that ever lived," he said, looking over the chld's head at Kei, the joke twinkling briefly in his eyes. "And what is this, an *ignis fatuus?*"

"No, a jack o'lantern, silly," said Dirk, holding it up for the priest to bend over, but Gino elbowed him aside and pushed his pumpkin into Father Barteau's face so that he had to raise his spectacles and peer under them to see it properly.

"Mine's more prettier," Gino boasted.

"Is not, you cuckoo!" said Dirk. A scuffle of kicking started up, and the priest held the boys apart while Garnett scrambled to his feet, brushed off his cutoffs, and came over to put a hand on top of each silky head, turning the twins toward the door.

"Don't hurt their feelings by comparing them, Garnett said. "Didn't you notice that I carved ears on them?"

The children gawked in dismay at their pumpkins and then took them along into the foyer, holding them with new respect, as if they were hypersensitive animated heads.

Kei excused herself to go change, leaving Simon to introduce Garnett and the priest.

The seraphic purity and spirituality shining from the boy nearly knocked the breath out of Father Barteau. He felt he was seeing the actual embodiment of the ideals he'd striven for when he'd entered the seminary so long ago, hoping to bleach out the inky stains on his soul. Quickly he covered up his shock at the vision and stretched out his hand. Seeing that Garnett was not going to take his hand out of his pocket to "press the flesh," as one of his Presidents had expressed it, the priest hastily converted his offered handshake into an awkward continuous movement upward to straighten his beret. Americans, he was aware, didn't necessarily shake hands in greeting and farewell like the punctilious French, and surely the boy must be incapable of impoliteness. Indeed, that warm smile was cordiality itself, and its innocence laid a toasty finger on Father Barteau's heart—that organ he'd begun to fear was permanently frozen, an icy pendant suspended in the black cosmic chill within his chest.

"You're not Catholic, I suppose," he said wistfully.

" 'Fraid not," said Garnett.

Father Barteau sighed.

While Garnett was in the kitchen overseeing the children's table manners before putting them to bed and Mrs. Eagleton—he must remember to call her Kei, since she insisted—was dressing, Father Barteau followed Simon into the foyer, where his host took a tweed jacket off the Giacometti nude torso and shrugged into it. "Kei's redecorated the salon," Simon said, motioning the priest ahead of him through the doors.

What a pity the Eagletons weren't Catholic, Father Barteau thought at his first sight of the room. Anyone with this much money would have had the parish house roof retiled without giving it a second thought. The cost of the Bäsendorfer Imperial concert grand alone would have repaired it completely, with plenty to spare, and one small corner of the Aubusson carpet must be worth more than the whole rickety little deux-chevaux that was permanently parked behind the parish house because it needed a new transmisison.

He recognized the Moody painting that covered an entire wall, having seen it in an art magazine he'd leafed through selectively in the dentist's office while waiting for root canal work, but its wild colors—laid on with a trowel by a blind man, one might think—was not to his taste. Nor was the luxury of the light yellow suede settees or the deep easy chairs covered in Florentine brown leather that crouched around an eighteenth-century Japanese trunk with gold and silver-gilt lotus seals serving as coffee table.

45

Close by, a mammoth rococo mirror over a gigantic fireplace drew in light and repeated the room's interior, making it appear even vaster, brighter, and airier than it already was.

With people starving the world over, how could anyone with clear conscience, the priest asked himself, litter a room with all these costly bibelots and pictures? Such prodigality! Those baroque gilt consoles with mirrors, the coromandel screen, the collection of crystals, too much, too much! And the knee-high Grecian stone head perched on its neck in the corner and the ostrich eggs in gold holders were simply ridiculous.

Hands clasped behind his back, he strolled across the carpet, wondering what noble soles had walked across it in its long history, and went over to look at a small picture by the bar while Simon poured him an aperitif. He recoiled at seeing that the painting depicted a woman with an exaggeratedly long neck and eyes like black watermelon seeds, who was not only as bare as the day she was born, but seemed to take reprehensible glee in displaying unpleasant parts of herself that were best kept concealed. He did an abrupt about-face, reminding himself that it was not his place to judge the Eagletons' spiritual development.

"A votre santé!" said Simon, handing him a glass and holding up one of his own.

"Cheers!" Father Barteau replied and took a hearty swig of the drink.

Mrs. Eagleton—Kei—came in, wearing a long honey-colored suede vest lined with muted apricot fur over a white silk tunic, and trousers stuffed into white boots. The mass of her tawny hair was swept to one side in back by a gold comb and fell in an uncombed-looking mass around her cheek and down to her shoulders. Sinfully ostentatious for a simple dinner, thought Father Barteau, and well calculated to tempt venery!

Neither she nor Simon knew what to do with a priest, he discovered, and there was a limit to how long they could discuss the weather. When the smalltalk faltered, he could no longer resist indulging himself by asking about Garnett.

"Don't really know much about his background, except that he's bummed around the world rather extensively," said Simon, handing a drink to Kei when she'd perched on one of the settees and sitting down himself in one of the easy chairs by the fireplace. He gave Kei a cigarette and offered one to the priest, who held up a hand in refusal. Tapping his cigarette on his thumbnail, Simon added, "I think he spent the summer in Alaska." He lit Kei's cigarette and then his own.

"Be it ever so humble, there's no place like Nome," said Father Barteau, instantly regretting it.

Simon fixed him with an eye and cleared his throat. "Yes, well," he said disapprovingly. "He's going to make a playhouse sort of thing of the folly that's going up in back, where he can give the twins lessons, more or less, and keep them out of Kei's hair. They've chased her cat until it's hysterical and has taken to hiding up on the third storey, where the items I've collected for the gallery are stored. In amongst the canvases and bits of sculpture is a good place to nurse a neurosis, I'd say."

"They only want to love it, but it doesn't get the message." Kei rubbed one hand lovingly up and down the silk of her sleeve, unconsciously giving a clue to her sensuous nature that was not lost on the priest. "They're really very well behaved on the whole, but they do giggle the livelong day, and when they stop I have to get up and see what mischief they're getting into. I guess I should be glad that they're so happy, but . . . " She touched two fingers to her forehead in a gesture of hopelessness. "Frankly, I don't know what I would have done without Garnett to keep them amused."

A door banged out in the foyer and a young voice called, "Anybody home?" An adolescent who looked to be sixteen or seventeen entered, wearing dark trousers and a white shirt through which could be seen the lettering on his T-shirt: SOCCER PLAYERS HAVE LEATHER BALLS. At reading the printing, Kei's eyes swung over to the priest, who twinkled determinedly to put her at ease.

The lad seemed to be a bundle of barely controlled animal spirits. In the priest's opinion, his good looks were coarse in comparison to Garnett's ethereality. He looked familiar, but why? Whom did he resemble? That film actor who was now a sculptor, what was his name? Ah yes, Tommy McKenzie. Eagleton's sister had had an illegitimate son by him, someone had said. This boy, no doubt. They'd married and thus legitimized their child, but they hadn't shown undue haste, to be sure. Just last month they'd been wed. In a pagan ceremony, it was rumored. Was the boy a pagan too? He had every appearance of it. Father Barteau could imagine him dancing around on cloven hoofs and playing Pan's pipes. Shaking hands with him seemed almost like a violation of principle, but there was no civil way out of it.

"His given name is Simon," said Kei, "but we call him Eagle. It saves confusion."

It saves scandal, thought Father Barteau. His name might be McKenzie now, but it must have been Eagleton before the wedding. Hence the Eagle. Well, better late than never.

"I don't know what to talk about around a priest," Eagle said. "Guess I can't swear, huh?"

"Well, I . . . " Father Barteau began, caught off guard by the lad's guilelessness, and then couldn't think how to end the sentence.

"Don't mind me," Eagle said with a grin. "Aunt Kei says I open my mouth and let everything in my brain float out without listening to what I'm saying. It drives her bananas, but I really don't mean any harm.

It was an explanation, not an apology, the priest realized. Eagle had the puppyish air of one who expected to be loved and appreciated, whatever he did or said. Not a logical stance when one has grown up as a bastard. His family, including the Eagletons, must have been infusing him with massive doses of love and approval, which he'd probably sucked up gratefully as soil absorbs welcome showers after a long drought. If so, they were not the tinkling brasses and sounding cymbals that they appeared.

"I can see that you have good intentions," said the priest. "I'm not sure I'd know what to talk to you about, either. Soccer is not my forte."

49

"Oh, this." Eagle looked down at the lettering showing through his shirt. "I'm captain of the team at the American school in Paris, but that doesn't mean I'm your typical jock. Like, I'm polishing up my French so I can transfer to the lycée and get my bachot and I'm studying Japanese with Aunt Kei on the weekends and she's teaching me to play the koto and I'm into making films a little and where's Gar?"

Gar? Father Barteau shuddered. Wasn't that the name of a long-nosed fish? To replace the word for a ruby-colored gem with that for a snouted fish? Desecration.

Eagle monopolized the conversation until Marthe announced that dinner was served, and kept it up all through the marinated shrimp in orange chive sauce, talking with his mouth full, until Simon laid down his fork and said kindly but firmly, "Eagle, have the grace to shut up."

His nephew looked startled but recovered quickly and grinned amiably, having been cut off before by adults who wanted a fair share of the action. Garnett leaned over and bumped his shoulder against Eagle's sympathetically, confirming the priest's impression that Garnett's sensitivity would be hightly tuned.

Of course, Garnett must be regarded impersonally as merely a happy addition to the landscape of human figures, the priest reminded himself, but one could hardly be tempted to the sin of particular friendship by a transparency for good who was as sexless as an angel. The boy was no more a personality to him than would be a shaft of sunshine. As Simon served the sorrel soup, Father Barteau searched his heart mercilessly and rejoiced to find no tendency within himself to be attracted to Garnett as a person. If anything, he was a springboard to a higher understanding of the perfectability of man. That in itself was a blessing, and how did the Biblical verse go? He couldn't quite remember. Something about the fact that, if a blessing is from the Lord, it can carry no sorrow with it. Good enough!

Simon hardly noticed the Black Forest ham as it came in on a platter, surrounded by shiny candied prunes and apricots, he was having such a wrestle with wanting to go on that collecting tour and yet wanting to stay with Kei. They hadn't even had a honeymoon yet because she'd been pregnant when they were married, but Australia was a long, tiring distance away, and he'd have to put in a lot of legwork chasing down the kind of things he was looking for. Moreover, as long as he was over there, it would be foolish not to pick up some of those carved wooden grotesques from Japan that were becoming a vogue in America, as well as some fabrics. The national treasure who made the indigo-dyed material had died a short time ago, so he couldn't waste any time in snapping up some bolts of it, providing the government would let them go.

As for the memoirs, he could dictate them on a plane or in a hotel room as well as he could here and send them via air to London. It wasn't as if he'd be leaving Kei alone, either. She was fond of Garnett because he made her laugh, and there was no one into whose hands he'd rather entrust her. Garnett had proved to be quite as responsible as Simon had thought on first seeing him, and with him in charge there would be no need to worry about Kei's welfare.

When Simon's favorite dessert, soufflé au Grand Marnier, arrived at the table as light and fluffy as a cloud, prettily browned, Kei congratulated Marthe, who smiled proudly and sailed back out to the kitchen to give Esmé instructions for serving the after-dinner liqueurs and cigars. Esmé, who helped out when extra people came to dinner, nodded respectfully, then Marthe had a last look around the kitchen and took a plate of leftover ham to the garage apartment to share with Hilaire for their evening meal.

Marthe's arthritic knee was bothering her lately, Kei had noticed. Maybe Céleste should come in on a daily basis to take over the housework instead of helping Marthe only three times a week. Simon wasn't a bachelor any more, and the enlarged household was working Marthe to death. Even without counting the room Garnett used as a schoolroom until the folly was finished and the ones devoted to storing things for the gallery, there was plenty of space on the third floor. The rooms there had been originally used for the household staff and could be again. While Simon was in Australia, changes could be made and everything would be running smoothly by the time he got back, which would save the fussing he'd make if he were involved in hiring extra servants.

Of course it would be wrenching to have him gone, when she'd hardly had time to get used to living with him, but he was getting entirely too soggy, poor dear, and she herself wanted to quit thinking about the miscarriage. Together, they exacerbated the situation and kept the hurt from healing. The sooner he left, the better for both of them, and the sooner he'd be back.

"About that trip . . . " they both said at the same time and then laughed. Already they were beginning to think alike.

"All right, it's fixed for me to leave early November first," Simon called, putting the receiver back in its cradle and sitting down on the fur spread to take off his socks and shoes. "You're *sure* that's what you want?"

Kei hesitated as a wave of panic washed over her at the thought of doing without Simon for a day, let alone two weeks! Even when he was in the same house, she had to know which room he was in, wanted to know what he was doing, and now he was going to be half a world away, without anyone to tell him where he'd left his reading glasses or to see that he didn't fall over a chair when he was concentrating on something else! How he had managed without her for fifty-eight years, she couldn't imagine. A hell of a lot better than I managed before he came along, she thought. The previous part of her life seemed as pulpy and unappealing as a rotten apple in comparison to the bubbling comfort of living with Simon. Finally she called back, "It's not what I *want*, it's what's best for both of us, isn't it?" Best for Simon anyway, and that was the important thing.

She took a tube of pink, strawberry-flavored lip gloss from the medicine cabinet in the tower bathroom, rouged her nipples carefully with it, and put her nightgown straps back over her shoulders. After spraying herself from head to toe with

Givenchy III, she went in to pad across the plushy bedroom carpet to Simon, who was down on his hands and knees, searching for the gold pencil that had fallen out of his shirt pocket when he'd taken it off. As his hand came down upon it, Kei leaned over and stroked his bare shoulder, and he reached out blindly to put it on the bedside table while he looked up at her transparent ivory chiffon nightgown and said, "Why are you bothering to wear that?"

The pencil rolled across the table and dropped noiselessly onto the carpet again as he put his arms around her hips, pulling her close to draw in the scent of the sea that she carried between her thighs. "My God, it's been so long!" he breathed against her.

Kei spread her legs wider. After a moment, she said, "Not so hard, darling! You're hurting me," and, sinking her fingers into his silvery hair, gently pushed his head away from the damp patch at her crotch. He got to his feet and she ran a hand lovingly over the contours of his chest, then let it slide down to his fly and heard him catch his breath. Putting his hand over hers, he made her hold him tight while he put his open mouth over hers and slipped his tongue between her lips. When he said hoarsely, "Get in bed," she obediently folded back the covers, let her nightgown fall into a frothy puddle around her feet, lay down, and waited for the warm weight of his body to press down on her.

"Since when do you taste like strawberries?" said Simon.

CHAPTER FOUR

Father Barteau leaned his bicycle against the ugly modern sculpture by the château's front doors and stood staring down unseeingly at its handlebars while the wind whipped the skirt of his surplice against his trouser legs. A cup of hot tea would be welcome after making his round of visitations in this raw weather, and Kei had urged him to drop by any afternoon, but was he being honest with himself about why he had come?

For two or three days after having dinner here, he'd ridden on an exhilarating crest of spiritual renewal, inspired to fresh insight into man as the vehicle for the expression of God's purity and love. But when Garnett's face appeared on the pages of the parish records as he made his daily entries, returning each morning, he'd realized with horror that the elation he'd been feeling had an insidious parallel in the effervescence that had coursed through his bloodstream those long years ago when he'd first met Christophe. Catching himself up short, he'd methodically, ruthlessly rooted out this threat to his vocation through anguished prayer and now felt

55

serene again, cleansed.

Or did he? He looked up at the château wall and thought that somewhere on the second storey, behind one of those windows opening outwards behind curlicued iron railings, might be Garnett's bedroom. A raven sitting on one of the tin banners that flew at the peak of the corner towers cocked its head quizzically at him, as if questioning his motives, and Father Barteau took hold of the bicycle handlebars, preparatory to putting himself out of the way of temptation, when one of the front doors opened and Garnett stepped out.

"I've been expecting you," he said with a sweet smile. "Marthe's put the tea things in the salon."

Father Barteau hesitated. The leap of excitement he'd felt at seeing the boy again was a sure sign that his prayers had been ineffective. All that to do over again, more earnestly than before! However, Kei would be puzzled and perhaps offended if he left now, after being invited in. Resolving to watch his thoughts rigorously, the priest parked his cycle again and followed Garnett into the warmth of the house.

The coffee table by the fireplace was laid with a silver tea set, plates of brioche and spongecake, and accompanying garnishments. Father Barteau removed his beret and seated himself on one of the settees before noting that only two Haviland cups had been set out.

"Kei's taken the twins into Orléans to shop for winter clothes," Garnett said, watching the priest's eyes.

The situation was awkward, but he couldn't be forever running away from a confrontation with

56

Garnett, the priest decided. The boy was not to blame for the weaknesses of others. It would probably never occur to him that a priest was a normal human being, and if he'd had the faintest inkling that his closeness might upset anyone's equilibrium, Father Barteau thought, he would be sitting over there on the other settee instead of beside me. Close like this.

The tea was finer than anything the housekeeper served at the parish house and was deliciously warming. After another cup and a wedge of buttered brioche, laced through with a murmuring of innocuous chat, the priest began to feel full and cozy and relaxed. Garnett's voice had a curious soothing quality that almost invited one to nod off into a pleasant, buzzy sleep.

"I wouldn't have your job for all the world," Garnett was saying as the priest found that he had indeed nearly dozed off.

"No?" He looked down at the hand that had been laid on his leg, thought that there was no point in getting fussed about it, and asked, "Why not?"

"It must be so lonely. Don't you get terribly lonely?"

A denial began struggling up through Father Barteau's mind but never quite broke through to the surface. Something about not being alone because something, somebody, was always at his side. Who was it? He knew it as well as he knew his own name, but it kept escaping him. But really, he *was* alone, wasn't he? There was nobody to greet him when he came in at night to take his dinner out of the oven where Madame Prévost left it warming. And he climbed the stairs to his bedroom at night alone, sometimes aching for the sound of another voice. Garnett understood that. Tears prickled behind Father Barteau's eyelids as he looked down again at Garnett's hand and thought how he had missed this kind of sympathy and friendly contact.

Looking up, his eyes met Garnett's in a long gaze, and Father Barteau felt as if his mind was being scanned, his secret thoughts being searched through like dresser drawers. But he was not ashamed. It was *all right* that he was what he was, and the sins that tormented him were really nothing at all, understandable human foibles of no consequence. Garnett's sweet understanding wrapped around him like a mother's arms.

"What I'd hate most of all," said the benevolent voice, "would be not being touched. Everyone needs to be touched."

Yes, Father Barteau said or didn't say, he couldn't tell whether his words had reached outside his head or not. Yes, human contact, we all need that, the touch of skin to skin. One hungers for it; yearns to be touched, caressed, enfolded; longs for that deep comfort, like the comfort that flows through this hand holding mine.

"Your mouth is beautiful," the voice said. Everything seemed muffled in a luminous blur except for Garnett's mouth, its finely traced upper lip, its glossy full lower lip so soft-looking and moist, the tiny golden hairs at the corners, and then Father Barteau felt the warmth of that mouth on his.

Cycling back to the village past the leafless poplars

lining the road the priest asked himself why he'd gotten so apprehensive at finding himself alone with the boy. Nothing could have been more harmless and impersonal than their conversation. He congratulated himself that his behavoir had been above reproach, although it had been a bit graceless of him to have fallen asleep like that. He must be more worn out than he realized.

As he rode along, working against the wind and watching flocks of black birds drift like plumes of soot from one grove of trees to another on the horizon, an uneasy feeling began coiling through his mind, but he couldn't quite catch the tail of what was causing it. Nevertheless, there was a little slippery sensation in there of something's being wrong. Perhaps it was the brioche, working subtle mischief in his stomach. He wasn't used to such rich food, not with Madame Prévost in charge of the kitchen.

Father Barteau awoke with a start, his linen nightshirt plastered to his chest with sweat, and stared up at the ceiling. The rapid ticking of the sturdy clock on the bedside table seemed to be synchronized with his heartbeat and sounded preternaturally loud, like whacks of a tackhammer driving nails into his eardrums.

We are not responsible for our dreams, St. Paul said that we are not. We are not to blame! He looked up at the wall, where the light of a waning moon threw silvery highlights on the modeling of the figure hanging there on its cross. Drawing strength from it, he relentlessly squeezed the memory of his dream back into that compartment of his mind where all the demons in his soul raged, snarling and pushing against his will, struggling to free themselves, to take over his thoughts and command his body. The effort made perspiration stand out on his upper lip and drip into the creases that formed a parenthesis around his mouth.

Still, the white dust of Aix-en-Provence trickled slowly black into his consciousness, bringing with it dappled shadows and the reverberation of a voice long silenced. The eye of his mind opened like a lens shutter to show a flash of golden inner thigh and snapped shut again. He felt a quick lurch in the base of his stomach and his pelvis thrust upward involuntarily. *Oh, my Christophe! Oh, my God!*

He groaned and sat up to reach for the clock. The luminous dial looked fuzzy, its numerals blurred. Slowly a face superimposed itself over the glass, the features gathering more clarity, like iron filings concentrating above a magnet, until he saw Garnett smiling at him. As he blinked to focus his eyes, the face faded and the clock's dial showed two hands pointing straight up.

CHAPTER FIVE

Ghosts weren't a very imaginative choice of costume, but Gino and Dirk would get more of a bang out of shouting Boo! when people opened their doors than they would be pretending to be Tweedledum and Tweedledee, Garnett thought as he cut a sheet in two. He wasn't skillful enough to sew anything that complicated anyway. Besides, their mother had been vocal about being careful not to emphasize their twin-ness, lest it impair their individuality.

He put half of the sheet over Dirk's head and marked where the eyeholes should go, then did the same for Gino.

Telling the twins apart was easy. They were fraternal, not identical, and Gino was the one who stuck his thumb in his mouth and twiddled his ear with his free fingers. A fraction smaller than his brother, he had a sweet, wistful expression that reminded Garnett of a dreamy mouse. Gino found life an exhilarating new experience that required a lot of rushing around at top speed so he wouldn't miss anything. Dirk, on the other hand, moved at a

61

graceful, stately pace and liked to ponder things. His I.Q. must be phenomenal, although Gino was probably just as intelligent in his own fanciful way. Sometimes when Garnett looked into Dirk's eyes, he got the eerie feeling that an enormously wise old man was staring back at him, imprisoned inside the child's head. Pink, prominent ears large enough to vibrate gently in a strong wind saved Dirk's classical features from looking girlish. They were cute kids, really, and sharp as a whiplash. Promising material, if used cleverly.

He'd already alerted the Americans in the expatriate colony down in the village that the boys would be trick-or-treating, so they'd be ready with handouts and the excursion shouldn't take long. That would leave plenty of time to take Eagle a step further before midnight, when the other meeting began.

"I'll tell you a Hallowe'en story, a true one, if you sit on your beds quietly while I get this done," Garnett said, taking a pair of scissors out of the pint-sized desk whose top was littered with bottles containing insect life they'd collected on gathering expeditions while exploring the estate: a Monarch butterfly's chrysalis like a tube of light green jade decorated with gilt dots, a crawling mass of bewildered ladybugs, a walking stick that was examining three jellybeans that Gino thought would be a suitable diet for it, and a praying mantis that the boys had taken a marked dislike to because of its gruesome custom of biting the head off its living lunch and munching it untidily while its victim's body twitched pathetically. "Now, this story is a secret, and you know what that means."

The twins nodded solemnly. They knew what a secret was, Garnett had seen to that. Bedtime tales of epic comradeship had quickly indoctrinated them with the heroic ideal of loyalty unto death, and that included keeping secrets. The concept had caught on so smashingly that they carried it into their games, and Garnett had had to buy a second dagger with a collapsible blade to stop fights over whose turn it was to shout "Death to dishonor!" before falling on the weapon and dying with melodramatic groans and leg-jerks. Still, a booster shot might be good insurance.

He looked to see that each boy was sitting cross-legged on his own bed before starting to cut the fabric. They were hunched forward in anticipation with their elbows on their knees.

"Okay," he began, "once upon a time there was a beautiful lady who lived in a château just like this one. Perhaps it *was* this one, who can tell? It was three hundred years ago, when the world still believed in magic. There really was magic then, as there is now if you know where to find it.

"This lady was so fair at birth that she was named Sélène for the goddess of the moon. Her hair was like black satin, and her eyes were as bright as the stars on a summer's night. She walked like a queen, for she was the daughter of a king, although her father did not acknowledge her as his own. Thus, though royal blood flowed in her veins, the beauteous lady was forced to marry beneath her, to marry a base-born merchant whom she hated, a black-hearted man whose only virtue was that he was very rich, who treated her like a slave, and who laughed when the poor of the village came begging bread. This wrung the heart of the kind Lady Sélène, who yearned to feed the ragged poor, who starved year-long and died in the harsh winters, curled like dead snails beside cold fires—for the merchant would not allow wood to be cut in his forest.

"Then one day the lady came upon a curious volume in the library of the château. Blowing dust from its cover, she discovered that she had in her hand a book of magic. Oh, if she could but learn magic, perhaps she could warm the bodies of the poor with magnificent perfumed fires, load their tables with pheasant pies and plum puddings, replace their pitiful rags with silks and furs!"

Finished with cutting, Garnett folded up the sheets and put them amidst the litter on the desk, then leaned back in his chair.

"And so she studied the book until she had unlocked every one of its secrets and had learned to conjure up wonders out of the air, to fly to the farthest corners of the earth on the currents of the wind, and to summon up a powerful friend who could grant her every wish." Garnett made grandiose abracadabra swirls with his arms while the twins watched spellbound, their large round eyes and heavy arched brows making them resemble small owls.

"At first, this friend frightened the gentle lady, for he was terrifying of aspect, but she soon learned that he was just and fair and kept his bargains. But, he said, if he was to grant her wishes, she had to pay a dreadful price, for nothing is given without something being taken away. She cried salty tears that burned her eyes at what was required of her. She must sacrifice that which she held most dear, her own babies. But, said her friend reasonably, how could she be so selfish as to mourn over a little lump of flesh that had not yet known life, when men and women who loved her were suffering long years of bitter deprivation?"

Gino put his thumb in his mouth and grabbed his ear with his fingers, and Dirk frowned at the lady's dilemma.

"And so the lady made a choice that seemed to tear her heart in two," Garnett continued, clutching his fists to his chest to illustrate. "She chose the happiness of the villagers over her own and learned how to use her newborn babies to make powerful spells, reminding herself as she sobbed through the night that they would have carried the black seed of cruelty from her husband and would have grown to be as heartless and tyrannical as he.

"When the people saw what she could do to make others happy, they wanted to learn her magical skills, and the Lady Sélène generously shared her knowledge with them, so long as they paid the very small price that her friend demanded: they must never tell what they knew. They must never, on pain of death, reveal Sélène secrets.

"Alas," Garnett said woefully, "some of them did. Weeping wildly, the lady obeyed her friend's command and destroyed those who could not keep a secret. Alas, alas, they had to be killed, and in such a way. . . " Garnett stood up and pointed a finger direly at the twins, who began backing away along their beds. "And in such a way as to be a terrible warning to others who might foolishly think of giving away the precious magic!"

Garnett put his head in his hands and shook it back and forth sadly, saying in a voice that sounded full of tears, "Alas again, there were those who did not understand, who thought the Lady Sélène evil for erasing those few miserable ones, for releasing them from their worthless lives. They forgot that the ones who died had broken their sacred promises, forgot that there is no good given without a price being paid."

He sat down heavily on the small chair, his legs stretched out before him, slumping as if he were exhausted by sorrow. "And they took the good and gracious lady, who was now heavy with child, to the grotto where the magic ceremonies were performed, stripped the clothing from her ivory body, and wound cords around her as a spider spins silken threads around a fly before sucking it dry of blood, leaving it an empty husk."

Dirk now popped his thumb in his mouth to comfort himself, which Garnett had never seen him do before, and Gino put his hands over his ears to shut out the story but then opened them out again cautiously, unable to resist listening. Lowering his voice to a hollow whisper, Garnett leaned forward.

"And the villagers destroyed the grotto, pulling its stones down around the lovely lady while she writhed in agony. And as the stones rained down upon her, bruising her poor body, she knew that her time was upon her, that the child was about to be born. As the grotto sank down in on her, a love such as she had never known flowered within her heart for the child that was to die as soon as it felt life. Because of her, it was fated to perish in this airless tomb, poisoned by her own breath, struggling for air while its lungs filled with dust as hers were filling now."

Garnett clenched his hands around his throat and made a strangling sound that set Gino whimpering. "With her last breath," he said hoarsely, gasping out the words, "the Lady Sélène cursed the villains who were murdering her child, asking that her powerful friend take their own children from them at birth so that they might know the evil they had done her and repent of their wickedness—as was only just and right."

Suddenly, Garnett jumped to his feet and threw the folded sheets onto Dirk's bed, and Dirk gave a little shriek and Gino covered his eyes with his hands. Garnett went to the window and looked out for a dramatic minute at the skeleton of the summer-house standing in the forest, while Gino took his hands down slowly to see what he was doing.

"And there she lay—out there—for three hundred long years, her spirit hovering within the grotto, keeping watch over the dead shell of the child she loved, whose spirit had been in the world just an instant before having to seek another body into which it might be born again. But on special nights like this one, when the moon is dark, Sélène roams the countryside, calling in the voice of the wind for her child, seeking the newborn babe who houses the spirit of the child she lost. When she finds this child, the love she bore for it will flow through her ghost body like pulsing blood, and the flesh body that she left behind will come alive again, and the Lady Sélène will walk the land with the child in her arms."

He leaned toward the window and cupped a hand around his ear. "Listen," he said in a thrilling whisper, "can't you hear her now in the wind, calling for a child? She's saying *'Cher enfant,* dear child! *Cher enfant!'* " He drew the shushing sound in *cher* out into a long, chilling whistle.

"She doesn't want *me!*" Dirk said in a quavering voice. "I'm a big boy now, I'm not a baby!"

"And *I* don't tell secrets!" said Gino, jumping off his own bed to crawl up with Dirk for company. The twins hugged each other tight.

Garnett whirled and smacked his hands together sharply, making the children jump. "Well now," he said briskly, "didn't I make up a nice spooky story for you?"

"But you said it was *true!*" Dirk wailed, and Gino asked if the Lady Sélène was out there in the woods now, waiting to get them.

"Hm, I don't remember saying it was true," Garnett said evasively, rubbing his chin. "Did I say that? Well, never mind, let's get your jackets on, it's cold out there in the wind. Then you can put on your costumes and go down to scare the folks in the salon."

"I don't want to go treat-or-tricking," Gino said, starting to cry and digging his knuckles into his eyes.

Garnett got their jackets from the red pegs on the wall and tossed them on the bed. "Oh, come on. There's no danger out there for people who can keep secrets. And Hallowe'en only comes once a year."

"Once is too much," Dirk snuffled, putting on his jacket.

When the twins shouted Boo! from the salon doorway, Eagle clutched his chest, feigning a heart attack, slid off the settee onto the floor, and flailed around on the Aubusson carpet before lying flat on his back, eyes closed and tongue lolling from his mouth. Gino tiptoed over to him, squatted down, adjusted his sheet so he could peer through the eyeholes, and pulled up one of Eagle's eyelids. At seeing one brown pupil whirling around in giddy circles, he went off into the cascade of giggles.

As Eagle got up to get a handful of peanuts from the bar and toss them up into the air, catching them one by one in his open mouth, and the twins went from adult to adult to get compliments, kisses, and admonitions about saying thank you politely when they got donations, Garnett came in from the dark foyer with a lighted jack o'lantern in each hand.

"You've got a bag for the candy?" Simon asked.

With a tightening of his elbow against the folded bag under his arm, Garnett indicated that he was fully equipped for the expedition. He handed a pumpkin to each twin, said goodnight, and shot a look at Eagle, who gave him a quick, almost imperceptible nod.

The twins were draggling along the last two dark, lampless blocks back to the château, hand in sticky hand and feeling passably safe with Garnett right behind them carrying the bagful of candy, when the candles in their jack o'lanterns guttered down and went out.

Galvanized by the sudden blackness, the children took off for home like two Kleenexes flying before a high wind. A claw of bridal wreath caught at Dirk's sheet and pulled at it. He left the sheet in the grasp of the bush and, not stopping to look back, speeded up so that his feet were outdistancing his body and he was running slanted backward, his knees pumping away as fast as they would go. Garnett loped ahead of them and cut in front, calling, "Hey! Slow down! It's all right, calm down!" But the twins simply detoured around him on the sidewalk and left him standing behind as they tore toward home.

"What's all this?" Simon asked when Gino jumped, sheet and all, into his lap, grabbed him around the neck, and burst into tears. Dirk headed for Kei and buried his face in her lap, sobbing, "She wants me! I heard her in the wind, calling *'Cher enfant, cher enfant!'* "

"Kei hoisted him onto her knees with a grunt and rocked him back and forth in her arms, patting him consolingly. "Who wants you, sweetheart?" she asked, looking questioningly at Garnett as he came into the salon.

"Nobody! Nothing! It's a secret," Dirk gulped, sneaking a look at Garnett and then hiding his face against Kei's neck.

"I think this child is hysterical," Simon said in alarm, trying to clear his lap of passport, tickets, schedules, and all the things he was organizing for tomorrow and reach them around Gino to put them on the coffee table. "What in heaven happened to get him into this state?" He kissed and hugged the child, making comforting sounds until Gino quieted down to hiccuping.

"Guess I'd better be more careful about what they

watch on television," Garnett said. He set the bag of candy down on the floor and spit on his handkerchief. Applying it to the streaks on Dirk's face, he said, "They watched a rerun of the Wizard of Oz last week, and the Wicked Witch of the West scared them pea green." Gently he pried Dirk loose from Kei and set him down on the carpet. "I'd better give them a hot bath and get them set in bed before I leave."

"I don't want to sleep in our room! I want to sleep with Grandad!" Gino bawled, nearly strangling Simon with a tightened grip on his neck.

"Me, too!" cried Dirk.

Kei sighed. "Yes, go ahead and bathe them and put them in our bed. Let them have some candy, but make them brush their teeth afterwards."

As the tutor took them upstairs, Simon put his travel documents into the holster wallet he wore under his arm on long trips and groused, "Dammit, Kei, this is my last night home, and I was looking forward to a grand roll in the hay. My God, I thought Eagle would never quit talking and go home, and now we're going to have those two between us all night! It just isn't fair!"

"Come on, Simon, don't you remember what it was like to be scared when you were little?" she said placatingly and got up to empty the ashtrays around the room into the silent butler.

"I was *never* little. Or if I was, it's lost in the mists of time," Simon grumbled and finished off the drink he'd left sitting on the coffee table.

"When I was their age, I was convinced that there was a monster made out of melting peanut butter in

71

the bathroom clothes hamper. Every morning my mother made me look into it to see that it wasn't there, but you couldn't convince me that it didn't slither away when it heard us coming. I've never been so scared of anything since, not even the IRS. Anyway, I just got my period." She straightened the colored pillows on the settees and plumped up the backs of the easy chairs with stout whacks of her hand.

"When has that made any difference?" Simon asked with growing annoyance, working himself into a lather.

Kei pulled him to his feet and put her arms around him. "Well, it means we didn't get me pregnant this time, doesn't it?" she said into his chest.

"Bloody hell!" he said, laying his cheek on top of her head. "But just wait until I get back!"

Just as he'd feared, the twins were waiting for them, plunk in the middle of the bed, so he and Kei would have to sleep on the outsides. A great way to spend his last night at home! Simon lay awake, glaring up at the ceiling, with Dirk a soft lump pressing against him, radiating heat like a pot-bellied stove. He waited until slow, heavy breathing had been coming from the center of the bed for about five minutes and then sat up cautiously and lowered one foot to the carpet.

"Where are you going, Grandad? You're not leaving, are you?" Dirk whispered. Simon put his foot back under the covers and lay down again. The little bugger must have been playing possum, waiting to catch him trying to get into the other room with Kei!

Ten long minutes went by until he felt sure it was safe to make another attempt. He was only *thinking* about it, not stirring yet, when Dirk turned over toward him, grabbed him around the waist, and said suspiciously, "Promise you won't go away!"

"I promise! I *promise!*" Simon snapped. The kid must be a mind reader! But dammit, was it so unreasonable to want to be alone with Kei? While Dirk lay with his arm around his neck and drooled on his chest, Simon plotted. Technically, he reasoned, if he moved the twins into another room, *they* would be the ones that went away, not he. But first he'd have to work Dirk's head off his chest, millimeter by millimeter. If he got that accomplished, then he'd have to creep out of bed and try to scoop the child up without wakening him, which was a risky business, particularly since a child's weight seemed to multiply tenfold the minute he was asleep. Would Dirk wake up at being put into a cold bed? And if that part of the maneuver went off without a hitch, there was still Gino to move. Now, how to go about that? Let's see. . . .

Simon fell asleep.

Father Barteau was afraid to go to sleep, lest he dream again of Garnett. In the cold study of the parish house, he put his elbows on the desk and leaned his hot forehead on his clasped hands. When he was awake, prayer was a weapon against the sickly sweet desire to think of the boy, but asleep he was helpless. At first, it had been memories of Christophe that had drifted in, filling the night with a pastel-colored mélange of anticipation, discovery, and delight from which he woke in the morning with a black feeling of loss and guilt. Now Garnett's face had replaced Christophe's and he woke with an overwhelming sense of yearning as painful as the return of sensation to frostbitten flesh. To lose his vocation for love—and for the love of a man—would be agony, but with the help of God's mercy, he might yet be saved from that. It was too late to be saved from the anguish of realizing that he had never wanted God as he wanted Garnett.

CHAPTER SIX

"What'll he do if he catches us?" Eagle asked in a low voice, zipping up his windbreaker so it wouldn't hang loose and catch on something when he went through the window.

"He won't, don't worry about it. Nobody's ever caught me yet," Garnett said in a casual tone that made Eagle more apprehensive than ever. If Gar had done this so many times that it was getting to be old stuff to him, by the law of averages the chances of disaster must be creeping up on him rapidly. "Give me a boost," Garnett ordered. "I left the window open a little the last time I was in there, but it looks like it's closed again. If he's locked it, we're out of luck for tonight."

Jesus, he wished he'd stayed back at the château with the folks instead of letting Garnett talk him into this again! And what if Aunt Kei called to check on him, as she sometimes did, now that he was staying in the house alone while his mother and Tommy were on their stupid honeymoon? Eagle made a cradle of his hands for Garnett's jogging shoe and heaved him up onto the outside sill, his ears pricked for sounds of alarm within the house, for the footfalls coming down the sidewalk outside the bushes around the house, for any strange noises that signaled catastrophe. This whole business was giving him the blue whimwhams!

It had sounded like fun when Gar had described his private game of slipping into empty buildings at night and walking around them, seeing them as no one else saw them—deserted, echoing, their inky blackness peppered with unexpected hazards like sudden stairwells without guard rails or old, unused doors that opened out onto nothing where fire escapes had been removed. The challenge of testing himself against unmapped, forbidden territory *had* been fun at first, when they'd tackled easy stuff like the one-room local library with its silent shelves of books whose smell of yellowing paper and protective varnish was acute in the absence of human odors, and the school, where he'd gone into a girls' john for the first time and had also discovered that the teacher kept a bottle of cognac hidden in his desk drawer. But though they'd worn soundless shoes and kept the rule about not using a flashlight once inside, a night watchman had gotten suspicious at the city hall, and the cone of yellow from his flashlight had come within two feet of Eagle's feet as he stood by a file case with his heart gonging away, so scared he thought he was going to barf. And sneaking into a private home like this was *really* dangerous! This wasn't a matter of discovering forgotten tower rooms in public buildings where pigeon shit crunched beneath their shoes or of exploring networks of heating tunnels running under the village. This was the big time—breaking and entering, in fact—and if they got away with it this once, he was bugging out of any more of Gar's explorations. No more leaving scraps of paper with his initials on them in the backs of desk drawers to prove he'd been inside, even though anyone finding one would probably simply wonder what the hell *that* was and throw it into the wastebasket. If he had any guts, he'd stand up to Gar right now and back out.

But Garnett was already inside, with his arm reaching down for him. Oh fuck, I'm in it now, thought Eagle, and stubbed his sneaker toes into the cracks between the bricks of the wall, clambering up as Garnett pulled at him. Sitting at last on the window sill, facing the outside, Eagle couldn't get his legs twisted around to go through the window and had to bring them up over his head and fall backward so that Garnett could catch him and lower him to the floor. After that scramble, they stood still a moment in the darkness, listening to be sure the noise hadn't alerted Mr. Grapes, the house's owner.

Except for the wind rising outside, there wasn't a sound other than the breath whistling through Eagle's open mouth, which seemed as loud as a calliope on the inside of his head. He jumped when the furnace went on, sending a blast of hot air whooshing through the registers. Christ, he hadn't expected that! Everybody else in the village had radiators, but Mr. Grapes was rich enough to import a heating system, having retired from film directing with a pile of money. In the dim light from the window, Eagle could see the top of the desk crowded with writing accessories and paperweights. Furniture crouched ominously about the room like sleeping animals. Squares of dimmer light on the wall were, he figured, the glass in framed photographs. A mass of white flowers made a luminous ball above the highlight on the curve of the case of a grand piano; and a pale line traced a rectangle with rounded corners around a TV screen near a dark, tall oblong of a door. Eagle had never been in the house before and wondered how the room looked in the daylight, when it was more than a jumble of variegated grays and blacks.

The silhouette of Garnett's head jerked to the right, and Eagle followed him silently across the carpeting to another dark oblong and into a place that had the vibrations of a hallway, where his sneakers encountered bare boards. A squeak told him that Garnett had stepped on a loose one. They both stopped, then he sensed that Garnett was turning around and felt his friend's hands come down on his elbows to guide him along, sliding up a little to indicate when he should step over the noisy board.

They proceeded cautiously into a room whose flooring sounded like linoleum, and a slice of light made Eagle blink as Garnett opened the refrigerator door, extracted a container of kefir, drank half of it down, and offered the rest to Eagle, who refused it, although his dry throat felt stuffed with bits of knotted string. There was a small click as Garnett closed the door after putting the kefir back, and he pattered across the room to open a door into another room, from which a snore was issuing. Eagle hung back and let his leader go inside alone, if he was that kind of a fool. After he'd held his breath a few moments, he felt Garnett slip something that felt like a rolled magazine into his hand and put his mouth against his ear to whisper, "It was lying right on the covers under his nose. Bet it's a girlie magazine. That's what a toad like Grapes's valet would read!" Garnett chuckled softly. Eagle put the magazine in a back pocket.

They covered the rest of the house, with Eagle's mouth getting drier and drier and cold beads of sweat crawling like a stream of ants from his armpits, until they neared what must be the master bedroom, where a crack of light showed under the door. Again, Garnett put his lips next to Eagle's ear and said, "He's probably fallen asleep with the light on. Should we chance it?"

"Holy shit, no!" Eagle whispered, forgetting to say it into Garnett's ear. At just that moment, something brushed around one of his legs and then brushed around the other in a winding movement, and the shock nearly made him wet his pants. Not waiting for Garnett, he tiptoed as fast as he could toward a lighter oblong and found himself in the room they'd started in.

Over by the window, panting, frightened to the verge of tears, Eagle waited for his friend and cussed himself out for being a pushover, for acting like one of those marionettes that Gar made dance by jerking their strings. The guys at school couldn't talk him into pot parties and they couldn't make him feel chicken for not gangbanging the ever-willing Mary Lou Crébillon either, so why did he go along with anything Gar suggested? Had his brain changed to cottage cheese?

After a couple of minutes, he heard something moving across the carpet and saw a darker shadow coming toward him past the denser shadows looming in the corners.

"Can't panic like that," Garnett's voice murmured. "Might ruin the game, you know." In the window's light Eagle saw him cradling a cat in his arm. That must have been what wound itself around his legs back there. Garnett was stroking the animal and crooning to it, as calm as if he'd been invited to afternoon tea. He let the purring cat slip over his arms and land on the carpet with a soft thump, then held out his hand palm up to Eagle, saying, "Got it?"

Reluctantly, Eagle dug into his windbreaker pocket for the scrap of paper on which he'd written his initials. Before handing it over, he whispered, "Where's yours?"

"I've explored this house before. I left one already, in the bottom drawer of Grapes's bureau."

"I don't think I want to."

Garnett snatched the paper from his hand. "Don't be a sap," he said, almost in a normal speaking tone, and opened the top drawer of the desk by the window and reached toward the back to deposit the paper there. But before closing the drawer he took something from it and held it up to the light. It was a silver cigarette lighter. Garnett closed the drawer noiselessly and slipped the lighter into his pocket.

"You can't do that!" Eagle protested.

Garnett laughed softly. "I just did."

Flustered by what had just happened, Eagle followed his leader through the window into the windy night, skinning his ankle as he dragged it across the sill, and heard a ripping sound as he jumped down onto the soft earth behind the bushes that surrounded the sleeping house. He felt his jacket and discovered that one of the pockets was missing.

A light went on over their heads, coming from the room they'd just left behind, but it was too faint to be the overhead fixture in the room itself. The bushes rattled as Garnett slipped through them onto the sidewalk beyond, but fear of leaving an incriminating clue behind made Eagle stifle his impulse to flee in panic. He could see the pocket, a dark square flapping between the closed window and the sill, caught by a corner. He made a couple of jumps at it, but it was just beyond his grasp. Cold with fright, he backed up as far as the bushes would allow and took a run at the wall, half walking up it when he hit it, and grabbed the piece of material before he fell backwards onto his rump with the pocket safely in his hand.

Now the top light *was* on in the room above! He turned over quickly and pressed his nose into wet leaves smelling like strong tea, hiding his face from the light, and waited while a spider crawled along his cheek and the hair on the back of his neck prickled. He could hear someone talking behind the closed window, then some agitated music, and the sound of screeching tires. Relieved, he rolled over and sat up. Mr. Grapes was watching television.

Eagle hoisted himself to his feet and, crouching, pushed his way through the bushes and came out onto the sidewalk, where he stopped to remove the spider and flick it off into the darkness, brushed off his trousers, encountered the rolled up magazine in his pocket and understood why one buttock had hurt so much when he'd fallen on it, and ran his fingers into his hair and shook them to get the leaves out. God, that was a close shave! The blood was singing through his veins. An odd feeling of elation spread through him, a sort of post-emergency intoxication at having gotten away with it, with a hair's-breadth margin of error. Hot shit! He laughed out loud and was still laughing when he joined Garnett, who was leaning against a street lamp half a block away with his hair riffling in the wind, his ankles crossed and serenely smoking a cigarette as he studied the monogrammed lighter in his hand.

"That was great! Just great!" Eagle panted, feeling a wave of comradeship for his friend, who had initiated him into the pleasure of tightrope-walking over danger. Garnett smacked his fist lightly into Eagle's shoulder and told him to watch himself the next time. "Yeah, I nearly blew it, didn't I? Sorry," said Eagle, still giddy from his narrow escape.

"Got the magazine?" asked Garnett, squinting one eye against the smoke blowing into his face from the cigarette in the corner of his mouth.

Eagle handed it to him and Garnett looked at it with a scornful eye, humphed and said he'd expected as much, and handed it back. Its lurid cover showed a girl with spread legs who was obviously giving herself a good time.

"Don't you want to look at it?" asked Eagle.

"I prefer doing to looking," Garnett said and yawned. "You have fun with it. I have some people to see."

As Eagle let himself into the empty house and snapped on the lights, he felt the excitement waning and a headache waxing. He went into the kitchen, looked with despair at the sinkful of dishes, and made himself a Dagwood out of paté, Gruyère, onion slices, peanut butter, and a fried egg, and wished—not for the first time—that he hadn't turned down Aunt Kei's offer of a bedroom at the château until the folks got back. He was tired of taking care of himself and of catching breakfast at the train station when he commuted to school.

He took the sandwich and a glass of orangeade out to the living room and lay down on the couch with his legs over the back to study the pictures in the magazine. Eye-bugging though they were, he couldn't keep his mind on them and kept thinking of what he and Garnett had gotten away with. In five minutes he was feeling absolutely lousy about it. They'd come too close to getting caught. Wouldn't it be really terrific to have a criminal record before he even got out of school, he thought sourly. A couple of rat-shit petty thieves was what they were! And what for? Who needed a silver cigarette lighter anyway? Who needed a stretch in the slammer? He'd come *that close* to messing up his life for a dumb magazine and a cigarette lighter that Gar had appropriated for himself! Jesus, when Gar was around, he hardly knew himself. Turned into somebody entirely different, a robot with no brain at all, unable to think for himself. Well, that was the last time, by God! If he had to put both fingers in his ears to shut out Gar's voice, he wasn't going to be talked into playing Gar's fucking game again. Let *him* get his ass burned if he wanted to, but no more of his crap for Simon Thomas Eagleton McKenzie! No way, nohow! Hey, get a load of those two girls on page 23!

He whistled, and still looking at page 23, went into the bathroom.

Father Barteau prostrated himself before the altar, pressing his face against the stone of the floor, feeling its chill spread up through his clothing. Cold as the stone was to his open palms, the howling emptiness of the arctic night within his soul was icier still. He lay there a long time, his mind blank, listening bleakly to the sound of his own breathing and the wind hissing through the crumbling sealing around the high, dark windows. In the Lord was mercy and fullness of redemption, but how could he reach out for it with this enormous weight of guilt and hopelessness paralyzing his will?

A warm drop slid over his cheekbone onto the stone, and finally he could bring out the words to plead for compassion, crying out that this temptation was too much for him, throwing himself on the mercy of Christ. In his agony he heard the wind die away, leaving silence behind it—the terrible silence when God does not answer.

At two in the morning, Garnett took a back pathway where he would encounter no one and started back to the château. Ceremonial oil darkened his face and hands as well as his body, but he could not afford to be seen coming from this direction at this hour of the night. Filled with a sense of mastery and power, he allowed himself to cover the ground at abnormal speed, almost floating in giant strides.

At the château, he let himself in and slipped up the stairs to his bedroom to peel off the clothing sticking to his body. His tower bathroom was at the opposite corner to the other one that Simon and Kei used, and they wouldn't detect the noise of the running water down at this end when he showered.

Simon would be gone tomorrow, he thought as he lathered down. Kei would be alone. He was looking forward to that. But first, he had still one other amusement ahead of him tonight.

Dawn was not far away when Father Barteau made his way stiffly up the stairs to his room, turned off the hallway light, and began undressing in the darkness. He took off his surplice, undid his rabat, and laid them aside, rubbing the wet socket of one eye with the heel of his palm. His cheekbone smarted and was fever-hot. Cold air prickled along his arms and shoulders as he looked out at a sliver of moon hanging low on the horizon and dreaded the rising of the sun on another day.

When he felt a soft touch on his shoulders and a warm, moist mouth on the back of his neck, he felt no shock, knowing who it was and knowing that, however much he denied it in his prayers, this was what he had been hoping for, waiting for. He stood still a moment and then turned gladly toward the strong embrace he had been dreaming of.

85

CHAPTER SEVEN

Christ almighty! He'd forgotten to set the alarm! It should still be dark, but the white light of early morning had already crept halfway across the ceiling. Simon sat bolt upright and shot a look across the sleeping bodies—Dirk snuggled into Gino's back, Gino with his arm around Kei's neck and his pink cheek squashed against the thick tangle of her hair—and saw a three and a zero click down into place on the black dial of the clock. Six-thirty! The plane left in an hour, and the trip to the airport would take half of that! Thank God, he'd packed last evening!

In ten minutes he'd showered, shaved, stuck a piece of toilet paper on the cut on his chin, and was in the Donegal tweed jacket and vest and dark trousers that Kei had laid out for him.

"Kei!" he said urgently in a low voice, holding out her amber satin kimono so she could step into it. She opened her eyes, blinked, disentangled herself from Gino, and was out of bed and into the bathroom while he still held the robe out to empty air. The children slept on in their yellow Dr. Dentons, curled like prawns in the middle of the bed.

Mitzi added to his panic by jumping at the door of the Mercedes Benz jeep, begging for a ride, and then romping away and back again so he had to chase her around before closing her into the foyer. As he slung his battered flight case into the back of the jeep, Simon looked up to see three ravens convened like black-robed judges on top of the black and white scupture by the gravel parking area. They opened their beaks, and a faint hissing sound came from their yellow-lined mouths. Simon was startled as their eyes met his. To make contact with such inhuman creatures, with the untamed minds inside those sleek ebony heads, made him feel he was looking into a dark, forbidden kingdom that man was not meant to know, and a shiver of apprehension snaked down his spine. "Cat walking over your grave," whispered his grandmother's voice from the past.

Uneasiness stalked behind him all the way toward town. He tried to evade it by giving Kei last-minute instructions on running things in his absence, but the sense of foreboding clung around him like a stale odor. Sitting beside him in her jeans and thick white cableknit sweater, she patiently absorbed what he was telling her, punctuating his monologue with cooperative-sounding mmhmms, though she'd heard it all before.

"I've opened an account in town for Garnett to draw on to pay for materials, furnishings, whatever he wants for the folly, and to cover the salaries of the men," he said, putting his hand over hers. "He'll supervise the completion of the thing. Should be finished on the inside in a couple of days now, with double crews working overtime. They can add on the porch and outside gingerbreading later, as weather permits. Good man, Garnett. He'll look after you and keep your spirits up.''

He braked in front of a farmhouse ringed by crisp brown oaks at seeing a flock of chickens littering the road ahead. Damned chickens were out to get him! He could have sworn the word passed around through the flocks when he was on the way to town and they all headed for the blacktop just to persecute him. Did the silly twits move over to the side at the approach of a car, like any sensible being? They did not, they invariably crossed in front just to discombobulate drivers. They were on an intellectual par with field corn, nothing more than a fast-moving plant. Nerves jangling, he looked at his watch as the flock dispersed and then sped off again toward the bridge over the Loire, where the river undulated along in a lazy current the color of penuche fudge between banks fringed with bright yellow willows. Beyond the bridge honey-white buildings with blue slate roofs fronted the street facing the river. They were so old that they might have witnessed Joan of Arc's entrance into Orléans, but the high-rise apartments looming behind them could have been transplanted from downtown Cincinnati. Over the city, a lowering sky glowered down, promising wind and rain and further blackening Simon's mood.

He couldn't shake off the feeling that he shouldn't be leaving Kei, even though he was sure she'd be perfectly safe, surrounded as she'd be by people who

88

loved her. She had a warm circle of friends in the village, Marthe doted on her, Eagle worshiped her, the twins tumbled around her like fox kits in the springtime, he suspected that Garnett had a bit of a crush on her, and even Mitzi had transferred her doggy allegiance from him to her. He'd have to keep in touch by phone every day to be certain she didn't feel too lonely for him. Actually, he already felt more sorry for himself than for her. She would be with the family, whereas he was going out into the cold, cruel world of impersonal hotel rooms, unfamiliar waiters, and Pepto Bismol. He had a tendency toward self-pity whenever he was in a familiar place, and his accustomed solace of crumpled sheets smelling of feminine perfume was out of the question now. He'd better be damned careful not to be photographed with any attractive lady curators he met in the course of his collecting tour, or Kei would think he'd reverted to old habits. Next time, she'd come with him. From now on, Kei was going to be in bed beside him every night of his life!

The airplane dwindled into a small white dot against the gloomy sky and disappeared. Kei took a moment to compose herself, then walked slowly back to the parking lot, and got into the jeep. Oh lord, she'd let him go off with toilet paper stuck on his chin! She laid her head on the steering wheel and cried. Finally, she blew her nose and drove into Orléans to their sidewalk cafe and snifflingly ordered Portuguese oysters on the half shell with her café au lait. Appropriate hour or not, she needed every creature comfort she could lay her hands on right now. Sitting in the raw, damp air, her eyes itching, she felt as abandoned as an empty house on a vast prairie, with the wind howling through its shattered windows. Oh God, she thought, looking at the peeling green paint of the chair across from her, why isn't Simon sitting there?

"Don't let me catch you looking through that keyhole again!" Garnett said severely, pulling Gino away from the door and motioning him into a seat at one of the school desks in the third-storey room that he'd appropriated for the twins' lessons until the folly was finished. "What's in there is a secret."

He put a container of transparent tape on each desk beside the apple baskets holding seeds and leaves they'd just collected on an early-morning tramp around the estate. Taking blank scrapbooks from the top of his own desk, he handed them to the children, saying, "We're going to make botany notebooks. So start sorting out all the seeds and burrs you've found and try to figure out how they get spread to produce new plants." He picked up a beggar's lice between his thumb and forefinger and held it up. "This one's got hooks on it that catch on clothing or animals' fur so the seed gets carried away from the mother plant, see?" He gave it to Gino and searched around in his basket for a parachute-shaped bit of thistledown hanging from it like a paratrooper. "This one blows on the wind."

"What about this?" asked Dirk, pointing to a cherrystone.

"A bird would eat it and it'd travel into its

stomach and out again in the droppings. A seed can be carried hundreds of miles away like that." He sat down at his desk while the boys messed about happily with their collections, conferring in their private language, and took up the copy of Juvenal that Father Barteau had pressed on him as a memento last night. "When you're ready, I'll help you put your specimens in the scrapbooks and label them for you."

The Juvenal was pretty dull going, and after a few minutes he put it aside and got up to draw leaves on the free-standing blackboard with colored chalks, circling the lobed and pointed tips to focus his students' attention on the differences between oak and maple leaves. That done, he brushed off his hands and returned to his chair, leaned back with his arms crossed behind his head, and ruminated on the events of the night before, savoring them. Smiling, he rehearsed Jacques' rusty passion and his poetic gushings of gratitude. His kind always got lyrical. He'd let the priest remember everything, no danger from that quarter. Jacques would be too frightened by his own sin to publish it. It was almost too easy, no challenge at all. His smile faded as he recalled the crucifix that hung over the priest's bed and the moonlight reflection from it that had kept getting in his eyes. He'd been tempted to do something spectacular to the cross to show his scorn for the ineffectuality of a hunk of molded metal, but that would have given away the game too soon, and he intended to enjoy Jacques and his squirmings with his conscience a while longer. And wasn't it about time for Kei to be getting in from seeing Simon off?

Garnett's smile slipped back into place.

After the twins trotted downstairs to show off their scrapbooks to Marthe, Garnett unlocked the door that had piqued Gino's curiosity and opened it onto a windowless room smelling of dust and dry wood. A jumble of dark shapes huddled together in the middle of the room and, in a far corner, something white glimmered in the wedge of light from the doorway. The antique boards creaked as Garnett crossed them. A woman's hand lay palm downward on the floor, spread into a claw. He reached down and picked it up by one cold, pale finger, looked up into black eyes glittering in deeply hollowed sockets, and then screwed the hand back into the arm of the manikin from which it had fallen. Two department store dummies, fashionably emaciated and sexless, stood naked beside the soft bulk of a giant panda that smelled of synthetic fur. Tomorrow would be a good day to dress the manikins, give them names and characters, and get them ready to be moved to the large room standing isolated in the oak grove. Space heaters and storm windows were already installed in the folly, and the structure was nearly inhabitable now.

He walked over to another corner of the room where he'd stored what was to be the central feature of the playroom and delicately lifted up the black cloth covering it. Looking down at his treasure, he regretted that he couldn't share the irony with Kei and Simon, but their senses of humor were worlds different from his, and he wasn't sharing this secret until the time was ripe. He would be the one to decide when that was. He would always be the one to call the turns, because he was in control.

November first was a feast day, and Father Barteau was dressing for high mass. The day was typical for the month—clammy and cold, with a dreary sky—but inside his head was springtime, dazzling and blithe. All the gray, laborious years since his youth seemed to have been wiped away by last night, seemed never to have even occurred. His accustomed emptiness was filled with singing warmth now. After putting the amice over his surplice, he settled the stole in place on his shoulders and reached out for the cincture. His hand paused above it. The girdle of chastity. He stared at it, struggling with self-accusations, then resolutely took it up and fastened it around his waist. No matter how unworthy the vessel, the sacraments remained valid. The disease in his soul would not infect the communicants. On the way to the altar, his intellect called out warningly that he was mired in sin that was corroding his eternal soul, but his heart sang too loudly for him to hear it.

Thunder cracked open the clouds rolling overhead and spilled large drops on the moat. Little silver fish flashed up out of the pocked water, wriggled as if delighted at the release of tension in the sky, and plopped back again. While Gino and Dirk reeled in their lines, Garnett rowed the flatbottomed boat to the bank, then jumped out to beach it and helped the twins onto the leaf-slick bank.

Kei watched them from the window of her and Simon's bedroom, leaning out with her elbows on the sill, and sniffed up the exhilarating smell of ozone accompanying the downpour. Thunder rumbled in a heavy chain along the west, and now the rain came down in sheets, but the sound of hammering from the oak grove never paused. The workmen were snug and dry inside the folly.

She'd had lunch in town after moping through the stores, trying to find something extravagant to buy to lighten her depression, so while Garnett, the boys, and Marthe ate in the kitchen, she went down into the salon and pulled her Japanese koto out from its hiding place under the piano.

Part of the art of living, she believed, lay in harmonizing with the seasons and the ambience of the day: she read Dickens only in the bleak fall and winter months, toasted the first snowfall in red wine, went barefoot in the grass at the dawn of the equinox, and otherwise marked the slow turning of the earth with small ceremonies. Now the sound of plucked strings would synchronize with the beat of the rain, and the sad slide of the Japanese diatonics would echo her melancholy. She knelt beside the long horizontal harp shaped like a split log, adjusted the ivory bridges holding up the strings, took a set of gold finger picks from the purple brocade at the end of the koto, and slipped one onto each finger. She caught her breath in a sigh that was almost a sob and began to play a mournful song about a courtesan watching her lover climb a misty mountain on his way to war. When a teardrop fell onto the koto, it occurred to Kei that she was getting a little too into the role of Madame Butterfly, and that if she didn't cut out this *shit*, she'd start wandering around looking for a volcano to jump into.

Maybe some Chopin would be more cheerful. She removed the finger picks, got up stamping her feet to get her circulation going after having it cut off by the oriental kneel, and shoved the koto back in place. Sitting down at the Bäsendofrer, she ripped into the posthumous Waltz in E Minor, giving the keys hell while she pretended to be Paderewski, tossing her head so her hair fell into her face. But the fireworks in the piece soon fizzled into a tinkly melody that sounded as if it were trying to be brave in the midst of woe, and the colors of the Moody oil on the opposite wall started to slide into each other, mingling moistly, as her eyes filled again.

Maybe if she pigged out, it would help. No, it wouldn't, she decided, looking at the island of strawberry ice cream Gino was drowning in butterscotch sauce and sprinkling with cashews. Garnett asked her to join them, but she declined and went upstairs, where her cat Maybe was rolled into a striped ball where the bolsters met on top of the coverlet. The alley cat unfurled himself slowly, stretching out his front legs and shuddering sensuously, and then yawned until his ears met at the back of his head, revealing a raspberry curl of tongue inside a pink mouth. Once Kei was nestled on the bed with her head in the warm hollow left by Maybe and had perched the cat on her sweater like a cozy fur meatloaf with his front paws tucked under, she didn't feel quite so lonesome. There was nothing like a loving, reliable cat to purr away the blues as it smiled smugly into its thistledown shirtfront in double-chinned contentment. Maybe gave a minute burp, emitting a smell of fish.

Kei was wafting off into a nap while snapshots of Simon flashed through her mind—Simon striding in from his morning ride, smelling of horse, his boots clicking across the foyer tiles; Simon in a lounge suit at a London theater, surrounded by members of the jet set and looking excruciatingly bored; Simon grubbing in the soil of Tommy McKenzie's garden, tenderly nursing chrysanthemum plants while his hair blew around his head like a dandelion gone to seed and the soaked armpits of his work shirt gave off the intoxicating smell of masculine sweat; Simon laughing softly as he rolled off her, satisfied—when the twins banged on the door and asked if she was awake. The cat bounced off the bed and fled into the closet.

They climbed up beside her on the bed and handed her *Winnie the Pooh* to read aloud. "May I listen, too?" Garnett said from the doorway, then sat down on the foot of her bed with one leg tucked under him when she consented. Stephen used to sit on her bed the same way, and he must be about the age Stephen had been when he was killed in the car accident. He could never take the place of her own son, of course, but already he seemed like family—a comfortable sort of person who fit in easily and made himself welcome immediately. Kei was feeling very grandmotherly, surrounded by the three of them, as she started reading about Piglet and Eeyore and was glad of Garnett's company.

After a while, she saw that Gino had fallen asleep with his thumb plugging his mouth and that Dirk's eyelids were going up and down slowly as he tried to keep awake.

"Hey, hey," said Garnett, shaking Gino's foot to rouse him, "better run along to your room for a nap." They slid off the bed and stumbled out the door, closing it behind them at Garnett's orders. Feeling overwhelmingly sleepy herself, Kei wondered vaguely why he had asked them to shut the door.

"I can tell you're missing Simon," Garnett said sympathetically, lying across the foot of the bed on his stomach and fooling with the laces of her tennis shoes. "Don't you want to take these off? They've got mud caked on the bottoms." He unlaced them, pulled them off, and let them fall to the carpet. "That's the thing you hate most in the world, isn't it—having Simon gone?" He drew off her socks and rubbed her feet where the laces and eyelets had left red imprints on her arches. "But wherever he is, you know he loves you. We all love you." His hands were warm and strong-feeling as he massaged her feet slowly. "All you have to do to bring Simon close is to think about him, you know," his voice said soothingly. "Just think about him."

Kei relaxed against the bolsters while hundreds of golden bees droned in her head, and closed her eyes. Feeling hands at her belt, undoing the clasp, she opened them again to see Simon's beloved face above hers.

"What went wrong?" she asked, alarmed. "Did the plane have to turn back? Are you all right?"

"Nothing to worry about," he said. "I'll try again tomorrow."

Everything was back in its right place again, she thought, looking up into the familiar fine dark eyes. As he kissed her, he undid her jeans and slipped them out from under her hips, taking her panties with them.

"The twins. . . " she protested as his lips moved to her neck.

"They won't wake for hours," he said against her skin and pulled her sweater up above her breasts. "Just think about making a baby now."

Her eyelids grew heavier as his hands and mouth traveled over her body persuasively, preparing her to receive him, and she closed her eyes, so near to sleep that she could hardly move. Was it because she'd feared she'd have to do without him that he felt so delicious, or was he really more artfully subtle than she remembered? He filled her more completely than ever before, and his gentle butting at the entrance to her womb seemed to go on and on and on as if it would never stop. A sweet humming vibrated through the honeycomb of her cells, gradually rising in pitch and heightening in intensity as his movements grew more rapid.

Floating up from honeyed slumber, she felt his arm under her neck and, without opening her eyes, turned to put her mouth against the hair in his armpit. Dearest Simon, she murmured and started sinking back into sleep, but a tiny worm of uneasiness wriggled in the back of her mind. Something unfamiliar was intruding on her senses. The body beside her had a different, animal odor unlike Simon's. Then she remembered the cold shock of the icy semen that had flooded her. Her eyes snapped open and Garnett's hand came down over her mouth as he raised himself on one elbow.

"Now, now," he said, amusement in his eyes, "it's done. You can't take it back now, so you might as well enjoy it. And you will, you will." Clearly unafraid that she might cry out, he lay back with an arm under his head, perfectly at ease, and watched curiously as she struggled against the overpowering lethargy that bound her in place at his side. "It's useless, can't you see?" he said. "From now on, my love, I pull your strings and you dance to my tune. Right now, you *have* to, I've seen to that. Later, you'll want to of your own free will."

The guilt that swarmed over her at betraying Simon grew into fear as she found her initial loathing of the long, golden body at her side changing into acceptance, then a craving for it. Languidly, Garnett drew a finger from her forehead down to her crotch, as if he were marking off territory that he owned, and then he mounted her again.

She lost count of how many times he used her, and always there was that rush of cold inside her that could not have come from a warm-blooded, normal man. She felt herself come to orgasm again and again, try as she would to suppress it, and hated him for jigging insatiably on top of her until she cried from exhaustion—and despised herself for grappling him against her, straining him into her, wanting him one more time, then another, then another.

CHAPTER EIGHT

Father Barteau stood waiting under his dripping umbrella for the front doors of the château to open, watching a drenched sparrow dart and plunge through the rain as it evaded the attack of a team of relentless ravens. His pulse was racing in anticipation of seeing Garnett. Each hour without him had been an interminable, aching yawn and, foolishly, knowing it would not ring, he'd listened for the telephone, hoping that his love was also finding their separation unendurable. Throughout the long day he'd devised imaginary conversations with Garnett, brilliantly explaining his innermost self while Garnett fervently declared his total commitment and passion in words that the priest edited over and over, meticulously revising them to get the right tone of abandon and lyricism.

When the door opened and Garnett stood on the threshhold in tight khaki pants and a white shirt, Father Barteau was suddenly struck shy and couldn't find words for a suitable greeting. Had he kissed that beautiful face? Had he held that lithe body in his arms? Why had he been singled out for such glory, ordinary and unworthy creature that he was? He looked eagerly into Garnett's eyes, expecting to find deep communion there, but the coolness that he saw made him step back a pace. His heart shriveled. What had he done? What had happened to cause this shield to come up between them? Then Garnett drew him into the foyer, set his umbrella down on the tiles to dry, and smiled at him. The singing warmth flowed through Father Barteau again. Garnett kissed him lightly on the lips, and the priest went rigid and backed away. Someone might be watching!

He looked around to be sure there were no spying eyes. What he did in his private life was on his own conscience, but the church would not countenance scandal. If anyone suspected this liaison, he'd receive notice from the chancery to present himself, and if rumors were confirmed by the testimony of witnesses, he'd be ruined. Worse, he'd never see Garnett again! But had Garnett thought his reaction to the kiss was a rebuff? No, he merely raised an eyebrow, chuckled, and gave Father Barteau's hand a quick squeeze.

The priest was shocked by Kei's appearance. She sat in an easy chair, looking sick, depleted, and stared ahead of her blankly. Great heaven, what had happened to her? She looked older than she had last time. Even taking into account that she was wearing a long black dress that took the color from her face, she seemed to have aged overnight.

Garnett was taking over Simon's role, pouring drinks at the bar and handing them around as if he were the host. Where was Simon? Father Barteau accepted his glass of sherry and went over to greet Kei, first checking to see that his shoes were leaving no wet prints on the carpet. She looked up, but no recognition registered in her eyes and she remained silent. Rather rude, actually, but if she weren't well . . . The peremptory tone of Garnett's voice as he told her to snap out of it was surprising. Something was going on between those two. The atmosphere had changed. Kei cleared her throat and the glassiness went out of her eyes as she made an obvious effort to collect herself.

"Simon's gone to the Orient, Father," she said. "There will just be three of us tonight."

That was a pity. He'd made up his mind to bring up the subject of the parish house roof with Simon, hoping he would see it as a useful writeoff on the American income tax. However, since women were reputed to hold the purse strings in the United States, it might be worthwhile approaching Kei about it. If he got into an earnest discussion, he'd be able to keep his eyes off Garnett, and he was beginning to worry that he might be giving away his lovesickness in any number of unconscious ways.

Kei listened, nodding, and said that her bag was upstairs but that she'd put a check in the mail tomorrow, and named a figure a few thousand francs above what he'd hoped for. He was about to shave it down to the actual estimated cost for repairs when Garnett suggested that she double the amount. Father Barteau was about to object, but a look of complicity from Garnett made him reconsider. He tossed back his drink, asking himself if all his scruples would start collapsing like dominoes now that his vow of chastity had fallen. The conversation

102

faltered, stumbled, and died. The three of them sat on in silence, absorbed in their own thoughts, as the rain drummed down. Marthe's announcement that dinner was served re-animated them, and they got up and went into the dining room.

The table was simply set with blue and white Quimper ware on a navy tablecloth and Kelly green candles in white pottery holders. Evidently, things were not quite so formal when the head of the household was not in residence. No soup followed the seviche of conch meat, and after Marthe brought in a saddle of rabbit with braised endives, Garnett told her she could leave, that he would take care of serving the salad and dessert. Kei raised her eyebrows. Marthe, too, seemed surprised to be dismissed so early in the evening, but when Garnett said he knew that she and Hilaire wanted to spend the evening with her sister and that the dishes could wait until morning, she beamed and kissed him on the top of his head before leaving.

"You and Marthe certainly have gotten clubby," Kei remarked bitingly, when the swinging door came to a rest.

Garnett shrugged. "She had a favorite nephew who was killed in Viet Nam during the French occupation, and she says I'm his spit and image."

Kei began carving the rabbit with expert, vicious strokes. "If you don't mind," she said stiffly in a low voice, "I'll be the one to give Marthe orders."

"As you please," Garnett said, unruffled. "I just didn't see the need to keep her on for the three of us when she wants to visit her family."

"That's my decision to make, I believe," said Kei,

handing the priest his plate. Garnett shrugged again.

This was very odd. Father Barteau speculated about what had happened between the two of them as he ate, not joining in the discussion about the furnishing of the gazebo. There was a sharp edge to the conversation, as if it were about to turn into a quarrel, that made him uncomfortable. Garnett cleared the dishes and brought in the salad, and the priest was marveling at the grace of his movements when Garnett set the bowl down in front of Kei and ran a hand caressingly down her neck. Kei shook it off irritably. The glass in Father Barteau's hand shook, nearly spilling the wine onto the cloth.

His face flamed. He was not the only one, then! The implications of that gesture were unmistakable. He was in love with a whore! A whore who slept with his host's wife! Had last night been merely one in a series of encounters that meant nothing to Garnett? He stared at his salad, trying to convince himself that he was jumping to conclusions, but then he looked at Kei and she colored and lowered her eyes. It was true! Father Barteau clapped his napkin to his mouth, trying to stifle the nausea that soured his mouth.

"No one seems very hungry," Garnett said after a while. "Shall I bring in dessert?" Kei nodded listlessly. "Maybe I can add waiting on table to my other duties as a servant," Garnett said, giving the last word a sarcastic twist. He picked up the plates and carried them out to the kitchen, where they could hear him open the refrigerator door and put the dishes on the sink.

The rain had slowed to a heavy patter, but sullen

growling overhead persisted, and thunder boomed periodically, shaking the house. The priest and Kei sat quietly while Garnett worked in the kitchen, their heads bowed as if in prayer.

Father Barteau wanted to smash the windows with his fists, to rip the cover from the table and send the china crashing to the floor, to scream, to grab Kei by the hair and pound her face on the table's edge until it was a bloody pulp, but most of all he wanted to go out into the kitchen, throw himself at Garnett's feet, seize him around the knees, and beg him to say that Kei had blackmailed him into sleeping with her, that he'd submitted unwillingly to keep his position and bitterly regretted it now, that he had only one love. The ecstasy they'd shared last night was not something he could have felt alone, Garnett *had* to have known the same consuming delight. A messy, squirming coupling with a woman could only disgust him. It *had* to have been her idea. How triumphant she must be feeling this minute, the bitch!

He looked up at her. As he watched, bile in his throat, he saw a tear form at the edge of one of her eyes and spill down her cheek. My God, had Garnett seduced her? Father Barteau closed his eyes, shaken by black despair.

A sharp crack of lightning set the crystal drops of the chandelier tinkling.

"They say that lightning kills more people than any other natural phenomenon," Kei's voice said, remote and mechanical.

Father Barteau looked at her. The tear was drying on her cheek. She looked past him, straight ahead, with the gaze of a sleepwalker. The dripping of the rain filled a long pause before he said in a strained voice that sounded unfamiliar to his ears, "I once saw ball lightning come through my window at the seminary. It floated out into the hall and disappeared."

Scarcely moving her lips, Kei said, "A golf course is the most dangerous place to be in a storm, they say,"

"I don't know what happened to it."

"Or under a tree."

"Yes," he whispered, "it just disappeared."

The swinging door banged open and Garnett, wearing a towel over one arm as if to emphasize his role as waiter, came in with a tray of banana and pineapple sorbets that he set before each place. Kei took no notice of him, continuing to stare into space. Garnett came over to the priest, leaned over, and reached down into his lap to fondle him. Father Barteau jerked back, nearly upsetting his chair, and looked fearfully over at Kei. The sudden movement seemed to bring her out of her trance, but the incident was safely past, she hadn't seen it. Stupefied, the priest watched Garnett walk over to his own place, bow, and ask in mock servility, "Does Madame permit?," then seat himself without waiting for an answer. As Kei toyed with her ice, Garnett put an elbow on the table and, shielding his mouth so that she couldn't see, moved his lips so that Father Barteau could clearly make out the words "I love you." The devil he did, or why had he stroked her neck, making sure the caress was seen? Torn between wanting to believe the words he saw and doubting Garnett, Father Barteau was thrown back and forth

106

between hope and searing anger.

Two plates of sorbet melted as Garnett ate his. Finally, Kei rose, said she wasn't feeling very well, and excused herself. Garnett waited until her footsteps had passed through the foyer and on up the stairs, then said, "Now we won't have to run the risk of my coming to see you at the parish house, we can have the run of the château. Since I did what she wanted, she's eating out of my hand. I hope you appreciate the sacrifice I've made to protect you."

Father Barteau's eyes prickled. What a fool he'd been! How could he have doubted his shining boy, suspecting him of such sleazy behavior, when all he'd been doing was to prepare the way for them to be together away from spying eyes? He should have been more patient, had more faith! But the way he'd stroked her neck. . . .

"You'll understand, won't you, if I pet her now and then to keep her in line?" Garnett said as if answering his thoughts. "It makes my skin crawl to touch her, you know that, but I know how dangerous it is for us to be seen together." Garnett wiped his mouth on his napkin, got up, and came over to run his hand over the priest's hair. "I couldn't bear it if you were hurt in any way because of me," he said.

Father Barteau looked up at him adoringly, caught his hand, and kissed it. Together, arms around each other, they went into the salon, and Garnett closed the shutters on all the windows.

Upstairs, Kei locked the bedroom door before putting in a trunk call to London. When the connection came through, she said, "Missy, this is Kei. Can you come stay with me for a few days? Simon's out of town and I need you, I really do, or I wouldn't ask." She pulled a tissue out of the box at the bedside and mopped at her eyes, listening for a telltale click that would signal that Garnett had picked up the phone downstairs. "As soon as ever you can. I can't go into the reasons on the phone, but I feel like my brains are unraveling." After a few words from Missy, she burst into tears and said, "Oh, Missy, you're a real friend! Don't let me down, I'll be waiting for you." She kept the receiver to her ear several seconds after Missy had hung up, to see if any sounds within the house were filtering over the line from downstairs. Then she lay back on the bed and swabbed down her face, wondering where Simon was now and if she could ever explain to him what had happened. If she couldn't figure it out herself, how could he possibly understand? She'd never concealed anything from him yet and, God knows, she hated to start now, but he'd be shattered if he knew, and he might never trust her again. God above, what was she going to do?!

Get rid of Garnett. That came first. But morning was soon enough to tackle that. Tonight, the bedroom door was going to stay locked.

She took her fourth shower of the day, scrubbing herself all over with the pumice stone she used to smooth her heels and elbows, darned near skinning herself, but she still didn't feel spanking clean. She felt covered in invisible, slimy fingerprints. For the next couple of hours, she tried to sleep, got up again to smoke a cigarette, paced, and lay down again. At last, worn out, she sat in the black leather chair by the bay window, put her head in her hands, and listened to the rain tattooing on the roof. The monotonous pattern of sound was soothing, and she was beginning to feel sleepy when the click of the front door closing downstairs made her straighten up. Was that gravel crunching out in the parking area? Had some spark of decency driven Garnett to desert? Maybe the problem of the tutor had solved itself.

Hopefully, she unlocked the door and crossed the hallway to look down through the window. A nimbus of silver shining around the lamp over the canopy struck glassy highlights from the raindrops on Father Barteau's umbrella as it passed into the darkness toward the gate. What in hell had he and Garnett been doing together all this time?

"I need to talk to you," a voice said behind her, and she jumped. "I'll get your robe," said Garnett and was in her bedroom before she could stop him. "Here, you mustn't get cold," he said, holding out her satin kimono. She put her arms into it warily, ready to break and run if he tried to lay a finger on her. "Let's go down and have some tea," he said as casually as if the events of the afternoon had never taken place. "That's what you always have when you're feeling under the weather, I've noticed." He took her firmly by the elbow and guided her toward the stairway.

While the water heated on the stove, Kei sat at the deal table in the middle of the kitchen, clutching her robe together at the neck and waiting fearfully to hear what was going through his mind.

This was Simon's kitchen. He'd designed it, ordered the terra cotta tiles for the floor, brought in the restaurant-sized stove, hung a ceiling rack for the copper pots and pans, and suspended strings of red peppers, garlic, and dried herbs along the walls. He'd even arranged the rusty late-blooming chrysanthemums yesterday in the copper bowl on the table, and that—that *thing* whose shirt had come unbuttoned to the waist, showing the dark blond feathering on his chest, whose hair was hanging into his face, didn't belong in Simon's kitchen! He was an alien presence that had to be gotten rid of, as soon as possible!

"I had a long talk with the priest," Garnett said, turning off the heat under the kettle. "I hope you don't mind my confiding in him, but whatever I said about us is under the seal of the confessional, and I really needed some spiritual counsel about what happened this afternoon."

Spiritual counsel? What was all this sanctimonious crap? Kei looked at him skeptically as he got a white bamboo-handled teapot out of the cupboard, scalded it with hot water, put in a handful of China tea, and filled the pot.

"It's got to stop, Kei," he said. "Don't be angry, but it's got to stop right now." He set out white porcelain cups and saucers, slices of lemon, and a pitcher of honey while Kei rummaged in her mind for the most blistering rejoinders she could find. Before she could speak, he sat down opposite her and said, "I apologize for the part I played, it was unforgivable. I should have remembered that you're a married woman and that you were lonely for

110

Simon, but you were so insistent that I make love to you, and I'm only a man."

Kei jumped to her feet, outraged, but he reached over and caught the sleeve of her robe.

"Please don't be ashamed." he said, pulling her back down into her chair. "I wanted it as badly as you did, but I never would have forced myself on you if you hadn't made the first move."

Kei's mouth sagged open. She wanted to say that he was wrong, that he was crazy, that it hadn't been that way at all, but only stammering sounds came out. "You're not going to deny it, are you?" he said sadly, pityingly. "Darling, don't tell me you don't remember?"

Muddled, she stared down at the tabletop. It *couldn't* have happened like that! It simply wasn't her style. But the last thing she could recall clearly was reading out loud to the twins, and after that things were foggy. She'd thought that Simon had come back, which didn't make sense right there, but what she really couldn't understand was why, when she realized it was Garnett, she'd kept urging him on time after time as if she couldn't get enough of him. She remembered clawing at his back, and wanted to vomit.

"Ask me to go. I want to hear you say it," he said, and his quiet voice was like a tranquilizer going into her bloodstream. "Tell me you don't want me to make love to you again, and I'll go." There were gold flecks in his green eyes, or were his eyes blue? Blue-green. No, more a dark gray. His face was getting blurry. She was too sleepy to see straight and there was a droning buzz in her head. Her eyes

111

slipped past the fine-link black iron chain he wore around his neck, down to the light plumage on his chest. His nipples pricked out against his shirt, showing dark under the thin white fabric. She watched her hand drift out and slide into his shirt.

CHAPTER NINE

Garnett sat in his terrycloth bathrobe at the kitchen table, watching the twins empty their bowls of chocolate and polish off their breakfast croissants as he wrung Marthe's heart with a totally fictitious account of his childhood in an orphanage, getting a kick out of seeing how far he could stretch her credulity with a story lifted straight from *Oliver Twist*, when the phone rang.

"I'll get it," he said, thinking it might be Simon calling. He unsaddled the receiver from the cradle on the wall and heard the crackling interference that accompanies a long distance call. "It's for Mrs. Eagleton," he said after listening a few seconds and hanging up carefully. Turning to the twins, he said, "Don't let Eagle keep you at the soccer game past noon. Thursday's a holiday for him, but it isn't for you. We keep school on the American system." The twins drooped. They perked up again when he added, "I've got a surprise to show you after lunch," and started badgering him to tell them what it was, but he said mysteriously, "You'll see" and told Marthe that he was going upstairs to dress.

Simon's first call from overseas was likely to be a long one, but he wanted to hear as much of it as he could to see how far under control he had Kei now. Knowing no one was watching as he stood at the bottom of the stairs, he gave a slight push with his feet and floated up to the upstairs hallway, hovered in the air a moment, and then came down on the floorboards. The temptation to use such shortcuts was hard to resist, but each one took a measure of energy away from him and he had to be careful not to expend too much before he had a chance to replenish himself. If he ever miscalculated, he'd be as vulnerable as any ordinary mortal.

Kei was lying with the covers up to her chest and the phone set between her breasts. She frowned at seeing him come in the door. "I've asked Missy to come over from London for a few days," she said into the mouthpiece. That would be Missy Hilliard, the singer who used to be one of Simon's amours, Garnett thought. She was getting a bit long in the tooth, but her boobs were internationally celebrated. This could be interesting.

Kei shook her head violently as Garnett took off his bathrobe and went over to get in beside her. "She's getting in this afternoon," she said crossly, watching Garnett throw the covers back and slide in next to her. "No, I'm not grouchy because you called too early. It's nine o'clock, and it always make me happy to talk to you, whatever the hour of the day or night, you know that." She pushed at Garnett as he straddled her, but he slapped her hand away and forced himself into her, enjoying the outrage and humiliation on her face. He took his time, listen-

114

ing to her side of the conversation and guessing what Simon was saying, working her up to a climax while she struggled against him as hard as she could, trying to keep her voice normal. She hadn't a chance of resisting him, though, and he nearly burst into laughter when she clapped the receiver to her chest to smother the sound of her cries as she came. When she ceased fluttering inside and the mottled flush receded from her neck and shoulders, she put the receiver to her ear again and said hoarsely, "Something went wrong with the line. Could you repeat what you were saying, darling?"

When he was finished, Garnett rolled off her and lay back to stroke his chest and belly contentedly, thinking that he hadn't been so amused in quite some time. She'd never be able to forget that she'd let him screw her while she was talking to her beloved husband. If nothing else could put the stopper in her, that would. She'd think it was the height of deception, and her guilt would keep her mouth shut. Moreover, in a couple of weeks she'd start getting morning sickness. She'd let fall that she and her mother both followed a familial pattern of almost instant nausea after becoming pregnant. Now that he'd put a child in her, all he had to do was to sit back and wait.

Gino's and Dirk's eyes popped when Garnet threw open the door of the folly and they saw the colored balloons and streamers standing out festively against the contrast of the black walls. Under the windows along all four walls were cases filled with books and toys. One had a long, narrow aquarium on top that was stocked with brilliant tropical fish moving around in a greenish twilight world. The children's desks and the blackboard were sober notes, but the red and gilt marionette theater, the giant black and white panda standing by the door, and the rest of the furnishings Garnett had selected promised fun and games. Fully a fourth of the floor space was curtained off by black velveteen drapes that concealed a stage.

"This is *ours?*" Dirk asked wonderingly, looking around him at the carnival of color. Gino was already rushing from one toy to another and jumping at the helium-filled balloons mingling with non-deflatable plastic ones hanging from the ceiling.

"All yours," Garnett said, "but we've got to keep the door locked when we leave or someone might get in and ruin things." He showed them the key dangling from his neck beside the black iron chain that he habitually wore. "Don't let me forget. This is our secret kingdom, just ours. Your grandmother and Eagle can have a look at it, but what goes on in here is just between us." He grabbed Gino's hand out of the aquarium, where the boy was trying to catch a tetra. "For Pete's sake, Gino, their scales fall off and they die if you do that! Have a little sense!" Obviously, he was going to have to work fast if they were to learn the things they needed to know about the animal realm. City-reared, they had almost no knowledge of nature and, to add to the problem of training them, they came from a long line of Christians. However, they were unusually quick to learn, and being able to impart his skills to two children at once was an extra windfall.

"What's in back of that?" asked Gino, pointing at the black curtains.

"Friends. Special friends," Garnett said. "'But first I want you to meet Gunther, who's going to look after you."

The panda was about six feet tall, so his size made him forbidding and the twins were hesitant to take his paw. "Now, now, we're all friends here in the folly," Gunther said in the growly voice that Garnett had chosen to use for him. "We're going to get along just fine, as long as you behave like little gentlemen."

"Little gentlemen!" Dirk said disgustedly, dropping the plushy paw. "I have trouble enough being a good boy," he complained, looking up at the glittering black glass eyes.

"That's what I mean, a good boy. It's just another way of saying it," Gunther rumbled.

"My mommy says a person ought to say what he means," Dirk said saucily.

"None of your lip, Buster, or I'll come up to your room tonight and *stomp* you!" Gunther roared.

Dirk backed off and Gino hid behind his back. Garnett knelt down and put an arm around each child, saying, "Don't worry, I won't let Gunther get you. You can always count on me to protect you. Remember that. And Gunther's very friendly if you're obedient and don't get out of line. If you're very good, he might even bring you a present now and then."

Dirk looked dubious. "Are those other friends like Gunther?" he asked. "On account of because if they are, I don't think I want to meet them."

117

Laughing, Garnett got to his feet. "Oh, no. You're going to love them." He went to the stage, took the cords that worked the curtain in his hand, and bowed. "Presenting Pierrot and Pierrette," he said, sliding the curtains open on a stage with ornate gold paneling at the back. Two life-sized masked manikins stood at either side of the stage, the man in a black skull-cap and a voluminous white satin clown costume with big black pompoms down the front. The woman had on a skimpy ballerina's costume with a short white tutu that stood out stiffly above her black net stockings. A frilly ruff was around her neck and on her shiny red curls perched a black satin tricorn hat.

"Bon jour, mes amis," Garnett said through the male manikin in a deep voice. "Je m'appelle Pierrot. I am your new French teacher. I will also teach you songs." He began singing about the Good King d'Yvetot who put on his pants backward, but Garnett, using his natural voice, cut him off, saying that it was Pierrette's turn to introduce herself.

"I'm you new English teacher," said the female manikin in a falsetto. "Monsieur Tobol, would you show our little friends how to move our arms and heads to change our costumes?"

"Nothing easier," said Garnett. He twisted her arms at the shoulder, elbow, and wrist joints and pulled off her head, eliciting gasps from the twins. Chuckling, he put the head back on backwards.

"You're not going to leave me this way, are you?" protested Pierrette. "Ah, that's better!" she said as Garnett turned her face to the front of the stage.

Garnett waved a hand toward a big trunk in back

of the blackboard and said, "That's full of costumes for you and your friends here. You can use Pierrot and Pierrette in your games, but you can't move them around much or they'll break. Now, the next thing I'm going to show you—the *best* surprise—you can't touch. It's too delicate, and besides," he said, adding something he'd just thought of, "there's an invisible force field around it that'll zap you if you get too close." That would scare them away so he wouldn't have to use his own energy to protect his treasure.

At the back of the stage, he made swooping circles with his hands over the gold paneling to conceal the exact location of the button hidden amongst the painted swirls. When he pushed it, a door slid open to reveal a small space too shallow to be detected from the stage.

"This is Lady Luna," he said reverently. The tiny room was just large enough to contain a table and a gilt rattan peacock chair whose back fanned far above the head of a figure seated in it, wearing a cream satin cloak that fell about her in folds. The cloak's hood came down over her forehead to meet a half mask of the same material, from which hung a shoulder-length chiffon veil. Crowning the figure's head was a lacy circlet of wax orange blossoms heavily scented with attar of the real flowers. The woman was bent over the circular table and seemed to be peering into the crystal ball set on the red velvet cloth reaching to the floor.

"Here is where she sees the stories that she'll be telling you," Garnett said, pointing to the ball. "They're invisible to anyone but her, so there's no use looking into it to try to see them. You're not to touch anything here, remember. If the force field doesn't get you, Gunther could get very nasty if you got too near Lady Luna." He could sense the twins' uneasiness and tempered what he'd said by adding, "It's just that she's so very old, you see, and so fragile. But she's a special friend who loves you very much, and I know you're going to think she tells the best stories you've ever heard." He indicated a stack of white leatherette pillows in front of the panda. "Bring up a couple of those to sit on, and she'll tell you the first story."

The twins each carted a pillow up to the stage and plopped them down a few feet away from the figure at Garnett's direction, then looked around at Pierrot and Pierrette, nudging each other and giggling, before settling down to listen.

"Good afternoon, beloved children," said a soothing feminine voice. "This is a story about Dirk and Gino and how they learned to do things that other mortals could not do. Magical things." The voice murmured on, sweet as honey, as the twins' eyes unfocused.

Pierre ranted on about the impact of American mortgage rates on the French economy and rinsed Kei's hair with warm water as she lay back with her head over a pink enamel basin and fed him neutral comments like "Tiens!" and "Vraiment?" so she could think her own thoughts. Having her hair done was an act of hedonism she resorted to when her morale was at its ebbtide. This afternoon she was morbidly depressed, and the self-indulgence wasn't alleviating her mood.

When for the umpteenth time Pierre suggested that she have a rinse to cover the gray, she snapped at him. When he ran cold water over her head to bring out the shine in her hair, she let out a yelp and he snatched his hands back, looking hurt.

The look of herself in the mirror with her wet hair plastered down all over her head was not uplifting, either. The pink-tinted glass was supposed to be flattering, but the face that looked back at her was forty-five years old, twenty years older than her lover's. And that she had a lover at all was an outrage against Simon, who didn't deserve to be cuckolded when his back was turned!

Before she'd married Simon, she'd had a husband, given birth to Stephen, and had lovers. There wasn't anything new left to give him but her loyalty, and now she'd betrayed that. Wasn't it reprehensible enough that she'd taken a man with an worldwide reputation for pleasing women and being pleased by them and tied him down to monogamy, without two-timing him as well?

If he'd been deficient in any way as a husband and lover, she might have been able to justify herself through a manufactured excuse, but Simon was loving, mentally exciting, thoughtful, insatiably sexy, generous, and witty. He had all the virtues and only the vices of a hot temper and an inability to suffer fools gladly. He was, in truth, an ideal she'd never hoped to encounter in the flesh, and she didn't deserve him before and assuredly didn't now, in spades!

What was she in comparison? A middle-aged

grandmother with a face far from classic beauty and a figure lankier than she liked. She came on too strong, and only a man like Simon, who was sure of himself and his position, could handle her without being intimidated. She kept forgetting to hide the sharpness of her mind and spoke her opinions too forcefully. She'd been the head of two publishing firms and, as a result, refused to take crap from anybody. A soft-bodied clinging vine who flattered men, she was not. Moreover, after Stephen had been killed and she'd gone through the divorce from Robin, she'd had a nervous breakdown that left her with a fear of going off the deep end forever someday. Even that hadn't unnerved Simon. He'd gone to bed with scores of women ten times more glamorous, more exciting and feminine than she was, and to this day she couldn't understand what he saw in her. She respected him and adored him to the point of irrationality. He was the center of her world, the focus of her thoughts, and her duplicity and betrayal would break his heart. How could she have done this to him?!

Garnett's intrusion in their relationship was as welcome as a migraine, yet she couldn't push him back out of it now. He was implanted in her thoughts, and she could no more get him out of them than she could keep her tongue off a new filling.

Pierre rolled her hair into curlers, making her look like a robot from Mars. An overaged, rusty robot. Twenty years older than Garnett.

What was she becoming, some sex-starved old hag slavering after youth?! She'd never been promiscuous, had been very selective in choosing lovers, and there had not been many of them. This obsession for Garnett was totally unlike her. She had strangely little feeling for him, and sex for the sake of sex had always bored her faintly before. Unless she cared about a lover, just getting her rocks off seemed about as thrilling as any other bodily function. Garnett's physical proportions were astonishing, but that really didn't make all that much difference to a woman, and as for technique, how many variations could be wrung out of a familiar tune? Why was she so obsessed by him?

When he was trying to turn her on—before he got absorbed in his own satisfaction—he was a marvelously skillful lover. But no more so than Simon. Lovemaking with Simon was a sharing, and with Garnett there was none of that. He performed and she reacted. It was rape without the struggle. She had no say in it, no control, only a basic animal response that shamed her as she heard herself gasping and tearing at him as if she were trying to destroy him. He awoke some primeval creature in her that she hadn't known existed, rousing a hunger that couldn't be satisfied.

Her parents had been progressive types who had raised her to believe that sex was a normal, healthy drive with nothing dirty about it. Sex with Simon was natural, clear joy. With Garnett it was the opposite: forbidden, intoxicating lasciviousness, and she was irresistibly drawn to plumbing its depths, to degrading herself with almost malevolent pleasure. She couldn't stop herself, didn't want to, knew she was on the brink of self-destruction and didn't care. She was addicted to Garnett as a user is to heroin and as helpless.

He knew it, of course. He'd hypnotized her into it and fed her addiction with calculated, insidious doses of himself until she had to do whatever he wanted. She kept trying to pull away from his influence, but his power over her was too strong and unremitting. He'd taken over her body and emotions, and now it seemed that he was trying to take control of the house and its affairs as well.

The conflict between what she knew she should do and what she couldn't keep herself from doing tossed her back and forth continually, keeping her in a constant state of guilt and tension, fighting a losing battle, feeling herself slide down into a chaos of warring feelings. She was exhausted from the struggle, loathed herself, and her mental state was teetering precariouly.

Pierre seated her under a dryer and handed her a cup of coffee. She wished it were hemlock.

Ye gods, Kei thought, amused, watching Missy get off the train from Paris at Les Aubrais. All in black, wearing knee breeches and boots, a leather jacket and motorcyclist's cap, with hubcap-sized dark glasses, her friend looked like a midget hit-man with stolen bowling balls under his shirt. If Missy was wearing that outfit as a disguise to escape from autograph hunters, she must have the I.Q. of an abalone! The chic Frenchwoman Missy stepped down beside on the platform flinched as if an alligator had crawled up to her from a sewer, clutched her purse to her chest with both hands, and backed away. Then recognition dawned in her face and dazzlement made her mouth fall open.

"You poor darling,' Missy said, kissing the air four inches from Kei's cheek, "you look positively grisly, we'll have to do something about that, where are my bags, I've got eight of them around here somewhere, just a couple of changes in case you have company, aren't there any redcaps in this Godforsaken place?" Spotting her suitcases coming off the baggage car, she barreled ahead of Kei, saying, "No autographs! No autographs, please!," thus guaranteeing the attention of puzzled onlookers. At the luggage cart, she said, "Holy cow, we'll never manage these by ourselves," swept off her dark glasses, shook her famous apricot-colored hair out from under her cap, and blasted out a few bars of "Stormy Weather." A gaggle of young men of dubious gender materialized from amongst the people milling around on the platform and chirruped around her. She handed the suitcases out to them while they fluttered and cooed at the honor of waiting on an international star. When everything was loaded in the back of the jeep, Missy gave each of the helpers a kiss, sighed "What a waste!" at the most handsome of the lot, and swung in beside Kei. "Whither away!," she said, undoing her leather jacket and letting her stomach out.

They squished along the wet streets on the way to Orléans in companionable silence, past gray buildings set flush to the sidewalks, Missy giving Kei's arm bolstering pats from time to time, until they got to the downtown section. "I'm famished!" Missy exclaimed. "Everything they were serving on the plane looked like it was made out of Play-Doh.

125

Is there a *patisserie* around here where we could get a bite and a cup of coffee, somewhere out of the way where I wouldn't be recognized? You know how I *loathe* being recognized. I'm bushed, I was up until all hours at a conference about producing this fabulous new musical. It's a nude version of King Lear, isn't that an interesting twist, should bring the crowds in. I thought a couple of seconds about playing one of the roles myself, but the dear old boobs are beginning to sag off in opposite directions, makes me look wall-eyed in the buff. Mustn't disillusion my public. Maybe I ought to have plastic surgery to hoist them back in place, what do you think? It'd leave a scar underneath for a while, but I'm in between men, it wouldn't hurt, who'd see?" She bit her lip in thought and then said, before Kei could comment, "No, I guess not. Suppose I met some gorgeous stud while I was healing and he grabbed a handful and I came unzipped? How about that place over there?"

The jeep yawed and the tires squealed as Kei braked suddenly by a parking place. They entered a shop heady with the smell of freshly-baked bread, and Missy looked around the marble-topped tables and wire chairs waiting in the unpeopled gloom. Seeing they were going to be alone, she dropped her public image and the scatterbrained stream-of-consciousness monologues that went with it.

"Nobody here, that's a relief!" she said, looking down through a glass case at pastries set out on fussy doilies and indicating the one she wanted to the waitress. "You know what it's like, trying to have a friendly dinner with someone while people are staring at you and waiting to pounce on you to introduce their Great Aunt Zelda? The crazy part of it is, if they *don't* do that, you start wondering if you're slipping. It's gotta happen someday, I'm getting older and the pipes aren't what they used to be. I keep having dreams about eating dogfood in my old age."

A cup of coffee and half a tart later, Missy said, "I couldn't be sorrier about the miscarriage," and lit a cigarette. "Simon's always wanted a child of his own so bad, it must have made it harder for you." She leaned over the tabletop toward Kei after blowing out a gust of smoke. "Listen, I know how you feel," she said.

Kei looked at the small, round face and its pansy eyes ringed with blue mascara, thinking that Missy meant well by saying that, but it was easy for her to dole out cheap sympathy. Missy was cocooned in luxury and glamor, surrounded by an army of idolators who kept reality at bay for her. How could she know what it meant to lose a wanted child?

"My baby lived three days," Missy went on, bringing Kei down with a bump from the superiority of her own suffering. "I was sixteen. That's a lot of years, and I don't say you'll get over it, because you won't, but whole days go by now without my thinking of it." She picked up her thick china mug and made circles with it, swirling around the thin wash of brown at the bottom. "The guy walked out on me. They always walk out on me unless I'm paying their salaries." She picked a flake of tobacco from her lip. "These Gauloise cigaretttes really stink," She began pushing her half-eaten tart around her plate with her fork. Finally, she said, "Listen, Kei, you didn't ask me to come here because you're down in the mouth. My mother was Irish and I got my little psychic streak from her. My antenna's been picking up bad vibes from you ever since I got in. What's going on?"

"Nothing." Kei's mouth went dry. Missy was still in love with Simon and simply wouldn't understand how this ravening lust for Garnett was bedeviling her. She didn't love Garnett, she didn't even like him. He was a weasel and a liar, he was far too young for her, and there was something abnormal about him. That icy sperm. The way he made crazy things happen in her head. And yet, just thinking about him made her want him so much that she felt as if her insides were dissolving and dripping out between her legs.

Missy put an elbow on the table, stuck her thumbnail into the small space between her front teeth that she capped for photographs, and studied Kei's face. "When I came over here," she said finally, wiping her nail on her napkin, "I thought you'd be moping around, but you're scared, aren't you? I can practically smell it."

Kei swallowed and shook her head. "I can't talk about it," she said. "You wouldn't understand."

"You'd be surprised what I'd understand," Missy said, motioning to the waitress for the bill. "I won't push it, but sooner or later I'll find out. Then maybe we can talk about it and I can help in some way. Your doctor got you on tranquilizers? Your eyes look sort of glazed.

Kei shook her head. "I try not to use drugs. Your

problems just lie in wait, snapping their jaws, when you're doped. I'm all right.''

"No, you aren't," Missy said flatly, adding up the bill herself to see that she wasn't getting ripped off. "But whatever it is, I've probably been there myself."

No, you haven't, Kei thought. Nobody's been here before. This is a private hell all my own.

"Can't Hilaire help with these?" Kei asked, sharing carrying up the suitcases with Garnett while Missy trailed behind with her makeup case and tried not to fall over Maybe, who was sniffing the toes of the new addition to the household.

"He's out in the fields with Guillaume, supervising the extra hands clearing things up for winter," Garnett said, heading for the yellow room. "I told him to hurry things along so we could get them off the payroll as quickly as possible."

"You might have left that to me," Kei said, irritated at the way he was taking over. "Simon asked you to oversee the crew finishing the folly, not the field hands." She put down the bags on the marquetry by the bedroom window and opened the draperies. It was beginning to rain again.

Missy sat down on the bed and began pulling off her boots. Kei felt a slash of jealousy at seeing that Garnett was looking down Missy's cleavage as she bent over.

"I should think you'd be glad to have me take some of the work around here off your hands," said Garnett. "But pardon me if I've overstepped the bounds. I must remember to keep in my place." He left to get the rest of the bags after giving Kei an insolent look.

"That's some gorgeous hunk of a tutor," Missy said, wriggling her toes voluptuously. "I wouldn't mind biting off a chunk of that myself. He could probably use some expert training from an older woman." She stood up and pulled off her blouse, baring an astonishing pair of well-preserved breasts.

"Leave him alone. He's only a boy," Kei snapped.

Missy raised her eyebrows. "What's eating you? You got dibs on him?" She hung her blouse in the closet. At Kei's silence, she turned around and said, "Just kidding. Don't get mad," but her eyes were less frivolous than the tone of her voice. She kicked her boots into the closet. "He's probably lousy in the sack anyway. They usually are, the young ones—staying power, but no artistry." Surprised by Garnett's rapid return with the bags, she whipped around so that her back was to him and said, "Gee whiz, that didn't take you any time at all. You must be able to fly!"

"How did you guess?" Garnett said, backing out the door. A second later, his arm reached around the door frame and deposited one bag, then another on the floor by the threshhold. "Sorry. I didn't mean to walk in on you like that," he said.

"Sassy little devil, isn't he?" Missy said to Kei as she looked through her bags for her robe. "I need to sack out for a couple of hours, if you don't mind. I'm really pooped, but I'll be bright-eyed and bushy-tailed by dinnertime, okay?"

Kei got up to leave, when Missy gave a piercing shriek and backed up against the window, snatching the draperies against her chest. "What in glory is that?!" she shrilled, pointing at a small gray oval like a live dust mouse moving out from under the bed.

For an instant, Kei was alarmed, too. Then she saw what it was and said, "It's just a baby hedgehog." She bent down to pick it up gingerly. Its thick quills, she knew, were harmless except to animals that tried to make a mouthful of it. "How did this little thing get up here?" She held it off at arm's length, repelled by its powerful odor of damp earth. The hedgehog tried vainly to roll into a ball on her palm and then sat immobile, a dark pincushion on her hand. "Once in a while animals get into the house. It's the price of living in the country. You have a nice nap."

Better be sure to keep the doors kept shut, Kei thought, carrying it downstairs. The continual rain might make the local wildlife seek the shelter of the house. She'd have to speak to the twins about closing the doors when they came in from outside.

She set the creature down on the glistening gravel on the back bridge and through the glass panel of one of the back doors watched it scuttle slowly over to the first step, disappear over the edge, reappear on the step below, bump down to the third, and curl into a prickly ball as a raven swooped down to peck at it. "Stop that!" she shouted at the bird, banging on the glass with her fist. The raven veered toward her and dashed at the pane as if to attack her, but sloped off just before impact and flapped back toward the oaks towering over the folly. The hedgehog rolled off into the leaf-coated meadow like a miniature armored tank.

The near assault by the raven made Kei think for the first time about the unending savagery that went on out there in the woods as each species preyed on a smaller one. Unheard in the château, death flourished in the dark undergrowth of the forest. Thank heaven, the house was a safe refuge from the little murders that went on day and night out there! Being a city girl, Missy had over-reacted to the hedgehog's wandering in from the cold. The little animal was harmless. Really, there was nothing to fear here.

Where was Garnett? It was three in the morning, and he still wasn't back. After dinner, he'd taken off without saying where he was going. He had a perfect right to do what he wanted after work hours, but what could he find to keep him out so long in the village, where they rolled up the sidewalks at nine o'clock?

He couldn't have doubled back and gone into Missy's room, could he? Kei tiptoed down the hallway from her bedroom, past windows that overlooked the front courtyard, and put her ear to Missy's door. No sound, of course. Feeling ashamed of herself, she went back to lean her forehead against the soothing chill of a window pane and, looking down through the monotonous rain toward the gate onto the road, asked herself wearily what she was doing, waiting fretfully for Garnett like a teen-ager being stood up.

If she had dared to tell him, Simon wouldn't have been able to believe what lengths her craving for Garnett was driving her to, how far out of control she was! Oh, Simon, Simon! Her eyes filled. Through a foggy film of tears she looked out at the midnight blue horizon beyond the wrought-iron gate and was puzzled to see a strange blackness gathering like a cloud in front of the iron bars. At first it looked transparent, then the patch of darkness became opaque and flowed across the bridge and onto the parking area like octopus ink spreading under water. Just before it reached the fuzzy halo around the light over the glass canopy over the front door, it shrank into a solid, man-sized shadow. She wiped her eyes with the back of a hand to clear her vision and looked again. It was gone.

The front door opened and closed again. He was back! She forgot what she'd seen and flew down the stairs without bothering to turn on the light. Outlined against the dim light coming through the glass-paneled doors, he looked bigger that she remembered, elongated by a monstrous shadow stretching before him across the foyer tiles.

She paused a few steps from the bottom, reluctant to seem too eager, and watched him take off his raincoat, hang it in the closet by the doorway, pull down his Welsh fisherman's tunic, and run his fingers through his wet hair. In the murky light with his back toward her, his hair looked black, and shadow fringed down along the bottoms of his arms, making them look like the shaggy forelegs of a beast.

"Where have you been?" she whispered, coming down the rest of the way to stand a few paces from him at the foot of the staircase.

Her voice must have startled him, for he stood still a moment as if to compose himself. Then he turned slowly toward her and she could see the familiar blondness of his hair and the smooth golden skin of his face and arms. It must have been a trick of the light that had made him look so dark and feral. Nevertheless, there was something strange about his eyes, something odd about the pupils. No, it must have been her imagination. They were normal now. What was happening inside her head lately?

He looked at her sullenly and said, "I was out. That's all you need to know. You don't own me just because you pay my salary."

"Don't be angry," she said quicky. "I was worried about you, can't you understand that?" She went over to him and, putting her arms around him, turned up her face for a kiss.

"I can take care of myself," he said in a more civil tone, drawing back from her without kissing her. "Jesus, it's raw out there!" He rubbed his hands together. "Let's get a fire going in the fireplace."

"It's late and it'll take forever to catch," she protested, wanting him to go upstairs with her.

"Not when I do it." He was right. Flames sprang up around the logs immediately that he set a match to the kindling.

"You're a magician," she said, hoping to flatter him into a good mood.

"Yeah." He smiled up at her from his squatting position at the hearth. "I have a whole bagful of tricks you don't know about yet,"

She joined him by the fire, tucking the skirt of her kimono around her knees, and sat looking into the dancing tongues of flame. "Everyone's asleep upstairs." She ran her hand caressingly up and down the smooth muscle of his thigh. "Let's make love."

"Make love?" Impassively he watched the movement of her hand until she grew self-conscious and took it away. "Let's cut the sentimental crap right now. Lady, I've screwed you, fucked you, but I've never made love to you. You don't think I *love* you, do you?" Kei shrank into herself. "You just want to be serviced, and there's a price to pay for that. For one thing, you've got to come off that mistress-of-the-manor act and quit treating me like a God-damned inferior! You shouldn't have invited Missy Hilliard here without asking me first. Don't you know she'll blab to Simon first chance she gets if she thinks we're fooling around? That's your worry, though." He stood up with his back to the popping logs and began to strip. "I heard you talking to Marthe about taking on extra help, but you'd better put that notion out of your head. I don't like people watching me all the time."

The light from the fire made a nimbus of the blond hairs outlining the lower part of his body. Kei's eyes traveled avidly over the strong curves of his shoulders and his shield-shaped chest where the soft flat cones of his nipples were set like ruddy exotic buttons in a cross of feathery hair that tapered from a fan on his pectorals to his navel and spread out again in a light bush above the magnificent cluster of his genitals. His skin was the color of old ivory, molded over his body like a thick, flawless plastic sheeting.

"If you hire anybody new for the house, you're not going to get any more screwing, is that clear?" he said. "You wouldn't want that, would you?" Kei swallowed and shook her head. "That's a good, reasonable little girl. Then it's a promise?"

As he'd been removing his clothing, the subtlety of the play of muscle along his thighs and calves had hypnotized Kei, making her impatient to run her hands over his young, warm flesh, to feel it against her lips. She would have agreed to anything he asked to keep him from turning away from her when she was so aroused. "I promise," she whispered.

"Good. Just for that, as a reward I'll let you blow me."

He took a pillow covered in gold-shot obi material from a settee and tossed it down on the floor beside the Japanese chest. Lying down with his head on the pillow and his feet toward the fire, he reached up languidly and brought her head down to his nipple. Then he closed his eyes, and his only sign of interest as she knelt over him was his enormous erection silhouetted against the firelight. He might have been asleep, he was so unresponsive as she rubbed her cheek against the hair splaying out on his chest and moved her mouth down his body, using all the art she knew to give him pleasure. When her lips reached his groin, the goatish smell there was so penetrating, so unlike Simon's clean male fragrance, that she felt a momentary repulsion and sat back on her heels.

Garnett grunted and put his hand on her head to bring it down again to his crotch. Afraid of what he'd do if she didn't comply immediately with what he wanted, Kei went back to work, but as she brought him nearer and nearer to a climax, she dreaded having to take that unnatural cold sperm into her mouth and slowed her pace.

Abruptly, he seized her by the hair with both hands and rammed himself down her throat. She choked and grabbed his wrists, trying to disentangle herself, but he was too strong for her and the pain in her scalp was agonizing. Brutishly, he worked her head up and down, faster and faster while sparkling darts of light appeared in the blackness behind her eyelids. She was slipping into unconsciousness when he gave a growl and filled her mouth with thick, icy fluid that tasted viler than anything she could have imagined. As he released her, she strangled for breath, coughing and retching, and grabbed up a corner of her robe to spit his poison out when he commanded, "Swallow it!" She obeyed, but her stomach lurched and she nearly brought it up again.

Garnett lay back, smiling to himself like a sleeping child, golden eyelashes curling up along the curve of his closed lids while he contently stroked the hair on his chest. Then he sighed heavily, said casually, "You give good head, old lady," and got up, gathering his clothing from the floor. With the bundle of clothes under his arm, he walked naked out into the foyer and up the stairs, deserting her without a further word.

Kei stared blindly into the flames as the logs spluttered and an owl screeched in the woods out back. The cistern on the third floor filled itself with a sound of rushing water. A car swished by on the wet road leading to Orléans.

After a time, she got stiffly to her feet and groped her way on trembling legs to the dark kitchen. Feeling around on the counter, she found a glass and ran water into it to rinse the ugly taste from her mouth.

For a long time she stood there numbly, listening to the thrumming of the rain beyond the kitchen windows.

Old lady! Realizing how tenuous her hold on him was, she felt seized with panic. She was years older than he was and, though she'd kept her figure and was proud of it, her breasts were not quite as high as they used to be. Her skin no longer had the bursting tightness of youth, and he could find younger, more appealing bodies wherever he looked. Was she only a charity case to him—someone he used because she was handy and laughed at behind her back? Did he sleep with her only because he wanted to keep on the good side of the person who employed him? How could she keep him, what wiles did she possess that would keep him coming back to her? If he tired of her, she didn't know how she could bear the monstrous hunger for him that gnawed day and night at her sex.

Simon or Garnett, she was going to lose one of them sooner or later, and she needed both of them! The guilt at betraying Simon that tormented her, peaking when he made his daily telephone call, seemed almost trivial in comparison to her fear of what the future would bring. When Stephen was killed in the car accident and her divorce from Robin followed, she'd had a breakdown and knew what madness was. This obsession for Garnett was already making her mind feel sick and bruised, and if he abandoned her or Simon found out and deserted her, she might be pushed over the brink into irretrievable insanity, never again able to climb back into normality. A chill blast of terror whistled through her skull as the kitchen windows rattled in the wind.

Father Barteau straightened the linen nightshirt that had become twisted around his legs during his vain vigil for Garnett and fell back into lonely dreams as Eagle woke up from a nightmare of wriggling, pimpled behinds and snapped on the bedside light. At seeing the familiar drapery of dirty clothing on the furniture in his room, Eagle humphed in comfort. Revolting as his dreams had been, they could barely top the reality of what he'd witnessed earlier that night at Mr. Grapes's house. It was one thing to see blue movies on a screen and a horse of a different color to have the same thing going around about you like theater in the round! Talking about turning you off on sex for life!

A ravishing vision of a peanut butter sandwich drifted into his mind. Immediately he felt an irresistible craving for a thick slice of limburger. Alone, each was beautiful in its own way. But together, ah!

Actually, the combination wasn't all that great. It needed pickles, and he was out of pickles. He looked into the refrigerator and thought lonesomely of his mother.

When were she and Tommy going to get back from their honeymoon? Maybe they'd get tired of hanging out together—it couldn't be that much fun staring at each other in hotel rooms—and cut it short. He was just about out of mayonnaise. Things were getting critical. Aunt Kei would shop for him if he asked her to, but after his big act about being able to take care of himself while the folks were gone, he'd rather eat mothballs than ask.

He sat down at the table, picked up the sandwich, and looked at the crescent of his toothmarks in the bread. Should he eat it because it was there, or not eat it because it didn't taste so hot? He ate it.

Damn Gar and his ideas about "broadening one's horizons"! Naturally, the stupid thing had wilted when he'd stood there feeling goosebumpy and gangly without his clothes, looking at all that freaky business going on around him. And when Mr. Grapes, naked as the day he was born except for a black chain like Gar's around his neck, had started coming at him on his knees over the carpet and telling him what a beautiful young boy he was, what did Gar expect him to do?

Everything between hearing Gar's roar of laughter at his horror and finding himself flying along the sidewalk in the rain, having one hell of a time locating the other armhole in his shirt, was a purple blur of panic. His jacket was still back there, and he didn't care if he never saw it again!

Gar had him in a royal bind now! A diamond pendant from Mrs. Van Dreuten's jewelry box was in the toe of a sock under the bed, and a slip of paper with his initials on it was in a back corner of her dressing table. Gar hadn't left *his* slip of paper behind. In fact, afterwards he'd admitted that he *never* had left any. He'd always palmed them, letting Eagle leave incriminating evidence in every place they'd visited at night. Gar had seen to it that Eagle had left a trail of clues behind him all over town.

The sandwich sat in Eagle's stomach like a chunk of iron. He'd known all along that Gar was bad news and hated him when he wasn't actually around.

Trouble was, when Gar was on the scene, he seemed so likeable that you forgot how you hated him when he was out of sight, and he could melt you down and convince you to do all sorts of things you knew you shouldn't. On top of that, the excitement of treading close to disaster was a marvelous feeling. And habit-forming.

Eagle shook his head and got up to place the plate and glass in beside the others that filled the sink. The gendarmes must be looking for the pendant right now. With luck, they might not think of looking through Mrs. Van Dreuten's dressing table drawers, where the initialed slip of paper was hidden.

He went into his room and retrieved the sock from under the bed, shook it out into his hand, and went into the bathroom with it. After wrapping the necklace in a thick wad of toilet paper, he threw it into the toilet bowl, flushed, and watched the water take it swirling out of sight. Never again! Absolutely never again, and—please—if they find that slip of paper with my initials, don't let them think of me!

He checked the alarm switch on his bedside clock before climbing back into the sack, feeling melo-dramatic at being up at such an ungodly hour, sleepless over his life of crime. What would his mother think if she knew he was a cat burglar? He lay back on the pillows, licked the peanut butter from the corners of his mouth, and wished she were in the next bedroom, even if Tommy had to be in there with her.

Do you suppose that when they were in bed together, they . . . Jesus, no! Not the kind of stuff that went on at Mr. Grapes's! *Please* not! Just the normal, good old-fashioned stuff. Oh, please!

141

Eagle's mouth fell open with a soft snore as he fed his last crumb of bread to a mouse he'd befriended while in solitary confinement.

CHAPTER TEN

Timorously, nervous at being alone on the empty third storey when the rest of the house was still sleeping, Missy turned on the switch that lit a bare bulb hanging from the attic ceiling. So that was what had been waking her through the night!

A motor whirred as rain water gushed into a chest-high cistern tank standing in the middle of the dust-perfumed room. It was a big one, about twelve feet across. Had to be, to serve a mammoth establishment like the château. It had given Missy the creeps, opening one door after another up here, seeing statues draped in dust cloths and faces staring at her from paintings stacked against the walls, until she'd traced the noise to its source here. Now that she knew what caused the periodic bubblings behind the walls as water rushed through the pipes down into the house, maybe she'd be able to sleep through tonight. She was a light sleeper, always had been since the early days of her show business career with its irregular hours, and at five o'clock she'd given up thrashing around and gotten up.

There was nothing to see in the room but unpainted, splintery walls and the huge copper tank with greenish verdigris around the bolts that held it together, so she snapped off the switch again. Just then, something ran over her foot and she gave a squeak of alarm. Hopping back into the lighted hallway, she scooted down the stairs to the second floor, turned off the attic light, and closed the door tightly behind her. This country life full of wildlife that turned up in unexpected places, had no charms for her! This morning, when she'd slipped her feet into her slippers, she'd been shocked fully awake by finding a mole nestled in one toe. Why Simon and Kei liked living in this big, echoing place of unoccupied bedrooms, where the hallway boards creaked at night as if someone were walking around out there just outside one's door, where just below the quiet of the countryside were subliminal rustling made by God knows what, was a complete mystery to Missy, who preferred city noises. At least, she knew what made them—traffic, people passing by, street repair work, maybe the scuffle of someone being mugged. Hefty locks on the doors kept her safe inside her mews apartment in London, but here she felt edgy both outside and inside the house.

Before Tommy had married Elaine, Missy had stayed with him in the village when she'd come to visit Simon and Kei. It was cozier there, and Tommy was an entertaining, sexy man, but outside of bed the village was boring. There was nothing to *do* in the country. She was perfectly willing to help Kei out in a crisis, but she didn't know how long she could flop around here without climbing the walls.

She went downstairs and wandered around, putting on the lights as she went. In the study, the birds in the aviary squawked and called for their breakfast as she entered. Idly she poked a finger through the bars and the pink cockatoo tried to bite it, thinking it was a small variety of banana. She sat down in Simon's chair at the desk and leaned back, rubbing her shoulders against the surface where Simon's shoulders must have left a trace of his presence. Running her hands across the leather desk top, she picked up his jade-handled paperknife, looking for his fingerprints on the blade. She sighed and blinked rapidly. Simon was Kei's now, no use sitting here getting the blues. Outside the casement windows over the moat, a gray light was coming over the meadow, bringing a low fog rolling before it. Why not go out and see what the folly looked like?

So far as Missy could see, the gazebo was finished, with a porch running around three sides. It wasn't painted yet, but it would be a pretty, lighthearted-looking spot in the summer if plantings could be persuaded to root in the raw soil around it that had been imported to fill in the grotto. Time and again Simon had tried to plant over the bone-colored mound out in the oak grove, but the earth over Sélène had been hostile to life and nothing had survived.

Missy stood on the back bridge, taking deep breaths of the invigorating air and watching the blanket of fog unfold toward the moat. She was glad to be out of the house. She could sense that something was wrong inside, something more widespread than the effect of its mistress's having a miscarriage. The house wasn't happy. The air in the rooms seemed filled with an electric tension, and the people within them moved about with a sort of listless expectancy like emergency-room attendants waiting for an accident to happen. The hollows under Kei's high cheekbones were unhealthily deep now. Her mouth had a twitch at the corner, and she jumped at the slightest sound, looking about her with haunted eyes. Missy was aware, too, that whenever the subject of Simon came up, Kei didn't look her straight in the eye.

Her boots made squelching sounds on the sodden leaves of the path as she hiked toward the folly and the oak grove, where a flock of ravens clustered like black fruit in the trees. As she approached, the birds rose in a body and swooped at her. Alarmed, she crouched down with her arms over her head, but they soared upward and scattered high overhead, then drifted down to settle around the château's conical towers and banners, along the roof edges, and on the bridge railings and window sills. A handful of them strutted on the grass bordering the moat, their heads turned towards her. She straightened up, her heart galloping, and trotted toward the folly, hoping to get inside.

She rattled the doorknob, but the place was locked tight. After looking back nervously to be sure the ravens weren't advancing on her, Missy walked around the porch, peering in the windows. All she could distinguish in the dark interior was a green patch of light where fish shapes undulated around a column of bubbles sent up by the aquarium's aerator.

Kei had said this was the twins' schoolhouse while their mother was in Spain. They were awfully young to be having lessons. At their age, Missy remembered, she was still having a heck of a time keeping the colors within the lines when she was crayoning in the pictures of her class worksheets. Chris was working on an advanced degree at the Sorbonne, though, and probably was pushing her kids for all they were worth. Academic types were like that.

Parents ought to let children play, Missy thought. Lord knows, they wouldn't be able to when they were grown up! Her own memories of school were ghastly. She'd gotten morning cramps when she couldn't for the life of her learn to read as quickly as the rest of her class, but her mother made her go every day anyway and then gave Missy hell for wetting her pants with fright when it was her turn to read aloud. They'd tested her eyes over and over without finding anything wrong with them that could explain why the symbols on the printed page carried faulty messages to her brain. She still read so slowly and painfully that when she got to the end of a sentence, she couldn't remember what the beginning was about and had to keep a social secretary to read letters and contracts out loud so that no one would know how defective she was. Missy hoped the twins weren't embarking on years of failure of the kind she'd suffered through before discovering her voice and how to use it to draw from an audience the love and approval she needed.

"What are you doing out here so early?" a voice said, startling her so that she banged her head on the latch of the window she was looking into. It was the tutor. The expression on his handsome young face was friendly, but the tone of his voice carried an edge that had Missy apologizing for looking around, as if she were some kind of sneak.

"Why don't we go and see if Marthe can rustle us up some breakfast?" Garnett said, taking her elbow and guiding her off the porch onto the path. On the way back, he told her he'd caught her act at the Palladium and collected her records, playing to her ego so absorbingly that she didn't notice that the ravens collected around the house rose up and obediently flew back to the oak grove when he waved a hand at them. Missy listened to him raptly, conscious of the sexual current that ran between his body and hers, and by the time they reached the back door, his charm had done its work.

"Please don't shut Lady Luna away yet! Just one more story!" Gino pleaded from his cushion on the stage.

Garnett touched the button concealed in the gilded paneling and the opening slid shut inexorably. "She's tired," he said, hoarse from using a falsetto voice. Jacques was due in ten minutes, and the twins had to be out and away promptly so they wouldn't run into him.

Dirk picked up his leatherette pillow and stomped off to put it away on the stack in front of Gunther, the giant panda. "Why do you only let her talk to us for a few minutes every afternoon? I love her," he said petulantly. "I want to see her more, 'cause I love her more nor anything in the whole world." He and Gino were completely unaware that they'd been with Lady Luna for two hours already while she instructed them in the arts they were to master.

"She's very delicate," Garnett said. "If you really love her, you ought to want to take good care of her. I know *I* do."

He set the twins to straightening up the folly and putting away the materials they'd been using. The evidence of today's lesson still littered the ground outside, but right now there wasn't time to search around for all of it. Jacques was probably so blind-eager to get to their rendezvous after having been neglected for the past couple of days that he wouldn't even notice if he stepped on one of the things. According to Mme. Prévost's abrasive voice over the phone, Monsieur le Curé was not to be disturbed during catechism lessons, but when she'd delivered the number of the château to him, Jacques had called back immediately, breathless from hurrying to his study. He'd be so anxious to answer his summons that he might arrive early.

"You boys are old enough to have dinner without me and get yourselves ready for bed now," Garnett said, lending a hand at picking up to speed them along. "Don't forget to put your clothes in the hamper. I'll try to be up to tuck you in after you've brushed your teeth, but don't wait up for me. I may be a little late tonight."

He looked intently at Gino, then Dirk, to curtain off the private lessons of the day, making certain that the information was securely stored in their minds but that they'd have no memory of it until he wakened it again tomorrow. It would be catastrophic, of course, if their childish lips leaked any hint that he was training them to be Masters.

That was part of Garnett's responsibility as Master of this region: training a replacement for himself. It was a lucky fluke that he could indoctrinate two at once. It was rare to start apprentices so young, but the body of knowledge he had to pass on to the twins was limitless. The *Necronomicon*, which outsiders supposed to be the Satanists' bible, contained but a few of the secrets that had to be imparted and was marred by intentional errors to befool the uninitiated. He himself was still studying ancient texts. Resurrecting Sélène from her present mummified state was the ultimate challenge, and he'd had to travel to the farthest corners of the earth to find the formulas he needed.

To have allowed Sélène's body to remain lifeless and buried in the grotto had been stupidity of the highest order, but the local cult had never been a strong one. The last Satanic Master, Rudy van der Zee, had been a dilettante who'd come late in life to the craft. Not only had he been inexpert, but he hadn't trained a replacement, so Garnett had been called in to take his place when Rudy had been killed. Only a hereditary Master, instructed early on in the black arts and with Satanic blood flowing down through both sides of his family, could hope to undo the mischief that the Eagletons had loosed on the local cult. It was poetic justice that Kei's own grandchildren would carry on the work of the cult she and Simon had nearly destroyed.

The children scampered out the doorway, hungry after a long day's work. Garnett was leaning down to straighten out a curled-up corner of the rug when he heard a squall of fright from outside. As he opened the door, a raven flapped up from something lying on the path, where the twins stood frozen in horror, and flew to settle on the edge of the folly roof. Annoyed, Garnett blanked the incident out of the twins' heads, sent them running happily along the path to the château, and kicked the evidence under the bushes, where it would remain unseen until he could take care of it.

His energy was running low, and he wasn't up to any fancy business until after he'd had Jacques. Odd how sex depleted ordinary mortals, he thought. It restored his powers. If he didn't discharge his semen regularly, the iciness in his groin spread through his veins, slowing his movements and seizing his joints in a painful arthritic grip. In that condition, he became as ineffectual as anybody else. No matter, there were always plenty of warm bodies to pour himself into, to use to recharge himself, as he was about to do with Jacques Barteau.

If the chocolate-frosted strawberry cream puff had been a child's mud pie, the priest would have eaten it equally as blissfully in his present state of euphoria. The advent of Missy, who was sitting next to Eagle in a black velvet pantsuit with a Pierrot ruff that fluffed up around her cheeks, was responsible for the bleakness of the past days, when he'd thought himself slowly dying from Garnett's neglect. Nevertheless, he smiled cordially across at her, unable to resent her for putting the château out of bounds for his meetings with the boy. Right now, Father Barteau felt, he loved the whole world. Kei's presence in the house during their lovemaking had made him nervous anyhow. As for Kei, he couldn't blame her for lusting after Garnett and forcing him into that brief coupling, now that it was over and done with. What a magnanimous sacrifice Garnett had made in doing that with her, a thing that had turned the poor child's stomach! True, it had been a kind of blackmail to make Kei compliant so that their privacy would be protected, but sometimes unpleasant means were necessary to break through the barriers that an ignorant society set up against his and Garnett's kind of love. Besides, it would never happen again. Once was too much, Garnett had avowed, and he'd sleep with Kei again only over his dead body!

This evening in the folly, Garnett had been like a man starved for love, and Father Barteau felt rapturously exhausted, as if all his bones had been removed. A few minutes ago, his giddy happiness had carried him into making a series of puns of escalating putridity until, after he'd said he'd vetoed the parishioners' plans to mount an American-style manger scene on the church lawn because he disapproved of créche diets, Missy had thrown a bun at him. That had shut him up, but the seductive glances Garnett kept sending him from under his golden eyelashes made the priest want to wriggle like a tickled puppy. Not even thrown buns could bring him down from the cloud he was floating on now.

"Did you ever find the body of the witch, what's her name, in the grotto when Simon dug out the foundations for the folly?" Missy asked Kei, accepting a demi-tasse of amaretto coffee to go with her cream puff.

"No, but there was some paraphernalia left from the old devil-worship cult down there. An altar and candlesticks, about what you'd expect, covered with obscenities. Simon wouldn't let me see them." Kei looked out of the corner of her eye at Father Barteau, not sure that such matters should be discussed before a man of the cloth, but he smiled cherubically, unperturbed. "He had them carted away and dumped in the canal a long way from here, I don't know where. He was afraid that if someone got hold of them, the cult might be resurrected."

Missy affixed a lipstick-colored cigarette to the end of a long ebony holder and lit it. "I wouldn't know a Satanist if he turned up selling Girl Scout cookies," she said, squirting a stream of smoke out of the corner of her mouth. "Would you be able to recognize a Satanist, Father?"

"I don't know. I've never come into contact with one." He took a sip of coffee and wiped his mouth with his napkin. "I've a romantic notion that they should smell of brimstone, but that's doubtless the result of reading thrillers in my youth. In any case, the local cult was obliterated with the help of your hostess and isn't likely to be revived again, so I'm not likely to be put to the test of recognizing one. Or so one would hope."

"Have you ever done an exorcism?" Missy asked. "I knew this family that had a haunted house in London, and they had to get a psychic in to get rid of their ghost, it was in the bathroom, and whenever a man tried to use the john, the lid would bang down. Nearly desexed their son-in-law, for crying out loud! They'd go in the bathroom at two in the morning and there would be this big black Thing squatting on the can, leering at them. Nearly sent the grandmother to the funny farm, but they could put up with that, the old lady was already saving cookies in her bloomers anyway in case sugar rationing ever started again. But there was only one toilet in the house, and when the ghost got to slamming the door in their faces and locking it, leaving them standing on one foot and then the other until they were ready to pop and had to dash next door, they called in the psychic. They never had any trouble after that with the bathroom except for stopped drains, could happen to anybody. Have you ever done the bell-book-and-candle bit, Father?"

"It's not been in my line of work thus far, I'm happy to say."

Missy persisted, waving her cigarette holder at him like a baton. "But would you know how to do it if you had to?"

Father Barteau coughed and said hesitantly, "Ye-es." doubtful as to his reaction if anyone actually prevailed upon him to peform the rite. Fortunately, the woman whose husband had been killed in the grotto had changed her mind and not pressed for an exorcism. Having to confront Satan and his cohorts was a challenge that would frighten a saint, and he himself wasn't the bravest of men. Speculation was vain, however. No one would ever call upon him to perform such an antique, superstitious rite. The only representatives of the Devil he'd ever have to struggle with were the ones with which he was already familiar—the imps that pranced in his brain, torturing him with quandaries about this accursèd-blessèd

154

love he bore for Garnett.

Why had God sent Garnett to him? Only God Himself knew, and who could fathom His thoughts? Was it a divine lesson to teach him that his proclivity for forbidden love, denied and stamped out so long ago after the affair with Christophe, still lingered on, waiting to have its embers fanned into flame? Was his adoration of Garnett a divine gift or a trial sent down to tempt him fatally, so that Christ in his infinite compassion could send forgiveness—salvation from hell—at the last moment? If their sweet congress was irretrievably evil, why hadn't he been struck dead at the altar before he could sully the office he was performing? In common parlance, if what they were doing was so bad, why did it feel so good? And what harm were they doing to anyone? He began to feel angry. What did God *expect* him to do if He put such temptation in his path? Not love Garnett? Who was to blame for the whole thing, after all?

"Don't you guys ever have chili?" asked Eagle, interrupting the moiling of the priest's thoughts. "I never know what I'm eating here, it's always so gussied up." He doled three heaping teaspoons of sugar into his demi-tasse to kill the coffee taste.

"I can teach Marthe to make it," Kei said affably, "but she'll put such a French accent on it that you probably won't know it's chili."

"And canned peaches for dessert? In boarding school back home, that's all we ever got. I didn't know there *was* any other dessert when I was young, and I kind of miss canned peaches." Eagle took a gulp of coffee and swished it through his teeth meditatively, thinking wistfully of chili dogs, hamburgers with everything on them, and milkshakes, and felt homesick for Cape Cod.

He wished his mother and Tommy would get back soon. The mayonnaise was all gone now, and he was tired of the French cooking he got here at the château. Most of all, he needed someone to talk to about what was worrying him. If he'd been a Catholic, he would have gone to see Father Barteau, even though the old bird with his awful puns and his way of sort of singing his words wasn't exactly the kind of guy he'd like to spill everything to.

"By the way," said Kei, setting down her empty cup, "I hope you're being careful to keep the house locked while you're at school. There have been some serious thefts in the part of the village where you are."

The coffee went down Eagle's Sunday throat. Missy hopped out of her chair and pounded him briskly on the back until he quit choking and could speak again. "Really?" he said in a strangled voice, trying to sound not particularly interested.

"Peggy Van Dreuten had a valuable piece of jewelry stolen," Kei said. "She says she'd rather have the insurance money than the necklace, but I suppose the company will be making investigations anyhow. She says she lives in dread of their finding the piece, because she's spent all the money already at the fall collections in Paris."

"Do they have any leads on who took it?" Garnett asked, relishing how shiny Eagle's nose and forehead had become.

"Not that I know of," Kei replied.

Marthe came in to replace the coffee server with a fresh one and cleared away some of the plates.

Kei wiped her mouth with a napkin. "We'll take our liqueurs into the salon with us, Marthe," she said. "The fire in there will feel good. This room's getting chilly in the evenings."

As they entered, the cat stirred on the hearth, unrolled itself, and got up to squeeze itself together like a concertina before weaving figure eights around Garnett's legs. Kei and Missy sat down opposite each other on the yellow suede settees before the fireplace, glasses of Cointreau in their hands. Eagle warmed his rear before the flames, and Father Barteau stood behind Missy's settee, sipping his B & B. As Garnett bent down to stroke the cat's back, it bumped up its rear to meet his hand and, after its ration of body contact, swayed over to the doorway, looked back, and gave an imperious neow.

"I'll let Maybe out," Garnett said, going out to open the door onto the back bridge. The cat slipped out into the dark rain.

"I wonder what Simon's doing now," Missy said, slipping off her shoes. "I never can figure out the time differences. He's probably sitting in some hotel room, feeling lonely. Golly, how he's changed since he met you, Kei! All those women chasing him for years, including poor little me, and he never gives one a tumble until you come along and he goes down like he's poleaxed, I mean really! What kind of magical double whammy did you put on him to turn an alley cat like Simon into a model husband?" She put down her drink on the Japanese chest and inserted another fuschia-colored cigarette in her holder as Eagle lay down in front of the fire and proceeded to go to sleep. "Anybody here play the piano, I'll sing, but I can't play. Can't read a note. Everybody ought to know how to play the piano. I knew this couple, he played the harp, and she got so tired of helping him schlep it on and off subways that she finally took up with a piccolo player she wasn't all that crazy about, it was just that he was portable. If the guy had played the piano, they'd still probably be together."

She raised her eyebrows at seeing Father Barteau seat himself at the Bäsendorfer. "What's your key?" he asked, rippling out a few introductory chords and adjusting as she told him.

Missy took along her ashtray and went over to lean back against the piano, facing the group. Garnett stationed himself at the other end of the instrument, hunching himself over his drink on both elbows after putting a coaster down on the closed lid. "You know 'My Funny Valentine'?" Missy asked. Father Barteau did, and she belted out in her acclaimed style an was a few bars into "Lili Marlene" when she stopped, patted her stomach, and said, "That's it for tonight. I shouldn't perform on a full stomach, makes me feel asthmatic." Taking her drink back to the settee, she sat down again on its yellow suede and stuffed an obi-covered pillow behind her back.

The priest rumbled into expert boogie-woogie from his lycée days, remembered that it was politick to keep his image polished while in Garnett's company with other people, and modulated into "Jesu, Joy of Man's Desiring," accompanying himself into a choir loft voice that was pure and true.

Garnett turned his head toward Kei sitting by the fire. As they exchanged a look of intimacy, Father Barteau's fingers stumbled on the keys. Kei saw that he'd caught the glance she'd given Garnett and reddened. The priest's voice trailed off into silence and the music died away. He folded his hands in his lap and looked at Garnett, who shrugged and smiled. It was practically an admission that his liaison with Kei had continued.

Father Barteau was capable of carrying hope to its furthest limit, but he was not an utter fool. He couldn't make excuses for Garnett any longer. He might have been able to tolerate a non-exclusive relationship, although that would have taken the self-discipline that only a great love could commmand, but Garnett had *sworn* he hadn't and wouldn't sleep with Kei again. And once trust was broken, it couldn't be repaired. Father Barteau's illusions about Garnett's affection for him shattered like a glass thrown against a wall, and widening cracks began spreading through his illusions about himself.

He got up from the piano, retrieved his B & B from the bar, and took it with him as he went to stand behind Missy's settee, leaning on the back with both elbows to steady himself. His head drooped. He'd broken his vows for nothing, conned by a beloved liar into thinking God had granted him a special blessing and an extraordinary dispensation. What was he going to do with the rest of the empty days that stretched before him on this earth?

Garnett left the piano to put his glass down on the bar before joining the priest behind Missy. Father

Barteau drew away from him, but Garnett first looked over Missy's head to be sure he had Kei's eye and then took the priest's chin firmly in his hand, kissed him full on the lips, and grinned back at Kei's white face. The glass leaped out of Father Barteau's hand and fell on the parquet beyond the carpet. His face flamed as he and Kei shared a look of despair.

Missy looked around the arm of the settee at the priest's hand frozen open while the amber liquid of his drink pooled against the baseboard. "Naughty, naughty, Father Barteau!" she said teasingly. "Can't you control yourself?"

"I'll get a cloth to wipe it up," Garnett said quickly. As he went into the foyer, Kei and the priest continued to stare at each other.

"Hey, it didn't get on the carpet, you don't need to look as if the world had gone smash," said Missy, who had missed the whole interchange. "You let things get to you too much, Kei. No wonder you look so rotten lately." She put two reprimanding fingers on her lips and then said apologetically, "I shouldn't have said that. Excuse me."

Eagle, awakened by the sound of the glass hitting the floor, sat up and rubbed his eyes with the heels of the his palms. "Guess I'd better be getting home," he muttered. "Anything interesting happen while I was asleep?"

"Not a thing," Kei said woodenly.

"That's Maybe bumping at the door to be let in," Eagle said, gaping and staggering to his feet. "I'll see to it and then I've got to be running along."

Garnett came back with the cloth and got down on his hands and knees to wipe up the drink as Eagle said from the foyer, "What you got there, Maybe?"

The cat dragged something almost as big as himself across the threshold, hauled it into the salon, and deposited it proudly on the parquet near Missy's feet.

"Get away, you nasty thing!" she screamed, jumping up on the settee and nearly knocking it over. "My God, *where's its head!?* Ye gods, take it away, somebody, do!"

Garnett looked up at the rocking settee and said, "It's only a squirrel, Missy. Calm down, I'll get rid of it." He carried it out to the door onto the bridge, feeling severely irritated with himself for forgetting to clear everything away after this afternoon's lessons, and slung it by its tail into the moat.

Missy climbed down from her perch, uttering moans of dismay, and resettled herself, bolstering her nerves with the rest of her drink. Maybe sat on the hearth, looking deprived and disgruntled, then lay down with his paws tucked under his chest and brooded.

"Some fun *that* is, with your after-dinner drink!" Missy said. "What kind of a monster have you got there, Kei, that can bite the head off a squirrel? His mouth isn't anywhere near big enough to do that, I should think." Not bothering to use the ebony holder, she stuck a cigarette between her lips, lit it, and then said around it, "Listen, haven't you noticed things creeping around the house? I found a mole in my slipper this morning, nearly jumped through the roof, and there was some little bitty animal, a shrew, I think, staring at me from a corner while I was eating breakfast. This place is a zoo! And

161

those black birds that sit on my window sill give me the willies!"

"Now, now, Missy," Garnett said coming in from the hallway. "We're living in the country, you know. Don't get yourself overexcited." As he left to take the wet cloth back to the kitchen, he said back over his shoulder, "It does make your bosom heave rather enticingly, though."

Missy looked after him consideringly. Assuming a self-consciously becoming pose with her neck stretched up, she unconsciously ran her hand down the side of one breast to her waist and pursed her lips thoughtfully like Betty Boop.

"Twenty-six. I asked him. He's twenty-six," Eagle said.

Missy's nostrils flared and her eyes narrowed. "Who asked you how old he was?" she rapped out, her Irish up.

"Nobody. I was just making an observation. Forget I said anything." Eagle held his palms out toward her in a calming gesture and backed toward the door. "As I was saying, I'm on my way. Good night, all." He bowed his way back through the door into the foyer.

"Smartass!" Missy snorted and stubbed her cigarette out in the ashtray as if she were trying to give it a painful death. The front door closed behind Eagle. "Twenty-six isn't all that young," she said under her breath, but the sound carried across the still room to Father Barteau and Kei, whose eyes met, bonding them in a sinking sense of inevitability.

Where was Garnett and what was he doing at this

162

hour? She'd heard him go out the front door hours ago. Where did he go at night? To another woman in the village? Or a man? Recalling the shame and despair in Father Barteau's face, Kei picked up the glass of Scotch from the bedside table, stared at it for a moment, and put it down again untasted. Did Garnett prefer men to women? Oh God, if he was basically homosexual, what chance did she have of holding him? Men knew how to please other men better than a woman could, never having experienced the sensations in a male body. She suspected that an ascetic like the priest, repressed for so long, would be ferociously passionate if he let go of the reins he kept upon himself. A picture of Father Barteau kneeling before Garnett flashed into her mind and sexual jealousy seared through her.

Missy would be next in line. Poor Missy, always looking for love wherever she could find it. Missy, with her magnificent breasts. Kei put her hands on her own and felt inadequate. A sudden thought distracted her from her worry about Missy as a rival: Had Garnett tried it on with Eagle?

She *knew* she should have insisted that Eagle stay at the château while Tommy and Elaine were on their honeymoon! She searched through her memory, trying to recall any secret glances, and clues that would have suggested that Eagle and Garnett had been up to funny business together. No, she hadn't noticed anything and, to judge from Eagle's conversation, he was so busy chasing girls at school that she doubted he had any gay leanings. Still, psychologists said that homosexual experimentation between boys was to be expected. But with Garnett, it wouldn't be experimentation, it would be enslavement. She knew that from her own experience. In any case, there was nothing she could do to protect Eagle. Perhaps Simon could have a talk with him when he got back. No, she daren't say anything to Simon about it, or he might suspect her own connection with Garnett!

What was wrong with her? She was suffering the torments of the damned over a boy—a man—she didn't even like. Garnett was—was wicked! Somehow he clogged the natural flow of her thoughts and made her do things she'd never do if she were in her right mind. Then he twisted everything around and made her feel that she was responsible for it while he skipped free of blame.

And then there was that cold gism. She didn't know everything about sex, who could? Perhaps some men—rare medical cases—had that kind of ejaculation, but she'd thought from the start that Garnett had something alien about him, and the sense that he was abnormal in some way was growing stronger. Sex with him brought an intoxication she'd never known before and couldn't do without now, but even as she'd lain writhing and wallowing in his arms, she'd always had an eerie feeling that she was in the power of someone unnatural, inhuman.

She lay back against a pile of pillows, looking at the tawny-faced madonnas in the icons on the emerald velvet wall as she stroked Maybe. The cat purred contently, vibrating gently under Kei's hand. Oh heaven, if only Simon were here to protect and comfort her, Kei thought. He would make everything all right again if only she could confide in him! But she couldn't. She could never tell him. It would hurt him too much, and he might walk away from her forever. She'd already lost a part of Garnett to Father Barteau, and now she'd have to share him with Missy as well, then God knows how many others. She could lose Simon and Garnett at the same time, and then would she break? She remembered the corridors in the psychiatric ward, the shuffling sound of her own steps along the floors as she'd paced back and forth, back and forth, wearing out the hospital slippers, and—for the first time in many years, whispered, "Now I lay me down to sleep; I pray the Lord my soul to keep. . . . "

CHAPTER ELEVEN

As he scuffed across the gravel parking lot in front of the château, Eagle looked at the ravens lined up along the roof like rows of black bunting, their feathers ruffled by the stiff November breeze, and thought that their ominous aspect was perfectly keyed to his mood. It was Sunday, two days after he'd been here for dinner with Missy and the priest, and those two days had been a delirium of conscience-attack that he'd spent debating whether to go to the gendarmes and confess—because he ought to, and anyway they'd get him sooner or later—or to keep quiet because he'd flushed away the evidence and maybe things would blow over eventually.

The outcome of that internal battle was still pending, but what he'd seen last night demanded immediate action. Having to face Gar with it scared him out of his gourd! Gar seemed to have some unhealthy power to make a person do things that were wrong, to get a person's thoughts all tangled up, and Eagle wasn't sure he could hold his own in an argument with him. Moreover, Gar was a strong son of a bitch, and Eagle didn't want to wind up on the receiving end of his fist if he lost his temper. Nevertheless, sometime in a man's life, he had to stand up for what was right. And this was the time!

Hilaire was by the marshmallow sculpture, sweeping bird droppings off it with a twig broom. He tugged politely at the front of his beret at seeing Eagle, took the cigar stub out of his mouth, and said *bon jour*. These accursed birds, he said, were a pestilence. He'd never seen so many before. They were taking over the place.

In halting French, searching through his inadequate vocabulary for the right words, Eagle suggested that an earthquake might be building up, having heard that animals acted very peculiarly before temblors. Hilaire looked doubtfully at him, stuck the cigar back in a corner of his mouth, scratched the gray stubble on his chin, and went back to his sweeping, muttering something about young intellectuals to himself.

Eagle stuck his nose in the doorway and shouted his presence. Faint voices answered, and he followed them to the kitchen, where Marthe and Kei were playing Old Maid with the twins.

"Where's Gar?" he asked, looking around to see if any leftover breakfast was visible, but everything had been put away neatly.

"I haven't the faintest idea," Kei said, slapping a set of cards down on the table. She looked cross.

"Garnett's playing games with Aunt Missy in her room. I heard them laughing," said Gino, taking a card from Marthe's hand and looking at it disappointedly. Kei's lips tightened and Marthe cleared her throat and straightened the brooch on her *tablier*.

Hm, thought Eagle.

He looked the twins over, trying to detect any change in their manner since he'd seen them last, but they looked intent on the game and otherwise the same as usual.

As he turned to go up the kitchen stairway, Kei said, "I'd knock first and wait a bit before you interrupt them if I were you."

Hm again, Eagle thought.

He did as Kei suggested. When Missy came to the door, clutching a red chiffon peignoir together in front, Eagle was astounded by the superb superstructure visible through the filmy material and hardly noticed the asperity in her voice when she snapped, "Well, he's certainly not in here!" in reply to his question.

As he walked down the hallway toward Garnett's room, replaying the scene of Missy in her peignoir in his mind, he heard the sound of a shower going. No one answered his knock at Garnett's door, so he stuck his head in the room and, seeing it was empty, crossed the Tabariz carpet and hollered into the steamy tower bathroom. The shower went off and Garnett stepped out, dripping onto the bathmat, and reached for a towel.

"What's up?" he asked, blotting his face and then rubbing his hair with the towel.

"I have to talk to you," Eagle said, and looked enviously at Garnett's equipment.

"Go ahead, I'm listening."

"It's about last night," Eagle began, more confidently than he would have if Garnett had been clothed. "I saw you taking the twins to Mr. Grapes's."

Garnett paused in toweling himself down, then scrubbed vigorously at his back and tossed the towel on the shell-shaped basin. "Well, aren't you the little bright-eyed boy, though!" He pushed past Eagle at the bedroom door and went to the armoire to get out his clothing. "Are you objecting to my keeping them up late?" He stepped into his briefs, pulled them up, and let the waistband snap into place noisily.

"That isn't it and you know it!" Eagle plumped down on the bed as Garnett went on getting dressed in black cords and a black turtlenecked sweater tucking the iron chain under his top. "I know what goes on there, and I don't like the twins looking into that snakepit!"

Garnett chuckled, looking into the armoire mirror to comb his damp hair. "*Look* at it! They were the main attraction! You're never too young to learn about life's delights." He put the comb in his pocket and looked approvingly at himself while Eagle gaped at him. "The twins seemed to enjoy it, and I know Grapes did. He'd never had any boys quite so young before."

Eagle sprang off the bed and grabbed a handful of Garnett's sweater. "You fucking bastard!" he shouted, enraged. "They're just kids! I won't let you do this to them!" Tears started to his eyes.

Garnett patiently pried Eagle's fingers open and then, seizing him by the collar of his shirt, lifted him off the ground and held him out at arm's length as easily as if the shirt had been empty. "You haven't

169

any say in the matter," he said slowly and distinctly as Eagle choked and clawed at his hand to loosen his grip. "They don't remember a thing about it, so no harm's done to your precious babies." He lowered Eagle to the floor but kept a grasp on his shirt as he gasped for air and rubbed his neck where his collar had bitten into it. "Now, if you don't keep your mouth shut about this, I may have to make a trip to the police," he said menacingly, relishing the look of terror in Eagle's face. "I'm sure they'd be interested to know what happened to Peggy Van Dreuten's diamond pendant." He let Eagle go and smoothed down the front of his sweater. "And that's the least that will happen if you give me any trouble." Grinning, he nudged Eagle's shoulder with his fist. "Let's forget about it now. I won't hold it against you this time."

His smile vanished as he turned Eagle toward the door and gave him a light push to get his legs going. That should hold Eagle for awhile, but the kid was getting tiresome. Maybe it was time to get rid of him altogether.

The day was bright and windy, but not too cold for a brisk walk around the estate. Kei was out riding and everyone else seemed occupied, so she'd have to tramp around by herself, Missy decided, although being alone was a bore. She was feeling high-spirited, though, having had her ego stroked nicely by Garnett this morning while she let him cop a feel or two. He'd said the difference in their ages didn't matter, but they all said that, the young ones. However, it was physically evident that he was all hot to trot, and if she hadn't been afraid of someone's blundering in on them, she would have let him have more than a kiss and a fumble. Holy Moses, what a body he had on him! And he could kiss up a storm, too, but she bet she could show him a thing or two tonight that he didn't know about. She'd picked up some pretty exciting exotic maneuvers from her numerous lovers. Not that she was promiscuous, understand! In the business, men were always leaning on you, it went with the territory. She was lonely almost all the time and just wanted someone to hold her and cuddle her. It didn't stop at that, of course. Men weren't built that way, so she had to take the one to get the other and be grateful for whatever came her way in the line of affection.

Mitzi the mastiff romped up along the pathway from the château and thrust her satiny muzzle into Missy's hand, sensing her dolor. Missy stroked the dog's ears and thought what a silky coat dogs' ears would make. She sighed. The only man she'd ever really loved was Simon, she thought, looking up at the black trunks bearing bouquets of yellow leaves over her head. The other men didn't count. And she had more fingers on her hands than the times Simon had made love to her. She couldn't make up her mind whether it was that he was so polished at the art or that he made her feel good about herself in a special way, but there had never been anyone else like him. Kei was so damned lucky she ought to be hanged! She picked up a soggy moss-covered stick from the leaves and chucked it away toward the folly. Mitzi dashed after it and brought it back, soggier than ever with drool from her mouth. Well, there was Garnett tonight, Missy thought, hurling the stick away one more time, and one of these days she'd better get back to London and start working on that album before she went broke again.

"Do they have to have lessons even on Sunday?" Kei asked, surprising Garnett as he was locking up the folly at four o'clock.

"They like it and it gives them something to do," he said touchily, worried because the twins were dancing away down the path without having had their daily instructions stored away behind closed lips yet. Oh well, Missy was taking a nap in preparation for their session together tonight and Eagle had gone off to take part in a polo match, so there was no one the twins could blab to.

"Can I peek inside? You haven't let me see the folly since you fixed it up," said Kei.

Everything vital had been hidden away, so that the interior of the summer house looked like a normal playroom again. Garnett gave Mitzi a light slap on the rump to chase her away and pushed the door inward, releasing a pent-up smell of fresh paint and new wood. "How do you like it?" he asked.

Kei hesitated. Black walls? Maybe they set off the gaudy colors well, but the place would look funereal in the summer without the twins' trappings in it. The walls would have to be repainted, and wasn't Simon going to have some choice words to say about that! "I . . . Gino and Dirk must love it," she said lamely.

The circus theme should have made the room look gay, but there was something grotesque here, something off-key that picked at her nerves. The black-curtained area at the end of the room looked unpleasantly like drapery around a giant catafalque, and when Garnett pulled the cords to show the manikins on the stage, Kei shivered. The figures looked just the other side of being human, bizarrely lifelike, ready to start sliding stiff-leggedly across the flooring like humanoids.

"You don't like it," Garnett said sulkily, watching her face, and picked up some picture books that had been left on the floor to put them in the bookcase under the aquarium.

"Yes, I do." Kei lied, groping for an honest but evasive adjective. "It's very . . . imaginative."

Garnett looked at her suspiciously and drew his eyebrows together in a frown. "Too bad if you don't like it, because if you want to get screwed, this is where we're going to have to do it from now on. Missy's watching us like a hawk. You shouldn't have invited her without asking me first, I told you that. She's a pain in the ass, and it's not going to be very convenient, having to come out here when you want it. And you want it all the time, don't you?" He went over to her, drew her against him, and bucked himself into her crotch enticingly. "We can't do it in the house any more, or she'll hear you," he said as she pressed herself against him. "You make so much noise when you come, you ought to hear yourself!" Sneeringly, he imitated her cries.

Humiliated, she wrenched away and caught him a stinging slap across the mouth. He said nothing, but the murderous look in his eyes made Kei catch her breath. He grabbed her hand and twisted it cruelly, making the bones grate together as he forced her to her knees. "Don't you *ever* do that again!" he said between his teeth. "You'd be dead now if I didn't need the child I've put in you." He dropped her hand and stood looking down at her with disgust.

Instinctively, her hand went to her belly. "What do you mean?" she said, horrified.

"I've got you pregnant, you silly bitch! Why else would I hump an old broad like you? I need a baby to bring Sélène back to life, and you're going to give it to me. You're the one who took the cult's talisman, you were responsible for breaking up the cult—temporarily—and your shitty husband had the grotto cleared out. He could have destroyed Sélène's body! You two have caused me entirely too much trouble. You *owe* me! You owe me that child!"

Kei got to her feet, knocking a jack-in-the-box off the bookshelf behind her. The toy fell to the floor with a clack and the doll sprang out with an accordion's wheeze, but she hardly heard it. Garnett's eyes had turned strange and animal. The irises were vertical black slits. Darkness spread through his hair, growing up from the roots, and shaggy hair hung along the undersides of his arms. The shock of the change in him collapsed Kei's chest, squeezing the breath out of her. She closed her eyes, trying to recover, thinking that this time she'd hallucinated, that she was worse now than she'd been when she'd had her breakdown. But when she opened her eyes again, Garnett looked the same as he always had.

He went over to the door and stood with his hand on the knob. "You don't have to keep this to yourself, you know," he said calmly. One side of his mouth curled upward. "Tell anybody you like!

They'll only think you've gone crazy again. Oh yes, I know about that. And I'm sure Simon will love to hear about the baby."

"You're lying!" Kei said faintly. "You're just trying to frighten me!"

Garnett clicked his tongue and looked at her pityingly. "Don't give me that innocent look!" he said. "You must have known the first time I came in you. Or didn't anyone ever tell you that the Devil's seed is like ice?" He motioned her toward the door. "Now, don't get any ideas about doing anything foolish like breaking in here when I'm not around. Get back to the house and start obeying orders, or I might change my mind about keeping you alive. There are other women who can make babies, but I like the joke of getting Sélène's child on you. I wouldn't push my sense of humor too far, though, if I were you."

He gave her a vicious shove as she stumbled through the door and locked it behind her, putting the key back around his neck. She didn't hear his footsteps on the path behind her, and when she looked around, he was gone. Only the ravens stared down at her from the trees around the folly.

Her legs grew weaker and more unsteady as she walked toward the château. When she reached the steps of the bridge, she lowered herself onto one and tried to pull herself together. What Garnett had just said was ridiculous, passing himself off as the Devil! How stupid did he think she was? The change that had seemed to come over him had been a momentary illusion, a product of her own fevered mind. Or a distortion of light in the dim summer house.

175

But that cold semen . . . She looked down at her stomach and put both hands over it protectively. Was something growing inside her? Something that Garnett had put there?

Gino's voice saying hello cheerily made her jump. He peered up at her from under the bridge with a happy grin and pulled himself up by the long grass growing on the bank of the moat until he stood by her feet, looking as fresh and healthy as an advertisement for multivitamins.

"Look what I can do!" he said. Pointing a finger at a squirrel burying a nut in the meadow, he said, "Boom!" The squirrel's head flew off. Blood spurted from the ragged stump of its neck as its body lurched about on the grass and finally lay twitching on a sycamore leaf.

Someone was screaming and screaming, and the sound seemed to fill the whole bowl of heaven.

"Oh, my God, oh, my God!" Missy breathed, trying to unbutton a dress from its hanger in the closet. Her hands shook too much to manage the buttonholes, so she tore the dress at the neck and took it to her suitcase and stuffed it in on top of the other things she'd crammed in there. That woman doctor had sedated Kei, who'd been sleeping for hours, and it was criminal to leave her like this, but it couldn't be helped, Missy thought, not even if Simon hated her for the rest of her life. She had to get out of here and get out now!

How long would it take a taxi to come at this hour of the night? Missy charged about the room, collecting things a piece at a time, making innumerable

176

feverish journeys back and forth over the carpet and, blind with panic, overlooking things set out in plain sight. She threw a slipper and shoe in on top of the other clothing and jammed down the lid of the suit-case. It popped open again. Nearly hysterical, she sat on the case to get the lock to close and then jumped up and looked in the closet again. Was that everything? Oh, the hell with it, she could only carry two suitcases. Marthe would have to send the rest on to London.

A note! She'd have to leave a note! She scrabbled in her purse and found a tobacco-covered stub of pencil and ripped a check out of her checkbook to write on the back of it. Standing at the dressing table, she licked the point of the pencil and painstak-ingly began writing in a trembling hand, trying to squeeze her normally flamboyant letters into the space on the back of the check.

> *Dear Kei*
> *Their's no excuse for leaving*
> *you like this when your in bad shape*
> *But I can't stay in the same house with*
> *Garnet! Get rid of him as soon as you*
> *can! And get Simon back home!!!*
> > *Love*
> > *Missy*

She couldn't tell Kei why she had to leave, not when she was already under a doctor's care for hav-ing a screaming fit. In fact, Missy didn't think she'd ever be able to tell *anyone* about what had happened between her and Garnett. She'd thought she could teach him about sex, but his knowledge of it included practices more bizarre and ancient than anything she'd ever dreamed of! She could never tell anyone about that. Ever. Especially what he was about to do when that thing had appeared outside the window. Seeing it, Garnett had let her go and opened the window to shout outside. Whatever it was disappeared before she could see it clearly, but it had given her time to skin out of the room into another and lock the door behind her so that Garnett couldn't get at her again.

Missy snatched up her bag and the suitcases and ran out of the room and down the hallway, hoping against hope that Garnett wasn't following her.

CHAPTER TWELVE

Three days later, an eye looked through the window of a Tokyo hotel at a man inside. "You're still sounding dreadfully odd, darling," he was saying into the telephone in a velvety voice with a shadow of English accent, but the eye couldn't record that. All it could transmit was the image of a white-haired man, reduced to the size of an aspirin tablet, who was sitting on the edge of a bed with a silk spread patterned in Japanese fans. The tealeaf color of the spread's background, the salmon and rust tints weaving through the fans, and the gold stitching registered in blacks and grays on the eye's lens, but that was enough. "Yes, the doctor called to assure me you're all right now, but he didn't know what triggered it. He said you wouldn't tell him," the man said, standing up and whipping the telephone cord out so he could pace around the room as he talked. "Mm." The man nodded, and in a brain far away, the nod was noted.

"No, I can tell you're keeping something from me, don't try to talk me around. I'm taking a plane home straightaway." The man turned his face toward the eye and his frown enlarged on the lens as he came across the room to the window, until his face completely filled the aperture of the recording organ. The sound of his hand batting at the window pane did not transmit, nor did his voice saying, "Absolutely not, I've already made the arrangements. Hold on a bit."

Simon opened the window with one hand and shooed the big black bird off the ledge. This time it had been close enough for him to see the one blind eye for certain. "Nothing, it was nothing," he said, closing the window, but a shiver slivered down his spine and he shook himself like a dog after its bath. "What? Oh, nothing as exciting as I'd hoped for, the urban abos seem to be trying to be second Andy Warhols. Tiresome. Nonetheless, I shipped some things to the London gallery by air from Australia. They'll take a few days to get there, so you might call Bony Foxworth and tell him not to get his knickers in a twist if they don't show up straight off." He walked back to the bedside table, trailing the telephone cord behind him. "No, all I've had time to pick up is some *shunga*, those pillow book sex pictures. Hard to get, mostly in private collections now, but I've an engagement tonight to trade some acquisitions with a gallery here. Think they'd better go to the Paris gallery. Too explicit for London. Yes, I'll be taking the morning plane. I love you."

After hanging up, Simon went back to the window and looked up through the smoggy haze hanging over the city, looking for the bird. It must be close by. It hadn't left him for long since he'd first noticed it in Sidney, a big bastard that stood out like an

180

oversized undertaker amongst the smaller birds. It was the white membrane over one eye that made him sure the same one had followed him over here to Tokyo. Yes, there it was, preening itself on the tiles of the opposite roof, the sun striking blue highlights from its feathers. It turned its seeing eye toward him and he stepped back, a bit unnerved. Time for a drink, by God, and the gallery rep would be waiting for him by the lift.

Inside the bar of the Okura, where there were no windows, he could forget about the raven and quit racking his brains to figure out why a witless bird was following him all over the map. Konrad Lorenz notwithstanding, he didn't think the bird had imprinted on him and thought he was its mother. The damned thing was full grown when he'd first seen it and was uncommonly large for a raven. However, other theories he had none. Oh, leave off, he told himself severely as he went to the cupboard to get out his jacket, or you'll go crackers! There was simply no good reason for the bird's shadowing him. Maybe it was crazy. In the event, there was no point in frazzling endlessly about it.

Miss Suzuki was waiting for him in the alcove near the bank of elevators, where seductively deep black and beige leather chairs invited guests to contemplate the tortured beauty of a full-sized pine bent to one side as if leaning before a stiff sea breeze. Sitting straightbacked with her miniature hands folded primly in her lap, Miss Suzuki looked freshly manufactured by a firm that permitted no flaws in its products. Not a hair escaped from the licorice pillow of hair on the nape of her neck, not a crease marred the drape of her tailored gray suit. The mandarin collar of her white blouse fit around her neck to such a nicety that it might have been glued to her skin. Simon could not imagine that she had ever been dirty in her life. That she had sweat glands was unthinkable.

At yesterday's meeting with museum curators and reporters, however, he'd discovered that she had one minor defect: unlike most educated Japanese, she hadn't completely conquered the letter L. Once in a while, she pronounced it as an R, and he'd had one brief moment of delighted fantasy when she said her brother was a pirate. Visions of her brother climbing aboard a junk with a snickersnee between his teeth vanished when she added that he flew the Tokyo-San Francisco run for Japanese Air Lines.

After bowing politely to each other, they repaired to the dark hotel bar to discuss business before dinner. The tables in there were made for people much shorter than Simon, who couldn't put his elbow on the tabletop without bending over double. He ordered two Scotch and waters and set about plotting how to arrange himself comfortably so he could dicker over exchanging acquisitions for a two-month term of display without being distracted by his body. The table was too low for him to cross his legs beneath it. Finally he hit upon a kind of pretzel twist with one arm over the abbreviated chair back and his legs wound around each other. The position was minimally satisfactory, and he had to hook one toe under the chair rung to lock himself in place, but it would have to do. Japanese bars seemed to be designed for pygmies.

Miss Suzuki drank down her Scotch and water like soda pop, pulled a tiny pad of paper and a tiny pencil from her bag, and prepared to bargain. "We agreed on three Harunobus for your Dufy watercolor," she said, reaching for the refill that Simon had ordered while he was still working on his first drink. "Those are men with women. Do you prefer prints showing men with women, men with men, women with women, group orgies, or masturbation?"

Simon cleared his throat, feeling awkward. For centuries the Japanese had given young virgins books picturing sexual acts on their wedding nights as training in being satisfactory bedmates, so they had a different attitude toward pornography than Westerners, but still! Miss Suzuki looked too puritanical to be talking about this sort of thing so matter-of-factly.

"I have an interesting one we just bought from a private correction," she said. "The man has a woman on top of him and is doing it to two others with his toes. Are you interested in that type thing?"

"Not personally," Simon said, trying to be humorous. But Miss Suzuki looked disappointed. "No, what I mean is—er—it depends on the artistic merit of the print."

"Oh, is very nice. Very pretty."

The Scotch was having a rapid effect on Miss Suzuki, who—like many of her race, was an instant drunk. Her cheeks, which had been cherry-blossom pink, were beginning to take on the color of the fruit itself and, as Simon watched, a wisp of hair detached itself from her bun and stuck out rakishly at the side of her head. Her conversation began to wander from the subject of exchanging art works.

After another drink, she admitted dreamily that she'd fallen in love with his pictures in the tabloids when she'd been an art student in Paris and still had something of a crush on him. She blushed furiously and quickly changed to talking about the problem of her grandfather's insurance.

"It was necessary, you see," she said in her prissy-little-miss soprano, "to have the body to correct the insurance. Yuki-chan saw him go into his room, but he never came out again. He didn't reave by another door, because there *was* no other door. Awr we ever found of him was his srippers and a charred spot on the tatami." She sniffled. "Poor Grandfather! It was spontaneous combustion! Poof!" Her lower lip pouted out and tears slid down her perfect cheeks. She pounded her tiny fist on the tabletop, making her glass jump up and down, and exclaimed aggrievedly, "Poof! Poof! Poof!"

She got out a cigarette and Simon leaned across for the gold-sealed box of hotel matches, forgetting his precarious position. His chair teetered and toppled forward, slamming his chest down on the table, and skidded backward, dragging him with it as he grabbed the sides of the tabletop and tried desperately to unlock his legs from the chair rung. The ashtray and drinks crashed to the floor, Miss Suzuki sprang to her feet with a canary shriek, and the bartender charged up to Simon's rescue as he sprawled face down, his legs still entangled in the chair rung. He felt the table turn in his hands and land on his head with a heavy *thunk*.

The bartender righted the table and gently unlaced

him from the chair before helping him to his feet. Simon stared stoically at the ceiling as the man brushed ashes from his suit and delicately extracted a cigarette butt from under the knot of his tie. It was, Simon decided, high time to vacate the Okura bar and take Miss Suzuki to dinner at that country-style restaurant he remembered from previous visits to the city. Maybe some food under her belt would sober her up—provided she could walk to the taxi. He had no intention of heaving her over his shoulder like a sack of grain and carrying her out to the street.

It had been broad daylight when they went into the bar, but the brief Tokyo twilight had passed and now garish neon signs squiggled with calligraphic symbols flashed on and off in the night.

The door of the taxi wouldn't open. "He opens from inside," Miss Suzuki reminded Simon, swaying perilously on her minute high heels. He helped her into the cab when the driver worked the mechanism controlling the door and she sat down next to the door as if she were never going to move again, so he had to clamber over her legs to the other side.

When he paid the fare, remembering that cab drivers weren't tipped unless the hour was unusually late, Miss Suzuki stood teetering at his side. Just before she keeled over into the gutter, he caught her and boosted her up a flight of fishy-smelling stairs to the second story, where the din from the *inaka-ya* trumpeted through the hallway.

The restaurant looked just as he'd remembered it. A chef in a navy blue *happi* coat and headband sat on a dais, stir-frying with theatrical gusto, dipping up ingredients from baskets of leeks, eggplant, other vegetables, and pink and white strips of fish. Waiters shouted orders at him from amongst the customers seated at the surrounding U-shaped counter. It made one's ears ring, particularly with a group of Aussies yelling Waltzing Matilda while they beat out the rhythm on the counter with cans of Suntori beer.

Simon hoisted Miss Suzuki onto a stool and sat down on one beside her. He ordered sake for himself, which came in a square bamboo box, and tea for his companion, who was beyond knowing what she was drinking. Pointing to various baskets to indicate what he wanted, he conveyed his choice of the menu to a waiter, who screamed the order at the chef. Simon winced. The chef's face split like a melon in a dentured smile, and he waved merrily at Simon. The man must be stone-deaf if he'd worked in this place very long, Simon thought.

By this time, Miss Suzuki had lost all of her L's and most of her inhibitions. Her hand kept straying into his lap as they waited for their order. Patiently, Simon kept putting it back in her own. Eventually, the tea and food straightened Miss Suzuki up as if she'd been a wilting daisy put into fresh water. Simon got the list of exchanges from her and, putting on his reading glasses, made a copy of his own in a pocket notebook before going back to dextrously manipulating his chopsticks.

"What do you do when you're not on correcting trips?" Miss Suzuki asked, tucking the errant wisp of hair back into her bun. That her shirt-tail was out escaped her attention.

"Live in France on a farm. Ride. Entertain once in a while. Nothing much. What do you do?"

186

Miss Suzuki smiled shyly. "I pray around. Do you pray around?"

"Great Scott, no. I'm not religious," Simon answered before realizing that she didn't mean making pilgrimages to Shinto and Buddhist shrines. My word, he thought, this is going to be a sticky wicket indeed when I take her home! He excused himself to go to the bathroom, intending to figure his way out of this one while he was in there.

The men's room, which also happened to be the women's room, was an old-style Japanese one with a slot on the floor instead of a w.c. Before stepping in, Simon rolled up the bottoms of his trousers, as he had learned to do before Western-style toilets became popular in the country. The floor bore shocking evidence of the customers' inability to hit a target. The light was dim and, though he tried to pick his way across the floor carefully, he miscalculated, skidded, and grabbed for the wall.

Next day, Simon was in traction with a wrenched back. Slightly hung over, worried sick about Kei, and furious with himself for his accident-proneness, he moved his chin cautiously in the sling holding it taut. Looking out of the corner of his eye at the hospital window, he saw a raven with one white eye push up and away from the sill outside. Slowly it winged away through the rain until it was out of his range of vision.

"Three weeks? You have to be in the hospital three whole weeks?" Kei's voice rose. Getting hold of herself, she said, "No, of course it's all right. The main thing is for you to get well. Everything's fine here, perfectly normal."

The bottom of the bedroom curtains were billowing out nervously, twitching. A small snout peeped out from under the material. Then a striped head darted out and back again. Only a chipmunk or some kind of ground squirrel. The twins were leaving the doors open behind them again.

"Are they taking good care of you? Are you in pain?" She drew her legs up and tucked her feet under her, in case the animal decided to make a tour of the room.

He was as comfortable as could be expected, Simon reported, except for a dozen itchy places that had cropped out as soon as he was immobilized. The doctors made regular rounds, but there were fewer nurses than in a western-style hospital, so he had to grit his teeth and do the multiplication tables in his head to take his mind off the itchies. The other patients' families, who scuffed in daily wearing cloth slippers provided by the hospital, brought their relatives gifts and food and supplied nurses' services to them but he felt shy about asking total strangers to get at that place right behind his knee that was driving him mad. Fortunately, he said, the representative from the gallery he was dealing with had taken him under her wing and was looking after him. She'd promised to bring him a long-handled bamboo backscratcher, and he was looking forward to that as pantingly as a wino anticipates his next bottle of muscatel.

There was nothing Kei could do for him, he said, that would justify her leaving the healing peace and quiet of the château to come visit him. The long and exhausting trip, plus the adaptation to a culture that had changed drastically since her childhood here, wouldn't contribute to her mental health.

Kei agreed with him gratefully. Much as she missed him, there were several reasons why she didn't want to confront Simon face to face right now. If her hold on reality was so shaky that she could imagine that episode in the folly when Garnett was transformed into a monster and the time Gino blew the head off the squirrel, she shouldn't be allowed out alone. Moreover, in her present state there was no predicting what she might blurt out to Simon. She needed time to straighten out her head.

She hung up and sat a few minutes longer with her feet up, watching the antics of the ground squirrel, which had gotten into the waste basket and was rattling around in there like crazy. Finally, she got the big book of Pissaro prints from the table in the window and capped the waste basket with it. Holding the basket out from her with one hand firmly on the top, she took it downstairs and tipped the animal free onto the wet gravel on the back bridge. It scampered down the steps and into the rain in a twinkling.

Kei set the basket and book down by the door, whose imperfect seal admitted a hiss of moist, penetrating cold air, and gazed through the veil of rain at the forest beyond the meadow. It looked as melancholy as she felt. The red and yellow leaves that had brightened the woods had had their season and lay in a discolored, slimy carpet beneath the trees. Only the sycamores and oaks retained their brown leaves, and the bare branches of the stripped

189

trees reached black fingers up toward an aluminum-colored sky that shaded into a sullen gray toward the northeast, where thunderheads were building up. The porch of the folly was covered with a moving mass of ravens taking refuge from the rain under its projecting roof. They fluttered up as Garnett and the twins came out, then resumed their places as the trio hurried down the path toward the château with heads hidden under a black umbrella.

Stifling an impulse to retreat before them, Kei told herself that there was nothing abnormal about Garnett or Gino. It had been the working of her own feverish imagination that had turned them into monsters the other day. If there was anything to fear, it was the machinations of her own sickish mind, not her own grandchild and her lover.

She opened the door for them, and the twins each gave her a hug and kiss before dashing into the kitchen to see what Marthe had prepared for dinner. Garnett shook out the umbrella and set it to dry on the foyer tiles.

"Anybody coming over tonight?" he asked, wiping moisture from an arm that had been unshielded by the umbrella.

"No, Eagles's staying in Paris with a school friend tonight," she said, "and I doubt that Father Barteau will be coming here any more." She gave Garnett a look freighted with resentment. She knew perfectly well that Missy had lied about having been called back to London by her agent when she'd called after fleeing the château. Thank heaven, Missy didn't know where to reach Simon, or that would have been another thing to worry about in addition to flipping out the other day. She knew Missy and Garnett had gotten it on together. He hadn't left a body unturned. But now he'd found someone new in the village or was spending all his time with Father Barteau, because he hadn't come near her lately.

"Now, don't get petty about Jacques," Garnett said in reply to her look. "I never said I was the exclusive type, did I? Neither are you, sweetheart, not if you fool around with me while you're still married to Simon."

He had her there. She felt like kicking him for making the comparison.

Putting his arm around her shoulders, Garnett guided her into the salon and poured her a Dubonnet at the bar before emptying the remains of Simon's favorite armagnac into his glass. "Any morning sickness yet?" he asked.

Kei felt as if a land mine had exploded at her feet. She'd been positive it had been an hallucination, the occurrence in the folly! She stood there thunderstruck, her glass halfway to her lips, as Garnett walked over to the cold fireplace where logs were pyramided, ready to be lit.

"Cold in here." Garnett commented, and waved his hand at the logs, Instantly, with a whooshing sound, the wood blazed up. Kei's legs nearly gave way, and she leaned back against the bar for support as Garnett crouched by the fire. "Well?" he said and looked up at her. When she didn't answer, he smiled at her ashen face and said, "It'll happen any day now. And this time you won't lose it, don't worry. I'll see to that."

Between his teeth, he began whistling an old

lullaby as Kei tried to get hold of herself. Then, as she walked slowly and unsteadily toward one of the brown leather chairs where she could collapse and try to reason things out, he turned to look at her and sang the words softly:

Baby's boat's the silver moon
Floating in the sky,
Sailing on a sea of blue
While the clouds go by.

Sail, baby, sail
Out upon that sea.
Only don't forget to sail
Back again to me.

Her mother had tucked her into bed with that lullaby years ago, singing slightly different words in her thin soprano. Kei remembered drifting off into happy sleep with that tune in her ears, feeling secure and beloved. Now Garnett's deeper masculine voice was giving the melody a sarcastic turn as his eyes bored into her, and the words took on a new and sinister cast.

He'd asked her about morning sickness, so their conversation in the folly hadn't been a figment of her imagination. If that had been true, had the rest of the nightmare taken place as well? Had he really turned into that shaggy beastlike creature with the goat's eyes? She could swear he'd made the logs burst into flame just now merely by waving a hand at them, but she mistrusted her eyes. He could have hypnotized her into seeing flames where there were none, just as he could have tricked her into believing the Devil had appeared before her that day.

She didn't believe in the Devil. He was only a theological fiction, a fantasy—nothing that actually inhabited solid flesh and blood. Garnett couldn't fool her with an optical illusion. He *didn't* turn into a beast and he hadn't really made fire spring up around cold logs, either!

She fell to her knees and crawled to the fireplace. The flames had to be illusory, something that Garnett was making her see, just as he'd made her see the Devil incarnate. To prove to herself that the fire wasn't real, she thrust her hand into it and drew it back with a cry. The pain was no hallucination! Gasping, she doubled over, hugging the singed hand to her waist, and covered it lightly, protectively, with the uninjured one.

Garnett sat down on his heels beside her and looked at her curiously. Then she could see realization of why she'd stuck her hand into the fire dawn in his eyes. He chuckled.

The momentary pain in her fingers would pass. She was tormented far more by her dilemma, wondering which was worse—thinking she'd gone crazy the other day or knowing that Garnett was what he claimed to be. It turned her whole conception of reality topsy turvy to believe that he was a creature of the underworld, but if it was a fact, she had to come to terms with it. Characteristically, in the midst of a crisis a cool clarity filled her mind, enabling her to think more efficiently than ordinarily. Perhaps it was a gift granted to women, who had to protect their young. Whatever caused it, she was grateful for it now. Almost with detachment, she asked herself what kind of semi-human monstrosity could be growing inside her if he *had* impregnated her. And if she gave birth to it, what did he intend to do with it?

"How . . ." Her voice failed her and she had to lick her lips to moisten them before she could ask him how he was going to use the baby.

"To bring Sélène back to life. I told you that." He helped her up into an easy chair, where she sat holding her seared hand by its wrist, trying to stop the pain by cutting off her circulation. "Leave the details to me. I know what I'm doing."

"You can't bring the dead back to life!"

"Oh, can't I? I've already started the preliminary work." A look of intolerable smugness came into his face. "I'm probably the only Master with the skill and knowledge to do it," he said. His expression reminded Kei of Jeremy Kirbottle's when he'd announced that he'd pulled off a merger of Landsend House with Neafie Publishers, Ltd. The self-satisfaction on Garnett's face was exactly the same as Jeremy's had been. Regardless of the vast difference between the two men, their male egos must operate nearly identically, Kei thought, and she'd had a lifetime of grappling with the male ego.

Grasping the thought like a weapon, Kei said, "If you can do that, you must be the most powerful man in the whole world," and watched for his reaction.

He clasped his hands in the small of his back and studied the floor as if considering the notion for the first time. A pleased smile played about his lips, and the resemblance of his expression to Jeremy's struck

Kei again. After a moment he raised his head and said, "You're a clever woman, Kei, and you're probably right. With Sélène alive at my side, I could rule the earth, just as long as I remembered to keep my energy level at its maximum." Narrowing his eyes, he stared across the room, apparently envisioning the infinite opportunities open to him.

So there was a chink in his armor! Kei hesitated, afraid of probing too obviously and incurring his wrath. Experience had taught her that most men could absorb endless amounts of flattery without suspecting the sincerity of the flatterer. Congratulate a curmudgeon on his sunny nature, and he'd believe himself a benevolent philanthropist. Assure a fat man that his physique was admirable, and he'd forget what his mirror told him and see himself as an Adonis. But Garnett was an expert in manipulating people. Would he detect her maneuvering, or was he as susceptible to appeals to his vanity as 99% of the men she'd known?

"Don't tell me you'd let your energy run down, I can't believe it," Kei said, not sure of what he meant. "You're too intelligent for that."

"Right again!" He laughed self-assuredly, looking at her as if she were a co-conspirator. "All I have to do is to screw every day to keep my powers intact, and I'm not likely to forget that! I can see how your mind's working."

Kei went cold. He'd seen through her ploy!

But he knelt down beside her and took her uninjured hand in his, saying, "You'd *like* knowing that the father of your child was king of the earth, wouldn't you? What a child that would be!"

195

Kei could breathe again. He hadn't understood her game, he hadn't caught her!

He took her chin in his hand and looked at her pityingly. "Unfortunately, my love, you'll never see him grow up. For Sélène to live, the baby has to die. Those are the rules." He stood up. "I'll see that you're rewarded for your service, though, I promise you that." He pulled her to her feet. "Now you'd better run along and put something on that hand. Tell Marthe I'm skipping dinner. Jacques is waiting for me, and my joints are beginning to feel a little rusty. Preparing the way for bringing Sélène back to life takes a hell of a lot out of me every day."

"Do you . . . Do you have to go to Jacques? Can't you stay with me instead?" Even though she knew what Garnett was now, that he'd be making love to someone else rankled. She wanted him badly. He could do no more damage to her than he already had, and he'd left her unsatisfied for days now.

He kissed her on top of her head. "I'll come to you after I've been with him. Wait up for me."

Taking the priest's leftovers was distasteful, but it was better than nothing at all. If only this ceaseless need for Garnett would stop!

She followed him out to the hallway, where he took up the umbrella.

"When's Simon getting out of the hospital?" he asked, turning at the doorway.

Startled, Kei asked, "How did you know he was in the hospital? I never said a word to you about it."

"A little bird told me," Garnett said. Then he opened the door and went out in the rain.

She had no appetite for dinner and went up to bed early without it. Thunder rumbled ominously overhead, cracking loudly miles away as the storm moved toward the château. Kei drew the curtains to shut out the sight of ravens sheltering from the rain on the window ledges.

There were more of them every day, gathering one by one, minute by minute, until she no longer liked to go out back, where they were thickest. Singly, they were large enough to be intimidating. En masse, they quite frightened her, particularly after that one had dived at her as she stood behind the window at the back door.

Perhaps they came here in flocks every year at this time, guided by some mysterious mechanism in their unfathomable brains. She hoped not. They were horrid birds, dirty and noisy, and she couldn't get it out of her head that they were symbols of evil, even though she knew that was a literary convention. In truth, they were meat-eating scavengers, and that was bad enough. They were known to every battlefield. The Norsemen had dragged the bodies of dead warriors to the woods and left them there to have their bones picked clean by ravens. If there hadn't been so many of them, she would have asked Hilaire to go out and shoot the disgusting creatures, but more would have come to replace the few he could have killed.

She went into the bathroom and got ready for bed, rubbing ointment onto her burned hand. The pain was already gone. She had lightning-fast reflexes and had withdrawn her hand from the fire before any real damage had been done. By tomorrow, the redness would have subsided.

Feeling a little queasy, she sprayed Givenchy III eau de cologne on her pillows and, as an afterthought, tucked herb-scented sachets amongst them as an extra protection against unsettling odors. She was not going to allow herself to think that a little upset stomach was the beginning of pregnancy nausea.

The pillows were an inviting nest after she plumped them up. She put an ashtray, cigarettes, a lighter, and a small glass of Drambuie on the bedside table, turned Simon's picture so she could see it from the bed, took up a copy of *The Tale of Genji* that she reread every fall, and got in under the fur spread.

> *"It was the first day of October," she read, "and, like a signal that winter was truly beginning, heavy rain was falling. All the day Genji had kept an eye on the stormy sky. Autumn had brought him almost unbearable bereavement, and now winter was taking away the one he loved so dearly: Now, as a traveler who has vainly tried two paths, I poise bewildered where these sorrowful seasons meet."*

The words of Murasaki's novel hit too close to home and Kei closed the book, putting a leather bookmark in to mark her place.

She put a hand on her stomach, trying to sense if it was inhabited. Garnett didn't know everything, despite his magic, or he would have realized that she'd led him into confessing that he had an Achilles' heel, the need to have sex if he was to remain powerful. He could be wrong about having impregnated her. It was too early to judge if there was life in her womb, but she could hope that it was empty.

She couldn't face the enormity of her situation all at once without feeling like screaming. But in the past, she'd discovered that she could cope with overwhelming problems by nibbling at them around the edges until they were of an unscarey, manageable size. She could start now by figuring out what to do if she *was* pregnant by Garnett. No, that was too big to handle just yet. But she'd found out that his energy was not inexhaustible and that his vanity made him as vulnerable to flattery as a normal man. That was a good beginning. She had something to work with. Now, if she could just break out from the sexual spell he'd cast over her . . .

A crash overhead shook the house and made the windows rattle. Gino was spooked by thunder and lightning, so he'd be dragging Dirk along with him soon to seek the refuge of his grandmother's bed. It disturbed her to think that her own grandson repelled her, now that she'd seen him make a squirrel's head explode. But was she certain about that? If the episode in the folly hadn't been an hallucination (God, how she hoped it had been!), the shock resulting from it could easily have unhinged her mind temporarily. After that, it wouldn't be surprising if the violence of her emotions had translated into imagining that she'd seen Gino's finger go off like a gun, destroying the squirrel. Gino had no Satanic powers. Whatever had happened or not happened out there on the meadow, Gino couldn't have been reponsible for it!

Sure enough, she heard a knock at her door. Dirk stuck his head in. "Gino's scared," he said, not looking too brave himself as another blast of thunder sounded close by the château.

"Don't forget that the little flags on the towers act as lightning rods," Kei said comfortingly and threw back the covers so they could get in beside her. They paused to take off their shoes and then scrambled in on either side of her, Dirk bringing a book with him. "Now that we're all cozy and safe," Kei said, "let's talk a bit first before I read out loud to you." She looked at Dirk's book. *The Wizard of Oz.* Wasn't that the one where Dorothy was carried away by a tornado? Not the best choice on a stormy night like this. On Hallowe'en Garnett had said that watching the screen version had petrified the twins, which was the reason they'd spent Simon's last night in bed with their grandparents. Oh well, the more familiar the story became to them, the less it might frighten them.

"Tell me about what Garnett taught you this afternoon," she said. What might he be teaching them out there in the folly? For all she knew, he might have instructed Gino in the fine art of killing squirrels.

"Bring, brang, brought. That's what we learned," Gino said proudly.

"I think it's 'bring, brought, brought'," Kei corrected him gently. However, when she thought the words over, they didn't sound quite right. How did foreigners ever learn English? Its irregularities could tie one up in knots. How many sounds were there, for example, for the letters "ough"? Bough, though, thought . . . ye gods! . . . and then there was hiccough, if you wanted to spell it that way. But she was getting off track. "It didn't take you all afternoon to learn that, did it?" Or mislearn it.

"We talked about what Monsieur Dubois bought at the market," said Dirk, snuggling up against Kei and looking up at the ceiling as a vicious boom shivered the windows. "Pommes de terre, un gros pain, des petits pois, stuff like that."

When it was quiet again, Gino added. "And Garnett taught us about horses, all kinds of horses. Do you know there's a horse called a zebra that's black with white stripes?"

"Is not!" said Dirk, his mind off the storm now. "It's white with black stripes!"

"You're a dumb dodo!" Gino retorted, sticking out his chin belligerently and glaring at his brother from the other side of Kei.

"I think maybe you're both right," Kei said soothingly. "Does Garnett . . ." How to phrase it? "Does Garnett ever teach you *unusual* things. How to do magic, for instance?"

"Oh, yes!" Gino said excitedly, and Kei's heart missed a beat. "He showed us how you can turn paper different colors by dipping it into chemical slushens! That was fun." He stuck his thumb in his mouth and fiddled his ear with his fingers.

Automatically, Kei pulled his thumb out of his mouth. "That's all?" she asked. "Nothing like . . . like how to make your finger work like a gun?" There, she'd said it! She held her breath.

Gino stuck his thumb back into place, puzzlement

making him frown. Dirk looked at his forefinger and wiggled it. "That would be neat, wouldn't it?" he said.

Gino uncorked his mouth and pointed his finger at Dirk. "You mean like this?" he said. Appalled, Kei grabbed for his hand, but he said, "Bang!" before she could stop him.

Nothing happened!

Kei slumped back against the pillows and started breathing again. She could see the front of her nightgown jump, her heart was thudding so hard.

Unaware that they'd caused their grandmother to come as close to fainting as she ever had, the twins pointed their fingers at each other, pretending to have a shoot-out and shouting "Bang!" and "Pow!" delightedly between giggles. Kei caught their gun hands and said, "Stop it! Stop it right now!"

Subdued, Dirk scrunched down under the covers and said, "I wish Garnett *would* teach us to do magic. I'd like to know how to pull a rabbit out of a hat. When I chase them out back, they always run away. I bet they really feel soft."

Maybe sidled in the open door and, seeing the party on the bed, leaped up and joined them. Dirk took him in his arms and rubbed his nose in the cat's fur. Maybe throbbed happily.

Of *course* it had been the aftereffects of the scene in the folly, Kei told herself. Garnett would never give his secrets away to the twins even if he could. Why would he want to teach little tykes like them to be monsters? It wouldn't make sense, and she was stupid to have fancied that he had. Her temporary insanity could simply have been hysteria, couldn't it? Anyone would have gone a little nuts under the same circumstances. She stroked Gino's hair affectionately, noted that his thumb was back in his mouth, and decided to indulge him. A thumb had no calories and didn't cause cavities.

As the storm moved off to the southwest, rattling its kettledrums, she began to read about Dorothy and Aunt Em and Uncle Henry.

Father Barteau had reached the conclusion that to know Mme. Prévost was to wish her bodily harm.

Every day she managed to devise some new, ingenious way to irritate him. This morning he'd discovered that she'd reduced the wattage of the bathroom light to the lowest limit she could without risking the sanctity of the floor around the toilet bowl. The old camel always produced some semi-religious justification for the little annoyances she instituted or explained their necessity with such tortuous logic that he'd given up trying to argue sense into her. This time, he supposed, she'd say that she was saving the parish money, that thriftiness was next to Godliness. In actual fact, she probably thought that the sight of his own body as he bathed would tempt him to leap out of the tub, red-eyed with lust for her scrawny body, and chase her screeching around the parish house. She should be so fortunate, the old crow!

If he hadn't known the terrain of his face so well, he might have cut his throat this morning while shaving for mass. Perhaps she'd hoped he would. Her constant references to his more thoughtful, more virtuous, and altogether more admirable predecessor were not designed to keep Mme. Prévost's resentment of Father Sarde's replacement a secret.

Now she'd straightened the drawers in his desk, which he had specifically told her not to do, and he couldn't find the notes he'd made for Sunday's sermon. He'd intended to treat the Biblical passage that urged the plucking out of the offending eye. The concept was thorny to grapple with, one he kept coming back to doggedly because he'd never been satisfied with his handling of it. Consulting the writings of church theologians left him mired in a morass of conflicting interpretations, and for years he'd been struggling to find a clear pathway to the intent of that statement. He needed those notes to recall how he'd planned to develop his argument this time! His irritation rose as he went through the desk drawers again.

Why, *why* couldn't That Woman keep her stubby fingers out of his things? And why did God insist on speaking in such obscure language? As one of the twins had said that first day at the Eagletons,' one should come right out and say what one meant. Mon Dieu, if the passage under consideration were intended to be taken literally, the population of the whole Christian world should be one-eyed or totally blind! And one might reasonably extrapolate to the cutting off of any offending part of the body.

He paused in his paper shuffling. In which case, he knew which part of him should go. Choppity-chop, like Saint Abelard, but others had emasculated the saint. It hadn't been his own idea. So much for literal interpretations!

By dinnertime, when Mme. Prévost put a charred entrecôte before him, Father Barteau was as touchy as if he'd spent the day rolling in a patch of nettles. "I see we are celebrating the martyrdom of St. Joan," he said pointedly. The housekeeper opened her mouth to make a retort. The sight of her mossy teeth and the anticipation of hearing the buzz-saw whine her voice assumed whenever he made the slightest complaint tipped the priest over the edge. He stood up, picked up the chop between his thumb and forefinger, and went over to dangle it accusingly before her eyes. "If I wished to mortify the flesh, I would wear a hairshirt," he said. "I do not intend to let you mortify it for me through indigestion!"

Mme. Prévost glared up at him defiantly from under pink-rimmed eyelids fringed with straight pale lashes. Pulling out the front of her dress, Father Barteau dropped the chop down it.

Her departure was swift but noisy, liberally larded with threats of what was going to happen to him when the authorities heard about this outrage. She went shrieking through the downstairs, weeping hysterically as she gathered up her things. Father Barteau stood by the kitchen sink, stunned with surprise at what he'd done.

When she returned to scream one last insult at him, a drop of mucus trailed down from her nose and vibrated on her upper lip. She looked so ugly that his fingers closed unconsciously around the handle of a meat cleaver she'd left on the counter. He was still gripping it tightly when the door slammed and the porcelain figure of the Holy Mother crashed to the floor from its shelf in the hallway, shattering into tinkling bits.

Father Barteau looked down at his hand and was horrified to realize how much anger had been building up in him, anger at the Mme. Prévost, at Missy, at Kei, at himself, at Garnett, and—worst of all—at God! He washed the cleaver under the tap, dried it slowly and carefully with a dish towel, and put it away in the drawer with the kitchen implements. Perhaps he could use that anger, channeling it into resistance against the lure of that two-timer who was expecting things to go on as they had. Tonight he was going to end this whole calamitous business!

As usual, he neither heard nor saw Garnett arrive. He simply appeared suddenly in the bedroom. Why hadn't he left his umbrella downstairs, instead of bringing it up here to drip on the rug? Well, at least there would be no Mme. Prévost to scold about the wet spot tomorrow. As Garnett went out to put the umbrella in the hallway, Father Barteau got up and put a bathrobe on over his nightshirt, calling out, "Don't put down the umbrella. You are not to stay!"

Garnett came back in the room empty-handed, sat down on the bed, and peeled off a black cashmere sweater that looked suspiciously like one Simon had worn.

Father Barteau felt his resolve shake. He'd never seen a man's naked chest that equalled Garnett's in sensual appeal. Licking his lips nervously, he averted his eyes and said, "I said, you are not to stay," more softly this time.

"What?" Garnett said, looking up from unfastening his belt.

"There is to be no more . . . no more of . . . We can't do this any longer."

Garnett looked searchingly into the priest's eyes. Then he bent forward, put his elbows on his knees, and clasped his hands together. He hung his head and slowly wrung his hands as if he were washing them. How very young he looked, with his rumpled hair and smooth golden shoulders!

After a long silence, Garnett sighed and said, his head still down, "You're right, Jacques." He sounded miserably dejected. "I thought one more time, one more perfect time to remember. But you're right, and I'm so glad it was you who said it." He looked up, and his eyes were wet. "I've felt so terrible about we've done. Especially with you being a priest." He sat up straight and ran a hand back through his hair.

Father Barteau was speechless with astonishment. A repentant Garnett was the last thing he'd expected to see tonight, but there he was, the very picture of remorse! The boy, too, had been suffering, the priest thought compassionately, watching a tear slide down the golden cheek. Father Barteau stepped forward and almost reached out a hand to comfort Garnett but, fearing that touching the child's hair or skin might reawaken forbidden desire, he tightened the sash of his robe instead and stood looking down at the boy tenderly.

"Don't blame yourself," Garnett said. "I couldn't bear it if you blamed yourself. I was curious, I didn't know anything about . . . our kind of love. So I'm as much to blame as you are, I didn't have to let you seduce me."

Joggled by the implication that he had been the seducer, when he could have sworn that Garnett had been the one who made the advances, Father Barteau searched his memory frantically. Something strange had happened between them that first day that they'd had tea together at the château, but he'd never been able to recall what it was. He *did* remember, though, that it had been Garnett who had come here to his bedroom, not the other way around. And he was certain that *Garnett* had made love to *him* then, even introducing him to some refinements that he'd never heard of!

Suddenly Father Barteau felt himself being clutched around the knees. Garnett was on the floor at his feet, kneeling before him. What *was* all this?!

"I couldn't help myself," Garnett said brokenly with his face against the priest's crotch. "I was in love with you. I would have done anything you wanted! I *did* do what you wanted!"

Father Barteau's head was swimming. While he tried to rally his thoughts, uncomfortably conscious of Garnett's face pressing against his groin, Garnett went one step too far. "Confess me, Father, for I have sinned," he sobbed.

Realizing he'd been conned again, all of Father Barteau's pent-up anger exploded. He brought his knee up sharply, savagely hitting Garnett in the chest with all his strength. Garnett's teeth clicked together as his head snapped back, and instantly Father Barteau was on top of him with his hands around Garnett's throat.

In the next moment, Father Barteau felt himself flying through the air. He slammed hard against the opposite wall and crumpled to the floor while incomprehensible noises came from Garnett at the other side of the room.

Groggily, the priest sat up and tried to figure out what had happened as he watched Garnett roll around convulsively on the floor. Finally, after shaking his head to clear it, he understood that Garnett had swatted him across the room with one hand as easily as if he'd been a tennis ball and that now the bastard was having a laughing fit!

The past few minutes had been a charade that Garnett had used for the express purpose of mocking and humiliating him! Father Barteau sat and listened to the rumble of thunder in the sky and the sound of Garnett's laughter. He was beyond anger now. Knowing that the man he'd loved so deeply—enough to lose his soul for his sake—had been scorning and sneering at him all along hurt too much. It took all the fight out of him. He felt too drained even to weep for himself.

Eventually, Garnett recovered himself and got up to sit on the bed. Then he took off his shoes and socks. Every few seconds, a jerk shook Garnett's chest. Incredulously, the priest watched him strip down to the buff.

"What . . . what are you *doing?*" Father Barteau asked weakly. Even Garnett wouldn't have the gall to expect lovemaking after that scourging performance!

"Hiccuping," Garnett said, tossing his clothes on the floor. "I laughed so hard I got the hiccups." He pounded his closed fist on his chest and apparently made them stop. Then he looked at the priest and sighed. "Now, Jacques, where's your sense of humor? Take that El Greco look off your face and get out of your clothes." When Father Barteau made no move to comply, Garnett leaped to his feet and shouted, "I said, GET OUT OF YOUR CLOTHES!"

The priest closed his eyes and shook his head. It was unbelievable, simply unbelievable! How could Garnett . . . A sound of ripping cloth made him open his eyes again. Aghast, he saw the seams of his bathrobe opening and the material falling to the floor. Then his nightshirt split across the chest and disintegrated into a substance like cigarette ashes, leaving him stark naked. He looked up at Garnett and saw darkness flowing up from the roots to the ends of his hair as the golden tone went out of his skin. His arms were becoming hairy, and the flesh of his chest was turning a greenish brown, hardening into scaliness. Instinctively, Father Barteau drew himself into a ball with his knees tight against his chest and his arms locked protectively around them.

"Come here, sweetheart," Garnett said in a new, hoarse voice, crooking a long finger at him. "I need to use your sweet Christian body, I'm beginning to run down. See? I'm losing my disguise."

What strange eyes Garnett had! Coldness spread through the priest's body as he huddled, unmoving, against the wall. His ears were buzzing. All the colors seemed to have gone out of everything in the room. He didn't want to look at Garnett. He particularly didn't want to see his groin again, not now. And when he looked at Garnett, the buzzing in his head got louder. Too loud. He wasn't going to look at Garnett any more. No, he'd look at the silver crucifix hanging on the wall behind Garnett's head instead. Then Garnett would think he was still looking at him. But he wouldn't be, he'd be looking at the cross instead. It was pretty. That thing on the wall was pretty. Oh, too bad! Garnett had caught him, and Garnett was angry. The pretty silver thing was melting and sliding down the wall like sparkly sludge. That was nice. That was good. If Garnett wanted the silver thing to melt, that was the way it should be. Whatever Garnett wanted.

Father Barteau uncurled from his fetal position, got up, and walked over to the bed. Then he lay down on his stomach obediently.

Oh my God!! What was he doing here on the bed? What was that metallic dripping that was sliding down the wall? Father Barteau sat up on his elbows, shaking with terror. With his face turned away from the creature standing at the side of the bed, he could think again.

"My, my, you *are* a stubborn case, aren't you?" the hoarse voice said derisively. "Obviously, you've trained yourself for years to discipline your mind. And you've believed everything they taught you. 'Resist the Devil, and he will flee from you,' isn't that what they said?" Garnett gave a chuckle that sounded as if it were coming from the mouth of a frog.

Father Barteau felt the side of the bed go down under the heavy weight of Garnett's body. He felt frozen to the bone. There was no doubt in his mind now as to Garnett's real identity. He should have known it from the start, should have sensed it.

Now he was lost! There was nothing he could do to protect himself. Then he remembered the rosary that he kept under his pillow and cautiously slid his hand under the pillow slip. When he found it, he felt along the beads for the crucifix as Garnett moved into a crouching position over him.

Whipping over onto his back, Father Barteau suddenly thrust the cross into Garnett's face.

Garnett recoiled, caught off balance. "Now you're beginning to get tiresome," he snarled and sat back on his knees, pinning the priest's legs under him. "I'm out of patience with your superstitious shenanigans! Looks like you need a little lesson."

The crucifix glowed red-hot and sizzled down into the flesh of Father Barteau's hand before turning into powdery ash.

Garnett winced at the priest's scream, waited impatiently for it to die away into guttural sobs, then flipped his victim back onto his stomach and proceeded to renew his Satanic power.

Traveling through the darkness in giant, floating strides, Garnett felt reborn, exhilarated. The cold rain was invigorating, and he carried the closed umbrella tucked under his arm so that he could enjoy the fresh wetness on his hair and face. Nevertheless, his spirits were not as high as they could have been. He'd never actually measured how much energy he could dispense without depleting himself, and today he'd come dangerously close to the edge. That meant he'd have to discipline himself more severely, and he hated having to put restraints on himself.

As he saw that some lights were still on in town, he released his bodily form and moved on through the business district in a shapeless cloudy mass that blended into the night. When he reached the château gate, he flowed through the bars and reassembled himself under the canopy that sheltered the front door. Shaking out the umbrella that had obeyed the laws of his transformation along with his clothing and everything he carried on his body, he opened the door with his key and went into the foyer. Kei had left the light on for him.

Another thing, he muttered to himself, wasting resources is damned foolishness! He set the umbrella on the floor to dry and brushed the wet off himself. It would take some time for Jacques to heal, he'd been so rough with him.

He'd let his pool of bodies run dangerously low. With Jacques out of action, he'd have to establish a new liaison or two, and setting up the groundwork took time. Finding a compliant lover was simple, but the logistics required in finding the right setup was bothersome. People tended to have families who couldn't mind their own business, or jobs that kept them occupied at inconvenient hours, or living quarters where he could be observed coming and going. He liked the security of having tried and true numbers like Jacques and Kei and supplementing them with a bash or two at one of Grapes's orgies for the coven. The Satanists gathered there only at night, though, and weren't always in session when he needed a booster.

At four in the morning, Garnett left Kei and went to his own bed.

The rain had stopped, but a strong wind was battering at the windows. As he pulled the covers up to his chin, he heard the cistern empty overhead and the pipes gurgle behind the walls. He felt snug, healthily relaxed, and ready for a good long sleep. He'd been gentle with Kei, whose eagerness was an ego-stroke, but not as spicy as Jacques' frenzied resistance. Rape was fun, but it was self-indulgent and left the victim considerably worse for the wear.

Determined to be less profligate with his powers and to conserve himself more frugally on the morrow, Garnett drifted off into enjoyable dreams that would have made anyone else wake up screaming.

CHAPTER THIRTEEN

Kei woke to a black and white world. An early morning snow had sifted over the last leaves blown from the trees in the night and was still filtering down in a fine powder. It veiled the air and whitened the sky, where a pale sun glowed like a lost moon.

She pushed the window open and stood shivering in her gown, her crossed arms goosefleshing, letting the clean air freshen the room. The animal odor that Garnett left behind him made her queasy. Was she starting to have morning sickness?

Ravens high-stepped through the snow amongst the naked black trees, searched the meadow for food, rooting under the buried leaves. A whinny came from the stable. Barney would be stomping in his stall, excited by the change in the weather and waiting for Simon to take him out for his morning canter. Waiting vainly. Just as she waited vainly for something to happen that would bring deliverance.

Soon it would be Thanksgiving. Thanksgiving for what? Simon wouldn't be home in time for it. Just as well. On the holiday when the family should be sitting around a festive table, everyone smiling and rosy-cheeked like a Norman Rockwell painting, she'd be harboring the germ of a monster child in her belly. Would it be fair like Garnett, or would it be dark like that creature he'd become in the folly? Would it have goat's eyes?

She shut the window and went into the tower bathroom to shower off his reek from her body.

In honor of the snow, Kei put on a V-necked white angora dress that was light as a kitten's breath but nicely warm for the first winter's day. Its fluffiness masked how bony she was getting.

Marthe had prepared eggs Benedict for their late breakfast, but the twins weren't interested. All they wanted was to get out in the white stuff and make a snowman. There wasn't enough of it yet and it was too dry and granular to pack down right, Kei said with the experience of one who had grown up in the Midwest, but they could lie down and make snow angels by sweeping their arms and legs up and down. Terrific! They left their eggs to congeal and ran out to the kitchen to ask Marthe's help in getting on their boots.

Kei was in the middle of the *Times* crossword, doing it in pen, and had finished her first cup of coffee when Garnett wandered in, yawning and scratching an armpit. He'd helped himself to Simon's cream-colored bulky sweater, just as he'd appropriated whatever he liked in the house, but Kei didn't want to bring up the issue and make him turn surly. If she nagged him, he might find another woman in the village who was easier to get along with.

This morning he looked about eighteen, but he

was no juvenile deliquent. How old was he, really? Twenty-six, Eagle had said Garnett told him. Hmph! Whatever Garnett told anyone was automatically open to doubt. Kei took off her reading glasses. No need to emphasize the difference in their ages, whatever it was.

"Lemme see the paper," he said, taking it away from her and bending down to kiss her on the neck. "How's the little mother this morning?" It was a rhetorical question. Garnett sat down and read the paper, consuming eggs behind its screen, without paying any attention to her except to ask for the butter.

Kei drank a second cup of coffee and toyed with the idea of asking Jeanne-Marie how to get an abortion. Knowing how Simon wanted a child, Jeanne-Marie would be surprised and she'd disapprove because of her devout Catholicism, but Kei couldn't afford to worry about Jeanne-Marie's reactions. She chewed thoughtfully on the stems of her reading glasses, wondering if the consent of both parents would be necessary. That wasn't the major stumbling block, though. *That* was sitting right across the table, stuffing down eggs as if a world famine were in the offing.

Garnett gave a loud belch and looked around the paper. "You shouldn't drink so much coffee," he said. "Bad for the baby. And why haven't you finished those eggs? You're eating for two now, you know." He went back to reading the paper, humming the lullaby about baby's boat. Kei had a feeling she was going to learn to hate that song.

In the folly, he'd said that the only reason he was

keeping her alive was that she was going to produce the baby. He didn't pretend any affection for her. He screwed her, but that was only because he needed to discharge his semen regularly. Why didn't he just masturbate, then? Well, apparently that wasn't the way it worked.

If she aborted the baby and he found out about it, would he really murder her? Oh yes, she said to herself, don't have any illusions about that! He had few normal human emotions, as she was coming to find out, and she doubted that forgiveness was one of them. He carried a massive resentment against her and Simon for destroying the grotto and for having had a part in putting down the Satanic cult in the village. *Temporarily,* he'd said. Did that mean there was a new one operating there now? Well, that was the least of her worries.

An appalling thought struck her. If Garnett was only keeping her alive because of the baby, *what about Simon?!*

A rustle of paper cut in on her interior monologue. Garnett was putting down the *Times*. He wiped his mouth with his napkin and said, "I'm going in to the village. Let the kids play in the snow until noon. We'll have lessons after that."

Whose children *were* they? Now he was giving her orders about them! Kei almost said something but realized it wouldn't do any good. He was in charge now, face facts! If she could have reached their mother in Spain, the twins would be in their own home now, out from under his influence, but Chris was traveling around in the Basque country, out of reach of the telephone. Kei didn't even know how to contact her by wire or mail.

He'd been gone only a few minutes when Jeanne-Marie dropped in and asked for a cup of coffee, her nose red with the cold.

"What a morning!" said the lady doctor. "Two normal deliveries, a Caesarean, and a breech presen-' tation! I have been on the feet most of the night." She accepted a cup gratefully from Kei and drank it straight down like a tonic before asking for another. "Oh, and there has been some excitement!" she went on. Before revealing it, she checked the neatness of her white hair and straightened the tie at her neck as if she were about to present a paper before her colleagues. Immured in the clinic most of the time, she seldom had gossip that she could impart without violating professional etiquette, and this was gossip on the grand scale!

She took a dramatic pause to whet Kei's appetite.

"There was no mass this morning!" she said triumphantly.

Kei raised an eyebrow and resumed sipping her coffee, unimpressed.

"Oh, but that is not all!" Jeanne-Marie said, her eyes bright, and reached over to grip Kei's hand. *"Au grande scandale de tout le monde*, Monsieur le Curé seems to have flipped his top! Not only did he fail to appear at mass, but he has barricaded himself! He will allow no one in the parish house. Mme. Prévost, his housekeeper, says he went quite mad last night and attacked her!"

"Attacked her? With what?" Kei asked, unable to imagine that the sad-eyed punster she knew could do harm to anyone.

Jeanne-Marie sat back, looking a little deflated. "With a veal cutlet, I believe." She leaned forward again. "But don't you see? That demonstrates exquisitely his state of madness. Anyone who knows Mme. Prévost well would have used a more substantial weapon." She wiped a moustache of coffee from her mouth and then looked at her watch. "*Tiens!* I must depart for the clinic. How late you breakfast! Or perhaps this is lunch?"

She stood up and gave Kei's hand a polite goodbye shake. "Ah, one thing more I have forgotten. With infinite regret, the police will investigate. It may be that Monsieur le Curé must be removed to the psychiatric clinic if he has become violent."

Father Barteau sat in his study as immobile and as deaf as a stone while one of the local gendarmes rapped politely, then more insistently on the front door.

Sometime in the early morning, the priest had come downstairs with his blood-stained bathrobe flapping open and, after taking care of some business that seemed imperative to him at the time, had searched the study until he found the missing notes. Now he stared sightlessly at the last page. The feverish whirl of his thoughts had slowed and finally stopped altogether, leaving a numb void within his skull.

He started, jarred back to life by the loud banging at the door. Stiffly he got up and went into the hallway. He stared at the boards that were nailed over the glass upper portion on the inside of the front door, wondered briefly who had put them there, looked at the door shake from blows on the outside, and walked into the kitchen.

At the sink, he opened the drawer where the kitchen implements were kept, and took out the meat cleaver.

Just as the front door burst open, the blade of the cleaver descended.

"I simply can't make it, Jeremy," Kei said into the phone. She traced the circles Simon habitually made on the desk blotter when he was talking on the phone, using the jade-handled letter opener he used to do it, and listened patiently to Jeremy complaining in London. "Look, you don't need me at the board meeting, I'm only a figurehead now. Just send me the monthly report to let me know how things went." She listened a minute longer, irritably tapping the blade of the letter opener on the desk edge, and then said, "Yes, I'm glad that Simon will be able to meet the deadline on his memoirs, now that he's laid up, but . . . but . . . Oh, Jeremy, shut up! I'm too worried about other things now to be able to think about the book business. What other things? Well, for one, I think a . . . friend of mine may have gone crazy."

The birds in the aviary began screeching. Marthe stood in the doorway, chest heaving, eyes popping. Kei put the mouthpiece to her chest and listening to the news that Marthe was gasping out.

"Where is he? *Where is he?*" she asked, dropping the receiver on the desk top.

The pink cockatoo cocked its head at the thin

sound coming from the abandoned telephone. "Are you there?" said a faint voice from London. "What's happening?"

But there was no one to answer.

Kei pushed her way through the crowd of people gathered around the door, trying to find a doctor who would let her in the room. Everyone stepped back a pace or two as one came out to face them. He stood looking down at the floor a moment, pursing his lips. Then he shook his head, and a communal sigh, like a musical note, went up.

Kei forced her way into the room just as the nurse was pulling up the sheet over Father Barteau's still face. His arm still dangled at the side of the bed, palm outward. A fiery cross burnt deep into the flesh.

Kei drove through the village, peering through the tears in her eyes and the falling snow, looking everywhere for Garnett, but she couldn't find him anywhere. When she got back home, she paced back and forth in the salon, looking at the ormolu clock on the mantel every few minutes. It was already past noon.

That poor, poor man! Blood everywhere, they'd said.

Now that he was dead, she was ashamed to have been jealous of him. He'd had such a sweet, sad face, and his life must have been so lonely and barren. Garnett's attentions might have been the only happiness he'd ever known. That Garnett! Taking advantage of the vulnerability of a man like Father

Barteau—a priest, at that!—was low even for Garnett!

Poor Father Barteau! Even a nonCatholic like herself knew what suicide meant for a member of the Church. What he must have gone through last night to have chosen such a way to die, to mutilate himself! How despairing he must have been!

At hearing Garnett come in the front door, Kei whirled, ran into the foyer, and flew at him. "*You* did it!" she cried, clawing at his face. "You made him kill himself!"

Garnett caught away her hands and held them easily while she struggled. "Now, now, don't get upset," he said calmly. "It's bad for the baby."

Kei burst into helpless tears and let him lead her back into the salon and deposit her in an easy chair. Humming the lullaby again, he poured her a glass of sherry and made her drink it. Then he got a glass of Burgundy for himself and, leaning back with an elbow on the bar, held the glass up to the light to admire its color.

"I don't know anything about it, only what I heard in the village," he said, revolving the glass slowly. "I always did think the old bird was loony." He took a sip of the wine and said with unquestionable sincerity, "I'm sorry he's dead." For a moment, Kei thought he might actually be having a normal human response to Father Barteau's tragedy. Then he ruined the effect by saying peevishly, "It's damned inconvenient!"

On her way upstairs, Kei met Hilaire coming down with the vacuum cleaner. Now that the work in the fields was over and the extra hands had been dismissed, he was taking over some of Marthe's household tasks to lighten her work load and keep her from aggravating her arthritic knee.

Garnett had frightened Kei out of hiring more servants, but the house and the grounds were really too much for Hilaire and Marthe to handle alone. Unbeknownst to Garnett, she'd upped their wages by a whacking packet as compensation and hoped they could manage until Simon could come back and deal with things.

Hilaire suggested putting poison out for the ravens, but Kei vetoed the idea, wishing he wouldn't carry on about something so trivial on a day like this. She tried to keep her impatience out of her voice. "Mitzi or Maybe might get into it," she said. Cities back in the States had tried everything to get rid of plagues of starlings—poison, artificial owls set on building ledges, recordings of predatory birds' cries played through loud-speakers. The starlings had stayed on. If whole cities couldn't prevail against an infestation of birds, Hilaire couldn't, and she felt too frayed to wrangle the issue.

She went to her room and, despite her prejudice against taking drugs to palliate emotional turbulence, popped a Valium. Her nerves were jumping like crickets.

Had Father Barteau been right? Was suicide the only way to escape from Garnett? She sat down in the leather chair by the bedroom window, lit a cigarette, and watched the snow fall.

She was in at least as bad a predicament as Father Barteau had faced, and he hadn't had one nervous breakdown already, as she had. Or not that she'd heard. Right now she was up against a situation that would have made the most robustly mentally healthy person worry for his sanity.

Here she was, pregnant by a devil who'd just as soon kill her as look at her if it wasn't for the baby. In about nine months, she'd be giving birth to a monstrosity. Garnett had said he'd reward her for producing the child, but his idea of a suitable recompense might be a quick death instead of a slow one. Garnett was loathesome, terrifying, and no one in her right mind would let him touch her. But she couldn't overcome this constant, sickly craving for him.

To top it all off, she was sure to lose Simon. There was no way out of it. If he was incredibly noble and accepted her pregnancy—which was not impossible, knowing Simon—Garnett would kill him sooner or later in vengeance. At six this morning, when Simon's call had wakened her, he was still alive, but that was because he was in Tokyo and out of the range of Garnett's powers. If she couldn't keep Simon away from the château somehow, he was as good as dead.

She brushed the tip of her cigarette on the edge of the ashtray. The Valium must be working. She didn't feel quite so jumpy now.

Poor, dear Father Barteau! If he couldn't hang on, how could she expect to? But he didn't have a family. It would hurt Simon too much if she took the same way out. She couldn't punish the family that way. And how did she know that Father Barteau hadn't found something even worse on the other side?

Either there was an afterlife or there wasn't, it was a fifty-fifty proposition. If suicide was a cosmic no-no, she could find herself on the wrong end of the odds, with a long, long time to regret her decision. There were a lot of people in the world who were convinced that if you didn't work out your life problem this time, your soul kept being reborn on earth until you got it right. How did she know that wasn't true? If it was, killing herself would mean one more damned go-around, and once was enough. And what if she got reborn into worse circumstances? Coming back as a deformed baby or a drooling idiot would be horrible, and there was always the remote possibility that the myth of hellfire and brimstone in the hereafter was a fact after all.

No, it was better to keep going until the last hope had faded. Besides, you never knew what might happen tomorrow. Something might turn up.

Besides, she thought—getting mad now—she wasn't going to give Garnett the satisfaction of driving her to suicide and then have him sniff that losing the baby along with her was "inconvenient"!!

As long as she was carrying the baby, she should be safe enough. Nine months should be long enough to plot a way out of this or at least take Garnett down with her. He was no Einstein, and that was a point in her favor. She must be brighter than he was, or he wouldn't have let her flatter him into giving away the information about how he got his energy. By heaven, she hadn't survived as a female executive in a man's world as long as she had without learning a few tricks! Now she was facing a formidable opponent, one with the powers of darkness on his side, but she wasn't going to go down without putting up a hell of a fight!

"You are just beginning to know how to use the powers of the air," Lady Luna was saying as the twins listened raptly to the figure shrouded in bridal satins and lace. "Use them wisely, only when you are not observed. It may be that, to serve some special purpose, you will wish to let these abilities be known, but be cautious in using them. Defying natural physical laws will deplete your reserves severely. The dark forces will aid you. Nevertheless, each time you must draw forth magic power from within you, and that must be renewed daily. Do you understand?"

The twins nodded in unison.

"At the present time," the falsetto voice went on, "because of your youth, you must draw on Garnett's strength. Therefore, you will be subject to the Master's commands until you have been prepared to use your own energies. Certain alterations must be made in your bodies before this is possible. There must be ceremonies and sacrifices while the physical adaptations are being made."

Gino wriggled uncomfortably and stuck his thumb in his mouth.

"Do not be afraid, children," Lady Luna said soothingly. "At the time you will be given potions to curb the pain, and the Master will remove your consciousness during the operation. You will not be aware of what is taking place. You need never be afraid as long as you follow the rules."

"We'll follow the rules," Dirk said quickly, remembering the hideous consequences Lady Luna had outlined if they were broken.

"Tonight, under the cover of darkness, you will practice what you have learned today," the lady said.

The panel slid shut. The lesson was over.

The children picked up their cushions, dashed off the stage, and piled them at Gunther's feet.

"Hot dog, this is going to be fun!" said Gino and gave a few bounces of anticipation. Dirk grabbed his hands, and they swung about in a circle, giggling.

"Time to pick up," Gunther growled, breaking up the celebration.

"Gunther is an old poop!" Dirk said, beginning to erase runes and symbols from the chalkboard.

"I heard that!" the panda rumbled, and Dirk twitched guiltily.

Garnett closed the curtains on the stage. "You'd better apologize to Gunther," he said. "You know he doesn't like impolite boys."

Dirk gave Garnett a rebellious look but bowed at the stuffed animal and said grudgingly, "I'm sorry, Gunther."

When the room was straight, Garnett gave it a final once-over and, satisfied that any outsider could see it without getting a clue to the nature of what went on in the folly, said, "Good job! Now see what Gunther's brought you."

Recently, because he'd overdone the panda's threatening manner to the point where the children insisted that the bedroom closet be inspected every night to be sure Gunther wasn't lurking there, Garnett had put a red knapsack on the bear's back for storing small gifts. Now the twins approached the panda timidly, edged around to his back, and reached into the knapsack for their rewards.

"Pâte de guimauve!" Gino said, rubbing his tummy and sitting on a carved carousel horse to enjoy a long lavender strip of tough marshmallow. The lady at the bakery said the candy was supposed to be used for babies' teething woes, but Dirk and Gino doted on it. Probably because it came in pretty pastel colors, Garnett thought, because it tasted like something that had been left on the shelf too long.

The boys were putting on their boots when a knock came at the door. Before going to answer it, Garnett locked the day's lessons in their minds.

"What do you want?" he said curtly at seeing Eagle standing on the porch, wiping his nose with a despicably dirty handkerchief.

Eagle looked at him hostilely. "Thought I'd come out and have a look around," he said, putting the handkerchief in a back pocket and giving a loud snuffle. "I didn't know you were here."

Ever the opportunist, Garnett put on his most winning smile. "Come on in," he said, holding the door open for him. "I've been wanting to talk to you."

"Oh, yeah?" Eagle said suspiciously but stepped over the threshhold. He looked around and said, "Really weird!" approvingly.

"Just wait until I get the kids outdoors, will you?" Garnett gave the twins a hand with their boots while Eagle seated himself warily on the edge of a window seat cushion on top of one of the bookcases. "What are you doing home so early?"

"I think I've got the flu, I ache all over. Even the roots of my hair hurt."

"Just don't give it to the twins," Garnett said. "Push!" Gino obliged and then stood up to stamp his foot into his boot.

When they were dressed for outdoors, Garnett shooed them through the door and they shot away to play in the snow before it melted.

To top off a particularly dismal day at school and getting the flu, Eagle had lost his house key and had to slog over to the château to get the spare from Aunt Kei. He felt dizzy and teetery and knew he had a high fever, but everyone back at the house was too preoccupied to be sorry for him. He gave a groan, put a hand on his hot forehead; and let himself down on the window seat until he was stretched out full length. His mother was due back in a few days. With a little cooperation, the flu might hang on long enough for her to bring him chicken soup and fuss over him.

"I wanted to talk to you about what you said the other day," Garnett said and squatted down beside him. "You sort of jolted me. It's funny how you can start doing things you don't feel comfortable about and pretty soon they don't feel uncomfortable any more and then you go one step further. You know what I mean?"

Eagle opened one eye and, pulling in his chin, looked across at Garnett. "The snowball effect, huh?" He closed his eye again.

"Yes, and until that day I didn't realize I'd got in so deep. I'm glad you shook me out of it."

"Oh, can it," Eagle said wearily. "Don't tell me you're going to reform, I can't stand it."

"I thought I'd try," Garnett said with a carefully

230

calculated amount of meekness.

After a period of silence in which Garnett thought he'd gone to sleep, Eagle said, "I suppose anything's possible."

"Will you keep an eye on me and give me a nudge if I go off the track again?"

Eagle sat up on an elbow and looked at him. "You really mean that?"

Garnett held up a hand as if he were taking an oath on the stand. "As God is my witness!" he said.

"Okay, we might as well turn over a new leaf," said Eagle and lay down again. With his eyes closed, he stuck out his hand, and Garnett gave it a shake of agreement.

The flush on Eagle's cheeks was becoming. Adolescent boys had never appealed to Garnett, so he hadn't considered Eagle before. The McKenzie house, a converted farm on the edge of the village, was isolated enough, though, so he could visit it freely without being seen, and Eagle's parents were away. Eagle came over to dinner several nights a week, and what could be more natural than that they hung out together? Garnett's natural laziness made him put aside his aversion to young boys. An immediate addition to his stable suited him marvelously well.

"If you want to take a nap, you'd better take off that jacket and your shoes. You're getting the window seat wet," he said.

Grunting, Eagle wriggled out of his heavy jacket without getting up, rolled it out from under him, and dropped it on the floor while Garnett unlaced his soaked suede shoes and removed them. The socks underneath were unsavory. Garnett held his breath as he pulled them off.

"What're you doing that for?" Eagle asked foggily. He raised his head at feeling his feet being massaged. "Cut it out, Gar, I'm ticklish!"

Undaunted that the sensuous approach that appealed to Kei only annoyed Eagle, Garnett got up off his knees and went behind the curtains to the costume box. "You'd better get out of those jeans, too. They're all wet around the bottoms," he said, coming back with a blue velvet Shakespearean robe trimmed in fake ermine. "Might as well take everything off while you're at it. This is heavy and will keep you warm." He tossed the robe onto Eagle's stomach.

Well, this was more like it! Somebody was finally paying attention to how rotten he felt! Feeling more in tune with Garnett because of his sympathy, Eagle stood up and disrobed, leaving on only his briefs. As he put on the robe and cinched the blue silk cord around his waist before lying down, he said, "I could use a couple of winks."

Garnett was pleased to see that, instead of having a milkwhite muscleless body, Eagle was almost fully developed and had a mat of fine fur already on his chest. He fixed his stare on Eagle's closed eyes and said in his magical voice, "Look at me, Eagle."

"Oh, buzz off, I was almost under," Eagle said sleepily, not complying.

"Look at me, Eagle," Garnett repeated.

Eagle opened his eyes. Garnett was gazing at him in a very queer fashion, and the pupils of his eyes were luminous. That was strange. He was also stripping down to his skin. That was stranger still. Eagle sat up. "What the hell do you think you're doing?" he said nervously.

"Just look into my eyes," Garnett said, kicking off his boots and standing naked before him.

"I *am* looking at you, Goddammit!" Eagle snatched up his jeans from the floor and began backing away along the window seat, trying to get a leg in his pants. "Holy shit, what's with your *eyes?!*" He fumbled at his fly and finally zipped it up, thoroughly alarmed by the glow coming from Garnett's pupils. "Stay away from me, you creep!"

Garnett sighed and turned off his power, seeing it was having no effect on Eagle. The kid must have a very high fever that was interfering with the electrical discharges in his brain.

"Sorry. How was I to know you weren't bisexual? Most people are." Garnett began putting his clothes back on as Eagle reassembled himself with astonishing rapidity and started for the door with his shoelaces dragging.

Garnett beat him to it and stood in front of the door with his arm stretched out to bar the way. "I'm not going to do anything to you, you idiot!" he said crossly, buttoning his shirt up with the other hand. "Don't get so excited. Hasn't this ever happened to you before?" He pulled on Simon's bulky sweater while Eagle spluttered. "My God, quit acting like a kid!"

That caught Eagle in a sensitive spot. He stood watching Garnett comb his hair, wondering how other guys acted in this situation. Almost everybody he knew had had a brush with this sort of thing—while hitchhiking, watching X-rated films sitting next to some guy with a newspaper on his lap, using restrooms in train stations. They just laughed about it. He'd laughed, too, not wanting to appear inexperienced. Well, now Garnett had made a pass at him, but he hadn't laid a finger on him. And so what if he swung both ways? Eagle liked and respected a couple of gays on the soccer team. They were as macho as anyone on the team and minded their own business. No reason to think Garnett would try to pull anything again.

But—ho! ho!—aren't we forgetting a little item, Eagle said to himself. Garnett *did* take the twins to that free-for-all at Mr. Grapes's, and saying he was going to mend his ways wouldn't undo the harm he'd done them. They might be scarred for life, doomed to spending years on a psychiatrist's couch. That couldn't be passed off lightly. They spent all day with Garnett, teaching them who knows what, and he didn't trust Garnett as far as he could heave him. Besides that . . . Eagle cleared his throat. "Uh, what's that crazy stuff with your eyes, that spooky glow?" he asked.

Garnett spent a moment being unnecessarily fussy about the set of his collar. "A blood condition that causes light refraction. Hereditary." He flicked a nonexistent bit of lint from his sweater. "I forgot to take my pills this morning."

"Jeeze, you aren't gonna go blind or anything, are you?"

"Not right away. The condition's terminal, though." Garnett turned aside to hide a smirk, then faced Eagle again with a gallant tilt of the chin he'd

234

picked up from an old Joan Crawford movie.

"Gee, I'm sorry I asked!"

"It's all right, let's not talk about it," Garnett said bravely. "I'd rather people didn't know." He gave Eagle a quick squeeze about the shoulders with one arm. Eagle went rigid. "No hard feelings about this afternoon?"

Instead of committing himself, Eagle took out his handkerchief and gave his nose a good blow.

At dinner that night, he kept away from Garnett as much as he could without looking unfriendly. He refused to let Aunt Kei and Jeanne-Marie talk him into staying at the château until his fever went down, on the grounds that he had a theme due Monday and all his reference books were at home. He didn't want to stay if there was the remotest chance of waking up and finding Garnett getting into bed with him.

The lady doctor drove him back to his house in Fay, which gave him an opportunity to question her about the unearthly glow that Garnett's eyes emitted. Knowing her propensity for gossip, he pretended that a friend had reported observing the phenomenon.

"Your friend said this happened in broad daylight, not in a dark room where the light struck the back of the eye suddenly?" She braked in front of the converted farmhouse.

"Mmhmm. Could a condition like that be hereditary?"

"Rubbish! Neither hereditary nor possible. Your friend is not a serious person. I would advise you to drop him immediately. He abuses the truth."

So that was that, Eagle thought, watching her drive off. Something very strange indeed was going on. Whatever it was, he had a feeling that the twins were in danger while they were with Garnett, and he'd better take fast action.

He hurried up the walk to the dark house.

By the time Garnett left her, Kei was too exhausted to sleep. Feeling cross and out of sorts, she got out of bed and started the shower so she could wash off his malodorous residue. Lately women's magazines were trumpeting the glories of multiple orgasms as if they were an earth-shaking new invention, but they omitted mentioning how drained one was after the fifteenth or twentieth. She couldn't imagine having the stamina to hang on longer than that, although some women reported having as many as a hundred per night. They must have steel parts, Kei thought, stepping into the hot shower. She, for one, was getting tired of having a sore crotch and being covered with nasty blue love blotches.

It seemed a million years ago since she'd made love with Simon, who didn't treat sex as an endurance contest or a freak show. Tears coursed down her cheeks along with the shower spray as she remembered how gently he always brought her down afterward, kissing and caressing and murmuring sweet words to her until she was quiet and ready to fall into a grateful sleep in the arms of her most beloved friend. Garnett simply left her when he'd had enough. Not even a word of parting, nothing. Made her feel like a toilet he'd just used. He was masterly at the introductory part, but after his first orgasm, he reverted to a jiggling rhythm like a dog mounting a bitch, and it was impossible to keep in synch with him. *People* didn't make love like that, only animals did. Oh, why couldn't she break out of this compulsion, with its aftermath of disgust and self-loathing?

She turned off the shower and toweled down. There was a dull ache in her lower back and a heavy feeling in her lower stomach. Perhaps she'd caught Eagle's flu. She paused in drying herself as cold flashed over her body. Those sensations were too familiar not to be recognized. She'd had them every month since she was thirteen.

The twins sat up in their beds in yellow Dr. Dentons, bright-eyed with excitement as Garnett finished going over their instructions again.

"You won't be cold," he said. "My strength flowing through you will keep you warm, whatever the temperature outside. It's dark, so you won't be seen. Now, this is just a trial run, over to the folly and back. You can do it twice if you like, but no going off on your own somewhere else. Got that?"

The twins nodded.

"Wow!" Dirk breathed.

She had approximately three days to live. It took about that long to get her period after those first symptoms appeared.

Hair still damp, knees trembling, Kei lowered herself into the chair by the window. The window rattled, shaken by the wind outside, and she drew her kimono close about her neck, beads of panicky sweat prickling along her upper lip. She was clean inside. No ugly growth had been planted after all. But her relief was swallowed up by fear of what Garnett had in store for her if he found out. She sat several minutes longer listening to the wind sweeping around the château, her thoughts paralyzed, before getting up to look for her suitcase in the back of the closet.

Tonight, while Garnett was still asleep, she could escape! Taking the twins with her, she'd get on the first plane that was leaving, no matter where it was going, and then somehow she'd get to Tokyo and Simon.

She threw the suitcase onto the bed and went to the bureau for her passport and traveler's checks. Something swooped past the window, catching her eye. A raven, a bat? Too large for either, but never mind. She went back to rummaging through the bureau drawers, pulling out what she'd need for the trip, when a movement in the darkness outside startled her again.

Slowly she turned her head toward the window.

Hanging in the black wind, swaying like a kite in the turbulent air, a child floated in the darkness. A strong gust whistled around the side of the house, shivering the window panes, and the figure receded, tumbling over and over as the current of air swept it away. Kei's knees crumpled under her. She pulled herself up by the side of the bureau, stumbled upright, and ran to the window to throw it open.

"Dirk? Gino?" she shouted, reaching out into the night as the window frames slammed at her arms. The sky was empty.

The door wouldn't open. Garnett must have locked it on the outside when she was showering. She threw herself at it, pounding on the thin wooden panels. Finally she heard the key turn in the lock and nearly fell into the hallway as Garnett opened the door. He caught her and held her fast as she struggled to get loose and see if the twins were safe.

"What's the matter?" he said calmly as she twisted in his arms.

"The children!"

"They're all right. Go see for yourself."

Kei ran down the hallway. By the night light she could see Gino standing by the open window. Dirk was snuggling down into his own bed.

"Where have you been?" she asked, kneeling down and hugging her face into the childish fragrance of Gino's neck as he yawned.

"I think I got up to get a drink," he answered fuzzily. "I'm too sleepy to remember." He wriggled away from her kisses and climbed back into bed.

She pulled the covers up around Dirk, who had already fallen back to sleep, and sat down beside Gino, "Were you . . . were you outside just now?" she asked.

"Outside?" He looked puzzled. " 'Course not!" He popped his thumb into his mouth and closed his eyes.

Kei shut the banging window. The room was frigid.

Garnett stood in the doorway. "I guess our secret's out," he said quietly, gesturing her toward him while he held the door, waiting to close it behind her. "Now, don't fret. The boys were perfectly safe.

Learning to fly is part of their training."

"What training?" she asked as he led her by the elbow back toward her room.

"To be Masters. Don't ask any more questions, I'm not going to tell you more than that."

As they reached her room, she turned toward him, blocking the doorway, and unobtrusively drew the door half shut behind her. The suitcase was out in plain sight on the bed!

"There's no use in asking them, either," he said, leaning a hand on the wall by her head. "I make them forget what they've learned between lessons."

"Is that what you've been doing in the folly, teaching them to fly and . . . and to blow animals' heads off?!"

He clucked his tongue. "My error. You weren't supposed to see that. Or the flying, either. But you know kids. Independent cusses, they are, always going just a little outside of the directions." He cocked his head at her. "And then there's you, always snooping around and interrupting." He pushed the door open, but his eyes were on her. "Just to be on the safe side, I think I'd better lock you in your room at night."

"Oh, please don't!"

"Sorry, sweetheart." He urged her into the room and she shut the door quickly behind her so that he couldn't look on the bed.

The key turned in the lock and Kei heard his footsteps getting fainter down the hallway.

The food was served attractively here in the hospital—on shiny black lacquer dishes, with an artistic attention to color and everything grouped in threes or fives because, Miss Suzuki said, the word for four sounded the same as that for death—but the preponderance of fish and seaweed had gotten to Simon after a couple of days. After trying to choke down a piece of raw squid that had the look and texture of a small cake of Ivory soap, he made arrangements to have a French restaurant cater his meals. The staff followed a laissez-faire policy in regard to orthopedic patients, who could eat anything they liked. The fellow in the next bed, who was trussed up like Simon, kept crunching tidbits that looked like black beetles, his family replenishing the supply every day. He'd offered one to Simon, who hid it under his pillow and munched his tongue appreciatively but refused any more, fearing that there might be tiny legs folded up on the underside. It turned out to be a cocktail cracker that tasted, to his tentative tongue, like a tidewater pool.

He was grateful for Miss Suzuki's visits, which kept him from feeling like an orphan amidst the chattering relatives gathered around the other bed. She brought him Swiss chocolates, French magazines, and read aloud to him. "Famous Art Critic Hospitalized," she translated from the Tokyo *Asahi*, showing him the newspaper article on the fourth page. Happily, the article did not mention the cause of his accident but concentrated on his biography instead.

She operated the tape recorder while he dictated his memoirs and combed his hair, parting it on the side and then in the middle to see how it looked. One day she drew a moustache on him with an eyebrow pencil and asked the family at the next bedside to come over and give opinions. It was decided that he looked better with a clean upper lip, and she removed the pencil with a paper handkerchief. All in all, despite the fact that she treated him like an oversized doll as he lay helpless in his harness, she was a delightful companion and kept him from expiring from boredom.

The only problem was that when she bent over him to adjust the covers—and she did it again and again, as if she knew the effect it had on him—he could see down the front of her dress, and he was getting horny as hell. This morning his reaction had been clearly visible, bringing a pretty blush to Miss Suzuki's cheeks and a titter from the grandmother at the next bed, who covered her mouth with her hand and rocked back and forth delightedly while pointing at the evidence, about which Simon could do precisely nothing. He begged Miss Suzuki to leave adjustments to the nurse, in case one ever showed up. When she left, he asked a passing doctor if he wasn't coming along well enough to be allowed the use of his arms. He was.

So when he got Eagle's call, he could answer it himself.

CHAPTER FOURTEEN

The parking area was mottled with melting snow. Crystalline clumps clung to the holly covering the air conditioner outside the kitchen, where two small European robins were engaged in a morning chat. Garnett's breath steamed as he squatted down beside Mitzi, who looked at him as he talked and then gave a shake of her head that set her chain collar ringing and pattered away across the gravel to the front door. There she lay down with her paws crossed and her silky ears flopped over them, guarding the entrance. A look from Garnett scattered the ravens clustering around his feet, and a pair flew to the holly clump to bedevil the robins as he stood up, pulled on lined doeskin gloves, and gazed up at the gray overcast.

On his way through Fay to the McKenzie farmhouse, he passed a young woman standing in a shop window, selecting knobs of celery root from a wire basket inside the store. Seeing that the low neck of her blouse exposed the thin black chain around her neck, he shook his head at her, and she quickly arranged her scarf to cover it. The woman looked worried, and rightly so, Garnett thought, nettled at seeing such slovenliness in a coven member. She'd pay for being so careless at the next meeting of the coven!

He stopped at the tobacconist's to buy a couple of smutty magazines and some bars of Cadbury's chocolates, and stepped back out into the street. The ravens were following him, flying up and settling again on trees along his route.

Eagle answered the door, fully dressed in jeans and a striped blue and green soccer shirt under a silvery velvet bathrobe meant for someone much taller than he. The underside of his rosy nose was fringed with fine shreds of skin, and his cracked lips showed that he'd been baked by a fever during the night, but he'd lost his flush and looked better this morning.

"Go away!" he said at seeing Garnett on the doorstep.

"I brought you some things." Garnett held out the magazines and chocolate. "Thought you said no hard feelings about yesterday."

They *had* shaken hands in the folly, agreeing on a new start, and it was friendly of Garnett to bring gifts. The full-breasted model on one of the magazine covers was really sensational! Eagle relented and opened the door. He took the presents reluctantly, feeling two-faced for having ratted on Garnett to Simon, and tinkered with the notion of making a clean breast of things at the diplomatic moment. Not very happy with himself, he ushered Garnett into the living room, where dust was collecting moment by moment on the furnishings and had fogged over a crystal ball on the coffee table.

Garnett wrinkled his nose at the faint smell of mildew and old socks pervading the air and seated himself on the brocade sofa while Eagle leafed through the magazines. The atmosphere made Garnett edgy. He was surrounded by props from Tommy McKenzie's movies—like the crystal ball that had been featured prominently in The Crystal Quest—and the paraphernalia of white witchcraft. An exquisitely illuminated pentagram gilded on Florentine leather was framed above the fireplace, and on a sideboard were mammoth silver candlesticks, a censer of the same metal, and incense burners everywhere. In the mullioned window hung a glass globe filled with colored string—a witch ball to entangle and entrap any evil influences that entered the house.

In the hallway, visible from the sofa, was a suit of armor Garnett recognized from the swashbuckling film, Cadiz, because of its blue-black sheen and the silver cross on the breastplate. Over the door hung a twig broom. Sourly Garnett thought that its owner would sprinkle salt on the threshhold and use the broom to sweep it out the door, purifying the house after showing out a visitor with negative vibrations. A visitor of the likes of himself, he thought resentfully.

To the untrained eye, the house was merely a pleasant, sunny place, expensively decorated by someone with eclectic tastes. Garnett knew better. Eagle's father was an hereditary white witch, the most powerful kind, whose life was dedicated to undermining Satanism through the use of positive, natural forces. He'd acknowledged siring Eagle and married his mother so recently that Garnett doubted he'd had time to pass on the teachings of Wicca to his son. To others, Tommy McKenzie was a retired movie star of considerable renown, who had gained equal distinction as a sculptor in the past few years, but to Garnett he was the leader of the opposition. One day they'd have to come to a showdown of strength, and it would be a point in Garnett's favor if he'd seduced Eagle by then. That would allow him to establish a spy and a saboteur within his opponent's household.

It would also supplement Garnett's supply of conveniently available bodies.

"How's your fever?" he asked.

"About the same," said Eagle, who had no idea. He had a French history exam coming up that he could miss if he kept himself sick enough. The folks were due back in four days. A good, strong case of the flu would take most of his mother's attention away from Tommy, who had had it long enough.

Garnett didn't like his answer. As long as Eagle's temperature was up, he was impervious to his influence. "Marthe's made you a big pot of chili," he said idly, considering going back to the store on the way to look for Colette. She was a good lay and would put herself out handsomely to make him reduce the penalty due her for being careless about displaying her iron chain, the badge of the coven.

"Chili, huh?" said Eagle, brightening. He took off the bathrobe that had been dragging around his feet and got his jacket from the hall closet. "Let's go!"

Garnett sauntered over to join him at the door. "Don't forget to lock up. Your aunt said there had been breakins around here," he said leeringly.

Behind his back, Eagle made a short lunge at him and then stopped himself. Jesus Christ, for the sake of a couple of girlie magazines and some chocolate bars, he'd let Garnett cozy up to him again! Would he never learn? He locked the door and put the key in his pocket, all the while figuring out how to phrase what was on his mind.

They clumped down the steps together and walked in tandem down the narrow, rivuleted sidewalk toward the street.

"You know I'm a juvenile, don't you?" he said finally, kicking a clot of snow out of his path. "I'll get off a lot easier than you will."

Garnett turned and looked at him scornfully, then continued on his way apparently unconcerned. Miffed, Eagle hurried ahead so that he could face him and, walking backward, said, "Your finger-prints'll be all over, same as mine!"

"Get out of the way!" Garnett brushed by him and continued, speeding up his pace.

Eagle was getting angrier and angrier at Garnett's lack of response to what he'd considered a blockbuster. When Uncle Simon had pointed out that Garnett would be getting the brunt of the rap, Eagle had nearly cried with relief over the telephone, but it wasn't fazing Garnett. "I called Uncle Simon last night and told him the whole story!"

That finally stopped Garnett in his tracks. Embellishing, Eagle added a few things he *hadn't* told his uncle because he didn't like to talk about sex long distance. "And I told him about you taking the twins to Mr. Grapes's and about you trying to—well, *you* know—in the folly. And that I thought he ought to get rid of you before you really screwed up the twins and everything else!''

Garnett's face was a study in rage. Looking at it, Eagle was cowed, sensing the malignant strength behind it. Garnett's hand shot out and caught him by the front of his jacket. The sturdy leather ripped as if it had been paper-thin plastic. For a moment, Eagle's legs turned to water and he thought his bladder would flood over, but the contorted expression passed from Garnett's face, leaving his features smooth again, and he let go of the jacket.

"If you're so interested in saving the twins,'' Garnett said slowly, ''maybe you ought to save them now. Come with me and I'll show you where they are.''

Garnett reversed direction and started out beyond the farmhouse, even farther away from the village, with Eagle trotting behind him, holding his jacket together and trying to keep up, wondering what new mischief Garnett had devised.

Just beyond the McKenzie house, but hidden from it by a tall stand of pines that were beaded with ravens, stood an unfinished three-story house, a hodgepodge of unfinished walls and partially-laid floors on the ground level, with only wall frames and flooring struts crossed by single board walkways on the other two. A chimney poked up through the skeletal structure, soaked black from snow melting on the half-completed roof. No stairs had been put in yet. Tall, rickety-looking ladders reached from floor to floor. The carpenters had vacated the site for lunch.

Garnett stopped in front of the house and looked up at the water-stained raw wood of the third story. Eagle blanched at seeing the twins sitting up there, dangerously high above a cement sidewalk, their feet hanging over the edge of the building. One false move, and they'd smash down onto the sidewalk far below!

"How . . . how did they get up there?" Eagle asked with stiff lips. He couldn't see how they got up those ladders without killing themselves, and now they were up at a tremendous height with nothing to hang onto, kicking their heels in the air unconcernedly as if they had no concept of the danger they were in.

"What does that matter?" said Garnett. "Have you got nerve enough to bring them down?"

He remained on the sidewalk as Eagle licked his lips and started for the house, keeping his eye on the twins, fearful that they might fall as he watched. "Don't move kids!" he shouted. "Just hold still where you are, I'm coming!"

Unnailed boards rattled under his feet as he entered the house and confronted the first ladder. It looked forbiddingly high, reaching up and up toward the bare struts that formed the second story. Only his concern for the twins gave him courage to quell his fear of heights. He laid his hands on the wet rung, gulped down a clog in his throat, and started climbing. He made it up the first ladder, talking soothingly to the twins and to himself all the while, then began on the second, the clammy sweat on his palms making his purchase on the rungs less secure as he went. Halfway up, his foot slipped and he nearly slid down the ladder, but he grabbed a rung, righted himself, and paused a moment while his heart rattled against his ribs before starting up again.

Reaching the third floor, he looked across at the twins, who were sitting on a wide strip of wood at the edge of the house frame, with nothing but air beyond them. To get out there, they had to have crossed the unanchored board that lay before him. Eagle looked down through the widely-spaced bare struts of the third story at the floor below, a geometrical pattern of narrow strips of wood like those up here, with the same perilously wide gaps between them. If he fell from here, he might crash through to the ground floor, but the twins were in even greater danger than he was. A mere tilt forward, and over they'd go onto the sidewalk, to be crushed like eggs.

He spread out his arms to balance himself like a tightrope walker and began teetering along the board toward the children, not looking down, trying to suppress his dizziness, drenched with perspiration.

"Hello, Eagle!" Dirk said gayly, turning six inches from disaster to look at him. Eagle inched toward him along the unstable board. As he came within about ten feet of Dirk, the child looked up and said, "Hi there, Garnett!"

Garnett?! No one had been behind him on the ladder, Eagle thought, stopping in surprise. The board rocked beneath him. He could feel a presence behind him, but he didn't dare turn to look. Who could it be but Garnett?

Suddenly the sky beyond the frames of the wall darkened as ravens swarmed out of the pines and flew in a screeching torrent around the house, nearly shocking Eagle into losing his balance. He panicked but managed to steady himself and began moving slowly toward the twins again. A bird wafted out of the cloud of ravens and dropped down on the end of the board in front of him. Fixing him with a glittering eye, it hopped sideways toward him. He couldn't kick it off, he'd have to keep going and hope it would get out of his way.

The board began to bounce slowly as someone put pressure on it from the end in back of him. "Stop it, Gar!" he cried, frantically shifting his balance, trying to match the up and down rhythm. Birds circled his head, screaming, as the board bounced faster and faster.

In front of him, the twins scrambled to their feet, laughing merrily, and leaped out into space. Eagle froze at seeing them hanging in the air like seagulls riding a current of wind. The board danced under his feet and he skidded along the wet wood toward the outside wall, fell twisting at the end of the board and caught it, tearing his hands on the sharp edges. Savage beaks slashed at his hands and head and the screams of the birds beat on his ears like heavy wings as he hung at arms' length a long, long moment with his weight dragging down on his weakening fingers. Then the sidewalk rushed up at him.

After sending the twins back to the folly by mental command, Garnett dropped down lightly to the ground floor and went out to the sidewalk to look at what he had wrought.

Eagle lay face down, spread-eagled on the cement

in a trickling splatter of blood. Garnett kicked him in the side to satisfy himself that the job was complete and left him for the workmen to find when they came back from lunch. They'd deduce that Eagle had fallen while investigating a vacant building, as inquisitive adolescents do, and be none the wiser. It was a pity, having to finish him off when he would have been a prime addition to the stable, but the damned fool had gone too far, phoning Simon!

Garnett's feathered minions scuttled around the body, pecking at it, as Garnett walked into Fay, his step lightened by the excitement of the kill. Seeing the carpenters coming back from the Café de la Place with wine bottles under their arms, he stepped behind a thick-trunked oak tree until they passed. Then, to be sure to disassociate himself from the incident, he took a deserted back path toward the château and joined the twins at the folly.

The call from the clinic came just after Kei had finished packing the twins' things and stored them in her closet. She raced out to the jeep parked by the front door. The momentum with which she pelted out of the house saved her from getting her throat torn out by the mastiff, who sprang up, fangs bared, and leaped at her. Kei's reflexes carried her beyond her shock at Mitzi's attack.

She was close enough to the car to open the door and slide inside, but the dog caught her by the left wrist before she could close it. With the mastiff's teeth locked in her arm and the animal's wiry weight dragging her off the seat toward the gravel outside, she pulled with all her weight against the pain, wedging herself against the other side of the steering wheel, and struggled to open the glove compartment. The tug of war was agonizing, but for a split second Mitzi opened her jaws to get a better grip, and Kei yanked her arm away. Grabbing the heavy flashlight from the glove compartment, she smashed at the jagged fangs lunging at her through the door, battering Mitzi back until she could slam the door.

The dog made a couple of futile charges at the car window, then whimpered and went back to sit down by the front door again and doctor her wounds. Mitzi gave Kei a sorrowful look as if she were apologizing, put her muzzle in the air, and whined mournfully.

Kei slumped over the steering wheel, shaking with shock, but feeling dampness down her side, she forced herself to bind her scarf tight around her wrist and then awkwardly reached over and turned on the ignition.

The jeep lurched out of the parking lot and through the gate. There was a filling station on the way to the clinic where she could call Marthe and tell her to get the twins to safety, if the road would quit weaving back and forth ahead of her.

Monsieur Topolini, the station attendant, alerted by the blood spattered on the side of the car door, hastily rebound her wrist with elastic bandage from a first aid kit, made the call for her, and drove her to the clinic.

It was late afternoon before the doctors thought she was far enough recovered to see Eagle. He was in intensive care, with tubes taped to his arm and upper lip, but he was alive. Kei stood at the foot of his bed and watched the almost imperceptible rise and fall of his chest, willing him to keep living. His head was swathed in bandages and his face was swollen around strange slash marks. Sticking plaster covered one cheekbone where, the nurse whispered, his flesh had been gouged to the bone. "Birds," she said softly in French. "He was covered with birds when they found him! He will need plastic surgery on his face and ears, but the doctor says there should be no major scarring, except for the cheek perhaps."

"Is he out of danger?" Kei asked, frightened by his stillness.

"You should ask the doctor," the nurse replied, "but I think he will tell you that the prognosis is guarded. The young man has a severe concussion in addition to multiple fractures. Fortunately, he seems to have a very sturdy constitution, so we can hope." She smiled encouragingly and patted the arm that was not in a sling.

The doctor's outlook concurred with that of the nurse. It would be touch and go for the next twenty-four hours, he said, but Kei should be home in bed herself, on medication for shock. Eagle's parents had been contacted at their hotel in Sri Lanka, thanks to Marthe's supplying the number from the itinerary they'd left at the château, and in the meantime, an aunt's presence at the hospital was superfluous. He would inform her immediately of any change in Eagle's status, he assured her.

Monsieur Topolini had been waiting in the corridor all this time and had nearly wrung his beret to extinction by twisting it in his hands from anxiety for Kei and Eagle and lack of faith in his wife's ability to make the correct change for customers back at the station. He drove Kei home.

Marthe and Hilaire were waiting at the door and helped Kei up the stairs to bed, though she protested that it was her wrist that was injured, not her legs.

"I had the veterinarian put Mitzi to sleep." Hilaire said in French as they went down the hallway. "Such an old friend," he said, taking a bandana from his pocket and wiping his eyes. "Such a gentle nature. I cannot understand what happened."

Marthe shut him out of the bedroom and helped Kei undress. "What a terrible day!" she said, plumping up the pillows after throwing back the covers. "What a terrible, terrible day! *Le pauvre garçon*, he will be all right?" Kei relayed what information the doctor had given her as she got into bed.

"I wish I could get hold of Chris," she sighed as Marthe got her smoking gear together on the bedside table and added the container of Placidyl from the doctor and a glass of water. "They ought to be home with their mother. I don't like having Garnett around them!"

Marthe raised her eyebrows. "That nice young man? Is he not satisfactory?" She folded her arms over her stomach, looking dour.

Kei put a finger on her lips and mulled over a way to retract the last statement. Marthe had been one of Garnett's staunch supporters from the first, but explaining her reason for disliking Garnett's association with the children would alarm Marthe. She couldn't count on the housekeeper's discretion, and one leak could bring Garnett's wrath down on Marthe's head as well. In dealing with him, one head was better than two.

"Just heard about Eagle," Garnett said from the doorway. "Do they expect him to come out of the coma?"

News certainly traveled fast, Kei thought suspiciously. Had Garnett precipitated Eagle's accident, as he surely had had a hand in Mitzi's attack? She gave a nod of dismissal to Marthe, who put a motherly hand on Garnett's shoulder before leaving, as if bolstering him for a dressing-down from Kei. He sat down on the bed and Kei put a protective hand on the sling over her wrist.

"I don't even know if he's expected to live or not," she said, doubting that his worried look was for Eagle's welfare.

"Do *you* feel all right?" This time his expression was sincere.

"Yes, I'm sure the baby's fine," she said bitterly. "No thanks to you! I suppose you gave Mitzi orders to keep me cooped up in here."

Garnett bridled. "She wasn't supposed to attack you, only keep you safe inside. Do you really think I'd want her to hurt you? You can't blame me for every accident that happens around here! I wish you'd try to understand."

He took her hand, and she acquiesced, not pulling away in repugnance, afraid of provoking him. He ran his fingers over hers, silent and thoughtful, then worked her large topaz ring back and forth with his thumb.

"Sometimes I have to do things I'd rather not," he said. "You see, certain responsibilities have been placed on me that I didn't ask for." He sighed. "I

256

didn't choose to be what I am. They trained me early, before I reached the age of consent, I suppose you could say."

He'd sat down on the back of his sweater so that it pulled away at the neck, showing soft golden hairs tracing down the top of his spine. Kei saw nothing strange in him as he was now, the way she knew him best. He was simply an ordinary young man—though an extraordinarily appealing one—who was feeling sorry for himself. Only once had she thought she'd seen the monster, and only for an instant. And it could have been a newspaper blown by the wind that she'd seen tumbling through the night sky, not one of the twins. All of her education, all of her experience in life, everything she'd ever read or known, told her that no devils walked the earth and that no children could fly.

She hardly knew what to believe any more. She had a natural faith that there was good in everyone, if you dug down far enough to find it. Somewhere under the overlay of learned evil that had been forced on Garnett, she thought, the original person—the one he was meant to be—must still be hidden, untouched, waiting for the right moment to struggle up to the surface.

"There's been a closeness between us, hasn't there?" he asked almost shyly. "I never learned how to feel the things other people do, never knew how to . . . to love. If you could care enough about me, maybe you could teach me, so I wouldn't feel so empty inside. Maybe you could even show me how to use my powers constructively." He looked at her beseechingly. "It's possible, isn't it? I don't have to be condemmed forever to this kind of life, do I?''

It was a beautiful act. Only the dull ache in her lower back that foreshadowed her coming period kept Kei from being lulled into believing it. In a day or two, those smooth tanned hands that were so gentle now might be around her neck, squeezing the life out of her. Having to deal with her rebelliousness for nine months would be deucedly ''inconvenient,'' she imagined, and he was doing a fine job of trying to get her on his side. She remembered a Casanova she'd once known, a heterosexual who cannily pretended he was gay. Convinced that the love of a good woman could correct his condition, many a gullible had bundled him into bed while he protested weakly, laughing up his sleeve all the while. The fellow had tried it on her and she hadn't been taken in by his game, and the one Garnett was playing now wasn't much different.

''I do try to see your side of it, you know how I care about you,'' she said, lowering her eyes so he couldn't read their expression. ''But it's all so new to me, you'll have to be a little patient.'' She drew his hand up to her cheek and cradled it there a moment, thinking that Garnett was so accustomed to manipulating people that he might not expect to be manipulated himself. ''You *are* the father of my child,'' she said, hoping she wasn't overplaying, ''so my loyalties will have to lie with you. I know that, but it means having to look at things in an entirely different way. You can understand that, can't you?''

She glanced quickly at him to see if he was buying it. He had a smug smile on his face that she recognized as the one a man got when he thought he had a woman in the palm of his hand. It usually preceded unbuttoning the blouse. She knew she'd pulled the gambit off when he slid a hand into the front of her nightgown.

"No, not now, Garnett," she said, moaning a little, as if she were getting aroused. "The drugs the doctor gave me are making me woozy, and I want to be able to feel everything. You do such gorgeous things to me, I don't want to miss a moment of it. So just let me take a nap first." It was almost impossible to lay it on too thick about a man's sexual prowess, she knew, and predictably, Garnett looked even more smug.

"All right, I'll come back later." He got up. "You're sure you couldn't stay awake?" he asked, giving her a last chance to partake of the wonderfulness of himself, Kei thought.

"No." She smiled. "I think I can just manage to call Simon and tell him about Eagle before I conk out."

He hesitated, looking speculatively at the phone on her bedside table, then bent over and kissed her before leaving.

So far, so good, Kei said to herself.

Garnett floated over the stair railing on to the floor below and was across the foyer and the salon, into the study, in two giant strides. There he took the phone off the hook and listened to Kei pick up the receiver upstairs and try to dial out. After five minutes of getting only the busy signal, she hung up.

Simon lay in the semi-darkness, listening to Mr.

259

Tanaka's gurgling snore, torn between wanting to call Kei and not wanting to disturb a man who was in pain most of his waking hours. He knew Peggy Van Dreuten wouldn't press charges against the nephew of an old friend, but Kei would have to tell his lawyer in Paris to negotiate a reimbursement with the insurance company. One way or another, if enough money was dropped in the right places, it should be possible to keep Eagle out of court and the affair out of the newspapers. Unfortunately, that meant letting Garnett off free, too. Somehow, though, Simon intended to see that no one would ever hire the rogue as a tutor again, not if his ass was studded with diamonds!

Great Scott, what a ballsup! Oh, to be home where he could sack Garnett himself, instead of being out of commission here, as helpless as a fly wrapped up and ready to be a spider's takeout lunch! The itching boredom and discomfort of being jacked up in these slings was maddening enough, without knowing that Kei—whose state of mind he was worried about to begin with—was having to cope alone with the whole bloody mess!

Now, now, he was whipping himself into a fine froth, and that would never do. Nothing had to be done this instant, it would keep a bit longer.

The overhead light went on, blinding him momentarily and further encouraging the rise of his blood pressure. Mr. Tanaka smacked his lips and coughed. There must be a universal law, Simon thought, decreeing that nurses come around to take temperatures at the most ungodly hour conceivable. Preferably while it was still dark. Over here they aired the rooms at the same time, just before the sun could take the chill off the night air.

The nurse skirted Eagleton-san's bed on her way across the room to open the window, hoping to avoid another argument about the necessity of freshening the air in a room where invalids had been exhausting the oxygen all night.

She wasn't used to taking care of patients as famous as he was, and it made her nervous. That he was handsome enough to make her heart flutter interfered with her coordination, so that she kept dropping things.

Since the newspapers announced his hospitalization, there had been a great coming and going of distinguished visitors, who brought him so many carefully-wrapped tokens of respect that the closet was brimming over with them. Reporters had come, too, but they brought no gifts, treated Tanaka-san's family like peasants, and left the ashtrays loaded with cigarette butts. It was all quite exciting, but cleaning up after Eagleton-san's visitors was an extra chore.

There was also that Suzuki woman, who ignored the picture of Mrs. Eagleton on the bedside table and never seemed to go home. The googly eyes she made at him were disgraceful!

Most of the time, Eagleton-san was so charming it made one's heart melt, and he was surprisingly polite for a foreign gentleman. But before he'd had his morning coffee—he refused point blank to accept tea for breakfast—he could be so fierce and explosive that it made one go to pieces. One had to have a good cry in the supply closet some mornings.

Gentleness and patience were supposed to accompany white hair, but Eagleton-san didn't seem to know that. Perhaps things worked the other way around in the Occident.

She opened the window and then, as she'd been instructed to do, pushed out the screen as well. Without warning, something big rushed in from the darkness and struck her in the face. She fell back with a sceam and heard a furor behind her as Tanaka-san shouted and a crescent pan hit the floor with a clang. Turning, she screamed again at seeing a huge black bird sinking it claws into Eagleton-san's face while its wings thrashed about his head.

Simon blinked, trying to keep looking at the mirror on the specialist's forehead as the light probed his eye. Thank God, the doctor had taken his degree at Stanford, so that his English was perfect! Medical diagnoses were mysterious even when not translated from the Japanese, and Simon wanted a clear answer as to whether or not he was going to lose his eye.

The doctor chewed his moustache thoughtfully as he worked the beam of light back and forth, and Simon's anxiety mounted. Finally the doctor handed the probe to the nurse and took off the mirror. "There is no damage to the cornea," he said. "You are very fortunate, Mr. Eagleton. Your eyesight will not be affected."

Only then did Simon realize he'd been as rigid as an ironing board. He relaxed, a cool wave of relief fanning through his veins, and felt a tear pool near his nose. The doctor sat back, took a packet of cigarettes from the pocket of his tunic, and offered one to Simon before lighting his own. Simon took a grateful drag and with his good eye watched a white blur of smoke float up above his head.

"It will take some time for the eye to heal, and you will need plastic surgery for the torn eyelid," the doctor continued. "A muscle at the outside corner of the eye—" He leaned forward and tapped the area gently, "—has nearly been severed, but we can take care of that. I hope you do not feel that we are backward here in Japan about this kind of surgery. We invented the contact lens, you know."

"I'm sure I'm in good hands," Simon said, meaning it.

"Thank you," The doctor smiled. "In a month or two, the eye should have repaired itself and very little scarring—if any—should occur. For a time, after the bandages have been removed, you will need to wear an eye patch." His almond eyes twinkled. "I am told the ladies think it is quite dashing."

The doctor leaned forward to wipe up a trickle of blood from Simon's temple with a sterile cotton swab and asked if he was more comfortable now.

"I'm getting quite numb," Simon said, fingering the bandage over his bad eye, "By the bye, what happened to the bird that attacked me?"

Dropping the swab into a wastebasket and motioning to the nurse to take it away, the doctor said, "It got away, I'm sorry to say." He held out an ashtray for Simon to tap his ashes into. "And I don't think the bird attacked you deliberately. Why would it? It must have been attracted to the light, got alarmed when the nurse screamed, and clung to the nearest object, which was you. The hysteria and confusion frightened it even more, of course. At any rate, it got back out the window while everyone was shouting and running around."

Simon disagreed with the doctor but kept his opinion to himself. That bloody bird had been laying for him since Australia. To tell a medical man that, however, would probably make him call in a psychiatrist.

"I'd like to phone my wife, now that I know I'm not going to be blinded," he said. "She'll be worried if I don't make my daily call, and I'm dreadfully late already." Without moving his head, he reached over toward the phone on his bedside table.

The doctor put a gentle restraining hand on his arm. "We've tried to reach her, but we can't get through," he said. "Perhaps there has been a winter storm and the lines are down." He consulted a large square Swiss watch on his wrist. "We'll try again, but you're due in surgery as soon as the room's free. Try not to worry. This was a serious injury, and it can't wait."

Goddamnit, thought Simon, how can I *not* worry?

It was snowing again. Illuminated by a circle of light cast by the window lamp, a throng of fluffy white flakes scurried across the black backdrop of the night. Kei sat up in bed, fresh from showering, thinking of Simon, thinking that if she hadn't urged him to go on his collecting tour, they would have toasted the first snow together. If he'd stayed, none of this would have happened.

The heavy feeling in her lower stomach and the

ache across her ovaries persisted. If Garnett had impregnated her this time, would she still be feeling this way? He'd brought up her dinner on a tray just as she was getting up to put in her diaphragm. Having set him up to believe that she was taking his side, she'd had to feign an eager reception. Though she thought she detected a foreign feminine perfume on him, her passion had not been a pretense. His spell still bound her, but she could feel it lessening. Sure of his power over her now, he might be loosening his hold on her mind.

For the first time since he'd set her thoughts swirling in a maelstrom of desire and fear, she could hear the voice of her inner self, sane and reasonable as of old. She welcomed it back, listening to it earnestly.

Now that she could touch the fringe of control over the privacy of her mind, she told herself, she must grasp it tightly and draw it back into her own power. Garnett must never take her over again!

If Simon ever found out what happened and left her, she would have to bear it. She wouldn't blame him if he did. Nevertheless, regardless of how much she loved him and how happy he'd made her, losing him would not be as catastrophic as losing herself. People came and went in one's life, sometimes sadly and sometimes gladly, and events altered one's destiny. The only permanent thing was one's own mentality, and having Garnett insinuate himself into her mind to twist it to his own purposes had been the ultimate violation of her selfhood.

If she'd been alert and put up a barrier, he couldn't have taken over control of her mind. Unthinkingly, freely she'd opened the door to him because he'd seemed guileless and boyish. If she'd thought of him as a man, she'd have been more wary, but his resemblance to her dead son had been like a password that relaxed her defenses. Then he'd slipped past her guard into the stronghold of her sexuality, that secret area where all the normal rules were off or didn't apply, no matter how strongly built and cautiously maintained her outer ethical stucture was.

Now that she could think straight again and was aware of how she'd let herself be maneuvered into surrendering her self control, Garnett was not going to master her again! The only power he had over her was that which she'd given to him, and she'd never relinquish now that she'd got it back!

Having reasoned it out with herself, she felt more like her old self and almost hopeful. If she could weasel out of this jam, at least she might not give birth to Garnett's child. Simon would understand how Garnett laid everyone waste about him and might even forgive her. Thank heaven, he was safe in Tokyo! But why hadn't he called? And was Eagle going to live?

She picked up the phone to see if it was still out of working order and heard the dial tone.

An hour later, she hung up and went to turn off the lamp on the table in the window. Back in bed, she snapped off the light by her elbow.

Attacked by a bird! A freak accident, maybe, but suspiciously coincidental with the incursion of ravens taking place at the château. "Oh, just some black thing," Simon had said vaguely when she'd asked what kind of bird it had been. She wished she were sure he wasn't pulling his old trick of minimizing. During his schooling in England, he'd picked up the British understatement thing, so she could never be certain that he was giving her the full story. If she hadn't insisted on speaking to one of the doctors to get professional reassurance, she'd be out of her mind with worry.

She wasn't in great shape as it was, but hearing that Eagle's condition was stable helped.

Was it at all conceivable that Garnett's powers extended as far as Japan? No, of course not! But if they did, then Simon was no safer there than he would be here at the château! The business about Eagle and Peggy Van Dreuten's diamond pendant seemed trivial in comparison to that shaking possibility.

She'd downplayed what was going on at home to keep Simon from worrying, and he probably was doing the same. Well, losing sleep over it would only make her more vulnerable to Garnett's tactics tomorrow. She'd need to monitor her thoughts carefully and see that he didn't worm his way back into manipulating her. And she'd have to start thinking up some strategies of her own.

She looked at the clock. Ten thirty. Plenty of time to get a good night's rest if she could. Another pill might make her logy in the morning, which could give Garnett an edge over her, so she'd better not.

She heard the cistern filling on the third floor. Her mother had toilet trained her by running water while she was on the potty, so a trip to the bathroom was imperative before settling down.

After getting back into bed, she started counting backward from one thousand. When she reached three hundred and six, she fell into a fitful sleep and dreamed of Father Barteau lying in a welter of blood with a cleaver by his hand.

CHAPTER FIFTEEN

She was back at the oak grove, with the cold leaves wet under her bare feet. Again the gray mist spiraled up and took the shape of a woman wearing a cowl. The taloned hand, reeking of decay, was beckoning.

Kei woke with the memory of smelling rotting flesh and looked at the illuminated clock dial. Only five minutes to midnight. This was going to be one of those nights of intermittent wakenings, interspersed with nightmares, that would leave her a wretched mess in the morning.

She shook a Placidyl out into her hand and got up to refill the water glass. On her way past the window, she looked out to see if the snow had stopped. The moonlight reflected back from a light covering on the ground, and fine pellets were tapping on the window ledge outside. She shivered and wondered if anyone had remembered to let Maybe in for the night.

Putting down the glass and the pill, she went to the closet for her kimono and slippers.

No need to turn on the lights, she knew the stairs and the foyer by heart. Maybe was in the door in a flash when she opened it onto the back bridge. After making some cutting comments about humans who forgot their duties and left the boss of the house out on a night like this, he stalked reproachfully into the salon, and Kei shut the door.

What in heaven's name was going on out there in the oak grove? Points of light were passing in front of the folly, winking out at either end. Then she realized that they must be circling the summer house. A black gap, larger than the rest appeared in the circle and traveled across the front of the building. Something solid. Faint light from the—candles, they must be—caught a spark of gold from the shadowy opaqueness moving at shoulder height toward a corner of the folly porch.

Holding her kimono together over her sling, Kei pushed the door open a crack with her shoulder. Was that the wind sighing through the trees? But the air was cold and still, while a dim musical sound ebbed and flowed in the oak grove—a chant of voices, so low it might have been a remembered melody in her own head.

She pulled the door to again and, with a sense of foreboding, went to the hall closet for her alpaca wrap and rubber boots to pull over her slippers.

The snow muffled her footsteps as she crossed the bridge and then the meadow, going the long way around, off the path, so she wouldn't be silhouetted against the house. Sleet was peppering down now. As she neared the folly, shielding herself behind trees as she went, the chanting grew louder and masked the crinkle of snow and sleet under her feet.

Hooded black robes preceded by candles flames

that trailed a stinking oily odor passed in a ring around the summer house as she watched, trying to quiet her breathing. Now the object that had broken the chain of candle flames lurched around the side of the folly, swaying on the shoulders of four black figures, like a religious idol being transported through the crowds on a high holy day. It seemed to be a woman in a high-backed chair. Covered in folds of white satin like a fall of snow on a pine tree, she bent forward. The moonlight frosted her back, the tops of her shoulders, and her head, where a delicate tracery of something lacy formed a crown.

The door of the summer house opened. The chair was lowered and passed through into the half-lit interior, where banks of candle flames flickered.

When the door closed again, the outside of the folly was dark except for a long slice of light where the drapes had not been drawn together. Kei crept up on the porch, testing each board before she put her full weight on it, and edged toward the bright slit where she might see what was going on inside.

By moving her head back and forth, she could see most of the room, although the stage wasn't visible from this angle. The woman in the chair had disappeared, but everyone inside was turned toward the stage, so she might be there.

By the light of candles massed on top of the bookcases, she could see a long, low sort of table covered to the floor in black cloth that had been set in front of the stage. At one end of it were set a gold candlestick with a thick, squat candle striped in brown and red; a brass box; a leather-bound book with brass fastenings; a golden chalice studded with gemstones; and a black-handled dagger whose blade gleamed in the candlelight. Kei's arms goosefleshed. The trappings on the table made it appear ominously like an altar. Garnett had said the Satanic cult has been quashed only *temporarily* earlier in the year. The scene inside convinced her that it had sprung up again from sturdy roots. She had a sinking feeling that this was the setting for a Black Mass.

The room inside was crowded with black robed figures blending together in a formless mass so she couldn't count them. The circus furnishings that looked gay and cheerful in the daytime were transformed by the dimness. Gunther loomed up in one corner and light from a candle picked out the varnished teeth of the carousel horse, whose lips seemed to curl back in a snarl. The balloons looked like giant black insect's eggs clustered across the ceiling.

A hood slipped aside and she recognized Malcolm Kidwell, the man who had recommended Garnett as a tutor, and that corpulent figure standing by the eldritch green glow of the aquarium must be Hamilton Grapes. Kei was not surprised to find him amongst the devil worshipers. His unctuous manner had alway made her shrink from his touch as if he was unclean.

Behind the altar stood three black robes, unidentifiable because of the hoods shadowing their faces. The two outer ones removed the robe of the one in the middle.

Dark ceremonial oil glistened on his forest of dark body hair and his goat's eyes glowed like marsh lights in the dimness. Although some semblance of

Garnett's usual form and features remained, the reptilian skin on his chest and shoulders was that of an alien being. The greenish horror protruding from his shaggy loins made Kei's stomach churn slowly. This was what had shared her bed, disguised in a thin veneer of golden flesh! If she died for it, she thanked God that he had not left his loathsome residue inside her to fester and burst into inhuman life.

A more exultant chant filtered through the window as a robe dropped to the floor and a woman stepped out to lie face down from the waist on the altar with her haunches toward the back of the room. Garnett walked around the table and bent over her. Kei looked away, but something had caught her eye. She looked back. Dirk and Gino were watching the ceremony intently.

She backed away, reaching out for one of the porch columns. Gulping in the chill night air to steady her heaving stomach, she fought down the vomit pulsing upward toward her throat. When she finally had herself under control, she left the porch as noiselessly as she had come and started back to the house through beads of sleet that bounced off her head and shoulders, falling with a whispering tinkle to the ground. No one back at the folly would hear her now, engrossed as they were in their vile ceremony, and her footprints would be obliterated by others that followed later.

Closing the door behind her, she leaned back against it with her eyes closed. A low, grating groan dragged up from inside her, and the door rattled as convulsive sobs shook her body.

273

CHAPTER SIXTEEN

"Where are Dirk and Gino?" Kei asked as Garnett stepped into the dining room. This morning she'd gotten up, put on cream woolen slacks and a honey-colored sweater after discarding the hampering sling, rewrapped her arm in a fresh bandage, and gone to waken the twins. Their beds had been slept in, but she couldn't find them anywhere in the house. Wondering if their disappearance was connected with the scene she'd witnessed last night, her imagination was going riot.

"Carolyn Kidwell picked them up earlier this morning, or should have," Garnett said, sitting down. Relieved, Kei let out the breath she'd been holding. He unfolded his napkin, put it on his lap, and shoved his cup over for her to fill, appropriating the *Times* with his other hand. "They'll be spending the day with her children," he said, looking at the headlines as he accepted the cup she handed him. "I have some work to do. Didn't want them underfoot."

Having the twins with a cult member wasn't what she would have chosen, but they'd be safe surrounded by the Kidwell brood, and Garnett wouldn't be subjecting them to more of his infernal teaching.

"How's your arm?" he asked.

"Better." It looked and felt like hell, but the swelling had gone down somewhat, and the Placidyl the doctor had given her helped numb the pain from the punctures in her muscles as well as relax her tension. The wounds looked ghastly, but no musculature had been torn, and the hospital staff had simply treated them and stapled the edges together.

She looked at him closely while he reached for the tub of sweet butter, spread some on his croissant, and looked down at the paper. No trace of the monster in him was left this morning. Bluish shadows under his eyes suggested that he hadn't had enough sleep, but otherwise he was the picture of blooming American youth. That enabled her to deal with him as a normal human being this morning, more or less, instead of being terrified of him. It must use up a portion of his energy every day just to keep up that false appearance, she calculated, to hide that scaly skin and convert those slitted irises to round ones.

Simon had already called to report that the surgery on his eye had been successful. That was a comfort, a ray of sunshine penetrating this nightmare, but Missy had finally located him and further upset him about Garnett. As soon as was humanly possible, he'd said, he was coming home. Kei had martialled all her powers of persuasion to keep him from considering it, knowing how dangerous it would be for him to return to the château. She *thought* she'd convinced him that she could handle affairs here, but if there was one thing Simon was, it was an independent thinker. She wouldn't lay any bets that he mightn't change his mind and hop on a plane, trailing bandages behind him. Naturally, she hadn't breathed a hint of what Garnett really was or what he was doing to the twins, or Simon would have left immediately, if he'd had to paddle his hospital bed through the Sea of Japan to do it.

The more she thought about the attack on Simon, the more she worried that Garnett had had something to do with it. If that was true, then Simon wasn't safe even in Tokyo, though Garnett's powers might be weakened by the distance. And it would certainly mean that her chances of getting herself and the children away without being stopped were very slim. The ravens outside were swarming all over the château now, particularly at the front. They crawled over the windows like a horde of black beetles, and if one could do so much damage to Simon, the sea of them about the house could be lethal.

"Garnett," she said, abandoning her anxieties about that, "if our child could . . . grow up, would he inherit your abilities?"

Garnett stuffed the end of his croissant in his mouth and licked his fingers before replying. "No, he'd have to learn everything from the ground up, as I did." His tongue traveled around the corners of his mouth, gathering up stray crumbs. "Then, when he was old enough, he'd have to have some physical alterations made, and infusions would change the structure of his blood."

So that was what was ahead for Dirk and Gino,

unless she could get them out of this!

She turned down the corners of her mouth. "I wish he could live," she said sadly. "He'd be extraordinary, and I guess any mother would want that. It's hard, knowing he's going to die." She blinked as if she were keeping back tears. "Perhaps we could have another one that you'd let live?"

"You're too old already to be having children," he said unfeelingly. "I'd want a young mother to give me healthy children. As it is, it doesn't matter much."

That was a blind alley. Nevertheless, she'd let him think that she was cooperative, and she could see him softening as he considered her change in attitude. She buttered another croissant and handed it to him.

"You can do *anything*, can't you?" she said. "I'll bet you could make this château float in the air if you wanted to."

He laughed with a full mouth and shook his head. "No, I couldn't, and why would I want to?" He washed down the bite of croissant with coffee. "That'd be stupid. Attract attention. Look, I don't want to disillusion you, but my powers are limited. I was born human, after all."

"Oh, don't get modest on me," Kei purred. "You're just pretending. You radiate power. I can feel it clear over here." She shivered, as if the idea thrilled her, and he smiled.

"Okay, I'll tell you what I can do, if you're interested." He wiped his mouth, put the napkin on the table, and leaned back expansively in his chair. "Maybe it'll keep you from trying to use that suitcase you've got packed in the closet." Kei paused with her coffee cup halfway to her lips, and he chuckled. "Oh yes, I found it. I keep a very close eye on you, you know."

"My, I'd forgotten about that," she said, keeping it light. "It completely slipped my mind in the past couple of days." She drank her coffee and put down the cup.

"Just so it's understood," Garnett said. He gave her a look of reproval and then went on, "Well, to begin with, my powers are linked to the animal world and the air, with a few extras like dematerialization thrown in for free. Like the twins, I can travel through the air—short distances only—and I can . . . well, it's hard to explain, but I can reduce air resistance, which makes for pretty fast going on the ground as well." He leaned forward again. "Bear that in mind if you ever get the urge again to take off somewhere."

"Then you couldn't fly around the world?" Kei asked, being careful to sound disappointed.

"Hardly. But far enough." He finished off the dregs of his coffee. "No, sweetheart, I don't do parlor tricks. Every bit of magic costs me something. Speaking of which, let's go up to bed. I've got something to do this morning that's going to take a lot out of me."

Oh God, what'll I do now?, Kei asked herself, getting up submissively and leading the way.

Her period still hadn't come, but cramps told her that it was on its way. When she got it, the jig was up, so she had only a few hours, perhaps a day, before she'd be staring death in the face. Her only hope, so far as she could figure out, was to run down Garnett's energy in some way so he couldn't keep her from escaping—if there was any safe place to flee to.

Her mind was going like an express train as she began to undress. She couldn't turn him down without arousing his anger. The hell of it was, she'd have to appear to want it, or he'd know her new cooperativeness was a sham.

He had something important to do this morning that was going to take a lot out of him, he'd said. That was why he needed the extra boost of bed right now. But if he didn't discharge his semen, eventually he'd be running on an empty tank. If she could keep him from coming to orgasm, whatever work he was scheduled for would drain him to some extent. Also, with luck, she wouldn't get pregnant. Now, how do you screw a man, seem to enjoy it, and still keep him from completing the act?

She lay down on the bed, thinking hard. Garnett sat down beside her to take his shoes and socks off.

"Is there anything I can do to give you more pleasure?" she asked at last. "Anything I've left out?"

"You're okay." He dropped his shoes on the floor and got on the other side of the bed. "No problems."

Accustomed to getting A+ on her report card for sex, Kei bit back a retort. Just one miscalculation could be her undoing.

"Well, do be frank," she said sweetly, "because we both want to have the best time possible, don't we?"

He rolled over toward her. "You're not suggesting

that my technique needs improving, are you?" His tone was playful. He knew he was superb in bed. He reached out for her and began his foolproof foreplay.

After a moment, she said, "There's just one little thing. . . ."

His hand paused.

"Oh, it's nothing, really," she said, stroking his chest, "just something terribly minor. Forget it."

He went back to what he'd been doing, arousing her skillfully, so that her automatic responses took over. When he entered her, she was eager for it.

She was digging her fingernails into his back when he stopped and said, "*What?*"

She opened her eyes.

"What is this 'minor' thing?" he demanded, lying motionless on top of her.

"Oh, never mind. Don't stop, it feels gorgeous," she said and ran her tongue around his ear.

He began pounding into her again. His movements were quickening when she remembered herself. "It's your rhythm," she whispered.

He stopped in mid-thrust. "What about my rhythm?" he asked crossly.

"Don't sound like that," she murmured soothingly and nibbled at his ear lobe. "It's simply that you go at it with the same beat as Khatchaturian's Sabre Dance right away and —look, I'm not really criticizing, but women like it more like The Blue Danube at first."

He grunted and slowed down his pace. "Like this?" he asked hoarsely.

They worked together until their bodies were slippery and she could feel herself coming dangerously close to losing control. "That's almost it," she gasped. "Now, listen, and we can get it perfect." She began to sing The Blue Danube, "Da dum-dum de DAH! Bum-BUMP, bum-bump!," marking the beat heavily with her hips while he tried to synchronize his lunges with hers.

"Goddamnit!" he groaned, grasping her by the buttocks and struggling to match the working of his hips to her direction. A bead of sweat crawled down his cheekbone.

"I'm only trying to help," she said against his shoulder. The sweat crept down his jaw, hung suspended from a stubble hair, and dropped into her eye. "Just on the downbeat, darling," she breathed, blinking.

She hummed the tune encouragingly while he strained into her, sliding back and forth across her belly on a slick of perspiration. "I think I'm beginning to get it," he muttered. "Yeah, yeah, *there* we go!"

"Yes, yes!" she sighed ecstatically, but she altered the tempo of her humming minutely and kept her own movements in time with the former one. Soon their hipbones were clashing offbeat again. He growled in frustration, and she said, "Don't be impatient. It's sort of a rocking movement, like a mother rocking her child." His breathing was getting labored, and veins were beginning to stand out on his neck. "Pretend I'm your mother, love. Don't I remind you of you mother?"

"Oh, *shit!*" he said, springing up off her. He sat down on the edge of the bed with his head in his hands and stared at the floor. "You and your fuck-ing Blue Danube!" he muttered and got up to put on his briefs.

"You're not going to leave me this way, are you?" she wailed. "Darling, I *want* you!"

"Tough!" he said brusquely, pulling on his pants. "I've got other things to do."

He stomped out of the room and Kei lay on the bed awhile with her hands over her face. When she heard the back door open and close, she drew them down slowly and clasped them together exultantly on her chest. Then she got up and, bareass naked, waltzed around the room, singing under her breath, "Da dum-dum de DAH! Bum-BUMP, bum-bump!"

Suddenly she stopped dancing. There was a spot of blood on the carpet between her feet.

A beak rapped on the window pane. Outside, the ledge was crowded with a moving mass of glossy black heads looking in at her.

"Where's Marthe?" Kei asked when Garnett came in from the folly at noon, his cheeks flushed with the cold. "She's laid a cold lunch out in the dining room, but I can't find her or Hilaire anywhere, and their extension in the garage doesn't answer."

Garnett looked tired. He hung his jacket in the hall closet and said, "You know their daughter's about to have a baby. I told them you'd given them permission to go visit her for a week or two."

Kei boiled over and snapped, "You know I can't run this house alone!" before remembering her precarious position. "Sorry," she said immediately. "I didn't sleep very well last night, worrying about

Simon and Eagle." She chewed her lip, looking to see if he was going to accept her apology.

He seemed to be still too absorbed in what he'd been doing out in the folly to give her temper his full attention. "Don't get yourself in an uproar. What else have you got to do but fix the meals and housekeep? You're a big, strong woman. You ought to be able to handle that without sniveling." He rubbed his hands together to warm them after the walk from the folly. "By the way, I fired Guillaume yesterday."

Kei stifled the sharp words that came to her lips and said in a reasonable tone, "Who's going to feed the animals, then, and . . . "

"One of my men," Garnett answered. "You needn't be afraid of him, I've told him to keep out of your way." He led the way into the dining room. "I don't want anyone around here interfering with me or stirring up people in the village."

There was nothing she could do about it. Now she was cut off, except for the telephone, and the catch there was that most of the people in Fay—except for Tommy and Elaine, who were gone—might be in league with the Satanic cult. She hadn't talked to Marthe about Garnett's true status because the housekeeper had been so besotted with him and would have been almost impossible to convince Marthe that her darling Garnett wasn't all that he appeared to be. Marthe assumed that because Garnett looked like her dead nephew, he possessed the same virtues. The nephew had been a tall, gawky young man with a potato nose, and how Marthe had seen any likeness in Garnett to that acne-ridden string bean was an enigma. Kei had taken Simon's word for it that Garnett reminded him of a fellow he'd known at school. But he really did share a remarkable similarity of physique and features with her son Stephen.

Or did he simply appear to an onlooker the way that the person wanted him to look, assuming a resemblance to a friend or someone much loved? It would be the quickest avenue to anyone's heart and confidence, and that would serve Garnett's dark purposes well. In any case, whatever he seemed on the surface, she knew what lay beneath.

They sat down alone to cold lobster, vinaigrette vegetables, and Brie with bib lettuce, laid out on teal blue hexagonal plates. If Garnett expected this kind of meal again, now that Marthe was gone, he was going to be sadly disapointed, Kei thought. She loathed cooking. Oh, once in awile when she wanted to get creative, it was all right, but twenty-some years of getting three meals on the table whether she felt like it or not had petered out the charm and challenge of the cuisine. Simon was a better cook than she was at her best. He chose the wines too, since distinguishing white from red and rosé was about the range of her talent. Growing up in the Midwest, where you had to drive sixty miles to find a restaurant that didn't serve up thousand-island dressing on chopped lettuce freckled with brown spots had not proved to be a finishing school for gourmets.

She was too nervous to eat and pushed her food around her plate as an imitation. If Garnett wanted to try bed again after lunch, this was her last meal.

She'd spent the time he'd been at the folly in putting her affairs in order as well as she could without an attorney present. Simon would need to know where she kept her safety deposit box key, her insurance papers, her will and all that legal claptrap after she was dead, so she'd made lists and gotten everything in order. It had helped keep her mind off the pending disaster.

Then she'd sat down at the desk in Simon's study and prepared to make peace with her Maker. Only she didn't know how to go about it. She didn't even have a nodding acquaintance with Him, who—if He existed at all—seemed to be too preoccupied with more momentous problems than to have time for the mere matter of her approaching demise.

Listening to the birds chattering in the aviary and staring across at the window, which was festooned with quarreling ravens, she envied people who had faith in a traditional deity. She'd never been able to buy the idea that some bearded, elephantine man on a cloud was looking after the afairs of little Kei. Simon's childhood notion that God was a giant horse appealed to her more. Some people felt that God was something inside, a part of oneself. In which case, Kei said to herself, How do you do, and Where have you been all this time while everything's been going to hell in a handbasket? Moreover, she ruminated, if I get confused trying to figure out which corner to stand on to catch a bus, no part of me should have anything to do with running the universe: if I *do*, that explains what a fine mess everything's in! All she knew for certain was that she'd tried to be the best person she could all her life, and if that wasn't enough, it was too late now.

She'd gone into the salon to have a drink, unable to summon up even a prayer with any conviction. What would happen, would happen. She just wished she knew *when*.

A feeling of suspense still gnawed at her, so she looked over at Garnett and asked, "Do you have any plans for after lunch?"

"I'm not finished with what I'm doing," he said, and Kei's heart gave a bump. She'd had a reprieve, however brief! He wiped his mouth and pushed his plate away. "Marthe leave any dessert?"

"There's a key lime pie on the table, I'll get it," Just as she rose, the phone rang.

Garnett got up and with a jerk of his head indicated that she should answer it while he went into the kitchen to get the pie.

"You *can't* come home now, you just can't!" she said sharply into the mouthpiece, panicking at hearing that Simon was taking a plane in a few hours. "Well, because you're in no condition to! You've just had an eye operation and you should still be in traction, what in the world are you thinking of?"

The birds in the aviary behind her were squawking, stirred up by the loudness of her voice. She swung around to look at them, unavailingly told them to hush, and turned back to the desk.

Simon was adamant. Both worried about the other, they were at each other yelling by now. He could be sick quite as effectively at home as in Tokyo, he said crossly, and he'd bribed a doctor into coming on the plane with him, as well as a nurse.

"They'll keep me blotto with painkillers," he said, lighting a cigarette and smoking it viciously. "They're making me wear a brace for my back, although I don't much fancy swanning around in public looking like a wooden soldier. What's the matter with you, don't you want to see me? What's going on there?"

Kei searched the desk drawer for the pack of cigarettes Simon usually had around, found it, and lit one. "I can handle things," she said, spitting out a column of smoke.

"Oho, I've heard *that* song before!" Simon said, annoyedly pressing down a strip of adhesive tape that had worked loose along the edge of the bandage over his eye. "You put off telling me about problems until they explode in your face, just because you think you have to 'handle things'. Would you do me the kindness to remember that you're not alone anymore, that we're suppose to share the burdens, now that we're married?" He tapped his cigarette irritably on the edge of the bedtable ashtray.

Kei studied the growing ash on her cigarette and wondered if now was the time to come clean with him. No, he'd be even more bullheaded about returning home if she did. "Just this once, please do as I ask and stay there," she said. "Eagle's still in a coma, so you can't do him any good. I'll take care of Garnett."

"Then let me speak to Marthe. If she agrees that everything's under control, I'll stay put."

"She's . . . she's not here."

"Well, if she's in her apartment, transfer this call there, would you?"

"She's not there, either. I . . . her daughter's having the baby, and she's gone to visit."

"Damn and blast!" Now he knew that something was not right. "No use our rabbiting on like this, then. I'm coming home!" He told her what time he'd be leaving, what flight he'd be on, his time of arrival, shouted, "I love you!" and hung up before she could argue further.

Stunned that she'd been unable to stop him, Kei held the receiver to her ear as if, although the connection was broken, she might still do something to dissuade him. There was a click on the line, and when she said, "Operator? Operator?," there was no answer. Garnett had been listening on the kitchen extension. Now he knew precisely when Simon would be at his mercy.

Kei stubbed out her cigarette, wrote down the numbers Simon had given her, and chucked the pen onto the desk, feeling helpless. What could she do to stop Simon from returning to certain death? Absolutely nothing! Even the doctors couldn't help Eagle. All they could do was wait and hope that his rugged constitution would pull him through. The twins were already under Garnett's sway. As for herself, she was resigned to the inevitable, but it made her furiously angry that racking her brains had produced no solutions for the people she loved. Events were rumbling onward like a huge machine of war, and she was powerless. However, there was one thing she could do—a small thing, but *something*. Even the most trivial gesture was better than flopping around and whimpering until the axe fell.

"Thought I ought to tell you," Garnett said from

the doorway, "I just called the business office and told them to cut off the phones, that the family was going on vacation. No more calls in or out." He smiled slyly and left for the folly.

Now, with Marthe and Hilaire gone, the phones cut off, and the guardians set at the gate, she was stranded. Alone with the twins and Garnett. Waiting.

Garnett worked ointment into the crumbling bones and shreds of dry flesh clinging to Sélène's forearms and slowly moved on to the hand, where the work was especially delicate and hazardous. Only brittle tendons held the small bones together. Three fingers were missing, lost in the destruction of the grotto. Sélène would be angry when she awoke to find them gone.

He recited aloud a formula, reading from a foxed, curling page of manuscript laid on the table he'd brought up on the stage. He was almost through. The rest of the remains were already coated with pungent dark oil that had taken careful weeks to prepare.

He wiped his hands on a cloth and put it aside to be burned with the rest of the oil afterwards. All of the magic infused in the oil had to be directed into Sélène, so none could be left that would drain away the potency of the spell. Now the only thing left to do for today was to lay hands on the body and send his own power into it to prevent further deterioration of the skeletal structure. Restoration of the bones themselves would come later, followed by the reconstruction of the network of veins, the muscles, the flesh, and all of the other parts of the body. The process would take months.

Putting his hands on the yellowed, porous hipbones, he concentrated, summoning up a surge of power that flowed down through his arms and tingled at his fingertips like static electricity as it passed through them. The effort of will made his muscles tremble and reddened his face.

After a few minutes, he relaxed with a sigh. Then he reclothed the mummy and carried it, frozen in its bent position, back to the chair behind the paneling. He placed her in it and arranged the folds of her dress about her. This was to be his partner in power when he completed the revivifying operations. He lightly kissed a cheekbone protruding through a webbing of papery skin and pressed the button that would hide her away.

Tired but satisfied that he'd done a meticulous job with the incantation and anointment, he put the table back and gathered up his paraphernalia, secreting some of it in a safe concealed in the wall in back of Gunther and gathering up the rest to put in the incinerator by the garage. The ritual had taken longer than he'd planned. It was already three thirty.

As he locked the door of the folly behind him and scrunched through a thin pebbled shell of sleet covering the path, Kei was watching him from the salon, standing back from the window. Above its companions jostling on the ledge, a raven beat its wings against the pane while trying to keep its balance on the wooden cross frame, and one claw scraped against the glass.

Garnett closed the back door behind him and

headed for the bar. He looked a little pale, Kei thought.

"Where are you going?" he asked at seeing her in outdoor clothing, and opened a new bottle of Simon's armagnac.

"To visit Eagle."

"Any change in his condition?" He splashed the liquor in a glass of Waterford crystal.

"No, but some member of the family ought to look in on him daily," she said. Seeing the indentations at the corners of his mouth deepen and supposing that he was about to refuse her permission to leave, she added, "The doctors will think it's very odd if no one shows up after I called and asked if he could have visitors." Surreptitiously, she ran a hand over the outside of her purse to be sure that her passport wasn't showing a betraying rectangle through the smooth leather.

"No, *I'll* go," he said and gulped down his drink. He set the glass down decisively on the bar. I'll be the token visitor. The twins are due back now, and I don't think it would be wise to let you go to the clinic alone. I'm not taking any chances on your not coming back."

"Don't you trust me?"

He laughed. "Of course not! I don't trust anybody."

Frustrated, she threw her purse down on an easy chair and began pulling off her gloves. "Well, while you're gone, could I at least take a walk around the estate? I need some fresh air after being cooped up in here so long." She took off the bushy fur hat she'd been wearing with her sable coat and fluffed up her hair.

"Go ahead, as long as you stay out in back and don't go past the stone wall in back of the folly. The ravens will leave you alone if you don't stray farther than that.' He went into the foyer and she followed him as he talked. "While I'm gone, I'll set some guardians on the front gate, just in case."

"Guardians?"

"Take a look and see for yourself." He went out the door and got in the car as she held the door. She looked at the gray, lichen-spangled stone pillars of the gateway.

On either side of the opened grillwork gate, columns of air shimmered like silvery gelatin. Although she could see everything around them perfectly well, when she looked directly at them, her vision blurred and she heard a buzzing in her ears like faint radio static.

Garnett got in the jeep, passed over the little bridge that spanned the moat, and went through the gate onto the highway. When he was gone, Kei walked across the gravel to get a closer look. The static in her ears grew louder.

When she was within ten feet of the columns, her vision cleared and she saw transparent milky forms standing like sentinels before the exit, leathery bat wings folded down along their sides. Their gargoyle heads had no eye openings, but through white membranes covering the sockets red pupils glowed like rubies in the sunlight. They looked slippery and soapy, vaguely formed, like something unborn. Kei took another few steps toward them, and the gargoyle mouths opened in a hiss. Reptilian tails uncoiled from around their clawed feet, and their wings began pulsing as if about to open.

She stepped back and hurried toward the house. Whether or not the guardians were some hypnotic image or solid substance, she didn't want to test them and provoke an attack. She shuddered. If they were creatures of Garnett's mind, she'd had a glimpse of what ghoulish visions peopled it.

She had her hand on the doorknob when a red car came through the gate and drew up before the door. The twins jumped out and slammed the doors behind them. Mrs. Kidwell felt chatty, and Kei surprised herself by carrying on a polite, inconsequential conversation without giving any hint of her actual state of mind. The twins sped inside and up the stairs to catch their favorite TV programs while she and Mrs. Kidwell discussed the weather, the scandalous cost of children's shoes, and the nuisance of having to drive into Orléans to shop, now that the village market was limited to seasonal local produce consisting mostly of root vegetables. Kei looked over the car hood at the gateway, where the silvery columns still wavered, and then glanced down at her watch. She had a job to do that would take an unpredictable amount of time, and Garnett wouldn't be gone forever. Accustomed to having to cut off longwinded employees at the press, she skillfully shut Mrs. Kidwell's flood of conversation down to a trickle.

"Two days to Thanksgiving. Got your turkey yet?" Mrs. Kidwell asked, like any normal American expatriate housewife, before driving off. Kei smiled grimly.

The car neither paused nor slowed down as it went by the guardians. Either Mrs. Kidwell couldn't see them because they were an illusion, or she was not alarmed because, like her husband, she was a member of the Satanic cult.

The TV was blaring upstairs, and the sound of canned laughter drifted down the stairwell. Kei went out to the kitchen, where she had a ragôut on a low flame. The room smelled mouth-wateringly of onions and herbs. In a drawer where household tools were kept, she found a glass cutter, putty, and some small steel triangles and put them in the pocket of her fur coat.

Garnett had said she'd be safe out back if she didn't go beyond the stone wall behind the folly, where the vineyard sloped down toward the road. The ravens, she could see from the window, had withdrawn to form a semi-circle at the limits he'd set and seemed quiet.

Doubting she could trust him about anything, Kei ventured out, flinching at every sudden movement in the landscape as she started toward the meadow, where blue shadows were lengthening across the paper-thin sheet of sleet. If she hadn't been compelled to do the job at hand, she wouldn't have had the nerve to face the ravens

Now that Garnett would find out that she wasn't carrying the child he wanted, her time on earth was cut down to only a few hours, but being clawed and slashed by a horde of birds was a frightening idea just the same, and she was scared stiff that he might catch her before she broke into the folly. If she had the opportunity, she could reputty the window and hope that he wouldn't discover her entry for awhile, but that was really beyond her hope. What he'd do to her afterwards didn't bear thinking about. She'd worry about that tomorrow. If there was a tomorrow. What she had to do now was not for herself, but for Simon and the twins. For everybody.

Reaching the folly, she went around the porch until she came to the windows at the back, where she couldn't be seen from the house. She took out the glass cutter, gritted her teeth, and ran the cutting wheel down the side of a window pane, close to the wood. When she'd done all four sides, she worked the putty into a ball between her fingers and stuck it on the middle of the pane like a handle before giving the glass a sharp, quick rap. It fell forward toward the room, but she had it by the putty and worked it around until she could take it out and put it down on the porch floor. That allowed her to reach inside and open the window. She was proud of herself for doing the job so swiftly and decisively, particularly since she had to close her eyes and make several timorous jabs before she could even puncture a balloon and had thought than smacking out a window pane would be more that she could manage. It had been easier than she'd expected, and the time factor hadn't allowed any internal debate about the matter.

Her sable coat was bulky, so she dropped it on the porch before climbing in the window.

The place still smelled of those nauseating candles, although no evidence of last night's ritual remained, except for a spot or two of candle wax on a bookcase top. The waning light outside made the inside somewhat dim, but she had plenty of light to find what she was looking for. The colors of the balloons and furnishings were still bright and circus-y, praise be! A spooky atmosphere, added to the fear that already made every nerve end as sensitive as an open sore, would have made it harder to go through with this.

She stood in the middle of the room, looking about her, then went to the stage and pulled the cord that opened the curtains. Pierrot and Pierrette stood upstage, wearing pirate costumes and smiling cheery painted smiles. Their arms stretched out toward her invitingly.

During the morning, while Garnett was at work in the summer house, Kei had been putting two and two together. She knew he had Sélène's body concealed somewhere, and before she herself was murdered, Kei meant to see that the body of the old witch was destroyed. Without Sélène, the keystone of the Satanic cult would be gone, and the cult's influence would be undermined. The Satanists had spread enough evil about the coutryside, mutilating, killing, and tainting everything within their reach. Kei refused to die without taking Sélène with her.

While Garnett had been working in the folly, she'd looked through all of the rooms on the third storey of the château, expecting momentarily to find the gruesome relic under a drop cloth or shoved into a corner, but she'd found nothing but art objects, paintings, the cistern, and the usual castoffs of a household. She'd been on the brink of a shriek the whole time, but here in the folly she knew the setting. This was the most logical place for the body to be, where Garnett could check on it every day as a matter of course.

When the cult had met here last night, she could see nothing of Sélène or any object that suggested the outline of a corpse. She suspected that the thing she'd seen swaying and lurching above the shoulders of the four black robes had been the mummy, wired together and fastened in the gilded peacock chair. It had disappeared by the time she looked inside, and the only place that she hadn't been able to see was the stage. It had to be here somewhere.

A screech from outside startled her, and perspiration broke out on her forehead, but after a moment she realized it had only been one of the ravens lurking out beyond the grove. Still, if Garnett surprised her, she had nothing to defend herself with. She looked around the desks and tables in the room, hoping to find some kind of weapon, and her eye fell on a hammer on a small tool bench. Picking it up, she went onto the stage and opened the costume box, which was large enough to stuff a body into. It held nothing but clothing and accessories for dressing up. Other than that, there were only Pierrot and Pierrette. Could one of them be Sélène, covered over cleverly with plastic?

Reluctantly, hardly wanting to touch them if something ghastly was underneath their colorful costumes and painted skin, she examined them, working their joints back and forth to be sure nothing was hidden there. What was that rhythmic rushing sound? She stopped, rooted to the floor, and then laughed weakly. It was the sound of her own breathing, loud in the silent room. Well, Pierrette and Pierrot were innocent, simply department store manikins. Now what?

In a horror film, about now the hero would be rapping the walls to see if any of them was hollow, she thought. Not that she'd know the difference between the sound of a hollow wall and an ordinary one. Weren't they *all* hollow, sort of? Nonetheless, being a member of the movie generation, she tapped her way along a side wall of the stage. The sound was uniform, whatever that signified.

And what if something or someone tapped back?, she asked herself. She'd go right through the ceiling. But there was no point in scaring herself more than she was already. She tapped the wall at the rear of the stage. It went *thonk!* So that's what a hollow wall sounded like! But what did you do if you couldn't get into it? There was no seam, no hinge, nothing that she could find.

She continued tapping along toward the middle of the rear wall when she noted a slight difference in the echo. Minute, barely perceptible, but there. And by her hand was a curlicue that ended in a circle of gold paint just like the hundeds of circles at the terminals of curlicues all over the wall—except that this one was slightly raised. An obvious button, if you knew where it was.

She pressed it. The panel slid back.

There she was, hunched over a crystal ball on a table. Not so gruesome after all. No more so than the manikins, in her elaborate costume and crown.

But this was the witch who had tortured living victims on the meadow centuries ago, who had caused God knew how many deaths then and the Devil only knew how many more since. For this little figure, smaller than a fullgrown woman of this century, Garnett would kill Simon and anyone else who got in his way! For this the whole family was threatened, and for this she herself would die, Kei thought.

She reached out and savagely ripped the mask from Sélène's face. Screamed as the motion wrenched off the head. Leaped back as the skull bounced by her feet and spun around before shuddering to a stop, rocking back and forth, its empty sockets staring up blackly as its skeletal jaws clicked.

Kei was on the floor, pounding the hammer into the grinning teeth before she was aware of what she was doing. Splinters of bone skidded across the stage floor. Her rage grew as she hammered and hammered at the skull, cursing, until it was a crumbled heap of fragments and shards. Then she got up and, hardly aware of the pain in her left arm, tore the cloak from the mummy, grabbed it by the front of its dress, and swung the body down to the floor, systematically reducing it to rubble.

"*That's* for Simon, and *that's* for Dirk, and *that's* for Gino," she said as her arm rose and fell again and again, "and that's for *me!,*" and the list of names went on and on. Covered with perspiration, with the banging of the hammer filling her ears, she worked on until every last bone was shattered.

Panting, eyes closed, she sat back on her heels when it was done. She ran her fingers through the wet strings of her hair and wiped her cheeks.

As she sat there exhausted, her chest heaving, she suddenly became aware that she was not alone.

Garnett towered over her.

CHAPTER SEVENTEEN

Sélène was gone! The only thing he loved was gone forever, never to be by his side! Everything that he had worked for, dreamed of, since childhood lay at his feet in a crumble of yellow dust and bone fragments.

Garnett threw back his head, and a howl of despair and unbearable loneliness tore from his throat, thundering to a bellow that shook the foundations of the folly. The walls swelled outward, quaking, and a seam ripped loose at a corner of the ceiling as the manikins crashed on their backs, crushing their hollow heads. The blast of sound hit Kei like a plank, punctured an eardrum and deafened her before she collapsed backward, senseless.

Gunther toppled on his side as desks, cushions, and books flew up from their places and stormed about the room in the whirlwind of Garnett's rage. The aquarium shattered in a splash of glass splinters. The windows quivered, rattled with increasing intensity, and burst out, driving blades of glass into the porch floor.

The cry wavered on the air and died away. Objects

clattered and bumped to the floor. Glass tinkled along the trembling wooden bookshelves.

In the quiet that followed, water dripped from a bookcase onto the upturned belly of the carousel horse and insulation fibers trickled from the rent at the top of the wall. The balloons swung slowly like bright, limp rags from the ceiling.

Garnett doubled over and sank to his knees in front of Kei. He felt empty, gutted like a fish. Scooping up a handful of powdered bone, he let it sift through his fingers, then stared at the hollow of his palm. Nothing, nothing was left.

Kei lay slanted diagonally before his knees, the hammer on her open hand. A thread of blood seeped from her ear into her hair.

In spite of himself, he'd felt drawn to Kei's vivacity and contrariness. Even under his thrall, she'd managed to keep a part of herself unreachable and unconquerable, nettling him and fascinating him as none of those fawning, eager lovers had. That unpredictable portion of her had evaded his grasp and had been his and Sélène's undoing. All by herself, Kei had smashed his dreams to bits.

He scratched at a tickling on his cheek and then glared at the wetness on his fingers. Was that a tear? An ordinary, mortal tear?!

Furious at seeing this evidence of the human side of his nature, Garnett leaned forward. He clenched his hands together and raised them over his head like a club, ready to crush Kei's face to a pulp. Then he paused, lowered his arms, and unclasped his hands.

She was unconscious. If he killed her now, she'd die without pain. It would be more gratifying to let her live awhile longer, stalking her like a running rabbit, driving her into a corner. Then he could kill her slowly, drawing out her suffering to wring every drop of agony out of her while she still had a breath left in her. Eventually that private place she'd locked up so tightly would burst its hinges, and his conquest of her would be complete. The baby was of no further use to him, and Sélène would have approved of this final vengeance.

And as for Simon . . .

Kei came to as Garnett dumped her on the bed in her room. She opened her eyes, shut them again, and flattened herself on the fur coverlet, expecting a blow that didn't fall. Instead, he stood there silently, letting the tension grow as she waited for her punishment. The only sound in the room was the scrabbling of the ravens on the window ledge.

After a breathless moment, he sat down beside her and rolled her over to face him. Without speaking, he stroked back the hair from her forehead, took his handkerchief out, moistened it with spit, and began wiping away the blood by her ear while he spoke softly. "I'm not going to kill you now, my love," he said as she turned her head to hear him better, "I'll choose my own time. You won't know when it's going to happen. It could be in the next hour, it could be in a week, I'll give you plenty of time to think about it.

Still working on her deaf ear, he continued, using the patient, measured tone of a loving father explaining to his child. "Now, let's review your situation. The phones are out and everyone's gone, except for the twins and Marc out at the stables. I wouldn't go near him, if I were you. He doesn't have a gun out there, but he does have an axe, and he's been told to use it if you stray too far. Now, that's a nasty way to die, so you don't want that."

He put his handkerchief back in his pocket and stroked her hair again.

"Then there are my friends, the ravens. They're all out back, guarding the perimeter there. There are thousands of them now, waiting in a ring. They'd tear you to shreds if you tried to pass them, and that would be a pity."

He took the clamp off the bandage on her left arm and retightened the gauze. "But the very worst are the guardians out by the gate. I once saw what they did to a man." He shook his head and clicked his tongue as he refastened the clamp. "I'd hate to have that happen to you. All that lovely skin." He brushed her cheek softly with the back of his hand. "Besides, I want you all to myself."

He stood up and shoved his hands into his pockets. "So you see," he said in a travesty of sympathy, "there's no way for you to escape. Oh, yes . . . " He drew a key chain from his pocket and dangled it before her eyes. "I have the keys to both cars."

He turned before going out the door. "No one's coming to save you, dearest Kei. Simon won't be coming back." He looked at her with the boyish, sweet-natured smile that had dazzled her so short a time ago. "Please accept my condolences."

Kei lay on the bed after he left, listening to his footsteps creaking down the hall. Was Simon already dead? If he were, wouldn't she know it? She got up and went to the bathroom, opened the medicine cabinet, took out the Placidyls the doctor had given her, and shook them out onto her palm. If Garnett was going to kill her, it would probably be a long, drawn-out execution, with ample torture to satisfy his longing for vengeance. The Placidyls had liquid cores. She emptied out a small plastic tube of Valium tablets, sliced the Placidyls open, and let the liquid drip into the tube. Waiting for the outer portions on the pills to dissolve in her stomach would give Garnett too much time to inflict pain on her. She capped the tube and slipped it into her bra.

Back in her bedroom, she could hear some kind of sound coming from the downstairs hallway. She couldn't hear it clearly with only one operative ear, so she went out into the corridor and looked down through the window onto the parking area in front of the house.

A lowslung black car stood gleaming by the front door, pulled up in front of the jeep.

As she watched, she saw the top of Garnett's head and then the top of another—this one with a bald spot—pass below her eyes.

It was Tommy! Her heart leaped as she recognized the configuration of the bald patch that makeup men had artfully concealed with hairpieces during his last few films.

The tall, deeply tanned man walked around the car to the driver's side and stood leaning against it with muscular arms stretched across the low top while he talked to Garnett. Kei tried to catch his eye by waving, but he didn't look up, and she was afraid of endangering him, too, by shouting out the window. Garnett would kill him on the spot!

Her heart plummeted.

"Yes, well, I thought I'd better come over and investigate when I couldn't get through on the phone," Tommy said. He crooked an elbow and thoughtfully scratched the stubble along a deep crease running from his cheekbone to his jaw.

He didn't like this Garnett Tobol, not even though his resemblance to Eagle was striking. Tommy's witch's eye detected a muddy aura hazing out around the fellow's head. If he could see beneath the sweater, he'd wager there'd be a fine iron chain hidden there. So the cult had sprung up again, despite the battle they'd had this summer!

"On vacation, eh?" Vacation, my arse!, he thought. Kei had found out what this Garnett fellow really was and made tracks for Missy's. Wise move, too. She'd never leave while Eagle was in hospital, not unless circumstances were extraordinary. "Well, if she calls, tell her Eagle's still in the coma." Something told him it was better not to let the tutor know that Eagle had taken a miraculous turn for the better. He was on the mend, and soon would be able to tell them what had happened. You can't keep a good man down. Good genes always tell.

He got in the car and started off over the bridge. A sound of static in his ears as he passed through the gates alerted him to the fact that something was not quite right, but he turned onto the highway and started for home.

The twins had given up scouring the house for Marthe, gotten the ragôut off the stove, and helped themselves to the drying stew.

"Want some?" Gino asked, hearing Garnett come in. "It's yummy!" He took one last spoonful before generously shoving the pot toward him, not taking his eyes from his plate.

"Give me a spoon," Garnett said wearily, and Gino handed him one without looking up.

Garnett ate directly from the pot, ravenously bolting down mouthfuls of scarcely chewed food and taking huge gulps of milk. His energy was dangerously depleted. After eating, he'd go up and use Kei to get back some of the strength that had been drained away. If she started singing The Blue Danube, he'd tear out a handful of her hair! The bitch was the first person who'd made him wilt in mid-screw, and he brooded while the strains of the waltz filtered through his thoughts.

"You look funny. What's the matter with you?" asked Dirk, who had been staring at him while he'd carried on his interior monologue. "I thought your hair was white, like Grandad's, and now it's sort of black. Are you dyeing your hair?"

Garnett looked down at his arms and saw the fringes of dark hair that showed his disguise was wearing off. Dirk had seen him this way numberless times, but only when the twins were under his spell. Garnett thought about renewing his likeness to Simon for the twins' benefit but decided it wouldn't be worth the expenditure of force. "Yeah, I'm using Grecian Formula. Thought I'd like a change," he said.

He'd hustle the twins up their room for more TV and then they'd go to bed, and what he looked like wouldn't matter. He wasn't going to stay around much longer. Once Kei was dead, this place wouldn't hold him, with Sélène gone. Now that his hope of finding a partner was blasted, he'd be alone forever. Tears prickled at the corners of his eyes. He blinked and cleared his throat.

This place was a lost cause. Maybe he'd go to India and spend some time with worshipers of Kali, whose devotion to blood and death made him feel comfortable. Then he'd look for another Satanic cult that needed a Master.

All that time and effort had been wasted on the twins, whose training would be broken off before it had hardly gotten started. The secret information stored in their heads would have to be erased so that it couldn't leak out, betraying the local cult, after he'd left and his influence over them had waned.

Summoning up energy from his tired body, he reached out and pressed a hand on Dirk's head, cleaning out every memory of what the child had seen and learned with him. He did the same to Gino and sat back, letting a sense of failure and desolation flow over him.

The twins looked puzzled. "What did you do that for?" Gino asked, but Garnett simply shook his head and told them to run along upstairs, that if they stayed in their room, they could watch TV until late. Pleased, they took their plates and silverware to the sink and went off, chatting in their private language about how weird Garnett was getting lately.

CHAPTER EIGHTEEN

Simon was in his hospital room, already dressed for the flight home. Without unfolding them, he held his reading glasses up to his good eye and looked through one lens at his timetable. Good! He'd ordered the taxi to arrive just far enough in advance—an hour ahead—so that he wouldn't have to lounge about the airport and listen to Dr. Yamashita, the generalist who was accompanying him, grizzle about how he shouldn't be attempting the trip home. Simon had made the trip out to the airport seven or eight times in the past few years and knew precisely how close he could shave it.

He was also convinced that he could have made it by himself from Tokyo to Paris without serious trouble, let alone doped the way he was. The drugs made him feel as if he were floating a few inches above the floor. He knew the limits of his own stamina better than the doctor did, who seemed to regard him as a fragile old person. The doctor might be a wizard medical practitioner, but Simon thought him rather dim. Christ, just a couple of months ago, his horse had fallen on him and pinned him down by the knee, but he'd walked away from that with only a slight limp that was gone in a day or two! And, once the staff had straightened out his back so he could walk upright again, he could have recovered from the accident by himself, without babying himself in a hospital bed. The eye, however, was another proposition. He needed the painkillers for that, and having Nurse Ozawa along to change the dressings so they wouldn't stick was a welcome addition to the trip.

He patted his jacket pocket to see that the three tickets were there and walked toward the bathroom to check the drape of his jacket over the brace. He seemed to be on a conveyor belt going in the wrong direction. His legs were going back and forth, but it was taking an unconscionably long time for them to get him anywhere. Finally he reached the bathroom and looked in the mirror. There was a faint ridge under his shoulder blades but otherwise the light aluminum brace was invisible under his clothing.

His head bandage had been reduced to a swathe that covered his bad eye and the flattened plastic bubble that protected it. He'd made enough noise to make the specialist omit the gauze on the top of his head, just to shut him up. Simon didn't fancy getting on the plane looking like Claude Rains in *The Invisible Man* and frightening little children.

It was a surprise to see the doctor and nurse in civilian clothes when they came in to take him to the taxi. They looked smaller somehow when not in hospital gear, one of them weedy and the other doll-like. Great Scott, Simon thought, if I have an attack of the vapors and fall on them, I'll squash them like a couple of popped blueberries! For the first time, he wished he had a Western-style doctor, in case he needed to do any leaning along the way.

There was a bit of a row about using a wheelchair to get to the taxi, but since it was hospital regulations, Simon sat down and let them wheel him out to the curb, feeling like a bloody fool, after saying goodbye to Mr. Tanaka and the nurse.

Sitting on top of the waiting cab was a raven with one white eye. Simon drew back instinctively, and Dr. Yamashita rushed out, screaming shrilly and waving his arms. The raven looked at the doctor contemptuously as he ran around shrieking and banging on the car. The driver craned his neck out the window, wondering if he had an escaped psychiatric patient on his hands. Finally the bird strutted lazily across the car's top and took off, soaring up and beyond the buildings across the way.

CHAPTER NINETEEN

Kei knelt with her elbows on the sill, watching her last hope drive away. Limp, too exhausted to cry, she felt overwhelmed by a desire to give up, to let Garnett do what he wished with her. It would be so sweet to die, to stop thinking, to drift into nothingness! There was nothing she could do to stop the tidal wave of evil surging toward the house. If Simon wasn't dead already, he was on his way home to be slaughtered. Eagle was on the brink of death. Only the twins would be untouched, as long as Garnett was training them to be Masters, but soon he'd turn them into monsters like himself.

She touched the tube of Placidyl in her bra. She could get it over with right now, painlessly. But there was still an outside chance that she could get the twins out from the house to safety, where they'd be beyond Garnett's influence. The gears in her mind began to mesh again.

Two cars had passed by the sentinels at the gate without being stopped, perhaps because the guardians had been set there for her alone. They might let the twins slip through unharmed. It was an enormous risk, but they'd be better off dead than growing up like Garnett. They were not her own children, they were Chris's. She had no right to make such a fateful decision for them, but what alternative did she have?

If she could distract Garnett long enough for them to run through the gate, they might run to a haven while she kept him preoccupied. After that, she could worry about Simon and herself, who had less chance of survival.

She heard Garnett close the front door and click over the tiling down in the foyer. Was he heading for the stairway, to come and get her? The footsteps receded. She went back into her room and looked down onto the back bridge over the heads of ravens roosting on the ledge.

Garnett was on the bridge, leaning on the railing over the thin scum of ice on the moat, looking out toward the folly and the scowling band of ravens drawn up in ranks behind it. The sun had left a lavender afterglow, and he wasn't wearing a jacket. Soon the cold would snap him out of his reverie and send him back inside.

She ran down to the twins' room. As they looked up in surprise from the television, she put her finger on her lips and frantically motioned them toward her with her bandaged arm. Stunned by the urgency in her face, they froze in their places, so she ran over and yanked them to their feet.

"Don't say a word. Just listen," she said, grabbing each by a hand and hurrying them toward the door.

"But . . . " Dirk began. She shushed him severely

and rushed them down the hallway to her room, pushed them inside, and closed the door behind her.

"I'll explain later," she whispered, going to the bureau for a couple of Simon's heavy sweaters, "but you've just *got* to be good and do exactly what I say." She began wrestling the sweaters over their heads. "You're in terrible danger here," she said, breathing hard, working their arms into the armholes. She had to frighten them into strict obedience, so she pulled no punches. "Garnett's gone crazy, and you've got to get out of the house before he hurts you." She rolled up the sleeves of the sweaters to leave their hands free.

The twins' eyes widened, and Dirk began to whimper. "Stop that!" she commanded. "You've got to be little men about this, real grownups. I want you to get down the kitchen stairway just as fast as you can. But you've got to be quiet, or he'll hear you, and then I don't know what he'll do to you. You understand?"

The twins nodded, too scared to answer or to notice that the bottoms of the sweaters hung down to their calves.

"When you do that, head for the gate. Now, you have to remember one thing, and don't ask why, just *do* it! You've got to run through the gate *with your eyes closed*." She held Gino by the arms and looked earnestly into his eyes. "No matter what, you're not to open them again until you're outside on the road. Promise me?"

They nodded again, their eyes watering as they grasped the seriousness of the situation.

"Once you're on the road, you tear toward the

village to Mrs. Van Dreuten's house—you know which one, the first one on the first corner—and tell her you're to stay until I come.'' Even if Peggy turned out to be a secret member of the cult, she wouldn't hurt little children, Kei felt sure.

She got up and looked out the window. Below, Garnett was clapping his arms about himself to get warm. Soon he'd be in the foyer again.

The children stood paralyzed, like wooden Indians, as she had a thought and snatched up a round crystal paperweight from the table in the window. She crossed to the door, opened it, and heard the door in the foyer below opening.

"Now, scoot!" she hissed, with a sweep of her arm. The twins tore down the hallway toward the kitchen stairs as she took off in the opposite direction toward the foyer stairway, pounding her feet noisily on the wooden flooring. At the top of the steps, she dropped the round paperweight, which bounced down ahead of her, hitting each stair with a smack until it broke in halves on the marble tiling of the downstairs hall. She had just reached the bottom when Garnett caught her by the arm. She jerked back at seeing that his hair was black and his skin was darkening. The monster was returning!

"Going someplace?" he asked affably. His voice was taking on the huskiness she'd heard at the black mass. He let her go and bent down to pick up the pieces of the paperweight.

Kei flashed a glance over his head and out the glass panel of the front door The twins were racing across the parking area toward the gate. Garnett was straightening up. The temptation to watch to see

314

whether or not they made it unscathed past the guardians was sickeningly strong, but she daren't attract his attention outdoors. She wrenched her eyes away.

"Going to brain me with this, were you?" he asked, looking at the pieces of crystal in his hand.

Let him think so! Its noise on the stairs had covered the sound of the children as they ran along the upstairs hallway. "You can't expect me not to defend myself," she said, flicking a look outside. The twins had vanished. Had they made it through the gate, or had something terrible snatched them away?

"The chase wouldn't be nearly as pleasurable if you didn't fight back," Garnett said with a grin, and set the broken crystal on the refectory table beneath the rococo mirror. Catching his reflection, he looked surprised and frowned at himself. Apparently, he hadn't realized that his energy had run so low that his disguise was wearing thin. "First, though," he said, and with a sinking feeling Kei knew what he would say next, "it's time for some bed."

"I . . . I haven't had any dinner," she said, hoping for a delay.

"You've already had your last meal," Garnett said, turning to her with a smile that sent cold trickling down her back.

"Well, could I have a drink? You can wait five minutes, can't you?"

He shrugged and let her enter the salon before him.

"It's cold in here," she said, pouring herself a scotch from a nearly empty pinchbottle. "Would you mind starting a fire? I'm freezing."

He shrugged again and went to squat before the fireplace. With her back turned to him, Kei slipped the tube out from under her sweater, poured the drug into the bottle of scotch, and secreted the tube again in her bra. Flames crackled in the hearth. "Wouldn't you like one?" she asked, turning around with her glass in her hand.

Chafing his hands before the fire, he looked up and nodded. There was only enough left in the bottle for one drink. She poured it and took it over to him.

"Bottoms up!" she said, and put her glass to her lips. Gratefully she watched him down most of his drink in one gulp as she took a small sip of hers. The drug should act in a few minutes. She'd used all the prescription the doctor had given her, but she didn't know its strength. If it wasn't a lethal dose, she hoped against hope that it would at least put him to sleep so she could get away.

"I forgot to feed the birds this morning," she said, watching closely to see if there was any change in him. "Do you mind if I do it now?"

"You're just stalling for time, but I'm in no hurry," Garnett said lazily. "Go ahead and feed the birds, but leave the door open so I can see what you're doing."

Carrying her glass with her, she went to the study and switched on the light. The birds, who had settled in for the night, sceeched at having their sleep disturbed. She left the door half open, which shielded her for the second or two it took to remove the second set of car keys from the desk drawer. If Garnett had ever been married, she thought, he would have known there would be another set.

"What are you doing?" Garnett growled, startling her.

"Setting my drink down and getting the birdseed, what do you think?"

The birds pecked desultorily at their second meal of the day, and some went back to their perches without eating and put their heads under their wings. Maybe the ravens out back were asleep. It was dark outside now, and they seemed inactive except in the sunlit hours. If she could get by them without disturbing them, she could get through the vineyard and down the hill to the road. The hired hand that Garnett had brought in to replace Guillaume wouldn't be able to see her in the dark, and the light around the stable didn't shine as far as the path.

When she came out of the study, the lights went out. In the darkness, Garnett's eyes emitted a yellow glow. Kei stood where she was, momentarily traumatized. Repulsive as his appearance was in the daylight, she could steel herself against it. But knowing that that reptilian abnormality was lurking in the darkness, waiting for her, started an involuntary shuddering along her muscles.

"I'll have to go to the fuse box," she said in a trembling voice.

Garnett's black outline uncoiled from its squatting position in front of the fire as he lay down on the floor. "Don't bother." His voice was a sleepy, rasping whisper. "I just short-circuited the system. The light was beginning to hurt my eyes."

"But I can't see in the dark!" Kei protested, hysteria rising in her voice.

"I didn't think you could, you're only human,"

he said sarcastically. "Besides, it'll add some fun to our merry little chase when you're falling over the furniture and caroming off the walls." She heard him chuckle. "I like it when you get excited, you know that." She saw the silhouette of his hands at his belt. "In the meantime, you know what I want. Come over here."

The squares of the windows were pale against the night outside, and from where she stood she could glimpse the glass panels of the doors onto the bridge through the foyer doorway. It was too soon to make a break for outdoors, and he could see in the dark. But another freakish coupling with that abnormality. . . .

"The hell I will!" she muttered and darted toward the door.

She was out and over the bridge, tearing toward the meadow. Ahead lay the black rectangle of the folly, then the menace of the ravens, and then—perhaps—freedom! Her breath raged through her throat in gasps as she ran up the path, her feet skidding and slipping on patches of ice.

Abruptly, two yellow circles of light appeared before her on the pathway. "If you don't want it by the fire," Garnett's voice rasped from the darkness, "maybe you'd prefer it in bed."

With a crash, the upstairs windows of the house banged outward and shattered glass spilled down, knifing into the moat. A suffocating gust of wind spun Kei around, caught her up, and she felt herself being swept up toward the château roof. She flailed her arms, clutching at the dark air, trying to right her balance, but the gale tumbled her over and over, sucking the breath from her lungs. She hurtled against the window frame of her room, slammed her shoulder agonizingly against the wood, and fell to the carpet. Stunned for a split second, she lay in a heap, gorging herself on blessed breaths of air. Through the open window, where the frames sagged on their hinges, she could hear Garnett nonchalantly whistling the lullaby as he sauntered down the path toward the house. He probably thought she'd passed out and was saving his energy by a leisurely stroll up to the bedroom. Painfully, she staggered to her feet and teetered back and forth a moment, holding her shoulder and feeling blood seeping through the ravelings of her sweater.

The back door opened and closed. His heels were clacking across the tiles toward the stairway. He mustn't find her here! One leg doubled under her as she started for the door, but she pulled herself up by catching at the bureau, tested her weight on the leg, and then limped into the hallway. The whistling had stopped. Which way had he gone? She made for the kitchen stairway, but when she reached the top, to her horror she heard the strains of the lullaby floating up and the sound of his feet on the creaking wooden steps. Panic-stricken, she got to the attic stairway, closed the door quietly behind her, and dragged herself up to the third floor. The lullaby drifted past the door, and she could hear his feet on the wood of the upper hallway. Now the steps were muffled by the throw rug. God, why hadn't she reversed her direction and run down the foyer steps? There was no exit here. Only rooms where he'd surely find her. The only chance was to hide in one near the stairs, wait for him to look in the other rooms—unless he found her right away—and then dash down the stairs ahead of him.

The cistern room was closest to the stairs. She stumbled through the black doorway, walked a few steps and bumped into the circular tank. A rush of water cascaded into the cistern from the pipe leading down from the roof, and she clapped a hand over her mouth, stemming a shriek of surprise. The water bubbled and hissed around the rim. She remembered that there was no furniture in this room, nothing but the verdigris-tarnished tank, but it was high enough to hide her. She felt her way around it and crouched down behind its shield, opposite the open doorway.

The door to the attic opened, and the lullaby drifted up into the dry, musty air.

CHAPTER TWENTY

At the Narita air terminal, nearly two hours by taxi from Tokyo, a dozen ravens bounced to a landing on the grass beside a runway as Simon's plane began loading. A huge flock appeared in the sky to the east, wheeled to avoid air traffic, and slanted in to settle at the end of the field. Immediately they were joined by countless others coming in from the south, and within minutes birds were drifting down like black snow.

After a moment of shock, commotion broke out in the control tower. Officials gathered in knots to confer about delaying flights while the field was cleared, but the air corridors were already crowded, and it would be a futile gesture to send out emergency vehicles and field maintenance men to try to control such an invasion. Flocks of birds were too volatile, too slippery to handle from the ground. Nevertheless, they sent out an alert signal in code over the loudspeakers, alerting personnel.

Every inch of space beyond the concrete was packed with black bodies, but only one bird broke ranks to venture onto an air strip and quickly hopped back onto the grass at scolding cries from its fellows.

Thousands of them were spreading across the grass in an incoming wave. Far too many to be dealt with effectively, management decided, but if the birds stayed where they were and were not frightened into rising in a body, scheduled departures and arrivals might be maintained.

Emergency services were directed to stand by but to keep noise and movement to a minimun to avoid disturbing the ravens. A westbound craft was due to move out in two minutes and would conflict with incoming flights if its departure was delayed. The ravens were quiet now, but the roar of revving motors or jets could provoke them into storming over the field and into the air. Sweating, a traffic controller spoke into the intercom mike at his lips, and Simon's plane began turning, preparing to move onto its designated taxiway.

Visitors and waiting passengers crowded to the observation windows, uniformed personnel hurried through the terminal at a jogtrot, and the sound level within the building escalated, while tinny voices calmly announced incoming and outgoing flights over the loudspeakers as if everything were proceeding normally.

Simon's plane trundled down the taxiway past a seething black carpet of ravens with their heads turned toward the aluminum and steel bird. Passengers tensed as they looked out the windows, and hostesses jolted down the aisles to soothe the few hysterical people who were demanding that the flight turn back. Like a well-disciplined army, the ravens

322

remained in their places on the ground, ominously quiet.

Stopping before the runway for flight backup, the 747 shook like a Doberman straining at its leash as power surged through the turbines with a screaming whine. Two or three birds flapped up in alarm but settled down again. The jet started down the runway.

As the plane lifted along the runway and climbed toward the sun, free and unmolested, relief bubbled through the men in the control tower. Cheering and laughing from released tension, they reached for cups of coffee and tea. Westbound Flight E47862 was on its way!

The plane circled the airport at low altitude, preparing to adjust into its flight pattern.

Without warning, streams of birds suddenly swarmed up from the field and drove up toward the nose of the 747. Masses of them zeroed into the turbines in a fatal kamikaze flight, and showers of feathers and blood shot back from the jets.

Obscured by the cloud of ravens, the plane faltered, hung for a moment in the sky, then fell back to earth and scattered across the field in a blast of shearing metal.

CHAPTER TWENTY ONE

Whisting through his teeth, Garnett slowly mounted the wheezing stairs and came up into the dusty-smelling blackness of the third storey. He was somewhat hampered in his search by the restrictions of his night sight, which allowed him to see only what he looked at directly, whatever the beams from his eyes fell upon, without peripheral vision. But he'd run her into a dead end, and she couldn't get away from him.

He was getting tired, felt strangely sleepy, and should renew himself. That could wait, though, until he went to Colette. He was back to his natural state now, and as his humanity faded, his repressed blood lust came forward. He hadn't killed in a long time. Too long a time. He ran his pointed tongue around his lips, picturing the exquisite excitement of seeing the terror in Kei's eyes as she died, anticipating the sweet taste of her blood in his mouth. If he killed her slowly, he could use her while she was still alive, and that would be the ultimate pleasure.

He looked first into the cistern room, but it was empty, and he passed on to the next, directing the light from his eyes behind the canvas and statuary. Every few seconds, he swept the hallway with his eyes, in case she were moving behind him. She was not in the next room, nor the next, nor the next. She couldn't have gotten by his continual inspection of the hallway. He retraced his steps and paused before the room with the tank, where the water constantly bubbled and rumbled. She might be hiding behind the tank, it was large enough for that. He entered, made a circle around the huge vat, running the twin beams of light along the floor. Not there, either.

She must have slipped past him somehow when his back was turned. She might have had time to get out to the back again. He hurried down the attic stairs.

With a huge sucking noise, the water in the cistern began draining into the pipes below. Lungs bursting, Kei raised her head and gulped in air, then climbed out of the tank, shook the water out of her ears, and ran her hands down her clothing to wring herself as dry as she could. The bastard had kept too close a watch on the hall for her to get out and away! Now she was behind him.

She emptied her shoes into the tank, slipped them back on, and squelched down the stairs cautiously, shivering as she listened for his whistle. The door creaked as she opened it onto the second floor, freezing her to the marrow, but she heard nothing down the hallway.

Going to the top of the kitchen stairs, she held her breath and cocked her good ear toward the stairwell. All was quiet in the kitchen below. The pounding of her heart seemed louder than her footsteps as she crept down the stairs, hoping that he wasn't waiting at the bottom for her. The air of the room was dead and still, devoid of any pulse of life.

Out the window she could see double spots of light on the bridge and could barely hear the faraway sound of the lullaby he was still whistling. My God, had she lost the keys in the tank upstairs? Frantically, she felt in her pocket and found them glued by wet in a fold of the fabric.

Shaking with cold, she went out the kitchen door into a blast of wind that set her teeth chattering. She longed for her sable coat, but it was still on the back porch of the folly where she'd dropped it getting in the window. Never mind, an icy skin was better than no skin at all. She sidled along the house to the car, got in, and pulled the door closed without allowing it to catch. Holding the door closed would agonize her arm, but she'd have to bear it.

The gelatinous columns by the gate were luminous in the darkness. Bits of denser material swam and swirled in the wavering silver like plankton, while the gargoyles inside turned their ruby-red eyes toward the car. Their leathery wings pulsed slowly, ready to open. Ignoring the pain in her arm and shoulder, Kei turned on the ignition and quickly whipped the wheel around to turn the jeep toward the gate. The milky bat wings cracked open with a sound like a flag snapping in a high wind and began beating the air. The white jaws opened as the monster guardians rose from the ground and started for her. With static crackling in her ears, Kei gunned the motor until the jeep was shaking, turned on the lights, then jammed her foot down on the accelerator. The car jumped forward onto the bridge. Claws scraped along the hood as it leaped through the gate and dove into the field beyond the road, shaking Kei like a mouse in a tin can.

Once she was aware that the jeep was still upright, she turned the wheel and charged back along the field. The canal was between her and the village, so she had to backtrack and get onto the highway again. She jounced up onto the shoulder, spun on the wet blacktop, and headed toward the village, anxiously looking in the rearview mirror and out the side to see if she was being followed. There was no sign of the guardians. As she'd suspected, they must have been illusions that Garnett had created. But Garnett was real, and he would have heard her start the car and crash into the field beyond. Was he in front or in back of her now? She grabbed the door that was swinging open, found it had slipped off the true and wouldn't close, and let it go.

Tommy's house was only a mile or so away. If she could make it. He was the only one she was sure of. He'd help her somehow.

CHAPTER TWENTY TWO

Simon watched one more stretcher go by. Then he couldn't watch any more and leaned forward with his elbows on his knees and wept unashamedly. There were no survivors, and it was his fault! His fault, even though he didn't know why. He knew in his bones that the white-eyed raven and the crash were connected, and he was drowning in inconsolable guilt and sorrow. Little children had gone down with men and women, hundreds of them.

Nurse Ozawa tenderly unwrapped the bandage over his eye, removed the plastic cup, and wiped it with a Kleenex. "You must not cry," she said softly. "Good for the eye. Healing. But the cup wets." She replaced the bandage and handed him a pill. "You can take without water?"

He nodded and took it.

"We are very lucky that you made a mistake with the taxi. If we had not been late, we would be like them," she said, looking at the solemn army of men carrying the dead out to the ambulances. The exits from the field were jammed with other ambulances flashing lights and with police cars. The usual bustle of the terminal was hushed except for the moans and sobs of the families of the victims and the flashing of camera bulbs.

Simon almost wished he hadn't been so tied to old habits that he'd ordered the cab in time to get out to the Haneda airport instead of Narita. Then he would have gone down with the rest and not have had to carry this burden the rest of his life. They'd been nearly an hour late and would have to take the next plane.

He couldn't stop the tears, and the cup was filling again. He pushed a finger under the bandage, pried up the edge of the plastic, and let the wetness slide down his cheek. Wiping his face with his handkerchief, he suddenly thought of the news of the disaster going around the world via satellite and of Kei hearing it and thinking he was dead.

He got out his telephone credit card and went to a phone. As always, the call seemed to take years to go through. When the operator informed him that the telephone at the château had been turned off, he put his fist to his mouth as a painful groan racked him. He yearned for the sound of Kei's voice.

Something was drastically wrong, and it was all connected, like strands in a web.

CHAPTER TWENTY THREE

Tommy's house was dark. Not a light anywhere.
But she didn't know where else to go. Anyone in the
village might be a Satanist, just waiting to turn her
over to Garnett.

Tommy and Elaine might have gone to bed early
after their flight from Sri Lanka, and she could rouse
them. In any event, the door of the jeep was hanging
off its hinges, exposing her both to the cold and to
Garnett, and she couldn't stay there. She switched
off the lights and turned off the ignition, pocketing
the keys.

She tried all the doors and banged on the windows, her anxiety getting out of hand as she knew
Garnett had more and more time to locate her, but
no answering light came on. Frantic because her time
to find a haven was shortening, she abandoned Tommy's house for a walk beyond toward the spot where
she'd heard a new house was going in. With a little
bit of luck, somebody might be living it it already,
somebody new to the village who hadn't had time to
be indoctrinated by the Satanists. If not and it was
still empty, Garnett might not think of looking for
her there.

When she saw the bare frame reaching up toward the indigo sky, she almost burst into tears of frustration and stood for a moment, hugging herself and shaking with the cold. Finally she sniffled back her tears and made for the house anyway. There was just enough moonlight for her to see her way to the ladder going to the second storey. Her instincts told to get as high as she could, where she'd have an advantage over Garnett if he found her. There was always the possibility that she could hit him with something or kick a ladder out from under him. His energy would have to run down eventually, and his powers of flight might desert him. It was a hope to hang onto, anyway. She could huddle by the chimney when she got to the top and let her body warmth take some of the chill out of her clothing. Heights had no terrors for her, and her shoes had just enough heel to make her progress secure, although her feet slipped around in the soggy leather.

It was a relief to get to the top and give her arm and shoulder a rest. Though the walls were still only frames that let the wind sweep through, there was a generous patch of flooring by the chimney, and she sat down with her back against the bricks, sheltered from the wind and facing Tommy's house. Convulsive shudders shook her body, but tension and nerves were equally to blame with the cold and wet clothing, and she could quiet them a little by thinking of something pleasant. She watched the road from the château and thought of being in Simon's arms, warm and cozy and loved, but that turned on the faucets of self-pity, so she concentrated instead on June week at the Naval Academy in Annapolis.

She pictured herself walking down the cobbled streets with Peter, who was gorgeous and trim in his dress whites. Why in the world had she turned him down and married Robin instead? Really crazy. At the dinner before the dance, there had been a white orchid at every One-and-Only's plate, and a pair of gold earrings that matched the class rings which were going to be put on for the first time that night. There had been a big-name band playing in the cavernous ballroom when she entered. She wore a black chiffon evening gown, really far too old for her, but she'd begged and begged her mother until she'd worn her down. In the middle of the dance floor was a gigantic gilt replica of the class ring with basins of waters from the seven seas placed around it. She dipped the ring on its ribbon in the basins and then she and Peter were lining up with the others, waiting their turn to walk up and stand framed in the ring as she put the ring on his hand and they kissed. Golly, how she was looking forward to that kiss! Peter was so handsome, those seductive dark eyes and that cruel-looking mouth, like Bogie's! God, he was ravishing! And so was the kiss. Her head was still swimming from it as they swirled off onto the dance floor. The other couples were spinning around them, white uniforms and gowns of all colors, like a field of flowers, going around and around and around.

Her head snapped up as a car door banged down the street. She blinked her eyes. The lights went on in Tommy's front room. She got stiffly to her feet, but her heart had leaped up ahead of her. Now she'd be all right! She hurried toward the ladder.

She was turning to put a foot on the rung when

she looked down and saw, on the bottom floor, two glowing pinpoints of light. My God, where had he come from?! She backed away and looked about her desperately, searching for something she could use as a weapon to defend herself. The moonlight shone across bare flooring. Still, she could see a short length of two by four out by the frame of the wall, where a couple of boards had been nailed down as a walkway. The danger of going out there to get it was nothing compared to having to face Garnett without anything in her hands. When she moved out to the edge, she'd be visible to him from the ground floor, so she'd have to move fast or he'd fly up to get her while she was still unarmed.

She got across the boards. Grabbed up the stick of wood. Not very heavy, but long enough for a good swing at him before he got too close. Take him by surprise, before he could call up his powers. Make him fall and hit his head on the struts below. Just one good crack at him before the end. Not too much to ask.

Taking a firm grip on the two by four, she set herself in the stance she'd used playing baseball on the neighborhood vacant lot.

Which direction was he coming from? Why was he taking so long? What was wrong?

She regripped the wood. Noticed she was standing in a loop of rope hanging from a rafter. Stepped out of it. Planted her feet firmly again.

Jesus Christ, he was on the ladder! Why not flying up through the frame of the house? Was his power giving out?

The beams of his eyes were dimmer. As if his battery was dying.

Why was he coming so slowly? Moving oddly, as if his joints needed oil. Sounding out of breath.

God almighty, he was big! She backed away, forgetting that nothing but air was behind her. Two inches from the edge, she remembered and stopped.

"Feisty little bitch, aren't you?" he said from the darkness with a shadow of a chuckle. "Thought you'd worn me down, didn't you? But I saved something special for you."

Abruptly the air whirled around her in a tight tornado, not touching him. Fighting for her balance, she swung out her left arm to steady herself as the wind spun her around. She felt a jolt in the arm with the two by four before she dropped between the struts of the flooring and jacknifed onto a joist below the ceiling of the lower floor.

It took a moment to realize she'd only had the breath knocked out of her. She was swinging on a slanted bar of wood just under the boards she'd been standing on. When she started breathing again, she looked up for Garnett and scrabbled for a hold on the joist. She couldn't see him anywhere above her.

It took all of her strength to hoist her leg up on the joist and haul herself up again on the walkway. She nearly fell again going back over the walkway, but fear that Garnett would swoop down on her from outside the walls gave her an extra spurt of adrenaline.

Without remembering coming down the ladder, she was flying along the sidewalk toward Tommy's. She ran up the front steps and pounded on the door until it opened.

"Good God, Kei, what's happened to you?!" The burred Scottish baritone of Tommy's voice was as sweet as a heavenly choir to her ear.

Finished with sprinkling salt around the walls of all the downstairs rooms and making incantations, Tommy sat down and loaded his Smith & Wesson. "White witchcraft is good protection on ordinary occasions," he said to Kei while she lay on the couch and Elaine dried her hair. "But this little number is sure to stop him." He put the gun on the table by his chair and leaned over to give Kei's leg a pat. "Don't worry about a thing, luv. He may have Satanic powers, but his body's human, and a bullet through that black heart of his will do him in, just like anybody else."

Kei lay there crying comfortably to herself with the blow dryer toasting her head, reveling in the feel of clean, dry clothing and the soft warmth of the blanket Elaine had tucked around her.

"I called Peggy Van Dreuten and told her you'd be over for the twins in the morning," Elaine said, taking Kei's head on her shoulder and putting aside the hair dryer to give her a sip of hot buttered rum. "Her husband's sitting up in the bedroom with them while they sleep, with an elephant gun on his knees. I don't think you have to worry about them."

Kei snuggled into Elaine's shoulder, which smelled marvelously of soft floral perfume, and enjoyed being mothered. "Is Eagle all right?" she asked.

"Coming along, coming along," said Tommy, draping a leg over the arm of his chair. "That's where we were when you came to call." He joined her in a bit of rum. "He was finally able to talk, and the doctor thought we ought to hear his story. Fellow couldn't figure out if Eagle was delirious, with the bit about the twins flying, so he said come see."

Kei drifted off as he related the particulars of how Garnett had nearly murdered Eagle.

Next morning found them in the same positions. An empty bottle of rum lay on the floor beside a half-filled twin beneath Tommy's hand, which was dangling over the chair arm.

Tommy jerked up out of sleep as a police siren boomed past the house. "Holy Mother of God!" he whispered, putting a hand to his throbbing brow. Kei's head slipped onto Elaine's soft bosom and they both woke up.

"What's that?" Elaine murmured.

"Sadists without mercy," Tommy groaned, getting to his feet. He rocked back and forth a couple of times and yawned. "Where do you suppose your famous tutor's got to?" he said to Kei, stretching to take the kinks out. The effort seemed to give him pain. "Good lord, I think a heart starter's in order," he said and went to a cabinet to pour himself a wee dram of whiskey. "Anyone else have one?"

"No, thank you," said Elaine, untangling herself from Kei, who sat up feeling very brittle, rubbing her shoulder. "*We* weren't drinking all night."

"Well, *we* weren't trying to keep awake all hours, keeping an eye on things, either," Tommy retorted and knocked back the drink. He gasped as the liquor went down his throat, patted himself gently on the diaphragm, and ran his tongue over his teeth, looking sour. He set the shot glass down, feeling better.

A loud knocking on the front door sent his hands flying to his head to protect its delicate condition.

It was a rain-spattered gendarme asking to use the phone to call an ambulance. Kei was the only one who knew French well enough to follow his rapid-fire, stuttering report of what had happened next door. Her translation impelled the three of them out of the house and along the sidewalk, jogging through the rain as Tommy held an umbrella over them.

Gray rain was washing away the remnants of the sleet and blackening the sky, where a watery sun the size and color of a Buffalo nickel was losing its battle against incoming storm clouds. Police and men in blue denim work clothes were gathered at one end of the skeletal house, looking up at a sodden, dark bundle twisting at the end of a rope. Ravens screamed down from the glowering of pines behind the house.

Kei ran ahead as a man in a beret shouted from the third storey to stand clear while he lowered the rope.

Kei looked up and saw the worn, dry soles of Garnett's engineer boots descending, then his soaked jeans plastered to his legs, his clawed hands swinging slowly at his thighs, the back of his jacket. A raven rode down on his shoulder, flicking its tail up and down to keep its balance. As his body turned on the end of the rope, empty sockets gaped where the ravens had done their work.

The bird flapped off toward the black line of firs, and the flock burst out from the trees, climbing toward the storm clouds. An undulating wave of birds floated from the direction of the château and joined the migration winging southward.

CHAPTER TWENTY FOUR

The twins, who had recovered from the fright of the night before immediately upon learning that Garnett was off the scene, were playing Gum Keepaway beside Kei in the back seat of Tommy's car, in turn probing each other's mouth with a finger to locate a wad hidden under the tongue or stuffed behind a tooth. Unsanitary, but it kept them quiet during the drive back to the château from the hospital.

"He certainly takes after you," Elaine said. "Did you see how those nurses were falling all over him? I hate to think what it's going to be like when he gets his full growth!"

"Oh, come off it, Elaine!" said Tommy, not displeased.

"You still get fan letters."

"Only from a few diehards. Probably old enough to have to gum their oatmeal in the mornings."

"Not since the reruns on television. Basketsful."

"Rot!"

"Nude photos and indecent proposals!"

"Well . . ."

"And his very first words to me after all this time were 'I'm starved!' Lying there looking like that and talking about mayonnaise!"

"Shows he's picking up. Bottomless pit."

"And the house, my God, the house! Like a whirlwind hit it!"

"Inexcusable. Harrowing! Don't know what I'd do if we'd lost him." He put his arm around Elaine's shoulders and she leaned her head against his neck as he drove. Not taking his eyes from the wet road, he kissed her forehead.

Not knowing if Simon was dead or alive, Kei couldn't bear to watch them. She turned to look out at the rainy landscape going by .

Last night, Garnett had offered her his condolences as if she was already a widow. This morning, she'd called the Tokyo hospital from Tommy's house, and Simon had checked out. She'd lost track of time when she was trying to elude Garnett, so she didn't know whether Simon had left the hospital before or after Garnett had made that remark. Anything could have happened between the time he'd checked out and the minute Garnett had fallen and caught his neck in the rope hanging from the rafter. Simon's plane was due in at Paris around six, a million long years away.

Her mixed feelings about being instrumental in someone's death added to the torment of waiting. Garnett had called up the whirlwind that had spun her around so that the two by four slammed into him and knocked him off the walkway. Accidentally, he'd caused his own death, but she'd *meant* to hit him. It had been his life or hers. She'd had to protect herself. He'd been a danger to society and someone would have eliminated him one way or another sooner or later. Kei just wished she hadn't been the one to do it. Human life—even *semi*-human life—was sacred. She was devoutly opposed to capital punishment, but she'd served as Garnett's executioner.

When they entered the château gate, Kei was bewildered by the number of cars on the parking area. One clearly belonged to the gendarmes huddling together under the glass canopy over the front doors. Tommy had told them that Marc was back at the stable, armed with an axe, and apparently they were waiting for his arrival before taking action. But why the rental cars, and what was Marthe doing, standing out there talking to the police, when she was supposed to be in Gien with her daughter?

Before stepping over the twins to get out of the car, Kei looked back at the gate. The guardians were gone, vanished along with Garnett. Ducks were sitting under the moat bridge, their feet tucked under their plumpness. A pair of robins was hopping about in the downpour on the holly outside the kitchen, picking exploratively at the red berries. Not a raven was to be seen.

Marthe swooped down from the excited group under the canopy and squeezed the breath out of Kei as soon as she put a foot outside, then transferred her welcome to the twins, brushing back the hair from their eyes, kissing them on their soft rosy cheeks, and thanking *le bon Dieu* for their delivery from Garnett.

"What are you doing home?" Kei asked

breathlessly. "Has Blanche had the baby?"

"*Pas encore*," Marthe said, wiping her eyes on a corner of her *tablier*. "The doctor thinks next week. However, tomorrow is the gala dinner, so I have returned to make preparations."

Thanksgiving! Kei had forgotten.

"If I had not been here, who would have let your inviteds in? Or turned the telephones back on?"

"*Mes invités?*" Kei hadn't invited anyone for Thanksgiving dinner. She hadn't expected to be around to eat it herself.

The gendarmes stood aside to let her pass into the house without interrupting their planning session with Tommy. She stopped for a moment at seeing two small blond heads looking out the panels of the front door. Michelle and Malcolm! Then their parents, Bony Foxworth, the head of Simon's London gallery, and his wife Margaret must be inside. Had she invited them over when she was half crazed and forgotten about it?

The children opened the door for her, shyly said hello, with Michelle giving a bob that was half a curtsey, and began getting acquainted with the twins, who were elated to see someone their own age at the château.

Half a dozen people stopped buzzing and looked up from an Imari platter of hors d'ôeuvres at the bar when she came in the salon and moved toward her in a mass.

"*There* she is!" shouted Mark Bowen's reedy English voice as his buttermilk-complexioned wife raised a convivial glass at her.

Missy outdistanced the rest, trotting across the

Aubusson with her breasts jouncing under her silk shirt like waterfilled balloons while she held out a dish of pickled shrimp. "Have some of these, get your strength up after what you've been through, not a calorie in a carload," she said, shoving the shrimps at Kei, who waved them away. "I knew Garnett was trouble, the guy was something out of a horror movie, you can't imagine the things he wanted to do! We didn't know he was dead until the gendarmes told us, and I wouldn't be here now if the rest of the gang hadn't come on the same plane, no matter what Simon said. What have you got a bandage on your arm for?"

"What do you mean, 'no matter what Simon said'?" Kei asked as the guests crowded around her.

Bony Foxworth poked his sleek blond head between that of his wife and Jeremy Kirbottle, the publisher from Landsend House, to plant a kiss on Kei's cheek. "I was absolutely shattered to hear what had happened," he said over the din of the other voices asking questions.

"I said, 'What do you mean about Simon?' " Kei repeated, getting shrill as claustrophobia clutched her. "Where's Simon?!"

The group fell silent.

"He called all of us yesterday and demanded that we rally round until he could get home," Jeremy said finally. "Haven't you heard from him? What's wrong?" His moustache twitched apprehensively.

"You don't suppose . . . " Margaret Foxworth began, speculation in her cowlike eyes. The group fell into a hostile silence, turning looks on her that were obviously meant to shut her up. Kei's antennae went up.

"Of course not!" Jeremy said curtly, taking command despite his pocket-edition size. "Absolutely not, and you're wretched to bring it up. There'll be no more talk of that, you terrible woman!"

"Now, see here, Jeremy, you're not to talk to my wife in that fashion!" Bony protested, putting a supportive arm around her and looking down at the top of Jeremy's head in a toplofty manner. Margaret snuggled against Bony, looking ashamed in her tactlessness.

Kei grabbed Margaret by the arms and said, dizzy with panic, "What is it? What don't they want you to tell me?"

Gendarmes charged through the foyer with a rattle of heels and the back door slammed open onto the bridge as the phone started ringing. The twins and the Foxworth children romped through the salon toward the study to get the telephone, and the birds in the aviary raised a clamor as the door opened.

"Is it Simon? Tell me, is it Simon?!" Kei demanded.

Margaret went pale.

Gino burst out of the study and began tugging at Kei's pants leg as Margaret stammered, "It was . . . it was on the news this morning. Yesterday a Japanese Airline plane crashed at Tokyo. Everyone on board was . . . " She almost swallowed the last word. " . . . killed."

Gino's tugging turned into yanking as Kei stared at Margaret. The group closed around them, protesting, assuring, comforting, while Kei staggered toward a chair, dragging Gino along with her.

"Listen!" Gino piped. No one paid any attention

343

to him, Kei least of all. He stamped his foot in frustration, then wriggled up on the arm of Kei's chair, took her face in his hands and twisted it around so she had to look at him, and said, "It's Grandad. He says he's in Vienna, waiting for his plane home."

Kei sat feeling as trembly as a girl on her way to her first prom, thinking of seeing Simon again, as the guests minutely dissected the events since his departure for the Orient, drinking their after-dinner liqueurs and smoking. While he'd been gone, she'd thought about him, longed for him so much that sometimes in the still of the night she could almost believe that the power of her thoughts would make him materialize before her. And just two hours from now, he'd be back! First she'd see the shock of silvery hair above the heads of the crowd at the terminal, then his dark eyes looking for her. He'd smile with that beautiful, smooth-lipped mouth and put his arms around her. She'd put her face against the rough tweed of his jacket and bask in his comforting personal fragrance, and he'd be warm and solid.

And she'd have to tell him about Garnett.

"Just so his body isn't buried in the village," Tommy was saying, lighting a cigar. "The Satanists would make capital of that. Rob the grave. Use the body as part of their rites."

"Not to worry," said Jeanne-Marie and took a sip of her chartreuse. "Sections of the tissue will circulate through medical laboratories for years, without a doubt. There will not be much left of him after every curious doctor has made his examination. The structure of the blood is puzzling, unique. And as for the reptilian texture of the skin . . . "

"Can't we change the subject?" asked Missy, looking ill. At the first news that the man she'd slept with had been a monster, she'd gone white and then gotten progressively greener.

"Got to get rid of Sélène, too," Tommy continued, ignoring Missy's sensitivities through ignorance of what had gone on between her and the subject that had been under discusison. "Even the dust. She's wreaked havoc for three hundred years now. Time to put an end to it."

The only topic that hadn't been gone over with a magnifying glass was why Kei had allowed Garnett to take control of the house and of her. Everyone assumed that he'd kept her captive by threatening her with his Satanic powers. Simon might make the same assumption, if she let him.

"Are you going to have the members of the cult arrested?" asked Margaret Foxworth.

"What for?" Tommy said around his cigar. "Prosecute them for belonging to a secret society? Sweet hope! No, and there's not much we can do about that fellow with the axe, either. He went back home quietly, leaving the axe behind him. The law's helpless."

"I should think they'd be massively demoralized," said Jeremy Kirbottle. "With Sélène and the tutor destroyed, what have they left?"

"The usual rubbish," said Tommy. "There'll always be somebody to tinker with the occult, to try to impress the public and to gain power for themselves. They're a vicious element, and they're everywhere."

"You mean there might be one next door to me?" said Margaret, aghast.

Tommy raised an eyebrow and stared at her cynically. "Anybody who's willing to manipulate another person's mind for his own ends is malevolent, wouldn't you say? And that takes in a lot of territory."

"But what can I *do*?" Margaret quavered, working her napkin nervously between her hands.

"Build a strong mental defense," Tommy said, tapping his cigar on the edge of a silver ashtray. "Watch your own thinking. Sounds a bit dim, but surround yourself with good thoughts in the morning. Put a white light around yourself. The only real shield you've got is positive mental energy."

"Lot of mumbo-jumbo," Mark Bowen said scoffingly and popped a stray pistachio in his mouth.

Tommy shrugged. "Have it your way. I'm not peddling tracts."

The conversation swirled slowly around Kei in an indistinct babble while she listened to the rain outside and the rumblings in the northeast. A storm was coming in. She hoped Simon's plane wouldn't run into it. She glanced down at her watch. An hour and fifty minutes. The guests hardly looked up, absorbed in their discussion, when she excused herself to go change.

Her hand shook too much to get her lipstick on straight. She wiped if off and substituted lip gloss. God, she looked haggard! Deep hollows under her cheekbones, smudges under her eyes, a twitch at the corner of her mouth—why was it that, when she wanted to look her best, she invariably looked like a mess of mealy bugs?

She put on a high-necked black dress with long sleeves that hid her bandage and tucked up her hair under her bubble-shaped sable hat. She'd retrieved her sable coat from the porch of the folly, where it had been showered with glass splinters, and there was a small slash under one arm, but it wouldn't show. She put it on, pulled on long black kid gloves, and opened the closet door to look at herself in the mirror on the back. Haggard but elegant. No one would guess she wasn't one of those moneyed, sophisticated women with ordered lives, who never encountered anything more unpleasant than a too-hot solution of wax when they got their legs defuzzed at Elizabeth Arden's. Pull up your socks, old dear, Kei said to her reflection, there's a dance in the old dame yet!

The headlights could hardly penetrate the silver curtain of drops ahead, making slow going back into Orléans. In between claps of lightning, Tommy gave a blow-by-blow account of the events Simon and his Japanese attendants had missed, while the rhythmic sweep of the windshield wipers provided a narrative tempo. The twin cords on the back of Dr. Yamashita's neck added their own accompaniment, standing out in tense relief at the high points of the story and receding at the lower ones. Nurse Ozawa's profile was thoroughly scrutable as passing street lights struck it. She nibbled her lips and gave little gasps of horror, screwing up her face. When Tommy got to Garnett's hanging, she offered Simon a calmative pill and, when he refused it, swallowed it herself.

Kei leaned back against Simon, nestling in the curve of his arm. The medicinal smell of the bandage over his eye obscured his natural signature aura of sunwarmed autumn leaves, so she sniffed deeply at his jacket, where his aroma lingered, and at last felt safe and serene, as cozy as a puppy napping on a sweater by a pot-bellied stove.

"I told you I could take care of things!" she murmured, looking up at the stubble on the underside of Simon's jaw.

He laughed. "You're utterly impossible," he said fondly and squeezed her sore arm. She turned her involuntary cry into a cough. "But what about the children?" he asked, leaning toward the front seat. "The things they've witnessed will be drifting around in their subconscious for years. Dreadful business!"

"I think not," Tommy said over his shoulder. "Garnett would have removed the memory so that the secret material with it couldn't be revealed later. He'd have the obligation to do that, you see."

"Shame about Mitzi," Simon said, relaxing. He leaned his chin on the soft fur of Kei's hat. "I loved that dog."

"How about me?" said Kei, feeling she deserved some sympathy for the injuries Mitzi had inflicted on her arm.

"Ah, yes. You."

Nurse Ozawa put her hand over her mouth and giggled softly as Simon directed his full attention to kissing Kei.

"A fine pair we are," said Simon, undressing for bed. "You with that arm and me with this." He touched the bandage over his eye. "However . . . " He took off his shirt and began unbuckling the aluminum brace that had chafed him all the way from Tokyo. "This has got to go!" He took it off and dropped it in the wastebasket.

"But your back!" Kei protested, sticking her head up through the neck of her nightgown as she pulled it on.

"Aha! Every cloud has a silver lining. When I was battling with the bird attacking me, I wrenched my back in the other direction. It rather evened me out, though I'm not going to be doing any grand ballet leaps for awhile."

A blast from overhead shook the house and Kei winced.

"Great Scott, I suppose we'll have the twins in bed with us again," Simon said crossly. "God knows, with jet lag and the pill Miss Ozawa forced down my throat, you can't expect any romance tonight, but I really wish . . . "

"Don't worry." Kei set the alarm and checked the clock with her watch, mindful that there was a turkey to get into the oven early. The backup bird would have to go in half an hour later. "The twins and the Foxworth children were having a pillow fight when I looked in. They wouldn't notice if a cannon went off in the next room. They shouldn't be up so late, but they'll sleep longer tomorrow." She sighed. "They can't go the folly, with the mess it's still in, so they'll be under foot all day."

She looked at Simon's bare back as he sat on the edge of the bed, taking off his shoes and socks. Two red lines went around his torso where the brace had dug into him, but otherwise his skin was as smooth as jade. She loved to feel it with her hands when they were in bed.

But when the pill and the jet lag wore off, she still wouldn't be able to make love with Simon, not while she concealed her relationship with Garnett from him. He hadn't asked and might never, but dishonesty on her side would curdle her feelings toward their marriage. And toward herself. It was all or nothing.

"I managed to get all the fucking tapes for the book done while I was in hospital," Simon was saying. "Just came in under the publication deadline, so now . . ."

"Simon," said Kei.

He sat in his robe in the leather chair by the window, smoking a cigarette as she talked. Now and then he put his fist to his mouth and nodded, but he said nothing. She sat at his feet, occasionally giving way to gusts of weeping, wanting him to touch her comfortingly, but he did not. He stared out the window at the storm, and she wondered if he was hearing what she was saying, with the thunder booming deafeningly.

Finally, she stopped. There was nothing more to say.

He was still silent, curtained off from her. A bolt of lightning plunged across the sky.

He stubbed out his cigarette in the ashtray and turned to look at her. His unbandaged eye was wet. "I didn't love you *conditionally*, Kei," he softly "I've lost count of all the women I've slept with, bu when I met you, it was like hearing a steel door clang

350

shut. A door I knew was never going to open again. It was final." He stroked her hair back from her face. "There's nothing you can do that would make me stop loving you. I'm only sorry you had to suffer through all that." A quiver ran down the side of his face. "Now, do me the favor of never mentioning it again."

He helped her to her feet and put his arms around her. They were on their way to the bed when there was an ear-shattering crack of lightning out back.

The tallest oak in the grove, crowned with fire, split open to its base, showing a pale heart of wood, and one half of the trunk collapsed onto the roof of the folly in a shower of shingles. Flame began curling along one end of the eaves as smoke spiraled up through the rain.

After a moment of shock, Kei said, "My God, the folly's going to go up! I'll have to phone . . . "

She started toward the bedside table, but Simon stopped her.

Standing looking out at the fire racing along the edge of the folly's roof, he said quietly, "Let it burn."

An early morning fog hung in the woods, mingling with smoke from the sodden rubble that had been the summer house. A charred beam quilted by the fire tottered and crashed down on shards from the crystal ball that had split in the heat. A blue jay strutted about in the wet ashes, looking for anything that was salvageable.

Hilaire had called for help as soon as he'd seen the flames, but the folly flared up like a matchbox, fueled by the melting wax figures and the chemicals Garnett had kept there. Firemen had saved the surrounding trees by hosing them down, but the wooden structure had gone up in a bright, fast blaze fanned by the wind, a fitting funeral pyre for Sélène.

Simon was standing by the window, looking out at the black splash on the forest floor. The storm was over and the sky was clearing for Thanksgiving Day. A slate-colored junco with a pink beak hopped along the window ledge with its breast feathers fluffed up against the gathering cold.

Feeling deliciously exhausted, Kei turned over and put her face in the hollow Simon's head had left in his pillow. *That* was the way it should be! Bloody marvelous, as Simon would say, and with no bitter aftertaste. She sat up, stretching like a lazy cat, and turned off the alarm. She felt tempted to ask Simon a question, thought she'd better not, then couldn't resist.

"Simon," she said, "does lovemaking renew your energy?"

"Jesus, no!" he said, turning from the window with a puzzled look. "I feel like I've just been run over by a freight train." He smiled. "Why do you ask?"

"Oh, no reason. I just wondered," she said, returning the smile.

She got up and put on her robe, planning to consult *Fanny Farmer*. She never could remember how many pounds to the hour when she fixed turkey.